About the

Kimberly Kaye Terry's love ~~...~~ at an early age. She holds a Ba~~...~~ ~~...work,~~ a Master's in Human Relations and has been a licensed social worker and mental-health therapist in various cities in the US and abroad – but she is happy to call writing her full-time job. She believes in embracing the powerful woman within each of us and meditates on a regular basis.

Maya Blake's writing dream started at thirteen. She eventually realised her dream when she received 'The Call' in 2012. Maya lives in England with her husband, kids and an endless supply of books. Contact Maya: mayabauthor.blogspot.com, twitter.com/mayablake, facebook.com/maya.blake.94

Approaching fifty Mills & Boon titles, **Dianne Drake** is still as passionate about writing romance as ever. As a former intensive care nurse, it's no wonder medicine has found its way into her writing, and she's grateful to Mills & Boon Medical for allowing her to write her stories. 'They return me to the days I loved being a nurse and combine that with my love of the romance novels I've been reading since I was a young teen.'

Postcards from Paradise

January 2023
Caribbean

April 2023
Costa Rica

February 2023
Brazil

May 2023
Australia

March 2023
Hawaii

June 2023
Bali

Postcards from Paradise:

Hawaii

KIMBERLY KAYE TERRY

MAYA BLAKE

DIANNE DRAKE

MILLS & BOON

First Published in Great Britain 2023
by Mills & Boon, an imprint of HarperCollins*Publishers* Ltd,
1 London Bridge Street, London, SE1 9GF

www.harpercollins.co.uk

HarperCollins*Publishers*
Macken House, 39/40 Mayor Street Upper,
Dublin 1, D01 C9W8, Ireland

ISBN: 978-0-263-31878-4

TO TAME A WILDE

KIMBERLY KAYE TERRY

To my beautiful daughter, Hannah, who always inspires me to be the best that I can be; I love you, Poohma...now go make up your bed! ;)

Chapter 1

Sinclair Adams was tired. No, scratch that. She was damn tired.

"And why am I so blasted tired?" she grumbled.

She briefly closed her eyes and inhaled a fortifying breath before allowing it to softly blow out of her full lips.

She had been expecting a car and driver, supplied by the Kealohas, to meet her at the airport. At least, that is what she had been told would happen.

And yes, a car had been sent—if you could call it a car. The one that had arrived for her shuddered and rattled so badly, she hadn't been the least bit surprised when it just...stopped.

A heartfelt groan slipped from behind her closed lips.

She closed her eyes again, knowing even as the driver,

an older man named Kanoa whose hands had shaken just as badly as the car, turned to her with a resigned look on his aged, weathered face.

"Guess I'd better go check under the hood." His voice registered hopelessness.

He hopped out of the car, spry for his obviously advanced age, and popped the hood. After a lot of noise, tinkering and mild curses, most of which Sinclair didn't understand, he walked to her side of the car and looked at her through the open rear window.

"Miss, I'm sorry, but old Mou Mou here…" Kanoa began, scratching his nearly bald head. "Well, she ain't gonna make it to the hotel. I gotta call a tow."

The look he cast toward the car was so sympathetic as he lovingly patted the rusted roof of…*Mou Mou,* that had Sinclair been in a better frame of mind, she would have felt sorry for the old man. *And* his obviously beloved car.

As it was, she barely checked her irritation. After all, it wasn't the old man's fault. She laid the blame squarely on one person: Nick Kealoha.

She groaned, but her choices were limited. She could either wait for another ride to take her to the hotel—which God only knew how long *that* would take—or climb out of the jalopy and wait alongside the road with Kanoa as the car was towed. She chose the latter, believing it the lesser of two evils and the quickest means to get to the hotel.

By the time she made it to the hotel where Althea Wilde had reserved a room for her, she was tired. And grumpy as all get-out, as her daddy used to say.

"Don't forget that part. I'm tired and I'm mad, and…" She paused in her verbal rant and lifted an arm, daintily taking a sniff as the elevator swiftly ascended. "Lord, I'm sweaty!"

After the elevator made it to her floor, she briskly exited, her high heels sinking into the lush carpeting as she strode down the hall. She slowed her gait, glancing at the slim credit-card-like key in her hand and up at the doors she passed, wanting to locate her room as quickly as possible.

"But at least I'm here," she murmured. Just as she located her suite, she heard a small ding. She glanced down at the Cartier watch, the last gift she'd received from her beloved father before his passing, and muttered a mild curse.

"Could this day get any worse?" she mumbled at the alarm notification. She was supposed to be at the A'kela Ranch in less than an hour.

Thank God she'd allowed Althea to make the reservation. Althea was married to Nathan Wilde—the oldest of her "Wilde Boys," as she collectively called the three men she considered brothers—and the woman was organized to a tee.

"No telling *what* the Kealohas would have had in store for me otherwise," Sinclair huffed as she dragged her suitcase inside the suite.

"Whose fault *is* all of this?" she continued her ranting monologue. To no one in particular.

"Him."

It was all…*his*…fault.

With a disgusted harrumph, her lip curled. She wasn't about to extend *him* the courtesy of saying his name out loud.

Name, image and everything about him had taken up too much of her energy, occupied way too much of her brain time than it should have, she thought, as she hauled her oversize bag inside the room and allowed the door to close softly behind her.

And there was no way she was taking the blame, even if only to herself, for the current state she found herself in.

"The ride-or-die girl herself, Sinclair," she said, releasing another disgusted puff of air from teeth clenched tight. "But...I have to take care of my Wilde Boys," Sinclair said, sighing heavily. "They're family."

She absently glanced around the room, taking it in quickly before dumping bags and her purse on the large king-size bed.

She slumped down on the bed, closing her eyes and arching her sore back.

But it wasn't the Wildes with whom she had issue.

One name, one face, came to mind and claimed *that* number-one spot: Nickolas Kealoha... Nick, as he went by.

Nick, along with his twin brother, Keanu, and father, Alek, owned and operated the A'kela Ranch in Hawaii.

Nickolas Kealoha...Wilde.

And there was the rub—along with the reasons she was far away from home and the Wyoming Wilde Ranch, and now in Hawaii.

Sinclair clenched her eyes tightly closed. And as

usual, what had become irritatingly familiar, the image of Nick Kealoha came to mind. She bit the corner of her lip. She knew what he looked like, every feature down to the lopsided grin he tended to have on his sensual mouth. The way one dimple would appear near his lower lip whenever he would smile, even the slightest bit. In that way he had—

Sinclair quickly opened her eyes, batting them several times as though *that* would scrub the image of Mr. Tall, Golden and Fine from her mind.

"Lord…help me," she muttered and reached down to slip the ridiculously high heels from her feet to massage her arches.

Okay. She was definitely tired. She'd become accustomed to blocking his image from her mind the minute it bombarded its way inside, as though he had every right to take up residence.

Increasingly, his image was the first that came to her mind in the morning as soon as she woke. And it was the last one she visualized at night, right before bed.

Right before dreaming.

"Arggg!" The groan rolled out from between her tightened lips.

She refused to admit how it was affecting her, how his image had been flirting inside her mind for the past several months, relentlessly. Without ceasing.

It had started even before she'd seen his family's show.

As soon as the Wildes had come to her for help with the situation, Sinclair had gone online to check out the

Kealohas in an effort to get an idea of what she would be dealing with. It hadn't been a hard task. As soon as she'd put their name into the search engine on her laptop, pages had filled the screen and she'd clicked through the various links and images. They were, in fact, quite… Google-able. Curious, she'd then decided to check out the show.

"Know thine enemy" had been a saying she had long learned to adhere to, even before completing her law degree. She'd settled down on her sofa and scrolled the various sites before finding the reality show.

That one show had done it.…

Oh, Lord. She swallowed deep, the memories making her face burn. Her self-massage came to an abrupt halt, her fingers pausing midrub.

She'd promised herself not to watch another episode. There was absolutely no reason for her to continue, after all. She had watched simply to see the men of the A'kela Ranch—to watch and observe for anything she could use against the Kealohas. Strictly research fodder for her Wilde Boys, no more, no less.

For reasons she refused to analyze, although she'd promised herself *not* to watch another episode, she'd been spellbound. Like a deer caught in headlights, she'd sat on her loveseat watching episode after episode.…

And what had started out as a mission simply to "know her enemy," had turned into a marathon TV session that had her viewing both seasons one and two of the popular cable network show. Episodes where Nick seemed to be most present, she'd watched twice. Sometimes three times.

The man was drop-dead fine as hell, no two ways about it.

After that, his image had been scored into her brain, from his golden-boy good looks to the bright blue eyes that seemed to show mischief even if the camera wasn't aimed in his direction. Even if he wasn't the one the scene was focused on, he seemed to attract all the attention to his broad shoulders, narrow waist and muscled thighs that even behind the signature rugged jeans he wore couldn't disguise the masculine appeal.

All of him had captured Sinclair's attention. And although she should have been irritated at the way he seemed to know it, the way he carried himself as though he was the only man on the planet, alpha to the nth degree...she'd found herself getting wet. Just from looking at him.

Sinclair had noticed that although the show featured the Kealoha ranch, the actual *Kealohas,* both brothers as well as father, were rarely on camera. However, when Nick glanced into the camera and spoke, it was as though he was speaking directly to her.

She felt a tangible...warmth invade her body. Sexual. Predatory heat...

Ingrained into her mind was the way his low-hooded, intense blue eyes would glance into the camera...his sculpted cheeks... And the hint of a dimple that would appear near his lower lip when he gave that ghost of a smile that Sinclair now associated with pure, raw, masculine…sex.

She sucked in a deep breath of air.

It all screamed that he was a man who knew his way around a woman's body.

Her face flushed. Her panties grew wet.

Hot mess? Nah…she was *way* past that.

"Uhhhh!" The growl of frustration slipped from her lips and Sinclair quickly snapped her eyes open and batted them profusely.

She needed help.

Nick Kealoha was a player. Straight. Up. Player.

No two ways around it. It was all in his image. The way he carried himself. She'd read his bio…and she was not going to be played. Never had, never would.

Sinclair straightened her spine and tossed her hair back over her shoulder. She ignored the way her thick, wavy curls refused to behave, and how the once-straight strands were a memory of the past.

She ran a hand over her hair and circled the bunch in one hand. After opening a pocket of her messenger bag she'd tossed on the bed, she withdrew a covered band and deftly secured the thick, dense mass of curls.

No. *She* did not see him as one part of the "dynamic duo" that he and his twin had so cheesily been dubbed by the media.

She only saw the irritating man she had come to truly…have issue with.

Their communication had begun when Sinclair had taken over all dealings with the Kealohas immediately after Nick's initial terse letter to the family, demanding retribution.

Although the Wildes, as well as Sinclair, had been surprised to find out that their adoptive father, Clint Jedediah Wilde, had fathered a set of twins more than thirty years ago, they had been happy, ready to meet their "brothers" and to hear their story.

Unfortunately, it wasn't long after that that they realized the Kealohas, in particular Nick Kealoha, was not exactly in the "family reunion" sort of mood. His demand was concise, to the point. He and his brother were demanding they get what was theirs legally: interest in the Wyoming Wilde Ranch.

"Not even gonna happen," had been the collective response from her Wilde Boys, big arms crossed over their large chests, faces set.

Although she didn't feel like smiling, the image of the big men, hard looks across their handsome faces, brought a smile to her face.

Although the Wildes were adoptive brothers, sharing no blood link, the men were just about as close as three brothers could be. And when they felt threatened it was quite an impressive sight to see them rally together.

Ready to kick ass first and take names later, if necessary, as Holt Wilde had once so eloquently put it.

Not that it would come to that, Sinclair had assured them, confident in her abilities as a mediator and the speed with which she'd contacted the Kealohas. In particular, Nick Kealoha.

Soon, her confidence had taken a radical turn.

With their first correspondence via email she'd known she was in trouble. She'd immediately sought out verbal communication after his rude response to what she'd viewed as a perfectly reasonable request for a meeting.

He'd ignored her, as well as her request for a meeting, to the point she'd felt every one of her back teeth would grind down to dust in her frustration from dealing with the irritating man.

Finally she'd gotten him on the phone and sparks had flown swiftly, strongly. After hanging up, Sinclair had felt as though she'd been skinned alive.

She'd felt...unnerved by the man. His voice had been the first thing to cause the dichotomy of feelings.

Low, sexy...rough.

She'd felt her heart slam against her rib cage, but had forced the crazy reaction to the side.

This was war. And from the get-go, he'd identified himself as the enemy.

Shelving the odd feelings, she'd at first wanted to walk away, but had known she couldn't, that she wouldn't.

She was not only the Wildes' lawyer, she was...family. There was nothing she would *not* do for her Wilde Boys. With resignation she'd gone to work, seeking to find out what she could about the Kealohas.

It hadn't been hard. As soon as she'd discovered they'd had their own reality show, the information had been relatively easy to acquire.

Not that she'd had to go that far for info. As soon as she'd plugged their name into her search engine, there had been pages and pages of information. And images...

For as much information as she'd uncovered about the men and their ranch, there had been just as many images, if not more. Identical twins who not only ran the most successful family-owned-and-operated ranch in Hawaii, but were also drop-dead fine? Yeah...there'd not been a shortage of images.

From the moment she'd laid eyes on him, she'd known Nick Kealoha was going to be impossible to deal with.

"And I was right," she murmured. "And now...time to face the devil," she whispered as she got up off the bed. And heard the excitement...fear in her voice.

That was the sum total of what she *would* allow herself to think about: the fact that he was nothing but an irritant. A sexy-as-hell irritant, but nonetheless an irritant. One she would deal with swiftly and be done with.

A mocking little laugh echoed in her ear. She swatted it away with her hand as though that would make *it,* and the reason for *it,* disappear. Nothing more than a nuisance.

Sinclair swiftly opened her suitcase and withdrew clothes to change into. Time was of the essence. She'd do a quick refresh and be out.

She ruthlessly tamped down the annoying fissure of delight she felt curling through her spine.

This was just a meeting. A meeting where she would do the best she could to make sure her Wilde Boys were not milked and taken for what was theirs, if not by true birthright, then by sweat, blood and tears.

Sinclair ignored the excited sliver of...*something*... that rushed over her at the thought. *Something* she refused to name. Yet, try as she might, that also refused to go away.

She hadn't met the man.... The thought occurred to her that by coming to the Kealoha ranch in Hawaii, she just might have bitten off more than she was willing to chew.

Even that thought excited her.

No one was taking anything from her boys, not if Sinclair had anything to say about it. And if that meant taking on the devil himself, she was just the woman for the job.

Chapter 2

Nick Kealoha frowned, his eyes scanning the computer screen, rereading the latest correspondence via email from the Wildes' attorney.

For the third time.

A sneer kicked the corner of his mouth upward into parody of a smile. The fools hadn't wanted to deal with him, so they'd sicced their lawyer on him.

"Damn woman," he grumbled as he strummed the fingers of one large, long-fingered hand absently against his desk. The other hand was poised over the keyboard as he thought about what he *should* have said instead of what he had said in response to the email.

As he reread the lawyer's message, despite his self-avowals to the contrary, the woman was getting to him.

That self-admission alone ticked him off.

His eyes studied the email from Sinclair Adams, the attorney for the Wilde Ranch of Wyoming.

Greetings Mr. Kealoha,
After consulting with the Wildes, I am informing you of the family's wish for a more personal approach in dealing with our...situation. Unfortunately, over the course of the past week you have ignored my certified mail as well as ignored my phone calls, and I feel as though the situation is degenerating versus improving. To prevent a complete breakdown in communication, and to continue with the path we've been on—resolution—we, the Wildes and I, feel it is best for a one-on-one approach. To this end, please expect a visit from me to the A'kela Ranch. It is our sincere hope that you and your family will be able to meet with me so that we may resolve this matter to the satisfaction of all parties. I will arrive Tuesday of next week in the hope that you and your family will work with me to resolve this matter.
Best,
Sinclair Adams, PLLC

He'd received the correspondence, spoken to his brother about it and promptly dismissed the woman from his mind.

Or tried to.

"Lot of damn good *that* did," he muttered.

He'd known she was on her way to the island. Known about it and hadn't told his family about it until it was too late for either his brother or father to call the Wildes or their lawyer to settle the matter.

He'd even told her he would send a driver for her.

He wanted her here, on his territory.

A feral grin split his mouth into a smile.

From the beginning of his…interaction with Ms. Sinclair Adams, Nick had found himself in a state of semi-arousal.

Didn't much matter when it happened. Whenever he either thought of the irritating woman or had *any* type of contact—written, emailed or verbal—his body reacted.

Hell, he could just listen to his voice mail and his cock was hard as granite.

The one time they'd had the Skype conversation…

Damn.

Even as he thought about it now, his cock hardened and his balls tightened in memory.

He'd seen pictures of her plenty. He'd known what she looked like, and had been intrigued. She had a different kind of beauty. Not traditional, but no less hot to him.

Then they'd spoken on the phone. They'd had conversations that had left him wanting…more. But the video interaction had taken it to another level.

Their conversation had been heated and he'd alternated between wanting *her* and wanting to strangle her pretty little neck. As soon as he'd gone to bed that night, he'd relived their exchange and the whole "wanting her" part had taken over.

And he'd promptly had one of the hottest dreams he'd

had as an adult male. He had woken up with his shaft, again, in his hand, his seed spilled over his stomach.

With a mild curse he'd reached over, pulled open the side table drawer and withdrawn a napkin, which he now kept at the ready for that very reason.

He'd had more wet dreams over the past few months because of her than he'd had, collectively, as a randy teenage boy.

It had gotten to the point he was beginning to think she'd cast some kind of spell on him. He'd never been so worked up over a woman he'd never met in person, much less one who was in the enemy camp, so to speak.

As soon as she'd begun to communicate with him, he'd researched who she was.

His initial thought had simply been to go by the creed of "know thine enemy." But it had turned into something…more.

Although calling the Wildes his enemy was a bit of a stretch. His anger had actually cooled toward the deception his mother had kept hidden for all those years: that he and his brother were the product of an illicit affair.

He cursed, low, his voice barely audible.

And no matter what his feelings toward Jed Wilde, whether he'd known about his and Key's existence or not, it wasn't his true father's—Alek Kealoha's—fault.

In fact, he'd been ready to call it off, and just let it all go. It wasn't as though he really wanted anything Jed Wilde had, or anything he'd left to his adoptive sons. Nick and his family had a ranch that was just as impressive and in no way needed anything the Wildes had. They were doing damn fine on their own.

He'd even told both his father and brother the same thing, much to the relief of both. They, too, didn't want anything the Wildes had, nor were they interested in dredging up old family dirt. They'd come to a resolution about it all, and now that both Clint Jedediah Wilde and their mother, A'kela Kealoha, had passed away, there was no need to protect anyone.

Even though there was still a small part of Nick that wanted to know what kind of man Jed had been, in the end, neither he nor Key wanted to hurt the man they'd called Father for their entire lives.

Yet, after the first encounter with Sinclair Adams, what he had found out about her through his amateur sleuthing had left him wanting to know more. So much so that he'd continued his threats.

Just because of her.

He wouldn't call himself a research nut by any means, but he damn well knew how to find out about a person if need be. He had taken to the internet in the hope that he'd learn more about her, assuming she was some high-powered attorney.

What he'd learned had left him even more intrigued.

The Wildes were easy to research. He'd simply entered the name of the ranch and, presto, a virtual flood of information was at his fingertips. It had taken a while, but he'd eventually uncovered information about Sinclair.

Pictures of her on the Wilde Ranch had shown a

young woman he didn't believe could possibly be the sophisticated woman portrayed in both the smooth-toned voice mails she'd left on his phone and the succinct emails she'd sent.

Further stealth-mode investigation had showed that it was indeed the same woman. Not only was she on the Wildes' website, there had been a hyperlink that directed him to her own website. Her bio had been impressive.

She appeared young, too young for the accomplishments listed in her biography. He'd frowned. Although young, she'd built quite a name for herself in her area of expertise in law.

Now working primarily as the lawyer for the Wildes, from what Nick had been able to learn from his internet search, she'd also had dealings in corporate law. She had interned with a prestigious law firm in Cheyenne, Wyoming, before returning home. She'd listed the Wyoming Wilde Ranch as home and he'd frowned, wondering if she had grown up on the ranch.

Just as on the A'Kela Ranch, Nick knew that many of the larger, successful ranches had generations of family members that worked and lived on the ranch. He'd guessed she was a family member.

He'd reached out and called her. In a voice low and sexy, feminine yet husky, she'd had him hard as hell, sitting up in his seat and listening intently to the low-toned voice smoothly inform him of her clients' wish to settle this unfortunate incident with as little "fanfare" as possible.

It had taken a minute for the insult to register.

And now, after four months of cyber interacting, she was on her way to the ranch. All that cyber *interacting* had him on edge.

He felt his cock stir at the thought. Unconsciously he adjusted himself within his jeans. If she made him feel in person even the *slightest* bit as she had during their previous interactions—verbal heated conversations, sharply worded yet oddly arousing emails and voice mails... He shook his head.

Hell, yeah. Things were about to get really interesting around the Kealoha ranch.

As he told his brother about his dealings with Sinclair Adams, Key remained silent throughout the conversation, down to Nick's informing his twin of the woman's upcoming arrival.

After he finished speaking, he waited.

It hadn't taken long.

"What?" Nick asked, mildly irritated and somewhat unnerved by his twin's silence and sharp regard—two things he didn't necessarily like linked when it came to his brother and his uncanny ability to know what was on Nick's mind.

Key simply raised a thick brow and shrugged, coffee mug in hand, his gaze steady and intense.

"What *what?* I didn't say anything," Key replied. He brought the rim of his coffee mug to his mouth and took a casual sip, his eyes still focused on Nick.

Nick's brows bunched.

"Nothing to say, bro?"

"What do you want me to say?" Key threw back the question, shrugging. "I have better things to do. Besides, you know my stance on that situation."

Nick pushed away from the counter where he'd been lounging, feigning a nonchalance he was far from feeling, and just as casually as his brother, refilled his coffee mug.

"Better things to do? Like you and Sonia producing the next generation of Kealohas?"

Two could play the game. Just as Key had an eerie ability to know what was going on with him, Nick could do the same with his twin.

One of the many perks of being an identical twin and for that same twin to be his best friend.

If he wasn't in such a *mood,* he'd laugh at the expression on Key's face.

"How did you…" Key began, only to stop. He shook his head and barked out a laugh instead. "Never mind."

Nick laughed along with his brother, breaking the tension. He then went on to tell him the details of Sinclair's impending arrival.

After listening to Key cuss a blue streak, telling Nick what he thought of his lack of brains, to put it mildly, for not letting the family know "what the hell was going on," the two men sat at the kitchen table.

Although he really wasn't up for a "*Dr Phil*" moment, Nick had haltingly opened up, slightly, to his brother. He was glad when his brother finally reacted.

He'd spared Key the more embarrassing details. Hell,

there was no sense in telling his brother what was going on with him. He wasn't sure what was going on in his own psyche, anyway. And to go into confusing feelings for a woman he hardly knew...? No. That wasn't going to happen.

He laughed even thinking about it. He could only imagine how Key would look at him. Nick had never really been the type of guy to share his thoughts that easily. Even with his brother, the closest person in the world to him, Nick was still, at times, the clam.

But there had been times in his life, like now, where he'd felt a real need to break the mold. So he opened up a little, at least enough to tell Key that he wasn't sure how to handle the situation with Sinclair. He'd known he'd have to come clean, if nothing else, to get a feel for his brother's take on the situation.

As he spoke, Key listened, not saying a word. When Nick finished his succinct tale, Key stood from the table and slapped his brother on the back...hard.

"I'm sure you can handle it, bro. In fact, I know you will," he stated, his voice emphatic, a tinge of humor laced in.

Nick sat back, puzzled.

His brother continued. "I'm so confident in your abilities that on behalf of the family I'm *giving* this to you." The evil gleam in his brother's eyes, blue eyes that matched his own, should have given Nick fair warning. "Consider this...'situation' solely your deal. Dad and I are out of it. I'm sure you'll figure it all out."

Again, his brother smacked him on the back.

"What the fu—" Nick bit off the curse, jumping up after his brother's hearty smack on the back, toppling his chair as he rose. Swiftly he righted the chair and turned to face his brother.

"What the hell, man…that's *it?*" he asked, staring at his twin as he calmly walked to the sink, coffee mug in hand.

"Yep. That's it, Pika," Key replied, snorting.

Whenever his brother used his nickname, it always set Nick's teeth on edge. Not because he didn't like his nickname… He'd been called Pika, which meant "strong" in the Polynesian language, since he was a boy.

Nicknames were nothing new. Key's legal name was Keanu, but he'd been called Key for most of his life. It irritated Nick because he knew there were times when Key used the nickname simply to screw with him. Something both men considered their God-given right to do: give his twin a hard time.

Nick had always thought of it as good old-fashioned fun. Until he was on the receiving end.

Just as Key placed the coffee mug in the sink to rinse—*no one* wanted to deal with their housekeeper, Mahi, the longest resident of the ranch outside of the family, and his rants if the kitchen was left a mess—Sonia, his wife, entered.

She quickly spied her husband. A wide grin split her pretty face as she made a beeline for her new husband and wrapped her arms around his waist.

"Hmm, last night was amazing, baby," Sonia purred,

her voice low, throaty and intimate, once Key released the death grip he had on his wife's lips.

"It's been way too long, baby," she murmured as Key reached down and captured her lips again. Finally he released her, enough to glance down at her, keeping her within the circle of his arms.

"Yeah, it felt like forever," Key agreed, his voice barely recognizable it was so low.

Key had been away on an overnight trip, so really it hadn't been that long, Nick thought, shaking his head.

"Little Alek isn't going to magically appear, you know. It's going to take dedication and hard…" He paused and unashamedly pressed his wife close to his body, allowing her to feel which part of hard he was referring to. "Work," Key murmured, stopping to give Sonia kisses down the line of her throat. "And work…" He paused again to capture an earlobe.

Nick wanted to throw something at the pair…maybe cold water. They were like two dogs in heat.

"And work," his brother *finally* finished. His voice was so low Nick suddenly felt uncomfortable.

He felt like a damn voyeur and desperately wanted to get the hell away from the pair. Yet… Against his will, he was fascinated with their play. He watched as his brother bent to kiss away the frown that appeared on his wife's brow before slanting his mouth over her lips.

"Oh, yeah?" she asked huskily when he released her mouth. Although she was obviously trying hard to keep the smile from her mouth, the dimple in her cheek flashed against her will.

"And who says *she* is going to be a *he?*" she asked with a shrug. "We could have a little A'kela in the cards for us," she said. But the look in her eyes told the real story. Just like his brother, Nick knew his sister-in-law didn't care either way, boy or girl.

Nick *had* to glance away; the intense look of love in his brother's eyes was too much for him to see and not react. And right now he wanted to be pissed at his twin. Not want to hug him.

It was no secret that the couple was trying to have a baby. Neither was it a secret that if the baby was a girl, it would be named after their mother, and if it was a boy, it would be named after their father.

He turned back to the couple and caught the soft look in Key's eyes and the small smile that graced the corners of his mouth as he steadily regarded his wife of six months.

Had he not loved his brother so much, and truly loved Sonia like a sister, he would feel real envy for the couple. Their love was so tangible; it wasn't unheard of for one or usually both of them to be totally oblivious of anyone else in the room when they were around each other.

Deep and real.

He turned to leave and would have made it away had he not bumped into the chair he'd just righted, sending it crashing to the floor. He bit off a curse and picked it up.

"Hey, Nick, I didn't see you there!" Sonia said, a deep stain of color washing over her sienna-colored skin as she realized he'd caught them in an intimate moment.

He grinned widely.

"Not like I haven't seen you two like this before…
disgustingly lost in the moment," he grumbled playfully,
not sparing her. She was family. The Family That Teased
Together Stayed Together was his motto.

"In fact, I don't think I'll be able to look at the hot tub
or the pool again in the same way after last week," he
said. He hadn't really seen anything. But he'd hazarded
a guess that, knowing his brother, something illicit had
taken place in the hot tub. Without a doubt. He'd bet his
last dollar on the fact they'd gotten busy there.

He brought his attention back to the pair.

His sister-in-law's eyes opened wide and her head
jerked, looking up at Key. Key leaned down, allowing
his mouth to hover near her ear.

She blushed even harder at whatever his brother whispered in her ear, halfheartedly slapping away the hand
that rested on her butt.

"Key!" she admonished, voice low, yet Nick clearly
heard the sensuality in it. "Stop it, we can't… I have
work to do," she stammered, but when he leaned down
to whisper something else in her ear, her eyes widened
and she bit the lower rim of her lip.

"Really? We can try that?" She gnawed on her lip,
as though considering whatever it was his brother had
proposed. "Okay…I'm game if you are. I can do edits
later today," she said, the blush growing. "Or tomorrow," she finished and, giggling, allowed his brother to
lead her away.

Leaving Nick to stare after them, shaking his head.
Freaks.

The grin returned to his face, but soon thoughts of Sinclair filtered back into his brain and how he'd *deal* with her.

And from the look of things, he'd not be getting any help from his family in "handling" the situation.

Which was perfectly okay with him, considering how...deviant he knew he could sometimes be.

He chuckled at the thought.

Good. He was flying solo. That had always worked best for him. It was best for others, even family, who probably didn't know *just* how wicked he could be.

It was time to work on his plan.

Chapter 3

Nick pinched the high bridge of his nose and pulled his glasses away from his face, frowning deeply.

"What's the problem, old man? Sight not as good as it used to be?"

Startled, believing himself alone, his thoughts still on Sinclair, Nick glanced up and away from the computer screen to see his foreman standing in his office doorway, arms folded over her breasts, eyebrow raised.

"Hmm… Last time I checked, you weren't that far behind me in age, Alli-oop," he replied sardonically, a small grin threatening to break free. "What's up? Come on in," he said, waving Ailani Mowry inside his office.

"Don't want to interrupt," she drawled, yet pushed away from the doorway and ambled inside his office nonetheless.

"Hell, it's not like I'm getting any work done, anyway," he growled. Although he wasn't about to disclose the true reason for his malcontent, he couldn't keep the irritation away from his voice.

He glanced at the monitor and realized Sinclair's picture filled the *entire* screen. He could only imagine Ailani's reaction if she saw that image as his screen saver. Like he needed that.

Swiftly, casually, he minimized the screen and maximized the previous screen he'd been viewing: a PDF showing the projected budget revenues for the upcoming quarter.

No sooner had the spreadsheet appeared on the screen than Ailani was standing beside the desk, peering over his shoulder.

"Looks like we're going to be up in revenue significantly for the upcoming quarter," she commented and, without asking, grabbed for the small chair near the desk. She dragged it over closer to his chair, her eyes never leaving contact with the monitor.

He glanced over at her as she peered at the screen, completely ignoring him and the chair. Ailani and he shared history. No two ways about it, she was a beautiful woman, even as she "hid" her beauty.

More often than not she was seen wearing her long thick hair in a tight French braid tucked beneath the battered pink cowboy hat she'd worn since the beginning of time.

Many had thought the two of them would end up together. But despite growing up together from the time they were children, and the short stint where they'd shared a romance, the two had maintained a platonic relationship.

He continued to watch her as her eyes darted over the graph. When she turned to face him, although her eyes were hidden behind the tinted glasses she typically wore to shield her sensitive eyes, he caught the scrutiny.

"So, tell me. What were you really looking at with such intensity when I walked in, Pika?" she asked, a smirk creasing the corner of her small mouth. "And don't tell me it was this projection. It's not even the one from this quarter," she noted, crossing her arms over her ample breasts and waiting.

His eyes flew to the screen. Sure enough, instead of the PDF showing the budget for the upcoming quarter, it was the one from the last quarter.

Damn. His head was most definitely not in the game.

Just as he had with his brother, he feigned a nonchalance he was far from feeling and tried to play it off.

"Comparing last month's feed budget projection with the actual cost, cross-comparing it with the upcoming fiscal year's budget to determine if we need to reevaluate the project. And if so, do we need to make cuts in other areas to make up the difference."

His response was quick and *sounded* knowledgeable. He hoped she actually *bought* his bullshit.

There was silence for longer than Nick liked, yet he kept his eyes glued to the screen.

Ailani leaned forward and brought her body closer to his. A hint of patchouli and hibiscus wafted across his nose; a scent she'd been wearing for as long as he could remember.

She jabbed a short but manicured nail at the screen, pointing to one of the columns.

"Who came up with this projection? No way is this budget anywhere near what we're looking at for the upcoming quarter, nor does it make any sense for the new fiscal year!" she huffed, her eyes scanning the document on the screen. "Between the hike in prices in grain and feed, as well as the new shipment of steers we purchased last year, we're looking at a number substantially higher than this," she proclaimed.

Nick breathed a sigh of relief.

An irritated Ailani was much more preferable to a discerning one.

Of everyone he was acquainted with, besides his twin, Ailani was one of the most astute individuals he knew. If she caught even a *sniff,* a *whiff,* that something wasn't quite right, she'd hunt it down. The woman could teach his father's best hounds the true art of the hunt.

Lucky for him, her hound-dog nose was holstered for the present.

She wasn't paying much attention to him; her attention was purely on the ranch's budget.

Despite himself, he bit back a grin. Good thing he now thought of Ailani like a sister, or her lack of attention would have been insulting.

She leaned even closer, the right side of her breast brushing against his shoulder.

"What are you thinking with these projections?

Geesh, what would you do without me, Pika? Knuckle-head…" she grumbled, pushing even closer, the side of her breast nearly colliding with his nose.

"I know you want me and all, but really, Ailani, could you get your damn boob outta my face?" he complained roughly. He barked out a laugh when she distractedly batted a hand at him, ignoring him as she continued to peruse the document.

"If I didn't know any better, I would think I didn't do anything for you, Ailani…but we both know that isn't true. What with you practically nursing me and all," he continued, knowing she wasn't paying much attention to what he said.

"Pika," she mumbled, her voice completely distracted. *"Whatever,"* she finished, dragging out the word, the frown on her face growing.

Without looking behind her, she blindly reached for the chair she'd dragged to his desk earlier. Moving it closer, she plopped down in the seat.

As she examined the document, Nick continued to make completely inappropriate, off-color comments to Ailani, chuckling when she continued to ignore his bait-ing.

If she even heard it. Which he doubted she did.

When it came to her job as ranch foreman, all else became background noise to her. Which made it even more fun for Nick to tease her.

Just as he grinned and opened his mouth to make yet *another* inappropriate comment about her boob pressing into his face, a cough at the door caught his attention.

"One of your men told me you were alone. But if I'm interrupting, I can…you know, come back later."

His eyes flew to the door and the grin slowly slipped from his face.

He jumped from his chair like a soldier would when his commanding officer entered. So fast that his chair shot out from under him and probably would have toppled over had Ailani not caught it.

Not that he was giving his foreman any attention.

That honor went solely to the woman who had claimed more of his attention than she had any right to.

The woman who had him waking up in the morning, rock-hard shaft in his hand, finishing off the job she'd started. If only in his dreams.

Her voice alone brought his cock to full-on "salute" status. Just like the good soldier that it was.

Husky and low…it poured over him like scalding rain. Even as it held a chastising note, it was turning him on in ways he'd never experienced from simply listening to a woman's voice.

Hell, maybe that whole chastising tone she had going on added to the overall effect.

Whatever it was, it—*she*—had him hooked.

Her voice was velvety smooth and sexy, the type that reminded him of rainy days and sleeping in with a lover. But then his glance ran over her, head to toe. As hot as her voice was, it was nothing compared to her body.

Damn.

Live and in living color. On his turf… With no more provocation than that, his cock stirred.

Although he'd only seen pictures of her from the internet, those pictures were scorched permanently into his mind.

One of those images came to mind. The one he'd found of her at the Wildes' ranch and had printed out on the spur of the moment. The same one he'd glanced at just last night before he'd succumbed to sleep.

The dream spurred from that image had been one that had haunted him as he'd wakened. His cock hardened even more as his gaze raked over her now.

There was no denying who stood in his doorway, one arched brow raised, small bow-shaped lips pursed, stiletto-heeled foot tapping.

Sinclair Adams.

Chapter 4

Confrontation time.

Sinclair kept her expression tight.

Closed.

Control... She had to keep it around her like a security blanket.

She was afraid if she didn't, she would lose it.

Control was her best friend. Especially now. Thoughts of what her last few hours had been like, from the time she'd arrived in Hawaii and the fiasco surrounding all of *that*...to now, as she observed the scene in front of her. In one all-encompassing swoop, from the large office with its floor-to-ceiling windows that faced a gorgeous picturesque scene straight out of a movie, to the desk in the center of the room...and the commanding man who sat behind it.

There was also a beautiful woman with massive breasts standing close by... Sinclair took it all in. Okay, so maybe she was being catty. The woman's breasts weren't all that *massive*.

No matter, she thought, tightly reining in her envy.

She was squarely in the middle of the enemy's camp. She felt her back stiffen as she lifted her chin, automatically "preparing." For what? She would wait and see.

Her gaze made a swift survey of the office, taking special note of the custom-built book cabinets and the obviously expensive furnishings.

The walls were painted a muted deep red. One wall was nothing but an assortment of mirrors in various sizes and shapes.

Bold decorating choice, just like the red. The color choice and the mirrors were oddly erotic to her.

She shook her head, negating the thought before it had a chance to bloom any further in her mind. She continued her quick assessment.

There was an array of beautiful oversize rugs covering the polished hardwood floor, and a variety of artfully arranged statues that she would love to get a closer look at, had she been here for any other reason than the reason she was.

She brought herself up short.

She hadn't come to the Kealoha ranch to admire the beautiful furnishings, the amazing scenery...or the exotic-looking woman who was now staring at her as though she knew her.

She was here for business. She turned her attention to the man she'd come to do battle with.

And that is exactly what it was in her mind: a battle. Her eyes narrowed as she watched the woman standing so close to him.

And it definitely wasn't any of her business who the woman was. The same woman whose breasts—breasts that Sinclair doubted were her own—had been pressed against the side of Nick Kealoha's face as if she were about to breast-feed the man, when Sinclair had approached the door.

Sinclair knew she was being unfair; she didn't know the woman. For all she knew the massive boobs could actually belong to the woman. She mentally shrugged, pretending not to feel the least bit of *anything* about the woman, her breasts, or where they had been pressed....

Nor the man they had been pressed against. Not really. None of that mattered.

She was just feeling a tad bit...irked. She took in a physical and figurative breath and silently recited one of her favorite quick-but-calming mantras. It took a few seconds longer than normal, but she got it together.

She turned her gaze to Nickolas Kealoha, after nodding to the woman next to him. His gaze was already locked and loaded on hers.

This time, the breath she took was anything but figurative. Nickolas Kealoha was breath-stealingly fine.

Bright blue eyes kept her regard from beneath thick lashes, lashes that from the distance she was from him seemed impossible...ridiculous for a man to possess.

Even though he was sitting behind the desk, the sheer…massiveness of the man was enough to make her breath catch at the back of her throat. She had to remind herself to breathe. In. Out. In…

Big arms, thick with bulging muscle, were pressed against the desk. His chest seemed carved from granite. She bit back the moan when she caught sight of the small tuft of hair that splayed from beneath the fitted black T-shirt he wore under his chambray shirt.

Her gaze cataloged the long, muscular, thick thighs that even the simple work jeans he wore couldn't disguise. At his lean waist he wore a belt and large buckle with some type of crest. From her vantage point she couldn't tell what exactly was depicted on the belt buckle.

Because, yes…she was only interested in his belt buckle and most definitely not the thick…outline…that lay just south of the buckle.

"Like I said… If I'm interrupting *anything*…" she repeated. She cleared her throat and allowed the sentence to dangle.

"Of course not," the woman cut in, before Nick could say a word. "I was just leaving."

Sinclair saw him cut the woman a quick glance, no doubt cataloguing the shit-eating grin on her face, just as Sinclair had seen the sly look on the other woman's face, as well. It hinted at a long association, a certain familiarity.

Sinclair noted the obvious closeness between the two, for future reference.

And completely forced herself to ignore the ugly stab of jealousy she felt. Along with the immediate desire to swipe the grin from the woman's face.

The woman grabbed the pink beat-up Stetson that sat on Nick's oversize desk and jammed it onto her head, grabbing the thick ponytail and negligently tossing the thick rope of hair in front of her shoulder, so that the ends dangled beneath her breasts.

The movement was so quick and casual, Sinclair knew that it was one the woman did a lot, without thought.

"Yes, please come on in. Ms. Adams, I presume?" Nick asked casually, one thick eyebrow raised in question, as though unsure who she was. At the same time his eyes roamed over her as though she was dessert on the dinner menu.

Sinclair clenched her lower jaw so tightly she feared she'd need an emergency visit to the dentist if she wasn't careful.

She inhaled a deep, fortifying breath.

Control, Sinclair… Control, she reminded herself. She was here for her Wilde Boys, and that was it. As soon as this was over she was out.

She simply had to remind herself of that fact.

"Ms. Adams?" he asked again, and Sinclair's eyes met his. He stood and began to walk toward her, his stride long, purposeful.

As though against her will, she backed up a fraction. When her back hit the door she stopped, embarrassed.

Even from across the room, it was as though his piercing blue eyes were drilling a hole into her.

He came closer, his long legs eating up the short distance in mere seconds. He stopped less than a foot away from where she stood in the doorway, his gaze leisurely traveling over her face and down the length of her exposed neck…to the deep V juncture of her silky blouse.

His eyes lingered on the swell of her breasts.

As though he had every right.

Sinclair cleared her throat.

"Please…come in," he murmured, voice low. Sexy.

She felt a shiver run over her body.

His eyes finally moved back up to lock with hers.

Sinclair fought with everything she had to keep her eyes open. It was as though an odd lethargy had invaded her body and the strange pull he had on her increased.

They had spoken on the phone many times, and his voice had captured her attention from the beginning. They'd even had that unforgettable Skype experience, one that still made her blush because of what she'd done that night, alone in bed, thinking of him and his deep, rumbling voice and handsome face. But seeing and hearing *him* live?

Dear God. The fascination she'd had…the pull he'd had on her…. The one that had been increasing over the past six months of their association was set to detonate. She could feel it.

It was a low, rich rumble that resonated through her body, catching her completely off guard.

It surrounded her.

Sinclair's eyes briefly closed, no longer able to fight it…

As though touching her, his voice reached out and…

caressed her. *Did things to her.* She felt a trickle of moisture dampen her panties.

A shiver of awareness slithered down her body and she struck out her tongue to dampen lips that had gone completely dry.

"Sinclair." His deep, rich voice made her heart catch. She forced her eyes open and realized he was close. Too close.

Back up! she silently yelled—begged—him.

She felt claustrophobic.

Her gaze met the level of his throat. His neck, thickly corded with muscle, worked as he seemed to swallow.

Immediately her breasts reacted. Heavy, they felt engorged, her nipples pressing urgently against the thin silk of her brassiere. One she should have thought twice about wearing, as it had about as much protection against the heat of his stare as a thong in a snowstorm.

It was as though she knew this man...really knew him. On a level that made no sense to her.

It makes no damn sense, Sinclair! she silently screamed at herself.

Come on...his throat is sexy, a mocking voice piped in, laughing at her.

As soon as the thought entered her mind, Sinclair rejected it. She dragged her eyes away from his throat. Since when did she find a man's throat sexy?

Frick!

Okay. Control. *Bring back the control, girl,* she admonished herself.

But, God... The combination of his voice and those

hypnotic blue eyes, along with his impossibly handsome face…not to mention his body—big, hovering, masculine body. It all summed up to making her feel like a house cat in heat. Trapped, with no outlet.

She hadn't been in the least bit afraid to bring the battle to *their* camp. She was just that type of woman. Bold. Without conceit she knew she could handle hers when it came to any sort of…battle. So when it had come time to battle the Kealohas, Nick in particular, she'd not thought twice about it. She had, in fact, relished the idea after months of dealing with the stubborn man.

Yet for a moment she wished to God she could reverse time. Rethink her "you don't know with whom you're messing" decision to fly to Hawaii and confront the Kealohas.

But she had no time for a redo.

She had to deal with the situation. And deal she would. She'd never been the type of woman who was afraid of a man, fine or not.

She placed a faux smile on her face and pushed away from the door. Allowing him to usher her inside, she walked in front of him, trying for a nonchalance she was far, *far* from feeling.

She was glad she'd decided against throwing on her flats. The five-inch pumps she was wearing were just what she needed to help give her a bit of an edge.

She knew his eyes were glued on her butt as she walked ahead of him.

She put just a hint of something extra in her walk

and shrugged on her confidence as she would her favorite sweater.

"I think you and I have some unfinished business, Mr. Kealoha," she said, firmly tamping down the ridiculous pull he had on her.

She was proud of the way her voice came off. Strong, confident…and not in the least bit showing the crazy nervousness that quivered within her belly…. A nervousness she'd never, ever felt when dealing with any other legal situation.

"Indeed we do, Ms. Sinclair," he rumbled in his "hot sex on the platter" voice. She felt…*something* slide over her as he spoke.

She turned to face him. Oh, yes… She was in trouble.

"Looks like you're going to be busy for a while, Nick… I'll catch up with you later," the pink-hatted woman said as she made her way to the door.

Sinclair barely registered her presence.

The woman laughed softly as she left, saying something that Sinclair didn't even catch, she was so caught up in…him. It was as though no one else was in the room.

"I'll work on the new figures and we can go over them later, Lani," she heard Nick murmur to the woman, yet his hot blue-eyed gaze remained fixed on her.

Neither one of them noticed when the woman left the room, quietly closing the door behind her.

Sinclair licked her bottom lip, her gaze still fixed on Nick.

His scrutiny was sharp, focused, the intensity making her feel off-kilter. Uneasy.

Suddenly, intuitively, she knew what a gazelle felt like caught in the stare of a lion.... A hungry, beautiful lion.

Dinnertime. And he looked like the type that would... Eat. Her. Whole.

She swallowed.

Chapter 5

The first thought that came to Nick's mind was that her pictures didn't do her justice.

The woman was mouthwateringly fine.

And she had swagger. She wore it around her like a familiar, favorite sweater. He felt his mouth fight not to smile. He liked that.

Before Sinclair had allowed him to usher her inside his office, as she'd stood framed in the doorway for a moment, he'd caught her fear. Despite the confidence, there was an undercurrent of…fear, riding her.

Hard.

His gaze swept over her, head to toe.

She nearly vibrated with energy; bravado, swag…and fear. A heady combination.

No damn way she could hide it from him. He was

the type of man that could smell it on a woman. That uncontrollable sensuality…fear. He prided himself on it being his gift.

He'd nearly pounced on her then and there. But he'd tamped his own need to conquer. *Down, boy,* he'd admonished himself. Time for that later.

She was in his camp, now.

The grin, unknown to him, broke free, tilting the corner of his mouth upward.

Nick stared. She was…tinier in real life than she appeared in photos. If he had to venture a guess, he would say she was just a few inches over five feet, which placed her more than a foot shorter than he.

His glance slid to the flashy stilettos on her small feet. Well, without those she wouldn't even make it to his chest level, he thought, frowning. Small, despite the taller-than-life heels she wore, the top of her head would barely reach him midchest without the stilettos.

As he walked behind the woman, his gaze centered on the sexy-as-hell sway of her round-but-tight butt.

So, this was Sinclair Adams. Sinclair. Sin… Yeah, that was a more apt name, he thought. She was the epitome of walking sin.

She wore a loose-fitting blouse tucked into a knee-length skirt.

Nothing overtly sexual about the outfit.

But on the woman who walked in front of him, her small hips swaying as if she *owned* the place…it was hot as hell. The skirt was a "business navy" color, as he liked to think of that particular shade of blue, yet the way it molded her hips, nipped in at the waist and curved over her rounded butt had Nick sweating as though he'd run a marathon.

She turned and he bumped into her. He reached out to steady her and realized she had come to one of the chairs in front of his desk. Realized he was holding on to her shoulders longer than what was really necessary.

But damn if he could stop himself, or remove his hands from the softness of her shoulders. Unconsciously his fingers rubbed the soft skin.

"Are you okay?" he asked. Although he knew she was, it was the best excuse he could come up with to keep his hold on her.

"Um, yeah," she said, seeming in no more of a hurry than he was to move away.

His gaze traveled over her face.

Her eyes were large and were the focal points of her heart-shaped face.

Almost too large. His gaze was stuck, as though he couldn't look away as he stared into the dark brown depths.

As he stood in front of her, so close to her, her scent drifted across his nose. Without benefit of the cracked windows or overhead swirling fan, he could *smell* her.

Damn. His nostrils flared. She had a scent unlike any he'd encountered before. Spicy and floral. A heady combination.

He forced his gaze away to take in her small nose. The small diamond chip in the crease surprised him. He cataloged that small rebellion for later contemplation.

His gaze moved on to her lips which, like her eyes, were a shade larger than would seem to work for her small face. Yet…it worked on *her*.

Full. Luscious.

The bottom lip of her perfect mouth stuck out a fraction more than the top, giving her an earthy, pouty look that had his cock pressing hard against the zipper of his jeans.

Nick had an urgent desire to grab that luscious lip and suckle it deeply into his mouth.

To see if it…she, tasted as good as both appeared to promise.

He reluctantly dragged his gaze away from her mouth to glance at her hair. Although it appeared thick, he couldn't determine the length. She had it pulled into a high bun, with soft curling tendrils hanging down her face on either side of her temples.

Something told Nick it wasn't by design that the tendrils had escaped capture. It was likely more that the strands were too damn stubborn to do as she'd instructed them to and stay confined.

Stubborn, just like the woman who had captured his attention.

The dark, soft-looking curl begged for him to reach out and touch it.

Nick felt his shaft harden. Felt the low thrum of arousal that he'd felt for her, even before he'd met the woman, sharpening, throbbing, his cock painfully erect and pressing against his zipper.

"What…what do you think you're doing?"

Her huskily asked question brought him out of his own musings. Nick's gaze caught hers and he dropped his hand.

What the hell was wrong with him? he thought. He'd been so caught up in whatever the hell was going on between them, what had been brewing between them for six months, he'd forgotten who she was.

Who he was.

He cleared his throat, motioning for her to precede him and offering her a chair that was a safe enough distance away from his desk that he could get his thoughts... and randy cock, firmly back in control.

What the hell had he been doing—thinking? He schooled his mind and wayward cock back into submission.

It was all about control.

Nick's control was legendary.

She was in his camp, now.

Yet the mocking voice inside his head whispered, reminding him how he'd felt about her, the growing feelings... After six months of foreplay—cyber foreplay—he was set to explode.

Chapter 6

Sinclair opened her briefcase, trying to still her shaky hands.

"The boys and I believe we can come to a mutually acceptable agreement, Mr. Kealoha. One I'm sure—"

"Nick."

"What?" she asked, a small frown on her face as her eyes met his, realizing he'd spoken. Damn, the man was a distraction.

"Call me Nick. I think we're past the 'Mr. Kealoha' stage, don't you?" he asked, and she found herself staring at his strong fingers as he poured coffee into a mug, then handed the mug to her.

Immediately after the odd yet sexually disturbing first introduction, she wasn't sure what she expected to happen.

Would he come on to her now? Was it all part of some weird game to undermine what she'd come here to do? To set her up so that she'd forget the purpose of the visit?

If so, he had another think coming. She was back in control and nothing, absolutely nothing, was going to make her lose it. It was not going to happen.

"And I'm assuming you mean you and the Wildes?"

She glanced at him, her gaze sharp. She frowned. "Of course the Wildes. Who else?"

He leaned back in the oversize desk chair. Despite the largeness of the leather chair, he still dominated it, as she would imagine he dominated any room, any place he was.

He was *just* that kind of man.

His lips were curled into a ghost of a smile.

She felt a shudder run through her body and suppressed it.

Business at hand.

If she continued to have to remind herself of *that* simple little fact…she was in a world of trouble.

A look passed across his handsome face. One which she couldn't determine the exact meaning of.

"Well…as you referred to them collectively as 'the boys,' I assumed you meant the Wildes. Or do you represent another group of *lost* boys?" he asked sardonically, one dark eyebrow raised in question.

Sinclair sat straighter in her chair, frowning, keeping his gaze.

She opened her mouth to snap out a retort before closing it, her mind going back over her words. She looked away from him.

She bit back a sigh of embarrassment and barely refrained from slumping back against the soft leather seat. He was right. Damn it.

She had referred to them as *the boys*. She silenced a groan of embarrassment.

Having grown up around the brothers, men who were like older brothers to Sinclair when she was a child, she had always referred to them in that manner as had some others in the small community in Wyoming. Although most people now just called them the Wildes, she, and a select few others, had the liberty of long association with the men and continued to refer to them collectively in that manner.

But Sinclair had never used the nickname for the men while conducting business. Particularly when the business she was conducting was on the Wildes' behalf.

Nicholas Kealoha had her so rattled that she'd slipped up and done something she never had before.

Control. She fought hard to bring it back.

She plastered a smile on her face and observed him. Just as he'd made the comment, she'd caught the look on his face. She hadn't missed his "Neverland" reference.

Sinclair decided to keep the peace and not call him out on his attempted slam. Calling three men who were the antithesis to Peter Pan's Lost Boys was a ridiculous insult and one she refused to even acknowledge…while praying to heaven that somehow the men hadn't developed ESP. Her Wildes were true alpha men, the kind of men one did not mess with, as her father had once put it, just not in such mild language.

Yet for as rugged and alpha as the Wildes were, Sinclair would hate to see any of them go toe-to-toe with *this* man.

Her glance stole over him.

He smiled slightly at her, one corner of his sensual mouth hitching up ever so slightly.

In that way he had....

The way that made her wish some resourceful designer had invented air-conditioned panties.

Damn, he was hot.

He took up way too much...space. She was hot. Damn, it was hot. She resisted the urge to retrieve a slip of loose paper from her briefcase to fan herself. Besides, the place she really needed to fan, she couldn't. She felt a blush steal across her face.

A knowing look passed in his aquamarine blue eyes, and the blush intensified.

Before she'd met Nick, Sinclair had never thought she'd meet another man who could come close to the Wildes in sheer masculinity.

She turned her attention away from Nick to the business at hand.

"Well, I'd like to start an initial dialogue on what the Wildes are offering, and we can go from there in the negotiations. I think you and your family will agree that it is a fair deal," she began. In control.

She deftly unclasped the hook of her chic custom-made briefcase, a gift from the Wildes upon graduating from law school.

She withdrew an e-tablet from inside and automatically removed the clamp, attaching it to the leather handles of her briefcase before hooking it to the arm of the chair.

She caught his look. She didn't feel the need to explain why she didn't want her bag on the floor.

"As I was saying, the Wildes have come to an agreement, and the proposal they have given me permission to offer you and your family is more than fair, we all believe," she stated clearly, redirecting the energy away from the direction it had been headed.

She had no intention of being at the Kealoha ranch, or in Hawaii for that matter, for longer than was absolutely necessary. Although Nate and the family had given her carte blanche in the way of time, telling her to take the time she needed to take care of the matter, she planned to be as speedy about the business as possible. Thorough, without a doubt, but with a quickness.

She handed the e-tablet over to him, ignoring the snap of electricity that zinged back and forth the minute their fingertips touched.

The ghost of a smile remained on his face as he took the tablet from her hands.

She kept her face neutral and after long moments he sat back in the oversize chair and finally released her from his stare.

Sinclair resisted the urge to wipe away the bead of sweat she felt running down the back of her neck. She also stopped herself from slumping against the cool leather chair; she continued to wonder if it was hot in his office or if it was just her.

Control.

Throughout the meeting, Nick sat back and listened to her, allowing nothing of what he felt, nothing of what he was even *thinking,* to show on his face.

With Sinclair, he had ascertained that beyond the beautiful face, the hot-as-hell voice and body made for sex, she was a force to be reckoned with. Intelligence and confidence fairly vibrated from her small sexy body.

Her sensuality was one he found intriguing; so far, he'd figured out that she allowed only tiny snapshots of it to the world.

The small nuances told him she was not the conservative button-down corporate attorney that she presented to the world, from the small diamond chip in her nose, to the matching pink-tipped manicured nails and toes, which he'd caught a glimpse of from the peep-toe high-heeled shoes she wore. She tried to hide her sensuality. But it was there.

Hell, her curves alone told that story.

Sexy, with an edge.

Earthy, yet restrained.

As she'd outlined the proposal from the Wildes, she'd pulled out numerous documents. He'd noticed that they were all in order, filed in an accordion-style folder, and mirrored what he was reading on the tablet she'd handed him.

Prim and proper. With hidden fire.

He had to force himself to listen, to concentrate on what she was saying. He knew that a lot was riding on the situation, but damn if she hadn't made it nearly impossible for him to maintain focus.

However, her next words caught his attention, snapping him sharply back to the present and the situation at hand.

"So we, the Wildes, feel this unpleasant situation can be remedied to all parties' satisfaction. In exchange for you and your brother signing the document, we will withdraw all charges against you."

He heard and swiftly cataloged what she'd said. But it was one word…one phrase that caught his attention beyond the rest.

Unpleasant situation.

That, and charges against them.

Renewed bitterness toward the man who was his and Key's biological father rose swiftly. He shoved the emotions—anger, resentment—down, and focused on the rest of what she was saying. Focused on what was really important. None of the rest mattered.

He ignored the pang in his heart at the cavalier dismissal of his and his brother's importance in the Wildes' eyes.

His jaw tightened.

"Hold on," he snapped, holding up a hand for her to stop speaking. He glanced at her quickly and saw that his gesture didn't sit well with her.

Good. Because her dismissal of him and his brother didn't sit well with him, either.

He took his time as he scanned the last page of the document. And then, although he'd caught the gist of it, he swiped a finger over the tablet screen to take it back to the previous page to reread.

He frowned.

"Exactly what charges are you talking about for my brother and me to drop?"

She sat back and gave him a *look,* withdrawing the half-glasses she'd perched upon the narrow bridge of her nose.

"Mr. Kealoha, have you not been paying attention to what I've been saying? What I've been proposing for you and for your family?"

Nick wasn't easily embarrassed. Yet at that moment he was, and the feeling ticked him off. He was irritated not with her but with himself for so easily allowing her to distract him.

He stared across the expanse of the desk at Sinclair Adams.

She smiled.

His eyes narrowed. He'd have to watch her. Her hold on him was one that he wouldn't tolerate. It had been... interesting, before he'd met her. The way he'd think about her, allow her to filter into his thoughts at night, mostly, when he was relaxing, and moments before succumbing to sleep. But that was as far as it was going to go, as far as he would allow it to go.

Damn. He needed his full attention on this matter. He

sat straighter in his chair, making subtle readjustments against his randy cock inside his jeans.

"Never had a problem with my concentration, Ms. Adams. Everything I do…" he drawled, keeping his gaze on her. "I do with extreme focus. Ma'am," he finished. And smiled at her.

He caught the way her light brown cheeks blushed fiery red at his words.

Good. Score one for Team Kealoha. Control was back in his corner.

Now that he had it, he knew he had to put his cock, and what he wanted to do to her with it, away for the moment to truly concentrate on what she was saying and what the damn Wildes were proposing.

"In layman's terms, the charge you and your family have levied against the Wildes claiming right of inheritance. We are simply proposing that, as the late Clint Jedediah Wilde had no knowledge of you or your brother, it was without malice that you and your brother were not included in the inheritance of his property as well as monetary inheritance. Because of this, your lawsuit is, in fact, unwarranted. However, we are willing to discuss a settlement."

"A settlement, huh?" he said, feelings of anger swamping him as well as his judgment. Making him completely put to the side that he had actually decided not to go forward with the lawsuit. "I'm not sure this… proposal is going to work."

"And your brother? Your father? What are their thoughts on this situation? Do they share your feelings?"

she asked, pinning him with a look. "And don't you have to show this to them first? To your brother?"

He felt the heat of her focused stare.

Discerning.

It was as though she saw right through him. He'd been right in his assessment of her: she was one to watch. He'd have to make sure at all times that he was the one in the driver's seat; he could tell she was used to that privilege belonging to her.

He subtly adjusted his approach.

"Of course I do. And I will, Ms. Sinclair. We are a united family," he said, deftly sidestepping the question.

She stared at him, not saying a word, simply holding his gaze.

She finally spoke. "That wasn't exactly what I asked, Mr. Kealoha."

He knew what she was asking. He simply had no intention of answering. Not until he had a hold on the situation and had decided exactly what he *did* want and how he planned to go about seducing her out of it.

His initial anger gone, he had been ready to tell the Wildes and their attorney to go to hell. But now, all of that had changed. Now he wanted to…play…with the Wildes' attorney.

"Just like the Wildes, the Kealohas are united." His mouth firmed briefly before relaxing, a smile crossing his wide lips. "In fact, in the spirit of the Hawaiian tradition of welcome, why don't you meet them? My family, that is," he said when she looked confused. "Tonight."

Before she could protest, he finished, "Have dinner with me." He smiled at the look of surprise on her face. "With my family."

Chapter 7

Have dinner with me.

The request caught her off guard and Sinclair tilted her head to the side. "For what purpose? I think you've made your position clear. And to that end, I think it best for me to wait for you to confer with your family before we go further, Mr. Kealoha."

The entire time she'd been in the meeting with him, her nerves had been taut, tighter than a string on one of her guitars.

The fact that she'd managed to speak in an intelligent manner was something she was eternally grateful for. The man had her on *edge*...

She struggled to clear her head. She couldn't say it was anything he was doing; couldn't really pin any one thing, one action or word that put her in the state she was in.

Nothing other than him.

She sucked in a breath, her glance stealing over his hard body. And he was enough.

She kept her attention on the estate matter, reminding herself of her years of concentrating on long, boring legal briefs that no matter how mind-numbing, she had to plough through to not only understand but to pass her exams.

"We can discuss this further. Nothing is set in stone, Ms. Adams. Besides, I need to speak to my brother, and sister-in-law, and of course my father, before going any further. It is, and will be, a family decision." For a moment a hard look crossed his handsome face and she felt her heart thump against her chest in reaction.

In that moment she saw how he and his brother, along with their father had one of the most prosperous ranches in Hawaii. Just like her Wildes, this man and his family were a force to be reckoned with.

But so was she.

She offered a broad smile.

"I think our work is concluded for now, Mr. Kealoha," Sinclair said, closing the fastener on her briefcase and preparing to leave. "If you could contact me once you have presented the proposal to your family, I would appreciate it. Although you have my cell, here is my card. On the back I have the hotel name and number where I can be reached," she said, withdrawing a card from her wallet and placing it on his desk.

He lifted it, examining the card, turning it over, his brow furrowed.

She had to get out of there. Now. She needed to collect her thoughts, set up a game plan.

The meeting had begun with a rocky start, yet over the course of the past hour and a half, it had gotten smoother and she'd relaxed. As much as one could relax with a predator in the room. One that looked ready to pounce at any moment, despite the relaxed manner he'd showed throughout the meeting. Sinclair shuddered.

Yet for all of that, Sinclair felt as though she'd been in a battle with a tsunami.

And she wasn't sure she'd been the victor. Unlike most times in her interactions and in her role as an attorney, when she'd felt sure, confident. Yes, she felt confident in her abilities as a damn good attorney and in her negotiation abilities.

She'd stolen a glance at him from beneath lowered lids on more than one occasion throughout the time of the meeting. The last time he'd caught her, she'd glanced away, pretending a nonchalance she felt anything but.

The entire time she'd tried to ignore the strong attraction she felt for him. Yet her glance would steal over his strong arms, braced on the armrests of his chair, and the soft-looking chambray shirt that lay open at the top, exposing a black, V-necked T-shirt stretched over a hard-muscled, broad chest. Not to mention the faded Levi's covering long legs stretched out in front of him or the large, cowboy-boot-clad feet casually crossed at the ankles beneath the desk.

Her gaze caught on the lean planes of his face, the intensity of his blue eyes, deep set and heavily rimmed by thick dark lashes. The lashes being so dark against his blue eyes, coupled with the way she'd catch him eyeing her, had been unsettling. Intense. It was as though he was looking at her and had discerned her deepest, most...private thoughts.

A tiny shiver feathered down her spine.

It was her ability to withstand him as a woman that she was concerned about.

Quickly she stood and, with nervous hands, clutched her briefcase closer to her body, as though it could ward him off.

"Staying at the Royale, huh?" he asked.

She felt as though he were mocking her somehow.

"Yes. The Wildes made the reservations," she murmured.

"Nothing but the best for their...lawyer," he said, and she felt her hackles rise.

Yes, it was a luxury hotel, with a spa, as well.

After Althea Wilde had made the reservations and Sinclair realized how luxurious the hotel was, she'd protested, to which Althea had hushed her and laughed.

"Girl, you may as well enjoy Hawaii while you're there. No sense otherwise! Besides, Nate agreed with me when I told him," she'd said with a wink.

Reluctantly, Sinclair had accepted the grand gesture. She knew that Althea had grown up with money as the only child in a wealthy political family, though she herself had had to work hard at minimum-wage jobs from mechanic to waitress for a stretch of time as she had been on the run from a crazed ex-lover before coming to the Wilde Ranch.

"Yes, well, as I said, there is my contact information," was the only thing she said in reply.

He stood, as well. She gulped down a breath as she gazed over at him. Unable to move, but knowing she should, she stood rooted to the spot, transfixed.

He kept her gaze.

Feet, move, damn it!

Nothing. She couldn't move an inch to save her life. She finally was able to stop gawking at the man and breathed a sigh of relief. She turned to pick up her purse and looped it over her shoulder before turning to face him.

"Beautiful." His deep, sexy voice said the word with an almost…reverent sound.

Startled, Sinclair met his gaze, her heartbeat racing at the compliment.

"The leather," he continued. "It's gorgeous. May I?" he asked.

Before Sinclair could respond yes or no, much less acknowledge the ridiculous disappointing feeling that he wasn't referring to her but her briefcase, he strode over to her.

He reached out and touched the soft case, running his fingers over the supple leather.

"Um…yes," Sinclair sputtered, caught off guard. "I suppose it is," she finished, unnerved by the interaction. "Okay, that is. For you to touch my briefcase."

She stopped speaking, feeling all kinds of crazy.

Instead of his eyes on her, he was staring at her briefcase. She didn't know if she should be insulted or not, she thought, a strange need to laugh coming over her.

His glance met hers, a wicked grin on his face.

"Soft, supple…smooth," he said, his voice lowering. "I like things… smooth."

As she watched him fingering her briefcase, her breath caught in her throat.

She moistened her lower lip. "Thank you," she replied, her voice low. "I think," she mumbled before lifting her eyes to his. She cleared her throat. "It was a graduation gift," she said and watched again as his fingers reached out and caressed the leather.

Her gaze was caught on the action.

His fingers—long, strong and masculine. Just like the rest of him. As she stared in hapless fascination as his able fingers caressed the leather of her briefcase, she found herself wanting, for a brief moment, to feel his fingers doing the same thing to her skin.

She swallowed the melon-ball-size lump that had formed at the back of her throat at the thought.

"Let me guess… Your *Wilde Boys* gave it to you?"

The statement barely registered, yet she nodded.

"Yes. A gift. For graduating," she said again and felt foolish for unknown reasons. Now, besides the breathless quality, she knew she didn't exactly sound like the Rhodes scholar she in fact had been.

The man was reducing her to a mumbling simpleton.

"Why don't you come to dinner with me…I mean, the family, Ms. Sinclair? What do you have to be afraid of?" he asked.

It took more than a moment for her to switch gears, snatch her mind from where it was headed to focus on the question.

"What do you have to be afraid of?" he repeated.

Her focus went to his sensual mouth.

A challenge.

He was issuing a challenge. One she knew if she were the smart woman she always prided herself on being, she would definitely ignore. Any business they conducted could be during regular business hours. End of subject.

She dragged her attention away from his strong fingers, and the way he was absently working the leather of her case.

Her gaze met his.

Yes, in them she saw the challenge. She also saw the look of something else in their deep blue depths. Something that was immediately shut down before she could truly see.

"What time?" she asked.

Obviously that something else she'd seen, or thought she'd seen, made her throw caution…and no doubt common sense, right on out the window.

A slow grin tugged the corners of his mouth up into a

grin that promised he was absolutely the bad-boy player she'd thought he was from the first moment she'd laid eyes on his image.

Chapter 8

"Have dinner with me. The family, that is."

The request was out of his mouth before he could retract the offer, not that he would want to.

Nick had read the surprise in her face, one that spoke volumes.

Had he not been experiencing that disquieting feeling that told him he was in trouble—deep-shit trouble—in the form of the petite, sexy woman who'd stood in front of him, he might have retracted his words.

Or *because* that same feeling, if he were a sane man, would have made him rethink the invitation.

What the hell had he been thinking, anyway?

Nick ran the brush over the horse's silky coat, his mind on the meeting he'd had the previous day with Sinclair Adams.

When she'd agreed, he'd known it was pride that had her doing so; she hadn't wanted to show any weakness. Which was what he'd been counting on. He'd known because, instinctively, he felt she was his kindred spirit in that vein; had the shoe been on the other foot, he would have done the same.

Then his glance had run over her face. The sharpness of her eyes had struck him, the slight shadows beneath them a testimony to her exhaustion.

At first he'd been prepared to try to ignore her look of fragility. A fragility he knew without having been told was one she tried to keep hidden. With a clarity that came from out of nowhere, Nick knew that for all the projection of confident lawyer—which he knew her to be—she was beyond exhausted.

And when she'd told him about the car breaking down, he'd admittedly felt a stab of guilt. It had been childish of him to send Kanoa. He'd known the elderly man's vehicle, as much as he loved it, was unreliable at best. Nick had told himself, tried to convince himself, that he'd sent Kanoa out there simply to throw some business the older man's way. But that was a lie. Between him and his brother, they usually kept the elderly man "busy" with work: odd-end jobs around the ranch that didn't require much in the way of labor.

He should have had one of the guys from the ranch go out to get her— Hell, he should have done it himself.

Nick refused to acknowledge, even to himself, that there was any reason beyond being too busy to do so himself.

He continued running the brush over the mare, his thoughts pensive.

In the end he'd retracted the offer, claiming that he'd forgotten an engagement he'd already agreed to, and promptly hid a masculine grin at the knowing look that crossed her beautiful face.

The fact that she'd thought his "previous engagement" was a date was easy to discern from her expression before she'd shut it down.

The fact that it had…upset her had been visible in her dark brown eyes, as well, before she'd shuttered her lids, lowering them as she fiddled with the clasp on her bag.

He'd felt an odd catch in his chest at the small action. She'd looked so vulnerable.…

From the moment their eyes had met, Nick had been like a damn fish out of water.

With a sigh, Nick began to water down the horse, his thoughts on the woman he knew was going to be more trouble than he'd originally thought.

And all because he couldn't stop thinking about her. She'd invaded his dreams; months ago, before he'd even met her. Sinclair had done that. Her hold on him was one he didn't understand, and a big part of him damn sure didn't like it. It was…uncomfortable. New.

He'd never thought of a woman nonstop, in the way he thought of her, and it had nothing to do with the Kealoha ranch or the Wildes and the Wyoming Wilde Ranch.

Damn the Wildes *and* their ranch; he didn't want anything to do with them, or it. It was all her. Sinclair.

What had started as a way to get back at the Wildes

was now something more. He wanted her to stay around for a while…to get her out of his system, to get her out of his thoughts.

And although he had no intention of pursuing the Wildes' inheritance, he had to make her think that he did. To that end Nick knew he needed his family's help, even if they didn't know they were helping him, or for what reason. They needed to go along with him. Be the united front he'd claimed them to be.

Oh, yeah, and added to that…Key needed to bring his new wife into the deception, as well. Just to make it more convincing. Yeah, that was going to be a lot of fun, he thought, convincing his twin of *that*.

Just as that thought came along, Sonia walked inside the stable, along with the horse her husband had recently purchased for her at auction.

He grinned, his mood improving.

He knew Sonia had a soft spot for him, as he had been rooting for her and his brother during their courtship as well as their breakup. He liked to think he was the reason his knuckle-headed brother had seen the light and hadn't allowed the best thing to ever happen to him walk away.

He hadn't cashed in on his favor…yet.

Sonia had gone out of town yesterday on a short trip to the main island to meet with one of the investors for the new show she was producing. He had to get to her now, convince her to help him out, before Key knew what hit him.

He felt suddenly like rubbing his hands together like a cheesy villain in a badly produced horror flick.

"Hey, you! When did you get back in town?" he asked, as though he hadn't been aware she was in the stable. He gave his own mare a final wipe down before closing and locking the horse's stall.

He threw Sonia a grin, casually, as he quickly strode to her side.

"Let me help you with that," Nick said, hustling to reach her in time to take the horse's reins from Sonia's surprised grasp.

She tilted her head to the side and stared up at him, a question on her pretty face.

"What? Can't a man help his favorite sister-in-law out?" he asked.

"Favorite sister-in-law, huh?" Sonia replied. One hand on her hip in question. "How about *only* sister-in-law?" she asked with a laugh, but allowed him to take the reins. As she followed him to the horse's stall, he felt her eyes on his back the entire time.

He knew he had about as much chance of getting something sneaky past Sonia as he did his brother: nil to no chance at all.

But unlike his brother, with Sonia he stood a chance of leaning, heavily, on the whole "you owe me" thing he had going.

As far as using the guilt trip for his brother... He wanted to save that one. For the time he *really* needed to call in a favor.

Not that he thought she truly *did* owe him for the coming together of her and his brother. He knew that eventually the two would have done so, with or without his help.

"So what's up, brother-in-law? What do you want? Want to meet one of the interns I just hired? Listen, after that last fiasco where we had to call the police, I prefer we keep business and personal separate!"

"No! I don't want to meet your intern!" he railed as he began to lead the horse away. "It's nothing like that. Geesh, does it always have to be me wanting to meet a woman, for me to want to help my sister-in-law out?"

Sonia gave him a look.

He swore.

"You know you're becoming more and more like my brother every day!" he complained as he led her horse inside its stall.

She laughed and went over to grab the feed for the horse as Nick began to rub it down.

"Sorry, Pika" she said, smiling affectionately at the faux look of offense on his handsome face. "Okay. Thank you for the help. I was wrong. You're sweet as pie. And so generous. And helpful... Did I mention helpful?" she asked, holding back a laugh.

The jig was up. She knew he wanted something from her. Hell, he might as well get on with it.

"Okay, here it is," he began, pausing slightly when he heard her choke back a laugh. "I want you to help me convince Key to attend a family dinner."

She frowned as she brought the feed pail over to her mare.

"What's so hard about that? That's cake. We eat dinner as a family all the time! And now with Dad out of the hospital and almost back to a hundred percent, family dinners are a regular thing. Which I love! In fact, I was thinking of asking Mahi to make me some of his delicious—"

"Sonia, wait a minute!" he broke in, laughing and shaking his head at his sister-in–law's enthusiasm for Mahi's cooking…and family. For a moment the smile lingered on his face as he glanced over at her and her face lit up. "I wasn't talking about just the immediate family. I was thinking more along the lines of inviting someone—" He stopped, inhaled. Finished, "A woman."

And waited for it. *It* being her reaction.

He didn't have long to wait.

Sonia spun around so fast on her booted feet she nearly did a three-sixty, her spin worthy of making any prima ballerina envious.

He snickered but leaped to where she stood, reaching out a hand to steady her on her feet.

"I'll take this!" he said, taking the pail of feed from her hands and hooking it on to the attachment on the wall.

He gently swatted her mare's rear end, encouraging it to go and eat.

"Okay. Now back it up, mister. Wh-what? You? Invite someone to dinner… A *woman?*" she asked, astonishment on her gamine face.

"Don't act so surprised. I don't know if I should be offended by your shock," he said, walking over to the supplies they kept nearby, grabbing a brush and returning. He began stroking it over the mare, but gave up the brush to Sonia when she held out her hand.

"Okay. Spill," she demanded.

She began to brush the animal, pleasure in her face as she took over the task. Nick leaned against the stall wall and crossed his arms over his chest.

She had taken to ranch life as though she'd been born to it. From the moment she'd set foot on the ranch he'd known she was destined to stay.

From the moment she and his brother had first laid eyes on each other, fireworks erupted and *everyone* had known she was there to stay.

He shook his head at his own sentimental thoughts, laughing at himself.

None of that was for him—the destined-mate thing. Immediately, Sinclair's image appeared in his mind.

Sonia chose that moment to glance at him over her shoulder as she continued to brush the mare.

She gasped, her mouth forming a perfect *O*.

"Oooh…. You're thinking about her now!"

Despite himself, he chuckled. "You know…you sounded like a little kid when you just said that, right?"

"I may sound like a little kid, but Pika has a *girrrrl-friend*. Pika has a *girrrrlfriend*." She giggled, further making her point, then laughed outright when he reached down to the floor, grabbed a fistful of hay and tossed it at her.

"Brat," he said good-naturedly.

She brushed aside the hay in her hair, laughing, "I just got my hair done, boy!"

He laughed along with her, thinking that only Sonia could get away with calling him *boy*.

Looking at his sister-in-law's hair that lay on her shoulders, unpinned, as well as the casual way she disregarded the hay, made him think of Sinclair.

He wondered if she ever let her hair down. Just completely relaxed, and allowed herself to be free like that. He knew she had it in her to do so.

He did a quick reality check, and admitted to himself that just about everything reminded him of the woman.

"It's Sinclair Adams," he said and carefully watched his sister-in-law's reaction.

She went back to the task of brushing the mare's rich dark coat, her expression sobering. "Oh…I see. Was she here, then?" she asked, knowing that the lawyer had been expected to visit the ranch.

He was counting on the fact that his brother hadn't informed his wife of all the details, and the fact that he'd given Nick the responsibility for "dealing with" Sinclair, as Key had put it.

He scratched his head, suddenly ill at ease. He'd have to tread carefully.

"She is. And thing is, I'm not all that sure what I think about it all."

"In what way?"

He sighed. "It's no secret how I felt about my mother and…Clint Wilde. The whole secrecy behind who our father was.… Why our parents never told us…" he began.

Sonya nodded, yet remained silent.

She, like Key and their father, as well as those other

few close members of their extended family, was aware of Nick's anger over the deception.

"What I do know is that I invited her here with the intention of getting what I thought my brother and I were due. I own up to that. But now that she's here... Hell, Sonia, I'm just not sure."

"Do you still feel that way, Pika? That the Wildes... owe you?"

"Not so much 'owe' as I guess I just wanted an explanation."

"For?" she asked, continuing to brush the animal, giving it her attention.

Yet Nick knew she was giving closer attention to what he was telling her. It wasn't every day that Nick opened up.

"For?" he asked, anger tightening his face. "For...why the hell Clint Wilde never checked up on Mom after she left. All this love he had for her... Why not check up on her to make sure she was okay?" he snapped.

She turned to look at him. The softening of her expression and the sympathy he saw there was something he didn't want.

Even from his sister-in-law, whom he loved; he did not want her to feel sorry for him.

His face hardened.

"Pika..."

He glanced down to see her hand on his arm. He hadn't even been aware that she had moved toward him.

He barely refrained from shrugging her off, instead forcing the frown he knew was on his face away and his muscles to loosen. He was so tense he felt an ache in his shoulders where his muscles had bunched.

"Hey, it's not a big deal. I'm a big boy. I'm good." He shrugged off the anger…the unresolved feelings he felt for a man long dead. "But now that she's here, I want her to know that my family is united. I want her to meet the family. If for no other reason than to let the Wildes know we are united."

"Are you sure it's her you want to know this?"

He pinned her with a glare. "I don't need a pop-therapy session, Sonia." He'd hurled the words and felt guilty when her eyes widened and her mouth turned down at the corners.

"I know, Pika… I'm sorry," she said as he reached over and gave her a quick impromptu hug.

"You didn't do anything, Sonia. It's me." He laughed without humor. "Just trying to figure all of this out. Figured us coming together, showing unity, would send a message, I guess." He rubbed the back of his neck in an unconscious gesture he and his brother shared when they were uncertain.

Sonia recognized the gesture and her face softened even more.

"That's pretty important to you, isn't it? The family showing unity?"

"Yeah," he said, turning to put away the supplies. There was a short silence before Sonia spoke.

"Well, that's good enough for me. What can I do to help? And, yes, Pika…I know that my husband put this ball in your court," she said.

He turned to face her, surprised.

She shrugged. "Doesn't mean I can't—or won't—help my favorite brother-in-law out," she said, volleying back his earlier words with a spin. "So…what's the plan?"

He glanced at Sonia as she rubbed her hands together, preparing to plot like that cheesy villain in a badly produced horror flick he'd thought of earlier.

He laughed outright.

Chapter 9

Nick was unlike anyone that Sinclair had ever met.

After the dinner with his family the night before, a few days after her arrival at the ranch, he was more of an enigma than ever to Sinclair.

She'd been glad for the reprieve; instead of facing his family that same horrendous day of her arrival, she'd been able to take a few days, acclimate to the time change as well as relax a bit.

She'd gone back to her room, unpacked and gotten herself "comfortable." She was a self-proclaimed "neat freak," preferring things be put in an orderly fashion.

It came from a lifetime of living in smaller quarters. She and her father had lived in one of the guest cottages on the Wilde Ranch, as many of the families had, and although the cottage was nicely kept—quaint—it hadn't been large. However, it had been enough room for the two of them.

Dorm life and a series of smaller studios and apartments had strengthened her habits. So, after making sure she'd put everything in its place, she'd also set up all of her gadgets: laptop, iPad, iPad mini and iPhone. She was a self-proclaimed gadget junkie.

Then she'd promptly fallen asleep after taking a long hot shower. The last thought on her mind: Nick Kealoha.

After waking up the next day, refreshed, she'd called the ranch. When Ellie Wilde had answered, she'd smiled. Sinclair loved all of the Wilde women. Each woman was unique, with her own very distinct personality, and they were all very loving women.

Yet, of all the Wilde women, she identified with Ellie the most.

Studious and serious, Ellie, too, had grown up around the ranch. Although she hadn't actually lived on the ranch, as she and Yasmine Wilde had, Ellie knew ranch life just as well, if not more. Her father had been the veterinarian for the Wilde Ranch and Ellie had followed in his footsteps.

The reason Sinclair identified with Ellie just a little more than Yasmine was that in addition to being an academic, as Sinclair had been, Ellie tended to be quiet, and had also grown up with only her father as a parent.

She smiled, now, as she took out a mug from the small overhead cabinet and poured herself a cup of the coffee she'd brewed. Taking it, she sat at the small table in the kitchenette of her suite and recalled their earlier phone conversation.

"Hi, ladybug, how's it going?" Ellie had asked in her low-toned, melodic voice.

"It's going!" she'd said, grimacing.

She'd laughed when Ellie replied, "Oh, Lord…what's happened so far? That didn't sound so good!"

She'd briefly retold what had happened to her during her trip so far, making light of the entire thing. As well as glossing over the effect Nick Kealoha seemed to have on her. She was close to the Wilde women, but not ready to disclose how she felt about Nickolas Kealoha.

She herself wasn't even sure how she felt.

"And how's it going with Nick Kealoha?"

The direct question had made her tense. Had Ellie somehow known about her odd relationship with the Kealoha?

"Nate mentioned that he was your point of contact? Or are you dealing with the other brother…Keanu?"

She'd felt her body relax. Ellie hadn't known. Sinclair had briefed her on what had occurred, and asked Ellie to relay the message to the Wilde men that she'd met with the Kealohas and everything was on task.

After that, she'd caught up on ranch life with Ellie. She'd smiled and given her loving congratulations when Ellie told her that she and Shilah recently found out they were pregnant.

"How is he taking it?" Sinclair had asked, a grin on her face as she'd pictured Ellie's husband watching her every move. Just as his brothers were when it came to their women, Shilah Wilde was fiercely protective of Ellie. Although she had a practice in the city, seeing domesticated animals of the town near their ranch, Ellie was not only the vet for the Wilde Ranch but would also lend a hand when needed on the smaller ranches nearby. The work could be hard and grueling, particularly when it was a difficult birth for one of the larger animals.

Because of this, Shilah tended to…worry about her. And that was putting it mildly. The man was crazy about his wife, she knew, which seemed to be a running theme with the Wildes.

Even before learning of the pregnancy, he would go with her when he could to help her in her practice, particularly when her father or one of her assistants was unable.

"Oh, my goodness…don't get me started," she had said with a wry laugh. "Now what do you *think,* Sinclair?" Ellie'd then asked, sounding exasperated. But Sinclair knew that the woman loved every minute of her husband's overprotective ways. The Wilde men were alpha men; no two ways about it, they protected what they considered theirs.

"I can only imagine." She'd laughed along with Ellie and listened as she'd filled her in on the other happenings on the ranch.

Sinclair sat back in the chair and finished her coffee, the smile on her face slowly dropping as she thought back over the dinner she'd had with the Kealohas and what she *hadn't* told Ellie.

* * *

Not knowing what to expect, Sinclair dressed carefully for her meeting with the Kealohas. Although he'd made it seem as though it were just a friendly meet-and-greet dinner at the ranch, in her mind, Sinclair firmly placed it in the business-only category.

It was bad enough she was having a difficult time separating business from pleasure with Nick, thinking not only of their six-month-long…foreplay, she thought, blushing, but of their over-the-top explosive first meeting, as well.

She still blushed thinking of their first meeting earlier that week. The way he'd been instrumental in taking feelings that she'd already begun to sense—feelings she didn't want to name—to the nth degree, turning her on, making her sweat…making her wet.

She ran her hands over her hair.

She'd spent the past few days learning as much about the Kealohas and their ranch as she could, all low key, not asking overt questions of anyone, just casual questions, as though she were another tourist. Her objective: knowing who she was dealing with from a different vantage point.

Which wasn't difficult; everyone knew the Kealohas, both the locals as well as the tourists. She'd learned more than she'd wanted to while on a tourist shuttle and listening to the two young ladies giggling in front of her. Twins, from the looks of them, they spoke loud enough for anyone to hear about how they were going to meet the "dynamic duo" and what they were going to do to them once they did.

Sinclair prided herself on being a grown woman, confident and accomplished.

Although somewhat inexperienced, she still thought herself to be sophisticated and aware...but after listening to the young women, she didn't know the last time she'd blushed and been more uncomfortable...yet strangely intrigued. Were some of the things they'd said even humanly possible to perform? she wondered.

Besides her encounter with the amorous twins, exploring the island the Kealohas' A'kela Ranch was located on had been an eye-opener for Sinclair. She had seen for herself the amazing impact their ranch had on their community as one of the most profitable family-owned ranches in all of Hawaii.

She'd gone into one of the local shops and listened as the owner had been on the phone with someone from the Kealoha ranch. After hanging up, there'd been a relieved smile on the woman's aged, dusky face. "Thank God for the Kealohas," she'd said and smiled at Sinclair.

"Something good happen?" Sinclair had boldly asked, yet kept her voice and question light.

"My grandson attends the University of Hawaii," she'd said, gathering Sinclair's small items and preparing to ring them up. "Money was getting tighter, and the Aloha Keiki Foundation is going to pick up the tab for his senior year!" she'd told her, a wide smile on her brown, leathery face.

Sinclair had smiled and congratulated the woman, yet

she'd been bothered by the idea that she had been wrong about the Kealohas. A pensive mood engulfed her for the rest of the day, as she'd toured the small town and learned of other small ways the Kealohas impacted the community they lived in.

She arrived at the family's sprawling ranch home on time and ready. She'd brought everything with her, armed herself with her beloved electronic gadgets as well as the documents she'd again gone over to make sure she'd covered all of the facts Nick had made bullet points about. She was ready for the family meeting with her guard up, ready to defend her Wildes *if* and *when* the opportunity arose.

Surprisingly, as the night wore on, the need for a swift defense would never come up.

She was greeted at the door by the housekeeper, who she learned was known simply as Mahi. Although concise in manner and speech, she felt the warmth in his welcome of her into their home.

She smiled at his demeanor. It reminded her keenly of Mama Lilly, the woman who had been the housekeeper for the Wildes from the time Clint Jedediah Wilde had bought the ranch. Like Lilly, Mahi's easy manner was one that instantly put her at ease.

And if she'd thought Mahi had been a fluke, she'd been mistaken, quickly.

"Come in, come in! You must be Ms. Adams. So nice to meet you. I'm Sonia Kealoha!" No sooner had she been ushered into the large, majestic-looking foyer, than a beautiful woman was headed her way, hand out-stretched. Close behind her was a man Sinclair knew had to be Nick's identical twin, Keanu Kealoha.

Forcing a smile on her face, and telling her feet to move forward, she placed a hand within the woman's and shook it, her grip firm.

"Mrs. Kealoha, it's nice to meet you," she said, keeping a pleasant expression on her face. "I saw the new documentary on ranching and the impact on the environment from a naturalist point of view that you directed a few months ago on the network. Very impressive."

The woman's eyes widened fractionally before the smile blossomed even more.

"Why, thank you so much. That means a lot! It's a new venture of mine, producing documentaries. It's been quite a change from my normal undertakings. A little scary, but hey, change is good." She stopped and smiled, her cheeks dimpling as she did. With a shrug she continued, "And not only did I direct it, I produced it," she said, and Sinclair caught the way her husband's hand tightened more on her waist and the pride in his blue eyes as he glanced at his wife as she spoke. "I'm very proud of the reception it has been receiving. I'm so happy you enjoyed it!"

"I did, very much. I rarely have time for television, but when I saw the reviews of your documentary, it was something I knew I couldn't miss. And I was right. It was brilliant!"

Everything she said was true. The documentary had

been riveting, and unlike many documentaries on the environment, it had been vibrant and at times even funny.

Sonia Kealoha was eating up the compliments with a big smile on her face. It didn't hurt Sinclair in her end game; *keep the enemy off guard.*

"And as I'm sure you know, this is my husband, Key...Keanu, that is," she said as the man came closer. He stuck out a hand for her to shake.

Okay, this is it, she thought. *No way is he going to be as welcoming as his wife, or even the housekeeper, for that matter.*

To say she was surprised with the honest warmth reflected in his blue eyes—eyes that were identical to the man she'd once referred to as a blue-eyed devil—was putting it past mild.

"Honey, I told you about Ms. Adams joining us for dinner, right?" the woman asked, upping the wattage on her smile a hundredfold.

He smiled down at his wife. The arm he had casually wrapped around her waist when he'd first come by her side tightened just a fraction, the long fingers massaging the indenture of her waist.

Hmm. Interesting, Sinclair thought.

She caught the passing glance between the pair. It was...a conspirator's look they had exchanged.

Sinclair cataloged it. And promptly pushed it to the back of her mind for later contemplation.

"You mean the text you sent to the phone I left on our bedside table this morning? The phone that got trampled when I broke in one of the new horses? The phone

I asked, since you were headed to town, if you could take with you to see about getting me a new one? That phone?" He said with a mischievous glint in his eye.

His wife's feigned look of surprise didn't even look real to Sinclair, and she didn't know the woman.

Sonia bit her bottom lip, fighting the grin that Sinclair could see was tugging the corners of her generous mouth as she grinned unrepentantly up at her handsome husband.

She reached a hand up to pat his lean cheek. "Oh, baby, I forgot about that!" she replied. "I'm so sorry. Is there anything I can do to make up for it?" she asked, and again she had the butter-wouldn't-melt-in-her-mouth expression on her pretty face.

If anything, her grin deepened.

Against her will, Sinclair found herself intrigued by the couple's playing.

"Hmm. Maybe," he said, his gaze catching on her mouth before sliding up to her face. "I'm sure I can think of something. We'll talk about your punishment later tonight."

"Am I in trouble?" she asked. But the way she said it... Sinclair fought against a blush. She felt like a voyeur.

"You might be."

Sinclair caught the way Sonia's eyes widened and the look her husband gave her made Sinclair's blush break completely free.

She'd seen that same look on his brother's face just two days prior, when she'd been in his office.

Directed at her.

She felt a fine line of sweat bead on her brow and trickle down her cheek.

If she didn't know any better she'd swear she had bypassed her productive years and been slammed straight into menopause with the swamp of heat.

She felt her entire body heat up, wondering if it had been a good idea to accept the invitation to dinner, after all.

"I see you've met my brother and sister-in-law.... Please, don't mind them. Come on in."

All three turned when Nick's deep voice interrupted. Sinclair had never been so glad to hear his voice.

She, along with Sonia and Key, watched him walking down a long stretch of hallway, his strides eating up the distance before he was standing in the foyer with the trio.

"Don't mind us? What is *that* supposed to mean? You weren't even in the room, anyway," his brother scoffed. "How do you know there is a need for you to excuse our behavior?" Key asked, staring at Nick.

As the two men faced one another, Sinclair took the time to look at them both and was struck by their similarities.

But she was even more struck by the fact that although the two men were indeed identical twins, she knew that, without a doubt, she'd be able to tell them apart.

Both were tall, equally so. She knew that some twins, even identical twins, would sometimes have one that was either taller or heavier, or sometimes both.

Not in the case of these two rugged Hawaiian cowboys.

Both men wore scuffed-up cowboy boots with equally worn heels, so there was no height advantage for either twin.

She discreetly ran a glance over them.

Just as with their height, both had an impressive breadth of shoulders; wide shoulders that tapered down to a trim waist and thick, muscled thighs. Her gaze trailed to their faces.

Both were drop-dead gorgeous, with startling blue eyes and light golden-tanned skin. Their eyes were made even more vivid by the darkness of thick eyebrows and ridiculously long, sooty eyelashes.

Their aquiline noses were similar, right down to the small bump in the middle. She'd noted that both had that same bump and assumed it was from a sporting accident. It wasn't uncommon, she knew, for twins to fall into the same type of injuries.

Although both men wore their jet-black, shiny hair longer than tapered, Nick's was a few inches longer, the ends curling lightly and brushing the top of his collar.

Chiseled cheeks and a square chin completed a picture of rugged, uncommonly fine-looking men.

But for all that…she caught the difference: the small dimple near Nick's lower lip when he smiled. The way his lids would lower when he looked at her, as though he had something so naughty on his mind that he sought to hide it. He knew better than to let her see his eyes, knowing it would show.

Or the way, when he smiled, just one side of his

mouth would hitch upward and again, his hooded eyes would stare a hole into her, making her feel like some kind of prey caught in a fierce predator's focused sight…

He chose that moment to glance over at her and she felt the heat of that predator's stare. She was helpless to look away.

"I'm glad you could make it, Sinclair," he said. His voice seemed deeper, richer. A low, sexy rumble.

She grew warm and sweat pooled between her breasts.

"I gave Mahi a list of your demands… I mean, the foods you might like," he said, and she caught the twinkle in his eye and fought the urge to laugh along with him.

When he put out his hand for her to take, she hesitated before placing hers within his.

She turned and caught Sonia watching her, an odd expression on her face. When their eyes met, the other woman smiled at her and Sinclair felt oddly embarrassed.

The other woman had given her the type of look only a woman could give another that she knew was attracted…to a man.

The evening meal and accompanying conversation went quite smoothly. No great surprises, other than the fact that Sinclair was having one of the best times in the company of other adults that she'd had in longer than she wanted to think about.

Nick mentioned that he and Key ran the A'kela Ranch, while their father Alek Kealoha was recovering from a stroke.

She was glad to hear the patriarch was doing well in his recovery and would eventually start to take a more active role around his ranch.

At one point, as they began eating the homemade coconut ice cream Mahi had prepared for dessert, the topic went back to the documentary that Sonia had produced.

"I have no problem using my man for my business endeavors. In fact, he likes it, don't you, baby?" the other woman asked, and Sinclair's eyes widened at the obvious double entendre.

"Yes, baby. In fact, I'm going to let you know tonight just how much, dear," he said.

Sinclair saw the other woman's reddish brown face flush.

"I told you…. Freaks," Nick said drolly, a bored look on his face as he nodded his head toward his brother and sister-in-law. "You get used to it, though, Sinclair."

Although he'd made the comment, a light of humor blazed in his blue eyes and she'd seen the love he had not only for his brother, but obviously for his sister-in-law, as well.

They had all laughed at his feigned offense, including Sinclair.

A small smile played around her lips as she enjoyed the rest of the conversation, any tension she'd thought she'd encounter a distant thought.

Chapter 10

As the night moved on, Sinclair had been amazed at how the time had flown and how much of a good time she was having.

She had found that the brothers, both, had a wicked sense of humor. One that, had she not known any better, would make her think they were in fact blood relatives of the Wildes.

Yet the Wildes were not actually blood brothers, despite the similarity in their personalities. A lot of that had to do with them being raised together as brothers, under Clint Jedediah Wilde as their father.

Guilt assaulted her from two different camps. On the one side, she'd suddenly, eerily, gained an odd understanding of what the twins felt, knowing that Clint Wilde was their father yet never having known him. She could understand the anger and betrayal both men no doubt felt. Although Nick was open about his anger, his brother was silent. Yet Sinclair had found him looking at her throughout the meal, occasionally. In his blue eyes was not anger or mistrust...it was the exact opposite.

She'd felt confused, unsure of what was going on, why he seemed so much like family...

It was a disquieting thought, which in turn presented her with the other side....

That one thought alone made her feel exceedingly guilty about her Wilde Boys. She was there for them... not to cozy up to the Kealohas, no matter how she may empathize with them.

After dinner and dessert, they took their coffee to one of the larger sitting rooms. Immediately, Sonia and Key sat, as though one, in a large chair that was meant for one but two could share. She smiled at the love between them. It was so palpable she felt as though, again, she was back home observing the Wildes with their spouses.

She felt Nick's eyes on her and her heart started thumping hard against her chest, a reaction she was starting to associate with him.

He reached out a hand for her to take, asking her, silently, to sit near him on the soft leather sofa. She took two steps before she halted and shook her head as though to clear it.

"Come and sit with me. I don't bite," he said and her face caught color as her eyes widened. She heard a choked-off laugh coming from Sonia but couldn't stop looking at him.

"Come on…you know you want to," he said and her blush deepened.

"Give the woman a break, Nick. She doesn't know you, yet," she heard his brother admonish from behind her, but still she was stuck, her gaze locked with his.

He smiled.

Her heart about stopped beating.

"Oh, yes, she does, brother," he murmured for her ears alone.

The blush intensified and she swallowed. She forced herself out of the odd trance he'd placed her under.

She straightened her back, lengthened her spine. Purposely she put on a sardonic look as she threw on her attitude like a well-worn coat.

"You're right…. I do," she said to Key before turning back to Nick. "Which is why I think I'll take this seat instead," she said, pointing a finger at the chair beside which she'd left her briefcase. Behind her she heard both Sonia and Key laugh outright.

Point: Sinclair.

Completely ignoring *his* knowing smile, Sinclair sat in the upright chair and brought her briefcase into her lap, strangely battling a smile she felt trying to break free.

She, with reluctance, pulled out the documents she'd brought with her.

"Listen…we trust you."

Before she could even withdraw all of the documents, Key had spoken.

Her eyes flew to meet Keanu's glance. "Excuse me?"

She could feel Nick's eyes on her and turned to see him sitting back on the leather sofa, a neutral look on his handsome face that didn't match the blazing look in his eyes.

"Of course we will look at the documents," Key continued, "but as I've told my brother, we are leaving this... decision for him to handle. We trust and believe in him." Key spoke calmly, as though not discussing what could be a volatile situation regarding millions of dollars at stake. "Whatever decision you two come up with is one that we, as a family, will agree to. Whatever that is," he finished.

His wife smiled down at him, kissed him. The moment was so private, a communication only the two of them understood, that Sinclair glanced away, her eyes colliding with Nick's.

"Looks like you're stuck with me, darlin'," he drawled, his hot glaze sliding over her body.

She fought the warmth flushing her body with his look.

"Hope that's all right with you?" he rasped, bringing the cup of coffee he held within his big, capable hands to his mouth.

"I think I can, uh, handle that," she said, putting the papers aside and toying with her own mug, her gaze locked with his.

"Good," he said, one side of his mouth lifting in that way he had, before he took a drink of the hot brew.

She watched in helpless fascination as he drank. The

way his throat worked the liquid down, the strong column of his neck straining as it slid down his throat.

She forgot for the moment that anyone was there but Nick. She even forgot why she'd come there.

There was *no one* in the room but the two of them.

"So, are you okay with that, Sinclair?"

Sinclair turned to see Sonia staring at her, a small smile lifting the corner of her generous mouth.

"I'm definitely good with that," she said, putting as much professionalism as possible into her voice and demeanor. "No problem for me."

The rest of the conversation proved pleasant, though before long Sinclair, surprised at the time, started to gather up her things. Standing, she said good-night to Key and Sonia and nodded when Nick offered to walk her to her car. It seemed natural for him to do so.

After walking her to her rental, he offered to shadow her back to her hotel.

"It's not a problem for me to do that. It's late, and although it's safe around here—the entire island is—I would feel better if you allowed me to see you back to your hotel safely."

She was already shaking her head no before he could finish.

"Um, no. I'm good. I mean, it's not that far of a drive. And, uh, like you said, the island is safe and—" She stopped as the dimple appeared near the lower corner of his mouth.

He was so sexy when he smiled like that. She nearly groaned out loud.

She knew she had to get away from him quick-fast and in a hurry. Throughout the evening they'd locked gazes and she'd known that he was too…experienced not to know she found him sexy as hell. And at this point, not only was it obvious that she felt attracted to him, but from the looks and his demeanor it was clear he was attracted to her, as well.

She was in a precarious position.

But she also knew his ego was just big enough that he would never think of forcing his attention on her. No, he was the type who enjoyed the woman chasing him.

She straightened her back, firmed her smile. Well, she wasn't that type of woman.

His eyes rolled over her face and stopped at her mouth.

With his gaze focused on her mouth, she licked lips gone completely dry, leaning away from him, fumbling in her satchel for her keys as her rear end bumped against the car door.

She glanced up in time to catch the knowing look in his vivid blue eyes at her telling response to his nearness.

"Well, thanks for a great evening. Your family is very nice. And I'll get back with you all on the new proposal. I mean *to* you, I guess, as it appears as though we're flying solo with this," she said in one long rushed sentence. She stopped and forced a smile she knew was twitchy from the nerves racking her. She turned, not wanting to make eye contact because she was too damn nervous to do so.

"Good night."

She would have gotten away with it, too, had he not stopped her, placed his big, warm hands on her shoulders and turned her back around to face him.

Goose bumps feathered down her arms when she felt his hands run down the length of her bared skin before holding her wrists.

She dropped her briefcase on the soft grass.

In a move that surprised her, he leaned down and captured her lips with his.

And just like that, she detonated.

His lips feathered back and forth over hers, casually, no demand, while his hands loosely bound her wrists.

When his tongue pressed against the seam of her lips she eagerly opened for him, eager for the feel of his tongue in her mouth. She'd imagined how it would feel, rough yet smooth.

She groaned when he lapped inside.

It was just as she'd imagined, but hotter. More intense.

He pulled her closer, one hand taking over as it kept her bound, the other moving to the back of her neck.

He was in control. Even as he kissed her, his lips making love to her mouth, a part of her recognized that he was a man used to being in control.

She allowed him the control, because it made her feel so damn good.

She moaned, leaning into the kiss and shyly meeting his tongue with hers.

He groaned harshly and brought her even tighter against his body, grinding against her so that she inhaled sharply against the sensation, feeling his shaft, thick, hard, against her stomach.

The kiss grew hotter and wetter as their tongues dueled.

A sound broke into her consciousness like an irritating buzz. She recognized it as the sound of men speaking, laughing, not far in the distance.

She brought her hands up to his chest and pushed him away.

Sinclair was so shaky she leaned against the car to lend her strength.

He reached out to grab her shoulders, and she moved away.

"I'm fine," she mumbled.

"I shouldn't have—"

"Look, it's fine. I'm a grown woman. I didn't let you do anything I didn't want done," she said, forestalling him from apologizing, her hand raised as she turned to lift her briefcase from the grass near the driveway where she'd allowed it to drop.

She glanced up at him in the dark, the moon highlighting his handsome face.

Instead of the look of triumph she expected to see, his was one of arousal mixed with something more.... That same thing she'd seen when they'd first met.

It was as though he was trying to peer into her soul.

Without a backward glance, she got into the car, reversed and skidded in her rush to leave before smoothly taking back control. Yet...she raced from the circular driveway as though the hounds of hell were after her.

With all of the heated stares and with all the sweating and panting she'd been doing the entire night, she felt just as though they were.

Chapter 11

She was a powder keg of sensuality, waiting to be lit.

He ran a hand across his face.

Nick couldn't take it anymore. The entire week he'd been on edge, his cock so hard he could use it to slice the Wagyu beef his family prided themselves on producing.

And the longer he watched her prance around his ranch, the randier he got. He didn't know how much longer he could take it before he would detonate.

And day by day it was getting worse.

It had been just a week, and he had it so bad for her, he was beginning to question his own sanity.

That morning he'd had a run-in with his brother. He'd known that his brother was aware that everything wasn't going exactly the way he'd planned with Sinclair the minute Key had opened his mouth.

* * *

"Everything cool, Nick?"

Without asking, he was asking…. It wouldn't take a rocket scientist to figure out that Key knew things weren't going that great.

Nick snorted. "That's got to be the understatement of the year."

He'd gotten up early this morning, earlier than the normal—5:00 a.m.—just to get out to the south pasture to look upon his land before it got busy and the ranch "came alive."

He often did that whenever something was heavy on his mind.

He glanced over at his brother. "How did *you* know?"

"That Sinclair is on your mind 24/7?"

Nick slowly nodded his head. There was no sense in trying to convince his brother that there wasn't something going on in his psyche regarding Sinclair.

His brother barked out a laugh.

"I remember the symptoms."

Nick didn't respond. He couldn't. He knew his brother was referring to how he had fallen for his wife. It wasn't like that for him. He wasn't falling in *love* with Sinclair…she just plagued his mind nonstop, he thought irritably.

At most, he was falling in lust with her.

The thought of how she'd feel beneath him had been his constant companion for the past week. In fact, it had been growing for six months, from their first communication.

"She's under my skin, man." Nick grumbled as the admission was torn from him. He knew that if he didn't just admit it, voice it, it would only get worse. Who better than his brother to admit it to? "Just not sure how in hell to get her out," he finished. He lifted the coffee mug to his mouth and took a swallow of the now-cooling brew.

"Who says she has to *come out,* so to speak?"

The two men stared out at the pasture, not looking at the other, both in their own thoughts.

Casually, as though it was no big deal, Key removed the large coffee mug from Nick's hand and took a deep swallow. Then promptly grimaced.

Before he could say a word and without even glancing his brother's way, Nick spoke into the silence. "You don't get to complain when you don't make it. That goes for when you steal it, as well."

Nick didn't *have* to look at his brother to know the look on his face after taking a drink of his coffee.

"Serves you right for taking such a big-ass gulp, anyway," Nick continued, snickering.

His lack of coffee-making skills was one of many reasons why Mahi forbade him from being in the kitchen when he was preparing any given meal.

"It's something about her…" Nick began, only to stop, shake his head. He paused for a long moment before continuing. "Something about how damn protective she is of her 'Wilde Boys.'" Nick picked the topic back up, unaware that one side of his lip had curled slightly downward when he mentioned the Wildes.

"Nick…brother, look," Key began with a sigh. He

took a careful drink of the coffee before he placed a booted foot on the lower log of the fence and propped his large elbows on the top rail. Although he'd complained, Nick noticed he didn't give him back his coffee.

"There are a few things you need to figure out, and one of them most definitely isn't how to 'get' Sinclair out of your head. One of them is how you feel about the Wildes," Key stated.

"Aw, hell, I don't need to hear—"

"And all this crap about being 'over' the fact that Clint either didn't know about us, or care enough to find out, is the major bee in your bonnet," Key said, talking over his brother's protest.

"It's not that, Key. I couldn't give a damn… Wait. 'Bee in my bonnet'? Really, bro, that's the best you have? You've been hanging around your wife too long. You're getting soft," he said, unable to let that one go.

When his brother gave him the middle-finger salute to his observation, he continued. "Look, if the man knew, cared, or otherwise, I don't care. That's all in the past." He stopped, his brow knitting in a frown. "A past I have…or had…no intention of dredging up. I'd decided to let it all go, anyway, to move on. Before…"

His brother turned to face him, an equal frown on his face. "Okay…this is new. 'Before'? Before what? What are you talking about?"

Nick ran a frustrated hand through his hair, feeling conflicting emotions as his brother stared at him, his eyes boring a hole through Nick.

"Damn. Look… Before Sinclair came around, before

she informed me she wanted to come out to the ranch to settle this, I was ready to let it drop."

"And?" Key prompted when it looked as though Nick wasn't going to continue.

He shrugged his wide shoulders. "And I didn't."

"No damn way. You can't just say that and not explain. You need to, if for no other reason than it's going to help *you* understand. Don't you see that?" The look in his brother's eyes was disconcerting. As though his brother knew something he didn't, as though he understood something Nick didn't.

Nick growled in frustration.

"It wasn't Wilde's...fault. He didn't know about us. Mom never told him. I know that. I just—" He stopped, clenched his teeth.

Although Key had asked the question, it was less than a minute later when Nick realized his brother had realized, come up with, surprised or Jedi-mind-tricked him. Either way his brother laughed.

Shaking his head, Nick turned back to face the south pasture. The sun was beginning to rise, and the two men observed it together. The ranch was beginning to come alive.

The brothers didn't exchange another word about the topic. Key instinctively realized his brother needed to get a handle on his feelings for not only Clint Wilde, but more importantly for the woman who was intimately involved with the family of a man he hated.

He glanced over at his brother, his twin. A small

smile pulled the corners of his mouth. He clapped his brother on the back.

"Yeah, well, I'm sure you can handle one little lady, brother, can't you?" he laughed, reminding Nick of how he'd once teased Key about Sonia. "Funny how karma and life find a way of getting us all eventually, huh?" Again his brother laughed. He laughed so hard he nearly choked.

Nick didn't think it was so damn funny.

Chapter 12

Sinclair stood at the gate closure, watching as Nick slowly approached the stallion. The animal tossed its head back, its nostrils flaring in agitation and its eyes on Nick, carefully watching as he approached.

The stallion was one of the most magnificent horses Sinclair had ever seen, which was saying a lot as she'd grown up on a ranch known for its acquisition of quality horses.

She frowned as she stared at the golden horse, trying to recall the name of the particular breed. She was no expert, but as she'd grown up around horses, she was very familiar with many types. It was magnificent: golden in color, nearly platinum, with a metallic-like bloom to its coat. The sun's rays bounced and played off the animal's body, enhancing the effect.

Yet, even with the natural majesty of the beautiful animal, it was Nick and Nick alone who held Sinclair's attention.

The man had more swagger than any man she'd ever met. Natural swagger, something that was innate to a man and couldn't be taught, learned or imitated; either he had it or he didn't. And Nick had *it*.

His natural charm was intoxicating.

She kept her eyes trained on the action ahead, blocking out everything else even as the noise from around her grew louder.

She'd known from the chatter around the ranch that he'd bought a new horse. A gorgeous and rare stallion, but one that was near wild from what she'd heard in the cowboys' excited comments.

When she'd heard Nick was about to "break" it, she'd carefully gathered the documents that she had been working on in the office and put them away. The fact that the documents weren't ones pertaining to the Wildes and the Kealohas, but related to another case she was working on made her feel uncomfortable.

She and Nick hadn't gone over the latest offer she'd put together. Each time she brought the topic up, he found something to distract her, from taking her to one of the orchards or gardens that his mother's foundation supported, to showing her around the small community, to taking her to hideaway cafés that the tourists weren't aware of.

All along she was getting to know him, discovering

that beyond the fine exterior, the player image she'd so easily bought into, was so much more.

It was that "more" that had her worried. But she kept her perspective, and although she'd contacted the Wildes, she was told, just as Nick had been told by his brother, that she was "in charge."

There were times, in the back of her mind, that she thought about it and wondered at both sides putting the situation solely into their hands. As well, she felt guilty for working on things for her few other clients, work that had nothing to do with the reason she was in Hawaii, but she forced the nagging feelings away.

"I think I'm going to head out and check out what's going on," she had said earlier as she'd stood from the leather chair and pushed away from the small desk.

She'd smiled at Ailani who had offered earlier in the week to share "office" space if she needed it, surprising Sinclair with her generosity.

"I heard the men bought a new mare. An Akhal-Teke," she'd said, frowning, hoping she'd pronounced it correctly. "I've never seen that breed in real life." She'd said that, knowing that it was best to at least tell a partial truth than a complete lie.

If Ailani decided to come out and saw Sinclair watching the excitement, maybe she wouldn't know that it was Nick who'd attracted her and not the animal. At least, that was her hope.

Ailani had glanced up from her own computer and smiled distractedly. "Oh, yeah, sure. It's a gorgeous animal! Nick and I bought it from auction a couple of weeks

ago," she'd said, smiling. Sinclair had nodded, returning
the smile. She'd felt just the smallest nod of jealousy but
put it away. After the time she'd been at the ranch, she
realized that Nick and Ailani were no more than friends.
In fact their relationship was close, and very similar to
what Sinclair had with the Wildes.

She'd been spending more and more time with Nick
this past week, getting to know him, learning his likes
and dislikes as he was learning hers.

She felt that queasy-good sensation in the pit of her
stomach that a woman felt when she knew a man was
as into her as she was into him. She'd hurried along to
check him out, in action.

She stood along with the others near the enclosure, a
gated-off area that she'd learned they used for the wilder
horses they often bought at auction. Horses that many of
the surrounding ranchers who attended the private auction thought were too much bother to buy. No matter how
good the bloodline, no one was willing to potentially lose
a great deal of money on a horse they couldn't break.

Her eyes left the beautiful animal and stayed on Nick.
He was all alpha male, from the top of his dark head to
the bottom of his big cowboy-boot-wearing feet.

Besides her own growing feelings, Sinclair saw what
the appeal was for him, his brother and the entire Kealoha ranch for that matter, and what made their reality
show the mega hit that it was.

Raw, masculine heat.

Her glance slid around the ranch. There were always

female tourists around, no matter what. Although they weren't supposed to be within certain staff-only areas, some wheedled the younger cowboys into giving them access and the young men had eagerly brought them, only to be embarrassed when Ailani read them the riot act for doing so.

Currently they were not filming the show, for which Sinclair was grateful. Yet there seemed to be an inordinate number of women on the ranch, hanging around the Visitors Only section. Although they allowed visitors on the ranch, most of the ranch was off limits to those who didn't live on, or work at, the Kealoha ranch.

She knew that the Kealohas more recently had begun to allow a small number of tourists to come to the ranch, outside of the visitors for the show, to a designated section. They'd even decided to give a few "dude" lessons, all for donations to the Aloha Keiki foundation they'd started in honor of their mother.

For all the sheer masculinity and testosterone teeming around the ranch, there was also heart. Although the locale and people were different, there was a similar, *familiar* vibe at the Kealoha ranch, one that reminded her of the Wyoming Wilde Ranch.

Most of the hands had been at this ranch for years, like Ailani Mowry, the ranch's foreman. Sinclair had not been sure what to expect from Ailani initially, but she had to admit she was all business when it came to the ranch. And the men she managed seemed to respect her, as well, from what Sinclair had determined so far, in the limited time she'd been at the ranch.

Sinclair still wasn't sure how she felt about the woman on a personal level; she'd wait and hold judgment. Although she had a feeling that behind the woman's reserved demeanor, the one she showed to Sinclair, was a more vivacious personality. One she chose only to show to those she knew and or cared about. Like Key and Nick.

Nick.

She sighed.

Piggybacking that thought was the realization that her thoughts and actions, from the moment she woke up excited to head out to see the Kealoha ranch…and Nick… had been so caught up in him, that she'd not missed home.

She experienced a pang when she thought of the Wilde Ranch. She'd expected…*wanted*…to miss it more than she did.

The truth was that since her arrival and during all the time they'd spent together, she hadn't. She put those disconcerting thoughts away, both about the Wilde Ranch and her confusing feelings toward Nick.

Just to watch Nick break in a horse.

Yeah…that makes a heck of a lot of sense, her inner voice mocked. She sighed again and leaned into the fence, her eyes glued on Nick as he slowly approached the stallion.

"He doesn't even use a blind."

Startled, Sinclair turned, surprised to see Ailani standing near her. She'd been so wrapped up in her own thoughts she hadn't realized the other woman was in the area.

"So I see," Sinclair replied, familiar with the term the foreman had used.

Having grown up on the Wilde Ranch, she was as comfortable with cowboy lingo as she was with legal briefs. "Is he an adept bronc buster?" she asked, thinking of Nate Wilde, who was an expert at breaking in the more unruly horses the ranch acquired.

The foreman tilted her head to the side, a small smile creasing her full lips

"Very impressive. Oh, that's right, you grew up on a ranch. I'd forgotten that."

Sinclair scrutinized her face, her voice, looking for any hint of sarcasm, but found none. Her expression was open, honest. Sinclair relaxed and turned back to the scene in front of her.

"Yes. Though all the men at the Wilde Ranch are adept at breaking horses, Nate is the best at it, to be honest. It was how he helped make money for the ranch when he and his brothers were young men," she replied, hearing the pride in her own voice and not caring if the woman heard it.

"Well, I guess the…brothers have that in common, as well?"

Sinclair gave the woman a glance, again wondering at her motive.

"Nate is the expert, but his other two brothers, Shilah and Holt, are no strangers to breaking in a horse. They've all worked hard to see the ranch a success." Purposely,

Sinclair included the three Wildes, although she knew the woman was linking Nick as a Wilde, alluding to the fact that he was the son of Clint Jedediah Wilde.

"They're like family to you, the Wildes, aren't they?" Ailani asked after a slightly awkward pause.

"Look, I'm not sure what is going on here. I don't know your connection with Nick, or how involved you are in this matter between the Wildes and the Kealohas, but for the record I am here in the best interest of the Wildes and their holdings. And that is it," she said, feeling on the defensive even as she was embarrassed, knowing good and well the foreman hadn't made the comment with the intent of being nasty.

"For the record, Ms. Adams… I have no pony in that race, as the saying goes," Ailani said.

Had it not been for the slightly reddish tinge to her café-au-lait skin, Sinclair wouldn't have known she'd upset the woman. She felt immediately chagrined at her own behavior and just a little bit ridiculous.

She'd been less than her normal cordial self with the foreman and she knew the reason for that was not because the woman had said or done anything besides be close to Nick.

Sinclair was woman enough to admit when she was wrong. "I'm sorry. I have a lot on my mind lately and… well…" She shook her head. "I didn't mean anything."

Ailani shrugged her narrow shoulders. "Hey…no problem. I get like that with my 'boys,' too," she said, laughing softly as she gazed over at Nick.

Sinclair refused to allow the kernel of jealousy to rear

its ugly head again. Enough was enough. Besides, she had no claim on Nick Kealoha.

He was just a job.

She paid no heed to the uproarious mocking laughter in her head that came with the thought.

Hush, she quieted the voice.

"I don't know anything about the Wildes except what's common knowledge. Just like my boys…the Wildes are just an internet search away. Information just a keystroke away. And as I'm sure you know, not everything you read is true," Ailani replied, her voice lowering, her gaze unflinching as she looked at Sinclair.

Sinclair kept her gaze just as steady on the foreman, reading the underlying message she was delivering easily. Then the other woman surprised her, her gaze softening.

"Your Wildes…they seem like good men. Just as the Kealohas are. And just as you are protective of them, I feel the same sense of loyalty for the Kealohas," she said. She pushed away from the fence post after glancing over at the scene in front of her, of Nick and the animal, surrounded by ranch hands as they cheered him on.

She surprised Sinclair when she finished with, "And just like you and the Wildes, they are the only living family that I have."

The two women held glances for long moments, neither one moving away, neither one dropping the other's gaze.

How the foreman knew that she was alone in the world, except for the Wildes, Sinclair had no clue.

She mentally shrugged. But, as the woman said…the internet was just a keystroke away.

Sinclair was adept at reading people. What she was now reading from the woman was…love. Love for the Kealohas' A'kela Ranch. The same love she herself had for the Wilde Ranch.

If for no other reason, this made her relax.

"I have a good feeling about you. I'm sure all of this will be resolved in a fair manner and…swiftly, Ms. Adams. Good day, ma'am," Ailani said. And with that, she jammed the beat-up, wide-brimmed, faded-pink cowboy hat onto her head, pulled the long braid from beneath and allowed it to flop in front of her shoulder—a style Sinclair had seen the woman wear each time she'd spied her on the ranch.

She stared after the woman, a contemplative look on her face.

Had she just been warned off and welcomed both at the same time? she wondered.

Sinclair felt an unreasonable smile threaten to break free. The longer she was on the ranch, the more she was strangely feeling like she was…home. The people reminded her so much of those at the Wilde Ranch.

"You got him, boss! You did it!"

Sinclair's attention was diverted from the woman and back to what was going on inside the small corral

In the short time she'd been in conversation with Ailani, Nick had been successful in breaking the horse. While she knew that it would take another session before the horse was ready to interact with the others, as well as be used by the other cowboys, she was impressed.

He was good. Damn good.

Her gaze ran over him. He was more than good…

His Levi's were dirty and had seen more wear than any pair of jeans should. Although he wore a belt, complete with a buckle that bore the Kealoha crest—she knew, as she'd noticed it when he'd worn it before—they rode low on his hips, his shirt bearing evidence of a long day's work.

Helpless to look away, Sinclair watched as he laughed at something one of the other men said to him, his strong white teeth gleaming in the sunlight. It was then he turned and their glances caught.

She noticed, peripherally, the same cowboy glance her way and then say something to Nick.

She couldn't hear what he said from the distance, although she had fairly good lip-reading abilities—abilities she'd acquired in law school during court sessions—and instinctively knew she was the topic of conversation.

She *should* be angry.

Or at the very least curious as to why the man was obviously talking about her…or what he was saying. When she saw another man join them, and all three glanced at her, she should've at least been uncomfortable.

Should've been.

But as she stared at Nick and their gazes held, she didn't really care what the others had said or were saying.

Nick and Nick alone captured and held her attention.

She watched as he blindly handed the horse's bridle and bit to one of the waiting men. After dusting his hands down the sides of his filthy jeans, he jammed his cowboy hat onto his dark head and ambled toward her.

She swallowed, taking in the sexy sight of him as his long legs devoured the distance. The man was the walking definition of sexy.

She felt moisture in her panties, a reaction she was now growing accustomed to having whenever she was around Nick Kealoha.

She should leave. She should go back to the assigned office space she'd been given to work out of if necessary and just...leave.

She couldn't. Instead she remained rooted to the spot.

And waited for him to come to her.

It had been a week of them dancing around each other.

She swallowed the excitement...and fear, biting her lower lip, tugging it deeply into her mouth, unaware of the picture she presented.

Chapter 13

Although the ranch was teeming with activity and men were gathered around watching as Nick began the task of breaking the stallion, Nick was acutely aware of Sinclair watching him.

His glance ran over the stallion as *it* watched him, warily. He needed to keep his head in the game, Nick knew. Breaking a damn-near-wild horse was no playing matter.

The horse threw its head back and snorted, before lowering its head. Its nostrils flared as it exhaled a deep breath.

Nick had known it the minute Sinclair had come within…smelling distance. He'd felt much like the animal in front of him. His sense of smell, as well as everything else, became acute, animalistic, when it came to Sinclair Adams.

They'd been sniffing around each other for the past week. It was all he could do not to take her to one of the stalls and have his way with her. But he'd played it cool. Let his guard down enough to let her in, to show her who he really was.

He knew what her thoughts were about him: playboy and wealthy cowboy. It was an image he'd carefully cultivated. But he'd found that with her, he wanted her to get to know him, not the image.

Damn. It wasn't the smartest move on his part: letting the enemy close.

But she'd never been the enemy. She'd been anything but an enemy. From the first moment they'd spoken, the first email, she'd sparked his interest.

He ran a gaze over her as he approached her.

Today she wore a pretty peach sleeveless dress, the color a perfect foil to her golden-brown skin, her arms and shoulders exposed, the skin looking so soft. He couldn't wait to get his hands on it.

He'd found every damn excuse in the book to touch her over the past week, casual touches, when she would come to his office or when he helped her walk over the plants in the orchard.

He knew that he needed more than just casual touches. He needed her beneath him as he rocked into her softness, felt her warmth surround him as he stared into her eyes while they made love.

He bit back a curse.

She made his cock rock-hard within seconds, while making him think.

Think about what it was he was angry about. Who? Why?

He frowned, pushing back the memories, the thoughts. Right now, as whenever he was around her, he found he didn't want to think of anything or anyone else that might interfere with them.

He knew he had it bad for her and didn't give a damn. Not now.

Although the corral was teeming with cowboys, it could have been a ghost town as far as he was concerned.

For that moment it was only the two of them.

And he knew that he had to do something about the way he felt about her. It had been only a week that she'd been at the ranch, but that, with the six months they'd been communicating, which felt like six months of fore-play, made him a powder keg ready to blow.

When he stepped outside the enclosure and approached her, he stopped, an unknowing smile on his face.

His gaze raked over her face, down the long line of her slender neck, to the deep V of her dress, where her small, perfectly round breasts crested over the top of her bra.

He saw her nipples pucker beneath the dress and growled low in his throat, dragging his eyes away to meet hers.

He loved that he could make her body react like that.

His shaft hardened uncomfortably in his jeans.

He reached out and brought her hand to his mouth. He knew some of his men were watching. Didn't really give a damn.

He'd had enough. He was about to claim what was his. Even if she was his for a short time, until it was her time to go, or when this fever that had claimed him relented. For now, she was his.

He was about to claim what was his. Tonight.

"Have dinner with me tonight?" he asked, his voice low, rough with need.

He saw her eyes widen and her pulse bang against the soft line of her throat.

He felt a need to conquer her. To take her and have his way with her.

He moved nearer, truly unaware of what he was doing, his actions one of a man going blindly on instinct. Like a wild animal.

He brought a hand up to her waist, bringing her close to him. To that part of him he wanted to wreak havoc with, claim and dominate her with, like a stallion claiming his mare.

In the background, as though from a distance, he heard the snorting of the animal he'd just broken as it allowed his men to take it away.

He kept his focus on Sinclair.

"You'll be coming home with me afterward." The promise was low, so low his voice was barely above a gravelly rumble within his chest.

He saw that little pulse of hers jackhammer against the soft skin of her throat before he ran a tongue over it, then lightly bit her, claiming her.

Chapter 14

When Nick asked Sinclair to go out again, this time with them alone, she could tell that her agreement surprised him.

Not to mention the hot words he'd whispered—no, promised—against her neck. She shivered at the memory. It was more like a heated sexual threat, one that shouldn't have turned her on as much as it had, as it still did. But, God, it did.

After he'd made his decree she'd known that he'd realized, too late, how it sounded.

So demanding.

Claiming her.

And even more, Sinclair had known her agreement surprised him, particularly after she'd followed it up with

a kiss, which she leaned on tiptoe to plant on his cheek.
Along with a whispered agreement against his ear.

She'd bit the lower flesh of his ear and he'd stared
down at her, the expression on his face one she'd never
forget.

Making her feel her *power* as a woman.

Yes, there was no denying he was a dominant, sexual, alpha man. One she just might allow to…lead her,
she thought, a purely feminine smile on her face as she
glanced at him over her shoulder and slowly ambled
away.

Knowing his gaze was straight on her butt, she'd put
a little extra something-something in her sway.

Two could play at that game.

If nothing else, the fact that she had been able to surprise him, turn the tables on him, show him that it was
she who gave him the power and that he wasn't taking
it from her…made her feel good. Damn good.

She grinned as she applied her lipstick. For a nano-
second, at least, she'd had the upper hand.

Her time at the Kealoha ranch had been one of lots
of twists and turns. From their first meeting to now, she
hadn't known what to expect from Nick Kealoha. And
she knew that was exactly what he'd wanted: to keep
her off kilter.

She stared into the mirror, a contemplative look on
her face.

"It might be fun," she said to her reflection. "A date…
with Nick Kealoha." She stopped, shaking her head and
laughing lightly, softly. That just sounded so tame, but

she knew it wasn't going to be. He had already told her. And although she'd flirted with the notion of going back to his home with him, to make love, as she knew that was what he meant—no grown man said he was going to take you home to play board games, after all—would she really go through with it?

Is that what this was? A date?

The first time she'd had dinner with him had really just been a meeting between her and his family, a time where she'd gotten to see with whom she was dealing.

She'd expected the worst. She'd thought that, like Nick, the rest of the family was as anti-Wilde as he was.

She'd been surprised to find out just how wrong she'd been and since then, the family had been just as welcoming to her as they had been during that first meeting. She'd even met the elder Kealoha earlier in the week. He, like his sons and daughter-in-law, had been pleasant.

She snorted…not that she was expecting "pleasant" with Nick.

Pleasant wasn't exactly the way she would call her interactions with Nick. That was entirely too mild a word to describe the way he made her feel.

Confusing, funny, perplexing, infuriating…hot. He brought a bevy of emotions and feelings to the surface. But pleasantness was *not* one of them.

"A date. Just the two of us?" she asked her image aloud.

"Girl, no. Get yourself together. This is just a business conversation and nothing more. The quicker we can come to an agreement, the better. What's the worst that can happen?"

Peering into the mirror closer, she examined her face, scrunched her nose, frowning... Was she looking for traces of self-denial, maybe?

She lifted a shoulder and made a self-mocking moue at her own reflection.

Maybe.

Or maybe it was the irritating little pimple that was trying its best to form on her chin. Just what she needed, dang it.

Carefully, she applied her favorite Mac cream-to-powder foundation over the red mark before lightly dusting her face.

Usually she wore a minimum of makeup: a light dusting of translucent powder, and mascara to darken her lashes and light-colored or sheer lip gloss. The lip gloss protected against both the harsh winters and hot summers back in Wyoming.

But this time she wanted—needed—the full "armor."

She wanted everything in her arsenal. She had an idea what the night had in store for her, and she wanted to look her best.

With the determination of a general preparing for battle, she unzipped the small makeup bag packed with all her favorites.

As she deftly, expertly, began to apply her makeup, she tried to remain calm about the night in front of her.

She frowned absently at her image in the mirror, turning her head to each side to make sure she'd applied the makeup subtly.

Sinclair wanted to look good. Not like a made-up clown headed to a rodeo.

She laughed at herself, thinking of one of the many colorful sayings Miss Lilly kept in her arsenal. "Locked and loaded…and ready to unleash."

A small smile played around her full lips as she thought of Miss Lilly…or Mama Lilly, as most of the kids who, like Sinclair, had grown up with Lilly as a mother figure, called her.

Before she'd left for Hawaii, she'd spoken with the older woman, gleaning wisdom from her, as usual. But she'd left…sad. It was as though she was saying goodbye to the woman she'd long felt was a mother to her. Which made no sense. She'd felt the same way after Nate had said his final words to her, before she'd left the ranch for the airport the following day. Her grief indeed made no sense.

As soon as her business was conducted and done… she was headed back home.

Yet, even as she thought about it, Sinclair knew that some major decisions were in front of her.

She'd come to realize that as much as she loved the Wildes—they were, after all, like family—as well as the ranch life—the only life she'd known for all of her twenty-seven years—she was ready for a change. Though she wasn't sure what that change was or what form it would take.

She sighed deeply, shoving those thoughts to the back of her mind.

One hurdle at a time, she reminded herself.

She felt that queasiness enter her belly again, the kind you felt when your belly bottomed out on a roller coaster. It was the same feeling she got when she thought of Nick and his hot sexual threat.

She slowly rolled her head from side to side and fought for composure, determined to hold on for the ride.

Chapter 15

"If you're on the menu, I'm going for takeout. Damn."

Sinclair's eyes widened at the very cheesy line that came out of Nick's mouth the minute she walked up to him, meeting him in the hotel lobby.

Her startled gaze met his and when she saw the humor lurking in his deep blue eyes, she laughed, relaxing.

"What? You don't like that one?"

She shook her head no, laughing.

"Damn. And I spent the entire day working on it!" he said and she laughed outright again.

"Well, keep on trying," she said, laughing again, immediately relaxing against him as he escorted her out of the hotel and into the warm breezy night.

She glanced up at him, smiling, and her smile slipped just a little.

He was such a beautiful man. Beyond handsome. The man was gorgeous.

He tilted his head to the side, silently asking what was wrong as he glanced down at her, his hand lightly cupping her elbow as they stood outside waiting for his vehicle to be brought to them by the valet. She shook her head, a smile on her face.

"Beautiful night," she said, glancing around.

She'd been to Hawaii once before in undergraduate school, and had even done a tour of the major islands, but she didn't recall it being so beautiful, the air so warm yet crisp.

"Yes, it is," he said.

She glanced up at him and felt her confidence slip at the discerning look in his eyes.

He brought a thumb up to touch her face, his finger caressing her chin.

He wasn't talking about the night.

He brought their lips together in a brief kiss, too brief, before releasing it when the valet smoothly delivered his vehicle curbside. After tipping the uniformed man, he escorted her to her door, then jogged to the driver's side.

"I have the perfect place to take you. You're going to love what's on the menu," he promised.

This time there was no double entendre, nothing at all that should have had her holding back a groan. Fear and anticipation warred for dominance as he smiled over at her, his white teeth gleaming in the dark cab of his truck.

Dear God. She was in trouble. Deep, deep…deep trouble, she thought, smiling back at him weakly.

* * *

Surprisingly, dinner had been amazingly...uncomplicated, for Sinclair.

Yes, the sexual tension was there. Wasn't any way it wouldn't be with the way they'd been dancing around each other.

She wasn't going to even try to pretend that she didn't find him sexually exciting...she was sure there wasn't a woman alive who could claim that. In fact, their banter had increasingly become hotter and more exciting. What they'd begun six months ago was finally being realized. She suspected even he hadn't been aware, to the extent they now were, of exactly what they'd been doing since their first communication.

But Nick had done something very subtle, yet she'd caught it. Initially his sexual energy had been raw, palpable...and nearly overwhelming. She remembered the feeling of being run over by a Mack truck. The feeling hit her and kept on hitting. Battering, unrelenting.

The feeling of being prey for the big lion she'd imagined him to be earlier.

But somehow, as the time they'd spent together had increased, and they'd been around each other more, something else had changed, as well.

Yes, he was still devastatingly sexy and overwhelmingly...male. And yes, he still made her panties wet with one heated look.

But he was more...approachable. Approachable as in the fear of being swallowed whole by him had slightly diminished, she thought.

She shook her head, an unknown smile on her face.

She took another small spoonful of the creamy custard the waiter had delivered right as Nick had left to take a call. She'd promised to wait for him before she tried the dessert if it came.

She'd lied.

"Hmm," she murmured. She'd never had coconut custard of this variety before. "Too good," she said aloud and ran the spoon back and forth over the dessert to smooth it out so he couldn't tell she'd tried it. She glanced over her shoulder to see if he was coming.

"Should I be jealous of the custard?" The deep voice that broke into the love affair she had going on with the custard, startled Sinclair, making her cough a little. She was thankful she'd managed to swallow before that happened, as the last thing she wanted was for him to see her spewing custard from her nose.

Not sexy.

"Started without me, huh? Can't say that I blame you."

She watched as he took his chair, a chagrined smile on her face. "Sorry. Couldn't resist," she said around a mouthful of the delicacy. She frowned. "For such a big guy, you sure can tiptoe up on a woman," she grumbled, and he laughed outright. She responded to his laugh with a grin.

Even his bark of a laugh made her squirm, she thought, watching as he began to dig into his own dessert.

God, is there anything he doesn't *do sexy?*

"Hmm... I don't know. My brother has lied for years that I snored as a kid. I didn't. He did." He spoke around the spoonful of custard, the smile on his face causing a fizzle in the area of her stomach.

It took a minute for his comment to register.

When it did, her face heated up. She ducked her head, so embarrassed she wanted to crawl under the table. And low-crawl all the way out of the restaurant.

"Did I say that out loud?" she was almost afraid to ask.

"Yeah," he said and winked at her. "I'm too sexy for this custard." The wink was so exaggerated along with the silly quip that again he had her giggling and at ease. If she wasn't careful she could really fall for him, she thought.

As she watched him eat, that half smile of his in place as he kept her gaze, she wondered if it was too late. The spoon dangled in her hand.

He frowned. "Don't get all delicate on me now," he said. "Eat your dessert!"

"Actually, I'm full. As good as this is, I'm going to have to have it wrapped up," she replied, forcing a smile.

He raised a brow. "So you're telling me the woman that managed to put away that feast we ate...can't take on a small helping of coconut-custard ice cream and whipped cream? No way! I'm not buying it," he replied as he picked up his own spoon.

The laugh that bubbled up was unexpected. There was something about him that at times made her squirm and at other times made her want to laugh.

Although she knew she needed to be careful around Nick, she couldn't help the way her guard seemed to naturally relax around him.

"So what are you trying to say? If I recall correctly, I wasn't the only one, um…enjoying the meal," she said tongue-in-cheek and laughed when he nodded his head in agreement.

"No, but in my defense, I am six feet five inches and weigh two twenty-five. But you…" He stopped and stared at her, his gaze running over her as though he was examining her. "What are you… like five-five and ninety pounds, wringing wet?" he said, his eyes assessing her.

Two things happened. She was only a few inches over five feet, so his giving her extra inches gave him points. And guessing her weight at only ninety pounds…well, she wanted to kiss him for saying that alone.

She knew he was being funny, lighthearted, but the way his gaze went over her, especially the "wringing wet" part…it was as though his hands were touching, feeling her.

Keep it light, girl, keep it light, she reminded herself. And purposely took a *big* spoonful of the custard and winked at him as she did so.

"I was hungry," she said, shrugging. "I may be small, but I can eat," she said and he laughed along with her. "And never let it be said that Sinclair Cross Adams allowed a little custard to get the best of her!"

With that, and with relish, she polished off the remainder of her dessert, keeping the silly giggle from erupting from her mouth at the faux look of amazement that crossed his handsome face as he watched her take the last bite.

And lick the spoon. Front and back.

"Delicious. Down to the last...bite," he said. Just like that, he affected her.

She decided that the idea of air-conditioned undies was something she was seriously considering inventing herself.

Chapter 16

"Well... Thank you for the evening. It was...nice," Sinclair said, the inane words that tumbled from her lips the best she could come up with.

She glanced away and searched for the keycard in her purse, pretending to have a hard time finding it, if only to give her that much more time to get it together.

When his big hand reached inside her bag and pulled out the small keycard, handing it to her, she smiled up at him.

The look in his blue eyes made her inhale a deep steadying breath of much needed air.

And to think she had thought him...tame...if even for a moment, she thought, her heart racing.

"Dinner was delicious, thank you," she continued, staring at his mouth as they sat inside his vehicle. She wondered how she would survive the ride back to her hotel, thinking of the hot sensual promise he'd delivered, wondering if he'd been simply trying to get a reaction out of her.

She could not stop staring at the lower swell of what had to be the most sensual mouth she'd ever seen on a man. Could a man's mouth be more perfect?

The thought ran in her mind and Sinclair licked her lips, which had gone dry.

He turned toward her, one finger poised over the button that would turn on the ignition. He paused in the act, tipped his head forward. His hand reached out and lightly grasped the back of her head, bringing her closer.

The kiss was light, smooth…and devastating. When he released her, she slumped.

"You're amazing…has anyone ever told you that? I wonder if your Wilde Boys know how lucky they are," he mumbled, his eyes trained on her lips—making her heart race even harder—as though he wanted to kiss her again. Although they'd just eaten, he had the look of a man ready to feast.

What do I say to that? Sinclair wondered, breaking contact with his eyes and licking her lips again.

She ducked her head, staring down at her feet, as though the answer could be found in the open-toe heels.

Still, he didn't start the engine. He simply sat there staring at her. They were parked in one of the more isolated parts of the restaurant's rear lot. As it hadn't been a tourist hot spot, the restaurant hadn't been overly crowded, so his truck was the only one of a few parked in the back lot.

He reached over and tilted her chin up, forcing her to look back into his eyes.

"This is not for any reason except that I've been staring at your mouth the whole evening... No, since the moment I first laid eyes on your picture and wondered if they were half as soft as they looked," he murmured.

Her heart nearly leaped out of her chest.

"But...we've kissed. You already know what they feel like," she whispered in reply, half teasing.

That lone dimple appeared near his lower lip when he smiled. "Yeah, but I need to kiss you again, just to make sure the first few times weren't a fluke," he replied, his voice low, sexy and deep.

When his head descended, she reached up and met him in the kiss, her arms circling his neck to pull him near.

That was all the encouragement he needed.

He surprised her when he lifted her from her seat and over to him, straddling her legs across his. The roominess of his luxury truck made it an effortless venture and her eyes widened.

"Nick!"

"I love it when you call my name," he said and laughed, claiming her mouth immediately.

In the position he had her, she was unable to move.

Her hands flattened on his broad, hard chest, as his mouth worked magic over hers, grinding their lips together even as he ground his hardening shaft against her.

Kissing and moaning noises filled the cab as they took their fill of each other, kissing with a ferocity that mimicked what their bodies craved from one another.

The moment was beyond magical. The entire evening had been like something out of a dream.

Static, erotic energy arced back and forth between them, shooting from his hard body to hers, igniting electric blazes in its path.

The hand on the back of her head reached up to loosen the pretty chignon she'd placed it in earlier. Within moments her hair fell and his hand was buried inside it, massaging her scalp as he claimed her mouth.

She grew warm, her body opening to his as his hands reached around her, both on the small of her waist... and moved her.

She moaned against the feel of him. Excited beyond measure at the thought of what deliciousness lay hidden behind the dark dress pants he wore. How it would look exposed.... That part of him that, as he kissed and caressed her, ground against her, hardened to granite against her, intimately pressing into her stomach.

His length excited her, as she imagined what it would look like unleashed.

How it would feel inside her.

He excited her in ways she'd not felt in a long time. In ways she'd never felt.

When his hand reached out and lightly pulled her dress up, it felt...good.

When he pressed her even tighter against his body,

his hand on her ass, her hands clenched his shirt and she moaned into his mouth.

Trapped, powerless...she was on fire. He released her and she cried out. In the dark she saw his nostrils flare as his breath came out in harsh gasps.

"I need more," he said, his voice like gravel.

She nodded and allowed him to reach between them, to put his hand inside her panties and touch her.

"Oooh, God, Nick!" she cried out, her head thrown back as he played with her. She lifted her head when he withdrew his finger. Her heart nearly skipped a beat when she watched in fascination as he lifted his finger to his mouth and tasted it.

His face descended, his mouth lowering until it was so near hers she could smell the sweet smell of coconut and her own essence that lingered on his breath.

His lips touched hers, and his tongue delved into her mouth, transferring the taste to Sinclair. As though he had the right.

Her eyes drifted closed as his unique scent reached out and claimed her, even as his mouth did the same. Even as he had, long before this night.

She shoved the thought away, only wanting to concentrate on the here and now, and the way he was making her feel.

He smelled...tasted *so, so* good. A mixture of coconut and...man.

And me, she thought, a feminine smile stretching her lips.

The man part had her senses reeling and her vagina,

with a mind of its own…clenching, as though in anticipation of something more. She doubted that any woman
could be anything but ready around Nick Kealoha.

He was lethal.

As he lay a light siege upon her mouth, his body hot,
hard, pressing into hers, the scent surrounding her, she
willingly gave in to his demands.

Hard, slamming…feral.

It was a wild, heady rush of need that slammed over
her, had her moaning into their joined mouths, their bodies creating a dance of their own.

Before Sinclair realized what she was doing, the wild,
unrepentant need that rolled over her had her rolling her
pelvis forward and rocking back and forth in earnest
against his thickness, a thickness that stole her breath.

The kiss took on an explosive quality.

Wild, hot, he devoured her mouth, tugging and dragging her lips within his, making love to her mouth in a
way that made her lose her mind. Thoughts of how good
he could make other parts of her feel rushed over her
like a wild cascade of water.

He broke the kiss and she whimpered, trying to re-
capture his mouth, but he brought her close, his hand
on her head, bringing it to his chest.

His heartbeat was thudding wildly against her face.

He was just as affected by their intimacy as she was.

Although he broke the kiss, he didn't ease her away.
His body was still tightly crushed against hers, his shaft
hard, pressed insistently against her stomach.

Their breaths were harsh. And both reflected a need neither was able to deny.

"Come home with me tonight."

The words were a rumble against her ear. A request this time.

Shocked, she couldn't move, much less form a coherent word.

She had only known the man for about a week, truly, despite the fact that they'd been in communication for going on seven months.

She chewed her bottom lip, remembering, thinking.

When he had showed her where his parents had met and had fallen in love, she'd seen the emotion in his eyes. She knew part of that emotion was from the loss of his mother. But she also knew there was a part of that emotion in his eyes that had to do with the way his parents had kept the fact that their biological father wasn't the man they'd called Dad for all of their lives.

The pain was raw and had made her reevaluate what she'd believed before, from their first contact and his reasons for doing so, to what had brought her out to the ranch to get rid of him, write a check and "Act like it never happened," as he'd said.

She felt…uncomfortable. A part of her, ashamed.

Nick had been an enigma to her, in the short time of their acquaintance. She'd briefly seen past the playboy he presented to the world to the cowboy who simply loved his land…

Yet, did she know him well enough to allow him to

do to her what his eyes…his kisses, promised would be unlike anything she'd ever experienced?

She wasn't here to get her groove back. She was here for her Wildes.

"This has nothing to do with them. This is you and me."

His voice had a hard edge that jerked Sinclair out of her thoughts.

She glanced up at him, licking her lips. She swallowed deeply.

He grasped her by the chin, forcing her to lift her head, forcing her to look deeply into his enigmatic blue eyes.

"And it comes down to the simple fact that you want me, Sinclair. You want me…almost as much as I want you."

He bent his head and recaptured her lips with his, briefly making a shudder rack her body.

When he released her, she was limp.

"As much as I've wanted you from the moment we began to communicate… It's fated… We are fated. Just give in to what we both have been waiting for…needing."

She glanced down at his open hand as he waited for her to place her palm within his.

Could this be happening?

Could she allow something like this to happen? With a man she barely knew…

She placed her hand within his much larger one.

His large, callused, work-worn hand grasped hers, holding it tightly. Even that sent shivers through her.

She imagined how those work-roughened hands would feel against her naked body.

Oh, God… She barely suppressed a shiver.

He didn't wait for her response.

He already knew. He'd known, just as she had, from the first moment they'd met.

Chapter 17

"You're one of the most sensual women I've ever met, ever known..."

She felt his hand on her shoulder as he came up behind her, his fingers toying with the thin T-strap of her dress. All of the air from the room seemed to be sucked out of it and Sinclair was left gasping, desperate for air.

"Shh, it's okay, baby. I'll take care of you. You trust me, don't you?"

He breathed the words against her neck, his honey-sweetened breath blowing warm against her ear. She inhaled sharply. When he kept still, unmoving, she slowly bobbed her head up and down.

"Completely untapped sensuality." His hypnotic, seductive voice was mesmerizing as he continued both his verbal and sensual assault.

She dragged in a fortifying breath of air and held it as his big fingers moved from the strap to ease around the front and cup one of her breasts within his large, able hand.

An air of expectancy had surrounded them as they'd driven back from the Rusty Nail, the out-of-the-way restaurant he'd taken her to. One that neither one of them attempted to "talk" their way around.

Both had known exactly what was going to happen, and the level of intensity, from the second they'd met until now...before they'd even met, had led them to this moment.

The time they had been communicating, before her arrival had been a buildup, a slow, wickedly hot foreplay of sorts that now had Sinclair so ready for him, she knew if they didn't make love... The thought of what would happen if they didn't escaped her mind when she felt his tongue work small circles around the lobe of her ear before laving a hot trail around and down the back of her neck.

"Mmm," she moaned against the wicked sensation.

"Do you like that? The way my tongue feels against your skin?"

Her voice in her throat, she was unable to answer, could only nod her head in agreement.

When they'd entered the grounds of the ranch, he'd driven directly to the house, yet he hadn't pulled his vehicle up to the main entry, surprising Sinclair.

The ranch house was a veritable mansion. And although she'd expected there would be more than the traditional two entry points into the home, she'd had no idea that Nick had his own entrance

He'd caught her surprise, and explained that there were what he called "master entries." Besides the front and rear entries, there were three others…one for each "master" suite: his father's, brother and sister-in-law's and his.

"For privacy," he'd said, briefly turning his attention to her as he parked the truck and shut the engine off.

In the dark cab, his blue eyes seemed to sear a hole directly into her, straight to her soul.

Coming around to her side, he held out a hand for her to take and again she placed hers within his and allowed him to lead her away.

He'd only turned on one small outside light, which gave just enough illumination to allow her to see enough so that she didn't stumble over her own feet.

Not that she would, with the hold he kept on her hand.

Sinclair felt strangely…safe, with him.

As they entered his massive suite, she squinted, trying to get a visual of what was a home within a home. His suite appeared larger than her condo back in Wyoming.

Yet when she tried, he purposely moved her away, blocking the full view of the room. He turned her toward the floor-to-ceiling windows that overlooked a picturesque view of the land and held her, mesmerized, in front of him.

Sinclair felt his hand move to her waist and stop in front of her mons, the silk of her dress doing nothing as protection against the heat of his palm.

"Raw, untapped sexual vitality," he rasped, both his words and tone putting her into a sensual coma.

Her body felt fluid and rigid at the same time.

A strange yet heady dichotomy of feeling.

He pulled her closer to his body, allowing her to feel the hot, hard, length of his erection against her buttocks.

Electric heat swamped her entire body, bringing a deep and staining blush she felt head to toe....

She needed this. As much as a part of her knew she was blurring the lines of professionalism and personal. Hell, she'd blown that line up. This was way beyond that.

This man had somehow imbedded himself into her very psyche.

"You want this as much as I do, Sinclair. Give in to me. Like you never have...for another man..." His deep voice breathed the words against her neck.

"Tell me you want it. That you want what you know I can give you," he boldly declared.

She licked excruciatingly dry lips, unable to say a word. Unable to admit that she wanted everything she knew he could give her, everything she'd dreamed about. And more.

She felt herself leaning back against him, as though some magnetic field was surrounding him....her, forcing her close, so close she—

She knew she should walk away, stop this before it could go any further, yet knew that would be an exercise in futility.

To make love with him would be an erotic exorcism....

She inhaled a hitched breath when he glided his hand

under her dress. His big hand on her bare thigh tickled the sensitive skin and stopped a hairbreadth from the band of her panties at the top of her thigh.

His fingers toyed around the thin ribbon, rubbing lightly back and forth until she felt her moisture increase, her panties now uncomfortably moist.

Her head was spinning and her body was already on fire.

And he'd barely touched her.

When he began to tug her panties down, she nearly sagged against him.

God, this is wrong...so wrong, so wrong, so... The cascading thought trickled in her mind.

Only to immediately have another override it.

But it feels...so good, so good, so...

When he fingered aside the edge of her panties and one thick finger brushed over the lower segment of her vagina, brushing over the hair, she nearly came.

From just that touch.

She felt her panties being pulled down, past her bottom, low enough so that he had better...access to that part of her that needed, desperately needed, to feel his torrid touch.

Sinclair held her breath, waiting to feel his finger. What he'd done in the car had been just a hint of what he—

Her mental imaging came to a halt. "Oooooh," she moaned at the feel of his finger inside her clenching heat.

Her eyes closed and her head sank back against the rock-hard chest that was now her pillow.

"I need to…play with you. Will you let me do that to you, with you, baby?"

She swallowed deeply. Dear God, what did he mean?

His hands were still, and cautiously she bobbed her head up and down in assent.

She heard his grunt of satisfaction.

Obviously that was what he needed before he would go on.

Seconds later she felt the hot stroke of his fingertips as he began to…play. Brushing back and forth against her mons, skimming over her clit that she felt engorging, as he began to *play* with her.

She moaned, her eyes fluttering closed as she bit down hard on her lower lip, nearly drawing blood as her heartbeat pounded and her vagina throbbed.

The moment Nick's fingers touched the core of her femininity he felt her clench and her body buck against his.

He knew she was questioning the sanity of what he was doing to her. Knew it as though he were inside her mind, reading it.

Just as he knew she wanted him as badly as he wanted her.

So responsive. She was so damn responsive.

Playing with her was going to be an experience unlike any other.…

"Easy, baby…we've just begun." He whispered the words from clenched teeth.

His job to seduce her was becoming more and more

difficult. He silently counted to ten as he continued to play, needing to keep his libido from going into over-drive. Although he knew it was too late for that; his cock was as hard as granite as it pressed against her back.

They were both still fully clothed, and had only ex-changed kisses…hot kisses, to be sure. Scalding-hot, make-his-dick-rock-hard kisses. But kisses nonetheless.

And with any other woman he could kiss and caress until he had driven her wild with need, so that when it came time to press and stroke, it would take only a few hard driving pounds and he'd take his lover over the edge.

Yet he knew it would take all of his considerable willpower to keep from coming himself before he got in her good.

Damn.

When he felt the sweet trickle of her cream against his fingers, he groaned against her neck. He brought her body closer to his, forced her nearer…his one hand lightly circling her throat.

Not enough to hurt her.

Just enough to claim her.

She mewled low in her throat, a kittenish sound as her head lolled back against his chest. His fingers continued to toy and play with her, while he yanked her panties down far enough past her plump buttocks to give him ac-cess to her, but not far enough that she could move away.

Captive.

He needed this to last. He felt his shaft throb.

He grit his teeth and with iron control forced his cock into submission.

"Do you like what I'm doing to you, Sin?" he grunted, barely able to speak. Without giving her a chance to respond beyond a shaky nod of her head, he pressed his finger deep inside her clenching heat.

One lone...long finger. One teasing, tormenting finger was all it took.

Deeper he delved, his finger easing inside her vagina, slowly, yet piercing it roughly. She bucked as heat surged through her body.

"God, you're so damn tight."

He added a second finger, easing it into her sex, and she cried out, her insides clenching and releasing against the hot, dual invasion, her entire body on fire.

Warmth gushed out, partly easing his thrusting fingers as they slid deeper, teasing the inner walls, until he was knuckles-deep inside her.

"Oooh, Nick..." The words were little more than a gush of sound as she felt even more of her own wetness ease from her body.

She felt more than heard his groan against her neck. She was on fire for him. In the position she was in, turned away from him, she was glad for the privacy. The thought of making eye contact with him was one she couldn't fathom. She knew in her eyes he would see her desperate need for him.

"I need more, Sinclair." His voice was rough. "So much more. I'm sorry...I can't wait," he said and before she knew it, he'd flipped her around, catching her off guard.

She would have fallen onto the thick Persian rug had he not lifted her in his arms.

With sure strides he strode with her across the vast room, and moments later she found herself bouncing on the bed.

The room was impossibly dark, yet Sinclair could make out the shadowy figure of his big body as he turned away from the bed and bent to open a drawer nearby.

She heard the sound of his zipper…releasing. The sound of ripping foil…unsheathing.

"This won't be…easy," he promised, his voice so low and rough she moaned just from the gravelly sound. The more turned on he was, the more scratchy and rough his voice became. She never knew the sound of a man's voice in need could do what his did to her.

It was nearly unbearable; her need for him was high.

"But I promise you won't be disappointed."

When he lowered his body above hers, she felt more than saw him ease her panties down the rest of the way, lifting her as he removed them completely from her body.

She was on fire for him, yet surprised at the way he'd carefully removed her panties. She'd feared he'd rip them from her.

He laughed roughly and her eyes sought his in the dark.

"They're too pretty to rip," he whispered hotly into her ear.

The teasing way he said it, coupled with the fact that he'd read her mind, strangely brought a hot blush to her cheeks.

She laughed with him, softly, intimately, in the dark.

"Thanks…they're my favorite," she admitted softly.

"Oh yeah?" he asked. "I like them, too. Peach looks pretty against your golden skin," he said huskily.

Although the words were negligible, and shouldn't have turned her on, they did.

God, everything the man said…everything he did, turned her on.

"Thank you," she said and felt the blush creep again along her skin. The soft pillow talk was the kind that was strangely intimate.

Something lovers said to one another that shouldn't be hot, but damn if it wasn't.

She inhaled a deep breath as he nosed his face against the side of her neck. She turned her head against the soft, silk-covered pillow. His unique scent was on the pillow, as well.

She felt her essence as it eased down her center.

The scent of him was surrounding her, containing her within a sensual box.

She lay back further on the bed as he followed her down, his body blanketing hers.

When he hitched her leg up to wrap around his waist, she inhaled a startled breath.

When she felt the press of his shaft at her entry she exhaled the pent-up breath in one long *whoosh* of air.

She swallowed. When he'd held her close she'd felt

the length of his erection, but now, unrestrained and sheathed, she knew it to be thicker and longer than she'd thought.

One part of her was afraid to feel it…to touch it and gauge the true length and girth, knowing he was well endowed and worried about him fitting inside her. The other part of her was eager to feel his weight in her hand. She decided that she'd wait to feel it inside her.

"But first, let me make sure you're ready for me," he said, his voice low, so low it was a deep gravelly sound, sensually abrasive against her nerve endings.

When she felt the press of one lone, thick finger slowly invading her heat, she inhaled yet another deep steadying breath. He added a second finger. Slowly he pressed inside her, until he was to the second knuckle.

"Oooh," she whimpered, her voice barely a whisper, and he paused.

He lowered his head and pressed his mouth close to her ear. "Baby…are you okay? God, you're so tight even on my finger," he said, the intimate words brushing against her skin.

She swallowed and nodded her head. Although he'd pressed inside her moments before, this time he'd added a second finger. "It's…been a while. That's all," she said, feeling her cheeks heat at the words.

"I'll be gentle with you. I want this to be good for you," he said.

His words, plus the feel of his thick finger swirling around her clitoris, not only helped to calm her, but brought forth a renewed moisture from her body as it prepared itself for him.

She'd been intimate with men before. But she'd broken up with her last boyfriend soon after law school after realizing he'd only been with her because of her connection with the wealthy Wildes. After that stinging realization she'd thrown herself fully into work.

Love…sex, had been the furthest thing from her mind.

Until she'd met Nick.

Chapter 18

He leaned over to capture her mouth with his.

The kiss he gave her was long, hot and sensual.

Whimpering, Sinclair's tongue came out to meet his. Dueling, lapping and suckling each other, it was one of the most erotic kisses she'd ever had.

He reached a hand up and placed it around the base of her neck, tugging her mouth closer to his. He slanted his head for a better angle, his tongue growing more insistent...aggressive...as it laid siege to her mouth.

"Oh, God, your lips taste so good...so sweet," he growled when he finally broke the connection with her mouth.

With one final twirl of his talented fingers against her blood-thickening bud, he slowly withdrew from her clenching sheath.

"How are you doing, baby?" he asked.

The question seemed even more intimate voiced in the dark room with nothing but the overhead moon shining through the skylight above to cast shaded illumination.

"I'm…I'm okay," she said, finally able to speak.

"Good, then you'll feel even better, soon…."

Before she'd had time to catch the meaning of his sexy promise, he'd eased his big body down onto hers, lifted her legs up and away from where he'd wrapped them around his waist, draped them over his shoulders and moved his head between her parted thighs.

"Nick…?" she questioned, her heart thumping harshly out of control in her chest. Was he going to…?

Her back arched sharply off the soft comforter and a cry tumbled from her lips with the first stroke of his tongue against her folds.

She felt his fingers as they separated her lips, felt the heat of his breath as he blew it, softly, against her heated center.

"Ohhhh…" She let out a soft, low moan when finally she felt his tongue, thick, rough, as he lapped once from the end of her cleft to the tip of her clit.

She held her breath, keeping it held, as she waited.

Her wait wasn't long. He dragged her pulsing bud into his mouth and lightly toyed with it.

"Nick…" His name was a husky moan of pure bliss.

He suckled her, delivering low licks and hot sensual glides of his tongue against her until she felt every nerve ending on fire. Her head tossed back and forth, her body grinding against his face.

"You like that, huh, baby?" He growled the question/statement against her mound, his voice so low and throaty she could barely make out the words.

"Hmm, *yessssssss*," she breathed. Her body was on fire. She squirmed around his talented tongue, whimpering when her soft cries elicited a deep male chuckle, one that rumbled and vibrated against her lips as he continued his sensual assault.

On and on he...played with her. He used tongue, lips and thick fingers to toy with her, making the most intimate type of love until Sinclair felt her orgasm hovering, threatening to break.

She pried her eyes open and looked down at him. His dark head between her thighs was such an intimate visual she closed her eyes again, her body slumping back against the thick comforter.

His mouth fastened one last time on her clit, his tongue giving one final stroke, and she went over the edge.

Her body lifted and she reached down, grasped the sides of his face and lightly ground into him, unable to do anything else, the moment overtaking her as she gloried in the feel of his tongue.

As she ground against him, her soft hands on either side of his face, Nick felt his own orgasm hovering.

Damn!

He'd always enjoyed pleasuring a woman in this way,

but as much as he had enjoyed it in the past, it was nothing compared to what he felt now.

She was so responsive, so damn responsive.

He'd only meant to prepare her for his invasion. After pressing a finger inside her warmth he'd soon realized that although she was not a virgin, her experience had been limited.

His cock had gone hard to granite-hard in 2.2 seconds.

And when he'd felt her dew cover his fingers, he'd had to taste it. The smell, taste and feel of her all added up to turning his world upside down.

It was then he knew that he had to take her over the edge. He wanted to see her when she orgasmed, wanted to experience it with her. He knew that once he was inside her, taking his pleasure from her beautiful, sexy little body, he wouldn't be able to think beyond the feel of her.

He watched through half-closed lids as her orgasm swept over her.

She was a beautiful woman. God, she was so beautiful.

He felt something beyond his cock react. A sharp pang hit him so hard in the chest he nearly moved off her and clutched his heart.

God...what was she doing to him?

When she finally lay limp, her head on the pillow, her eyes closed, he reached down and made sure the condom was still on his cock.

Rising, he covered her, lifting her legs and wrapping them around his waist.

"I think you're ready for me now, baby," he whispered, the words barely recognizable even to his own ears.

A soft smile spread her pretty little bow-shaped lips apart. "Yeah…"

He would have laughed a masculine laugh of satisfaction at the look on her face, knowing he was the one to put it there. His cock, if possible, hardened even more.

"I'll try to go easy on you," he said huskily.

Her eyes snapped opened when he began to press inside her.

He knew, without ego, he was large. And she was so damn small.

He'd have to ease inside her, take his time—

The thought cut off the moment she clamped down on his shaft, her walls milking him the minute he entered.

He bit off a curse and grasped both of her wrists within his hand, lifting them and bringing them above her body

The action brought her small breasts together and his hot gaze centered on them.

"Ohhhh." The distressful little cries were wrought from her lips, yet he pressed on.

"Just hold on, baby, it'll be okay," he promised roughly.

Unable to resist the temptation of her pretty brown breasts with their tight, perky, dark wine cherry-topped nipples, he bent and brought one into his mouth and sucked.

Hard.

At the same time he pressed all the way home, deep inside her tight and clenching walls, until he felt his balls tap against the soft underside of her butt.

"Nick!"

He took one of her breasts within his mouth, and with his free hand, palmed the other. Perfect.

She was perfect in every way.

Her breast, although small, was big enough to spill over his hand cupped beneath it. He tugged on her nipple, groaning when she began to grind against him in sexual excitement.

As he suckled one breast, the hand that held its twin pinched and massaged the other, before alternating, his mouth giving up the connection with one only to transfer its attention to the other.

"Nick. Nick. Nick… Nick…" she cried in little whimpers as he made love to her curvy body.

Her tight little squirms, mewls of sexual distress and overall feel of her body against his was one he feared would make him end their lovemaking *way* before he wanted to.

"Baby, please… Stop. Moving. Just for a minute." He grunted the words, the admission torn from him as he dragged his mouth from her sweet breasts.

He was afraid if she continued to move the way she was, it would be over in a stroke or two.

She felt incredible. Perfect for him.

It had been very taut pressing in, and she fit him tighter than any woman ever had. It was unlike anything he'd ever felt before.

For the first time in his adult life, he resented the use of the condom he'd automatically donned. Although he knew it was a necessary evil, he wanted to feel her naked on his shaft.

He doubted he would have lasted longer than a few strokes if they hadn't used one.

If anything, that imagery immediately made him even harder. He shoved the notion away.

No time for any thoughts beyond the way he felt, balls deep, inside her sweet warm center.

"So damn good… Feel so good, baby." He knew his words were barely intelligible, but at the moment he was damn near beyond human speech.

He bent and captured her lips with his. He kissed her slowly, passionately, the connection he felt with her unlike any he'd ever felt with another.

He released her hands and allowed her to let them drop to the bed.

One arm reached behind him to stroke against the soft skin of her thigh where her legs were wrapped around his waist. Although she felt good like that, her legs wrapped around his waist, he wanted to go even deeper inside her. He needed a different angle to penetrate her in the way he wanted…the way he needed.

It was almost a desperate need to reach as far into her as he could. Until they melded so tightly it was impossible to tell where one left off and the other began.

He wanted to *breathe* inside her.

If possible, his cock grew longer, harder, at the thought.

He deftly untangled her legs from their position, and in one smooth move, pushed them up and to the side, so that her beautiful body was spread out in front of him, her legs to either side of his as he began to stroke inside her sweetness.

"You feel so good, so good. This is the real deal," he grunted. His breathing grew ragged as he held her legs apart to receive him as he plunged deep inside her body.

He took her with a gentleness he was far from feeling, trying his best to hold back, fearing if he took her the way he wanted, he'd hurt her.

"Nick… God… Nick…please," she panted, her voice a coarse whisper as she pleaded for something he instinctively knew she was too inexperienced to know what it was.

She needed him to go harder.

He smiled into her throat, nipping the tender flesh there out of instinct, clamping down with a small sting, he knew, but not so much to hurt her.

Just to claim what was his.

As he picked up the tempo and his strokes became harder, stronger, he growled against the hollow of her throat. Her wet, velvet walls opened and closed in a sweet welcoming rhythm as he pumped inside her relentlessly, testing her to see how much she could take, still holding back.

He felt the sweat began to drip from his body, dropping down upon hers.

He didn't know how long he could hold back. As much as he was giving her…he needed to give her more. Needed to take more.

He grit his teeth as he continued to stroke, grunts of pleasure escaping his mouth as he drove into her sweet welcoming heat.

His body began to shake with the need to go deeper. Harder…

He felt her soft hands on the sides of his face and opened his eyes, staring down at her beautiful face.

He groaned at what he saw. Her limpid brown eyes stared at him, passion-filled and begging for…more.

"I…I need you, Nick," she whispered and her soft little cries were nearly his undoing.

Still, as he stroked inside her, he kept his thrust measured, tempered.

He didn't unleash all of his passion on her.

"And I'm giving you all of me, baby," he said, laughing roughly, hearing the need in his own voice, one that reflected what he saw in her eyes, felt in the quivering of her body against his, the warmth of her flesh burning into his.

When she lifted her body from the bed and pressed into him, grinding herself against him, she pulled his head down to meet hers. Moments before their lips connected she whispered hoarsely, "I need you deeper, baby."

With a harsh groan he latched on to her lips at the same time his hands grasped her curvy hips.

He feathered his tongue back and forth over hers, licking across the seam, asking for entry. With a moan she granted it, and swiftly he buried his tongue within. As he invaded her mouth and as she opened her mouth to his, her legs widened even more to accept more of him. To accommodate him.

He ran his tongue within the moist walls of her mouth, the length behind her perfect teeth before plunging his tongue deeply back within her

Against her mouth he replied, "Hold on, it won't be... easy."

"Hmm," she moaned, her lips curving upward even as he took them with his own.

When he'd first pressed inside her, Sinclair felt as though he was tearing into her, his shaft so thick, hard and long she'd felt it in her womb.

Now her eyes drifted closed and a soft breath of need escaped her lips as he kissed her, made love to her mouth and began to increase his depth of stroke.

It had taken a few minutes for her to adjust to him, but he turned her on so much, her own cream helped ease the way for him to feed her more of himself.

It wasn't long before she was greedy to feel all of him. She could tell he was holding back, afraid he'd hurt her.

Maybe she should be afraid, as well; his cock was so hard and thick, she felt stuffed.

When he pulled her tighter, kissing her, one of his

hands reached down, curved to the swell of her hip and palmed one of her buttocks, bringing her closer as he ground and stroked inside her.

"Hmm, yessss," she moaned helplessly.

"Like that?" he asked, the intimate question making the moment even more erotic as he stroked and rolled inside her. She could only nod her head up and down, the feeling too intense to allow her to say much more than a moan.

Her arms crept up and circled his neck, pulling him down closer as he continued to pin her to the bed, as he stroked inside her, his thrust becoming longer, more... intense.

Her breath caught in her throat when he angled her body to his, agilely moving her, shifting her slightly even as he continued stroking. Although the feeling was incredible, it was as though he were searching for something.

"Ahhhh!" she cried harshly into the dark room when he found what he was looking for. "Oh, my God...oh, my God...oh, my God..." The litany continued as he stroked inside her heat. "Oh, please, keep it right there... Nick, pleeeeease," she keened long and harsh as the side of his shaft brushed against a softness inside her body.

When she arched her body up in surprise, she heard his masculine rumble of satisfaction. He knew *exactly* what he'd done.

No man had ever found her...spot.

She swallowed deeply, her body no longer hers. It

now solely belonged to the man who was making it feel so incredibly good.

Again, she heard his low masculine laughter.

It brought out an answering, very feminine need to respond in kind.

She'd only read about it, but…

She reached down, blindly, and with only a few awkward moves, finally was able to grasp what she wanted.

She held his balls lightly in her hand and feathered caresses over them.

"This will be over before we both want it, if you keep that up." He growled the words, his voice nearly inhuman it was so low, like sandpaper, it was so gravelly.

"Turnabout and all that," she laughed softly, barely able to keep it together. What they were doing to each other was something she couldn't have imagined in her most erotic dreams.

He removed her hand and replaced it with his.

Nick moved his hand around and inserted it between them, finding her clit and rubbing it softly as he rocked her, on and on, until she felt her orgasm hovering.

When he found her clitoris, her soft laugh turned to a moaning scream. He slammed his mouth against hers, grinding against her, and within seconds she released.

Her cries of completion echoed his as he followed her into ecstasy's path, the tsunami they'd created together, sweeping them both along in its wake.

Chapter 19

"The Aloha Keiki, your family's foundation... How did that start?"

She felt his body tense and immediately regretted asking.

Sinclair knew through her research that not only was the Kealoha ranch the most profitable family-owned-and-operated ranch on the islands, but that the foundation his family ran in his mother's honor was one of the most successful nonprofit organizations that helped youth on the island.

He'd shown her the fields and orchards, and during her time on the ranch she'd also met some of the adults and young people who volunteered. But she hadn't heard from him the way it had started.

She had a desire to know as much as she could about

him, knowing their time was short together— She shooed that thought aside.

"I…I'm sorry. If you don't want to talk about it, I understand."

She felt his body relax, and his hand continue the stroking of her skin, in the way that he'd been doing since they'd come down from the erotic wave their mutual orgasm had taken them to.

It had been a long time before either one of them could speak, and when they'd finally been able to, it had been the talk of new lovers.

Pillow talk. Talk about nothing of any real importance; just enjoying the feel of sated bodies against each other and soft voices spoken in hushed tones.

Whereas before, in her limited experience, Sinclair had always felt a bit uneasy in the moments after sex. Not sure what to say… She'd never known the "protocol."

Neither of the two men she'd been with had made her feel in the least the way Nick had. To even compare them was a joke.

He was definitely in a league of his own.

Before, what had constituted pillow talk with her two previous lovers, had ended up an aborted attempt at best.

But it wasn't just her. It had been them, as well. They hadn't been much more…experienced in post-coital chatter than she had been.

So, she thought she should feel more…intimidated with Nick.

He was so much more experienced than her.

Additionally, he'd definitely been with more partners than she had. There was no way a man as fine as he was hadn't had plenty of women throwing themselves at him.

Not to mention his sexual skill… What he'd done to her body, how he'd made her feel…

"It started before my mother passed away, as you know. We've kept it going, built it and nourished it to see it thrive in the way it is now."

She forced herself to put her thoughts to the back of her mind so that she could focus on him speaking.

She listened as he, haltingly at first, started to talk about the foundation.

When she mentioned the foundation, a part of Nick had rebelled. He hadn't wanted reality to come barging in on the pleasure they'd just given one another. He hadn't wanted to think of anyone or anything else beyond the incredible, erotic encounter that had just occurred between them.

It was no secret that he was the one considered of the two brothers to be the "clam."

He'd never been what you would call "comfortable" opening up and baring his soul.

Just wasn't his thing.

With the exception of with his brother, it was not going to happen. And even with Key, the closest person to him, there were times when he felt more at ease keeping a barrier erected, or at least trying to.

Not that his brother had ever allowed that, he thought,

a small smile lifting his mouth. And to that end, most people thought he played it loose and easy.

He'd always been comfortable with folks thinking he either was a player or had no emotional depth. He'd never really given a damn what others had thought of him.

He frowned, recalling the words of one of his partners.

"Nick, you are unable to connect emotionally." She'd hurled the words and they'd bounced off him like eggs on a non-stick fry pan.

No effect.

It wasn't as though he didn't care about other's feelings; he didn't like hurting people, and particularly not women. The truth was that he had a very soft spot for the gentler sex. He simply preferred remaining...unattached.

He didn't need a psychotherapy session to tell him why that was. He knew it was because of his parents, what he'd always known to be true about them: that although they loved each other, there'd been something... missing.

He shoved the thoughts aside.

He glanced down at the top of Sinclair's head, her soft curls now lying in thick waves on her shoulders. With her, he found himself strangely okay with talking about his family, at least in this limited way.

Nick laughed, remembering his brother's reaction when the reality show's film crew had come to the ranch.

"What?" Her soft question brought him out of his thoughts.

"My brother wasn't exactly...welcoming when they

first came. The film crew, that is. But Dad and I knew it was a necessary evil. Eventually, Key saw it the same way. The end justified the means."

"'Necessary evil'?" she questioned, tilting her head to the side.

"Not exactly my feelings. Didn't really want them around, truth be told, but the idea didn't piss me off like it did my brother. You would have thought the hounds of hell had been loosed on the property with the way Key acted." He laughed outright. "Yeah, but then he remembered why he'd allowed the TV film crew on the ranch in the first place."

"And why was that?"

He smiled, thinking of his mother…his father and brother. Their history and love for Hawaii.

He recited the words that were ingrained in his mind, heart and soul.

"Family, ranch and the preservation of Hawaii," he murmured.

Although it was dark, he could feel her confusion.

"Those were the reasons Key finally agreed to allow the film crew on the ranch. Kinda became the family battle cry," he said, and she laughed softly along with his low chuckle.

"I remember reading something online that stated the reasons for the show were to make more money for the ranch…and maybe exploit two of Hawaii's 'dynamic duo,'" she murmured when their chuckles had died out.

Nick heard the question behind the teasing words.

He groaned. "Please, if you like the fact that my

brother likes you…don't mention that ridiculous nickname," he advised. "That is a surefire way of getting you escorted off the premises," he finished.

"I'll keep that in mind," she laughed. "At any rate, you're the one with the more…" Her voice trailed off and instead of being offended he laughed outright.

"I'm the 'player'? Yeah, I know," he replied.

He was well aware of his reputation as a "player." Hell, his own brother at times bought into the image he so carefully portrayed. Although he knew that his twin knew him well, and was also aware that behind the player image was a man who loved his family, his ranch and Hawaii as much as he did, and took it just as seriously.

And in reality, he'd carefully built up the playboy image as a way to discourage anyone from trying to get too close to him. Although his mother and father loved each other, had always showed love to him and his brother, a part of Nick had seen something else in his mother's eyes when she'd thought no one was looking.

"Yeah, a lot of folks think that. I don't really give a damn, though. By any means necessary." He paused, considering, before he continued to speak.

"The attention from the show brought in an awareness we couldn't have paid for—an awareness to the Aloha Keiki foundation our mother started. We wanted to honor her and to see her dream, her desire, to help those who are less fortunate prosper. And if my 'player' image helped bring in donations, who am I to complain?"

"Of course. All those beautiful women hanging

around the ranch, fawning over your every word, was a sacrifice you were willing to make, huh?"

She surprised yet another laugh from him. "Exactly!"

Her tinkling responding laughter made his smile linger.

He felt an odd little feeling in the pit of his stomach.

He'd been getting more of them lately, funny little feelings in his stomach; his chest would even ache oddly at times. There were even times he felt his heartbeat literally race, times when he wasn't doing anything extraneous.

He frowned. He'd visited the family doc a month ago and knew he was healthy as a "damn horse," as Dr. Pedersen had put it. Heartbeat regular. Blood pressure normal. Cholesterol count perfect.

When he felt her snuggle deeper into him, as she burrowed against his side, he felt the smile return to his face, and the odd thought that he was ill passed.

It was such a sexy thing to do, he thought, snuggling into him in the way she had.

"And we have my sister-in-law to thank for the extra publicity for the foundation," he said, bringing her closer to his body. If that were even possible.

"How so?"

"She made sure that when it came to the PR for the show, it was included that the true reasons we agreed to another season was for the foundation. Initially we kept that within the family—our real reasons. The executive producers thought it made for good PR when Sonia 'accidentally' let it slip 'our real reasons.'"

"Accidentally on purpose?" she said and he grinned.

"Yeah, something like that. We trusted her. And with that, she helped the foundation prosper even more," he said, pride in his voice for both the foundation and the woman he now called sister.

"It's an amazing foundation," she murmured, her words creating a warm spot in his heart. He felt his… feelings…for her grow.

"Thank you. Its purpose is to help disadvantaged youth by bringing in donations to the poorer communities on the island."

"It's admirable. Not just that your mother started it, but that her family loved her and their community so much they sacrificed to see it prosper," she stated simply, the sincerity in her words real, touching.

Nick felt that weird ache in his chest again.

Unconsciously he clutched at his chest.

She reached up, as though she, too, had felt the pang… or felt his pain, and placed her hand over his. Their intertwined hands lay on his chest.

He frowned down at her. The only other person he'd ever experienced that type of mental kinship with had been his brother.

The fact that she knew the information showed that beyond finding out what she needed to to help her Wildes, there had been more to her research than a way to "take care of" the Kealoha problem.

"Yeah," he began, and she burrowed even closer, bringing an unknown smile to his face.

"The money we get comes from both donations as well as what we generate from the farms," he told her.

"Farms? Like the one you showed me, the orchard?" she asked, softly interrupting him.

He nodded.

"Yes, like the one I showed you, baby. We have a few other ones. New ones we are creating on other islands to benefit other communities. All the proceeds are designated, targeted and used to help with agriculture for the youth, for them to learn a usable skill. It's also used for scholarship opportunities for the high school students who want to attend a college or university," he continued. "But the kids know to tap into the resources they have to help out."

"Through their volunteerism," she said, and he nodded. She'd been paying attention.

"Sure do." He was aware of the pride in his voice. "Most do so in the gardens, but we have a small group who come to the ranch and one of the hands supervises them, gives them tasks to do, to help them learn more about ranching."

"You're an amazing man, Nickolas Kealoha," she murmured, her voice thick with sleep.

Her words caused another kick to his heart.

He didn't want to think of her in those terms. Soon, she would be leaving the ranch. Soon, she would be leaving him.

The thought brought back that pang in his heart, this one so strong he grumbled. She sleepily laid a hand over his chest.

In the center of his heart.
He bit back a curse.
He was falling in love with her.

Chapter 20

"What a nice way to enjoy an afternoon break," she breathed, the words fluttering against his chest as soon as her heart had calmed and she could speak again.

She felt more than heard his rumble of laughter.

She groaned. "That sounded so flippant, didn't it?" she said as she lifted away from him to gaze down at his face.

The smile on his handsome face made her catch her breath.

He was such a beautiful man, and when he smiled, his entire face lit up, making him breathtaking.

He was the perfect specimen of manhood.

"Hey, I like it," he said and reached up to touch one of the curls that had, as usual, managed to ignore her attempts to keep it restrained.

His vigorous lovemaking had made sure the rest of her hair had followed suit, and now it hung around her shoulders in kinky, curly waves on her shoulders.

It was the weekend, and although a rancher's workday didn't preclude the weekend, she was surprised when he'd asked her if she'd be interested in going out with him. She'd agreed and they'd spent the day together.

He'd taken her to one of the floral orchards, as well as one of the small gardens that provided his mother's foundation with its supply. She'd been touched when he had brought her to the foundation gardens, knowing how much it meant to him, to his family. A part of her heart opened up that much more to him, despite her desire to take it one day at a time and enjoy what they had without bringing too much...*feeling* into it.

She feared it was too late for that.

"Oh, Lord, I must look a mess!" she said with a groan, brushing aside the gloomier thoughts and searching, in vain, for a ponytail holder.

"I like how you smile, laugh...how comfortable you are with me. I also like this," he said, continuing to finger the curl. "Why don't you leave your hair down more?"

She smiled over her shoulder at him as she pulled her shirt over her head and continued her search. "Not exactly the image I try to project, at least back home," she said, distracted.

"And what is that? What kind of image is it you're trying to maintain?"

He got up and tugged his jeans up the length of his

legs. She stopped as the sight of him dressing was nearly as exciting as him undressing. He caught her staring and gave her a knowing look, which made her blush.

"I happen to like the way you look, too," he said, reading her thoughts. They held glances, mutual smiles on their faces. He leaned over and kissed her softly before patting her naked rear end.

"Finish getting dressed, woman. We have the entire day ahead of us," he said and her smile returned.

Later.

Later they could talk about what was going on between them. How he made her feel.

She felt the changes within herself, knew that no matter what the outcome of her visit here, on a personal level, she wasn't the same woman.

"The image I 'try to project'?" she mimicked, not really paying attention to what she was saying in her vain attempt at finding the band to secure her hair.

She pulled her panties up her legs as she considered the question.

"I don't know. Just one of a professional woman, I guess, is as good as any way of describing it."

"I would think that would go with the territory, what with your profession. Don't your Wilde Boys treat you that way? Like a professional woman? Or do they still see you as the little girl who grew up on the ranch?" he asked.

She turned to look at him, wondering if there was anything in his question besides a simple question.

His look was the same. From his expression it didn't

look as though he was mocking her, or the men. She relaxed yet felt tense, not because of anything on his part, but her own.

Her Wilde Boys.

She hadn't thought of them in that way in a while. She bit on her bottom lip, uncomfortable with the thought.

He caught the way she was worrying her lip and his head tilted to the side.

"You okay, babe?"

"Um. Yeah. Just thinking, that's all," she said as she finished buckling her pink wedge-heeled sandal. "They do. It's not that the brothers don't treat me as a professional. They do. It's just hard sometimes, growing up in the same hometown, with the same people," she finished.

It wasn't always easy to voice her feelings to herself, as she'd been struggling with the conflicting feelings she'd been having lately regarding her career, the Wilde Ranch and the feeling that she was ready, in a lot of ways, to leave.

She'd felt a sense of guilt when she realized that for as much as she loved the Wildes, her life on the ranch and in her hometown, since the death of her father she'd found herself ready to move on.

"You know, sometimes change is good. Doesn't have to be bad, or make you feel guilt-ridden, either. We all need change sometimes," he said.

Again it was as though he was reading her mind.

Her gaze flew his way with a deep frown on her face. God, had she been that transparent? Had her feelings been that clear to read?

And if he'd guessed, did that mean the Wildes had known, as well? Had that been the reason Nate had encouraged her to fly to Hawaii, and not only that, encouraged her to take a small vacation?

Nick wasn't even looking at her, she noticed, her body relaxing at the realization. He was busy buttoning the remaining buttons on his shirt.

She exhaled. Despite the sexy sight of his muscled chest exposed to her, the beautiful lightly tanned skin thick and corded with muscle, she closed her eyes.

She thought back over her last conversation with Nate.

"So do you think this is the best course of action?" she asked as she leaned against the kitchen counter, her arms braced on the granite countertop as she held the mug of coffee between her hands.

The kitchen was the gathering place for the Wildes.

All three of the brothers lived on the ranch, and over the past year they'd completed the construction on the west wing, so that the house—mansion, really—had an extra three thousand square feet added to it overall, as each master suite for the couples had been expanded.

The brothers' rooms had already been large by most home standards, but now each one was like a home within a home, each room reminding Sinclair of a luxurious suite in an upscale hotel, complete with its own small kitchen area.

It was a retreat, and although they rarely did so, if at any time the brothers and their wives chose to break away from the family for a night or weekend on their own, their private suites allowed them the luxury without feeling stifled or restricted due to size.

There was no expense the brothers had spared. No expense when it came to their new wives and their new lives together. As much as she loved them, there had been a small part of Sinclair that envied them their love.

"I think if *you* feel it is, that's good enough for me, Sinclair. You know that I—we, the entire Wilde clan, trusts your judgment," Nate replied.

He brought his own coffee mug in hand over to where she sat perched on one of the stools near the low, circular granite counter they often ate and drank around, in an informal setting.

He eased his long frame onto one of the tall bar-stool-style chairs.

"So… Nate, what you're saying is, it's up to me, this decision?" she asked and bit down on the bottom of her lip.

Nate laughed. "Okay, so what's up?" he asked before taking a drink of his coffee and grimacing. "Told Holt to stay the hell away from the coffeemaker," he complained.

She smiled, despite her ambivalent feelings, before her face became serious again.

"How do you know there *is* anything wrong?" she asked, putting her own cup to her mouth. She grimaced, as well. Holt really did make the worst coffee she'd ever had.

"Little sis, whenever you bite your lip, I know something is on your mind," he said with a smile.

For whatever reason, that brought tears to her eyes, tears she fought against.

"Hey, what's wrong? Something is really troubling you!" he said.

Sinclair could only shake her head.

Smiling a shaky smile, she began to speak. "It's this whole situation," she told him.

He frowned. "With the Kealohas? You don't need to be upset about that. We have confidence in you, and at the end of the day, we've had to deal with situations a lot more complicated than this. We'll survive."

"It's not that so much as…one Kealoha, to be exact," she finally admitted.

And with that, she opened up to Nate in ways she hadn't even admitted to herself. Telling him that she was confident in her abilities, that it was Nick she was having problems with. Not the Kealohas as a family.

Just one Kealoha.

Nate listened carefully, without interrupting her once.

She poured it all out. The situation with the Kealohas was one she could handle, she assured Nate. In fact she had no issues with anyone in the family. After her initial interaction with Keanu Kealoha, it had been Nick Kealoha with whom she had dealt. And *that* was the problem. How Nick…affected her.

When she finally finished, she felt as though a weight had been lifted from her shoulders.

With an odd look on his face, one she didn't understand completely, he gathered her to his big chest and hugged her. When he set her apart from him and stared so intently into her eyes, she felt the rash of tears return.

"What?"

"Nothing. It's just wonderful seeing how you've grown into this amazingly wonderful young woman, so confident, so smart and capable..." He stopped, laughing and shaking his head. "And so beautiful, that if I hadn't grown up with you like a sister, and didn't have a wonderful woman I love more than life itself, I'd be a little jealous of Nick Kealoha," he said to her utter astonishment.

"What are you talking about, Nate Wilde?"

He smiled. The smile had been tilted down at the corner, as though he was sad in some way.

She frowned. If she didn't know better, she could have sworn in Nate's eyes was a mist....

"Nate?" Her voice cracked on his name.

"We have all the confidence in the world in you. Go to Hawaii. Do the Wildes proud as we know you will, baby girl," he said and hugged her.

They small-talked after that, and when he left her to go to work, she stared after him, a bemused look on her face, wondering what he knew that she didn't.

It was as though he was saying goodbye...with his blessing.

Unaware, a tear slipped down her face as she watched him walk away.

Now, as she watched Nick Kealoha get dressed, waiting for her to finish, a part of her wondered what Nate had known that she hadn't.

"Ready, babe?" he asked, smiling and holding out a hand for her to take. She again brushed aside the odd feelings she got whenever she thought too hard about the Wildes.

With a nod she placed her hand in his and allowed him to lead the way.

Chapter 21

"Ever saved a horse and ridden a cowboy instead?"

"Nick! You scared the hell—" The rest of her rant was smothered in his kiss. With a blissful sigh, she turned, wrapped her arms around his neck and kissed him back in earnest. Really getting into his kiss, she stood on tiptoe to get better access.

He didn't just kiss. He made love to her mouth, just like he made love to her. Hot, sweet and incredibly naughty.

She smiled around his kiss. He broke away, staring down at her.

"What?" he asked, his finger coming up to trace the smile.

She shook her head, "Nothing. Just thinking."

"About?" he asked, releasing her. She sighed, turning to face the documents on her desk.

Sinclair had been in the middle of going over the final documents she was sending off to the Wildes for their inspection before giving it to Nick for him and his family to go over.

His gaze went to the papers on the desk she used at the ranch.

It had been more than a week since they'd gone over it, and she had begun to wonder if Nick was holding something back. Every time she mentioned the settlement he would either divert her attention with lovemaking...or divert her attention with lovemaking.

She frowned. The man made her feel like the easiest woman on the planet, she thought.

He turned and caught the frown. Leaning down, he kissed it away.

"What's up? I know that look," he said, yet something in his eyes troubled her.

"You know what's up, Nick. What I can't figure out is why?"

"Why, what?" he asked, but she saw the way he evaded her eyes.

"That right *there!* Every time I bring up the settlement you go weird on me!"

When he folded his arms over his chest and stared at her, looking at her as though *she* was the one being strange, she'd had it.

She stomped her foot, feeling all of ten years old, but she was at her wit's end. Although Nate hadn't said anything, nor had any of the others, she knew they must be wondering why a matter that should have taken three days, a week tops, had turned into a weeks-long adventure.

The fact that no one had actually said anything to her was a mystery she didn't understand, but the fact remained: she needed to wrap it up.

Every day she was in Hawaii, the Kealohas were making it harder and harder for her to think of the time she'd have to leave.

"Come on, baby, we have to deal with this. I don't like that I have to keep trying to get you to look at something that will benefit you. The settlement is fair, but if there is something you don't like, you or the family, let me know, I'll let the Wildes know and—

"What?" she asked, her frown returning.

"What if I told you I don't want a damn thing from your Wilde Boys? My family and I are fine."

She frowned and moved toward him. She placed a hand on his arm and looked up at him. "What's going on? What are you talking about? I'm well aware of your family's wealth, baby. No one is saying you 'need' anything from the Wildes," Sinclair said, shying away from calling them her Wilde Boys without even being aware that she did.

She hadn't referred to the brothers in that way for a while yet that she was aware of.

"Listen. We need to talk. Really talk," he said, taking her hand and guiding her toward the desk.

He opened his mouth and began to speak, his eyes locked on hers.

"I...well... See, the thing is," he began and stopped.

"Baby…are you okay?" she asked and he looked at her, helpless, looking lost.

"Nick?" she asked, her voice lowering, fear threading it.

"I…I want to make love to you, baby," he blurted the words. "I've needed you all day. You know how I get," he said and buried his head in her neck, his hands shaky as they rested on her waist.

Even as she allowed him to lift her enough to remove her panties, she felt the fine tremble in his hands.

"Nick, baby, we really need to go over the papers," she moaned as his finger delved inside her, withdrawing her cream, her body already preparing for his.

Before she could question him further, before she realized that he had once again diverted her attention, her panties were on the floor and he was reaching for the box of condoms they kept in her desk.

It hadn't been the first time he'd taken her in her makeshift office.

Condom donned, seconds later he was easing his thick, long length inside her welcoming body.

As he rolled his hips she accepted him, rocking into him, their bodies swiftly catching one another's rhythm. Natural-born lovers. She moaned as he groaned, their voices sighs of passion even in sync.

Lazily she rolled back and forth on his shaft, her body calling to his.

The lazy sway of their lovemaking didn't stop the inferno from building and it wasn't long before their orgasms hit simultaneously.

As he came, he wrapped his big arms around her waist, bringing her close as he pumped, once, twice, three more times, his voice muffled as he growled his release.

It was long moments before her heartbeat returned to normal.

Not just because of the mind-blowing orgasm, but also because of what she thought she'd heard him growl against her neck as he came.

"God, I love you," he moaned in a heartfelt whisper against her neck.

Simple. Direct.

And, oh, God…she loved him, too.

Tears threatened to fall.

"How's everything going, Sinclair? Haven't heard from you. Thought I'd give you a ring, girlfriend!"

Sinclair smiled, leaned back against the soft down cushions on the bed in her hotel room and withdrew her glasses from her nose.

"Hey, Yaz girl, how are you?" she said, glad for the interruption, her mind not on the brief she was finishing, but on Nick, the Kealohas, the Wildes…and the tangled mess she found herself in.

"I'm doing well, babies are doing well, too," she said and Sinclair smiled.

Yasmine was pregnant, and had recently learned that it wasn't one Wilde, but two little Wildes growing in her tummy, a fact that had Holt, her husband, with his chest swollen with pride.

"How's Holt?" she asked, ready to giggle. Holt and Yasmine had always cracked her up, as Holt had a wild sense of humor and could make anyone laugh with a few well-chosen words.

"Girl, he got his chest all poked out, proud, like he *did* something!" she said.

"Yeah, well, girl, he kinda did help. I mean, it takes two and all that."

"Yes. True. And that is exactly what I'm talking about. It takes *two.* Not one. *Two,*" she emphasized. "With the way my husband is walking around the ranch talking about how potent he is…how, if it wasn't for his Superman sperm— What, baby? I'm on the phone, I *can't* talk to you!" she said, yelling at Holt, one hand covering the mouthpiece. Despite the ambivalent feelings Sinclair had due to her own personal situation, she fought back a laugh.

Holt and Yasmine always, without fail, cracked her up. When Yasmine got back on the phone, the two women caught up on what had been going on at the ranch in her absence.

Finally she opened up with Yasmine. She hadn't told anyone what had been happening between her and Nick, not because she didn't feel like she could, but mainly because she hadn't figured out her own feelings. Until he'd told her he loved her.

She knew without doubt she'd heard it.

After she spilled her guts, told Yasmine everything, she waited. Then said, "I love him, Yaz. I really love him."

She waited for the scream.

It wasn't a long wait.

"*Oh. My. God!* They were right, Althea and Nate were right! Wahooo! Wait until I tell them. Oh. My. *God!*"

Despite the yelling and hollering, Sinclair picked up on something, a frown making her sit straighter.

"Nate and Althea were right? What do you mean, Althea and Nate were right?" she asked.

She wondered if Yaz's pregnancy was affecting her in some weird way she had never heard of. There was a pause, and she could feel Yasmine's discomfort.

"Oh, shoot. Me and my big mouth," she mumbled.

Oh, no. This wasn't good.

Of all the women, Yasmine was not only the worst to know a secret, she was the worst to keep a secret. Which was why she knew that what she was about to hear wasn't going to be something she necessarily wanted to hear.

"You might as well come clean, Yasmine. Cat's darn well out of the bag. Almost, anyway. Besides…you know you always feel better when you do," Sinclair said, cajoling the woman and not feeling the least bit bad when Yasmine, in her pregnancy-induced emotional state started to whine, sniffing while saying, in a very small voice that Holt was going to get her when he found out. Then she stopped to giggle at her own words, repeating them.

"Holt's gonna *get* me," she said around her giggles. "Maybe the babies will come quicker if he does!" she said, her mind already on something else.

"Focus, Yasmine," Sinclair said, trying not to snap at the pregnant woman, knowing that it was truly the hormones racing in her body that made her the way she was. Kind of...

"Okay," said Yasmine, sobering. She began to whine again, begging Sinclair not tell, and on and on...until Sinclair forced the truth out of the woman. Finally.

And the truth made her face blanch.

When Sinclair was able to get off the phone, adroitly avoiding an agreement not to tell the brothers, she in fact wondered who she should confront first. The three men whom she considered brothers...

Or the one she was beginning to love like one: The one who was the identical twin brother of the man she was in love with.

All four men were not only in cahoots with each other, regarding the Wildes and the property, the inheritance and all, but were also responsible for her being there in the first place. They were responsible for all of the time she had been there, and for purposely throwing her and Nick together.

Chapter 22

"I messed up, Key."

The admission was made reluctantly as Nick found his brother in one of the stables, after looking for him the entire day.

He'd wrestled with the issue of the Wildes and, more importantly, Sinclair, for the better part of the day.

Hell, he'd been wrestling with it for longer, much longer than that.

"I was wondering when you would come and find me," his brother replied mildly.

"Am I missing something here?"

"No, Pica. I just figured you would make your way here eventually. Grab a broom. Menial work clears your head," he said.

With a frown Nick grabbed a broom as his brother'd asked, and began to help him clean out a stall.

"Okay, so what gives? Why are you doing 'menial' work, as you put it? Everything okay with you and Sonia?" Nick asked, putting his own troubles to the side to make sure his family was okay.

Key threw him a smile. It was strained in the corners and Nick began to worry. "We're fine, Pika… No fears. Just shoot. What's on your mind?"

Again, Nick hesitated. Two times his brother had called him by his nickname, one was to purely tick him off, the other time was as if something was on his mind, bothering him.

He continued to sweep after Key refused to say anything more.

Nick spilled his guts.

Opened up to his brother in ways he never had with anyone else.

He told him how he felt about their parents, how he felt about Clint Wilde.

"I know you don't feel the same way that I do, Key. I get that. And, man, damn if I know why it affected me like that—that he never found out about us—but it did," he finished, glancing toward his brother.

"Did?"

Nick laughed. "Yeah, did. Crazy thing is, it doesn't even matter anymore," he said, running a hand over the back of his head. "And the reason for that is because of Sinclair," he admitted, his voice gruff, raw.

His brother said nothing, just continued to work, but

Nick knew he was paying close attention to what he was saying.

"I love her more than I thought I could ever love a woman. More than I thought it was possible to love," he said, and turned away. As much as he loved his brother, he felt exposed admitting his feelings about Sinclair in such an open way.

"Have you told her?" Key asked.

Nick shook his head no even before he'd fully asked the question.

"No. Don't know how. Hell of it is, I don't know if she feels the same way."

"Man, come on. You know the woman loves you. Hell, the whole damn ranch knows how you two feel about each other. Damn sure you haven't hidden it."

"I tried. Damn if I didn't. It's just that whenever we're together, it's like there's no one else. I love her more than I love the A'kela Ranch."

When he made that admission the brothers locked gazes. The emotion in his eyes was one he couldn't hide, not from his twin. The A'kela was not simply their ranch, it was them, who they were.

By saying he loved her more than the A'kela it was clear that his words were deep and heartfelt.

Key smiled. The smile was one of relief, mixed with something more.

He grabbed his brother and hugged him. They hugged for long moments before Nick lightly shoved him, making him laugh as he pushed his twin away.

"I can't keep her here forever. She has to know the truth soon."

"Don't be an idiot like I was with Sonia. Tell her. Don't let her leave without telling her. And tell her the truth—that you don't want the Wildes' ranch. That the Kealohas don't want the Wyoming Wilde Ranch."

Nick blew out a breath after patting his brother on the back. "Wish it was that simple. How the hell do you tell somebody you love that you've been keeping something from them, just because you wanted to get to know them…? That what you felt from the first time you spoke was something you'd never felt for another person before?"

"Just like that, brother," Key said.

The brothers locked gazes. Nick laughed. "Just like that, huh?"

"But before you do, there's something I've got to tell you. And I don't think you're going to like it," he warned, rubbing his hand over the back of his neck.

Although he felt dread, Nick recognized the gesture, one that he himself made whenever he was unsure of himself.

"Oh, hell…what is it? Don't tell me… You and the Wildes have been talking?"

The look Key gave him was almost worth the ass-whooping Nick was going to give his brother for going behind his back to talk to the three men Nick had professed to dislike.

Even as he began to roll up his sleeves, Nick knew

that as far as ass-whoopings went, this one would be fair and evenly matched.

"Aw, hell. Okay, let's get this over with so I can tell you everything and you can get your woman," Key grumbled and began to roll up his own sleeves.

No one knew him like his brother. It was a natural thing to do, to go to him. Even if his brother was an ass sometimes.

Chapter 23

She was on fire with need for him, unsure if she could hold off until they got back to either her hotel or his home.

Her glance fell over him. In the dim light of his truck cab, she was still able to make out how able his big hands looked as they gripped the wheel.

He must have felt her gaze as he turned enough to glance over at her. He smiled and reached over to lift her hand up and bring it to his mouth.

He surprised her when he turned it over and placed a kiss in the center of her palm.

She felt the…intimacy of the kiss. Erotic. Different. But so hot.

"Today was amazing. Don't know the last time I enjoyed myself like that, Sin."

She smiled at his words. When he'd first called her the nickname it had startled her, so different than what she'd been used to in the way of nicknames.

"Sin," he'd called her.

She was the sensible one. The responsible one. Definitely not a woman with a nickname like Sin.

No. She was the girl who studied, sailed through undergrad and law school easily. The one who worked hard and...worked hard.

Family had come first. Her own. She and her father, as it had been the two of them since her mother's passing years ago. Then her extended family. The Wildes.

Now that her father had passed away, what kept her at the Wilde Ranch was the Wildes themselves. After everything they'd done for her, from the financial assistance that had allowed her to go to law school, to the position as their attorney, she felt a sense of...obligation to them.

Sensible Sinclair. That was who she was and, more importantly, who she was comfortable being.

She turned away from Nick, but allowed him to keep her hand within his much bigger one.

Sin.

One side of her lips hitched upward into a secret little smile. Lord knew the man had made her sin more than a little bit. And she'd loved every minute of it, she thought, holding back a sigh.

She'd decided to talk to Key first, after hearing everything that Yasmine told her that happened, from the beginning.

Assuming her friend's pregnancy-addled brain had it right, a part of her felt gratitude for what they'd done.

But she still was unsure about how Nick was going to respond. She knew that his dislike for the Wildes ran deep… How was she going to tell him that his brother had been in communication with them from the get-go?

Yasmine had informed her that after his initial communication, Nate had reached out and, believing he was speaking to Nick—and not realizing it was Keanu he was talking to—had told him that they—the Wildes—looked forward to meeting the Kealohas, and had nothing to hide. They wanted the brothers to come to the Wilde Ranch to see it. He'd invited them to become part of the family, to move to the ranch if they had a desire to.

The Wyoming Wilde Ranch would welcome the twins with open arms, sharing in the wealth as they knew their father would want them to.

She'd wondered how and what they'd had to do with her, and how the second part of their odd but well-meaning plot had evolved.

She bit her lip, wondering how she was going to tell Nick that part, as well. It got kind of tricky, there.

She'd searched for him all day and finally found him in town, and the two had decided to come back to the A'kela. It was then she noticed that he was quiet.

More quiet than usual.

"Baby…can we talk?" she asked, and he turned to her, his blue eyes filled with lust and need. A heady combination; one she knew too well.

"Yeah…after."

She knew what "after" meant, and felt her body respond. She also knew something was on his mind, as well.

"I promise, baby. We'll talk…after," he said, his eyes holding hers, and she nodded. Again he brought her hand to his lips to place a soft kiss in the palm.

For some reason the sweet gesture brought tears to her eyes. She batted them away, and stared out the window, wondering how he was going to feel when she told him.

The truck came to a smooth halt and Sinclair began to unbuckle her seat belt when his hand on hers made her stop. She turned to face him, a question on her lips.

The look in his eyes made her ask, "Baby…what's wrong?" Dread pooled in her gut, afraid she knew the answer.

"I think you're right. You've been right all along," he said, searching her eyes. "Let's talk." He squared his shoulders. "Hell, let's get it over with now. I don't want to wait," he finished.

"Here?" she asked, wondering at the urgency. It was as though he thought he was going to face the firing squad.

She swallowed. Afraid. She knew that what she had to tell him he wasn't going to want to hear. He may even question her motives, but she had to tell him.

She was opening her mouth to tell him when he forestalled her.

"My brother…the Wildes…have all been in communication with each other, for the entire time we have been," he began.

Promptly her mouth formed a perfect *O*.... He knew.

She listened as he told her, his head hung low as though he was afraid, or ashamed. She felt the love she had for him grow even more, and the decision she had made, to stay at the ranch, she prayed was one he wanted, as well.

"Baby, it's okay. I know everything!" she said, but realized he wasn't listening. When he continued speaking, she frowned. The happiness she felt began to fade as disbelief took its place as he continued to speak.

Nick knew that if he didn't say it in one big rush, get it all out, he would never do it.

After he and his brother had nearly come to blows, he knew it was the least he could do to tell her the truth, the entire truth.

As his brother had told him, he knew he could hold back, not tell her of his part in it, how he'd already decided long before she came that he wanted nothing from the Wildes. But if he did, there would be no other reason for their continued communication.

"And I couldn't do that. So I went along with it, pretended I still wanted to sue the Wildes," he said, finishing stoically. He hadn't been able to look at her, not since he'd seen the crestfallen look cross her pretty face.

"Why did you do that? Why did you lie like that?" she asked, her voice so low he felt, for the first time in his adult life, like damn near bawling, she was pulling at his emotions so.

"I'm sorry. It was the only way..." He stopped.

"Revenge was that important to you? To waste my time...?"

"No. It was because I was already in love with you. Which is what my brother saw. Which is why he went along with the Wildes in sending you out here, as well," he said, praying to God it was as his brother had said: that the Wildes had seen her love for him, as well, the spark they hoped would flourish for a woman they considered a sister.

She frowned. "Okay, let me get this straight. Your brother and the Wildes put this all together because your brother believed you were in love with me, and the Wildes thought I was in love with you?"

He nodded his head.

She chewed her bottom lip, frowning at him.

"And did you? I mean, uh, were you falling in love with me then?"

Her eyes were lowered and he was unable to see the look in them. But he heard the uncertainty, the small catch.

"God, yes, baby. I didn't know it, but I knew I'd never felt like that in my life. It wasn't long before I started to suspect I was in love with you."

"Falling-down-drunk kinda love?" she asked.

He felt a grin tug at the corner of his mouth. Humor was good. If she was laughing...

"Falling-down, begging-please-baby-please in love with you," he said, hope blossoming.

"Well...I guess since you put it that way," she said and

laughed when he dragged her across the seat and into his lap, swallowing her laughter with a kiss.

"Oooh, yessss." The wail of pleasure was ripped from her lips in one long hiss.

For long, hot moments, there was nothing to be heard in the stable but the sound of horses softly neighing, providing background noise to what was going on in one of the empty stalls.

"Shush, baby. You're going to wake up the ranch if you keep that up," Nick said, his deep voice husky and low, intimate as it and he brushed over her skin. "But I do like how you respond," he said.

Before she knew what he was going to do, she felt him stroke deep inside her in one fatal hot slide, deep inside her welcoming warmth.

They hadn't made it to the ranch before he was dragging her inside the stable, a wicked grin on his face.

"We haven't done it here, yet. Want to?" he'd asked, a wicked smile on his handsome face.

The request was just what she'd needed. Light, sexy and fun...before she would have to tell him something he wouldn't want to hear.

Now, as he stroked inside her, she met him thrust for thrust, as they made love facing each other, his legs thrown over hers as she rode him.

"You're my perfect match, baby...you know that?" he asked, his voice low and rumbly, just the way she liked it when he was really turned on.

She grinned, asking, "Oh yeah...how's that? Because

I can do this?" she asked, performing a move that had him growling so low she giggled. Her giggle turned into a long purr of satisfaction when he mimicked the move. With a twist.

He lifted her, easily, and stroked inside her, and soon there was no time for laughter. There was nothing but pleasure and moans, sighs of delight and hot glides of skin against skin.

He placed his hands on either side of her face, his face strained with pleasure. She gasped as he stroked, widening her legs to take as much of him as she could, his shaft thick, long and hard as it speared inside her wet, welcoming warmth.

When she tried to look away, the feelings, both physical and emotional, became overwhelming, too much for her to handle, too intense, but he wouldn't allow her that luxury.

"Yesss. Oh, God, yes," she moaned, her head rolling back in pleasure.

"You like that, baby? Like the way I make you feel?" He breathed the words more than said them and she bobbed her head up and down in eager agreement.

"Yes, Nick, I do…I love it, and I love you," she cried out sharply when he pinched her nipple before grasping the turgid tip into his mouth and sucking away the small pain.

"Good…so good," she moaned. Her body was on fire with need, and he was the one, the only one, who could put out the flames.

When he widened her legs, she took in a breath. The

tip of his shaft was tapping against her bottom as he deep-stroked her. "Before I give you what you need…" he said, and pushed a fraction deeper inside her. "You have to tell me what I want to hear," he said, taking her nipple back into his mouth, swirling his tongue around it.

Her mouth went dry. "Wh…what are you talking about?" Coherent speech was nearly behind her.

"The Wildes. Tell me I'm more important to you than they are. Tell me they are no longer your Wilde Boys," he said.

She inhaled a shuddering breath. Not because of his demand, but because he pressed inside her quivering lips.

She was shaking so badly, so filled with lust and need…and love for this man, that she would say any-thing, do anything, for him.

"Tell me I'm the only man you'll ever need, ever want." His voice was like graveled sand. Low. Demand-ing…yet filled with uncertainty.

"God, yes, yes, yes!" she cried in agreement, hearing his chuckle as he lifted her hips and began to press all the way inside. "Baby, I love you," she cried, and forced the red haze of lust to the side so she could see her man.

She grasped the sides of his face this time, forcing him to look into her eyes.

"I love you. Only you."

His eyes closed briefly. When they opened again, the blaze of love in their deep blue depths was nearly blind-ing in its intensity.

"That's what I wanted to hear, baby," he said, no triumph in his voice. Only love.

At the moment of climax she felt it, reached for it, her eyes glued to his, swaying as they reached the summit together.

On a long wailing cry she released as he did, with him inside her...

"I love you, baby. God, I love you!" he shouted and she allowed the tears of emotion associated with good loving and even more than that, being in love, to freely fall.

* * * * *

BRUNETTI'S
SECRET SON

MAYA BLAKE

CHAPTER ONE

THE HIDEOUS MANSION was just as he'd recalled in his nightmares, the gaudy orange exterior clashing wildly with the massive blue shutters. The only thing that didn't quite gel with the picture before him was the blaze of the sun glinting off the grotesquely opulent marble statues guarding the entry gates.

Romeo Brunetti's last memory of this place had been in the chilling rain, his threadbare clothes sticking to his skin as he'd huddled in the bushes outside the gates. A part of him had prayed he wouldn't be discovered, the other more than a tiny bit hopeful that discovery would mean the end to all the suffering, the hunger, the harrowing pain of rejection that ate his thirteen-year-old body alive from morning to night. Back then he would've welcomed the beating his reluctant rescuer had received for daring to return Romeo to this place. Because the beating would have ended in oblivion, and the bitterness coursing through his veins like acid would have been no more.

Unfortunately, the fates had decreed otherwise. He'd hidden in the bushes, cold and near catatonic, until the ever-present hunger had forced him to move.

Romeo stared up at the spears clutched in the hands of the statues, recalling his father's loud-bellied boast of them being made of solid gold.

The man who'd called him a bastard and a waste of space to his face. Right before he'd instructed his minion to throw him out and make sure he never returned. That he didn't care whether the spawn of the whore he'd rutted with in an alleyway in Palermo lived or died, as long as he, Agostino

Fattore, the head of the ruling crime family, didn't have to see the boy's face again.

No…not his *father*.

The man didn't deserve that title.

Romeo's hands tightened on the steering wheel of his Ferrari and he wondered for the thousandth time why he'd bothered to come to this place. Why he'd let a letter he'd shredded in a fit of cold rage seconds after reading it compel him into going back on the oath he'd made to himself over two decades ago. He looked over to the right where the towering outer wall to the late Agostino Fattore's estate rose into the sky, and sure enough, the bush was exactly as he remembered it, its leafy branches spread out, offering the same false sanctuary.

For a wild moment, Romeo fought the strong urge to lunge out of the car and rip the bush out of the earth with his bare hands, tear every leaf and branch to shreds. Tightening his jaw, he finally lowered his window and punched in the code his memory had cynically retained.

As the gates creaked open, he questioned again why he was doing this. So what if the letter had hinted at something else? What could the man whose rejection had been brutally cold and complete have to offer him in death that he'd failed so abjectly to offer in life?

Because he needed answers.

He needed to know that the blood running through his veins didn't have an unknown stranglehold over him that would turn his life upside down when he least expected it.

That the two times in his life when he'd lost control to the point of not recognising himself would be the only times he would feel savagely unmoored.

No one but Romeo knew how much he regretted wasting the four years of his life after the bitter night he'd been here last, looking for acceptance anywhere and any way he could find it. More than hating the man whose blood ran through his veins, Romeo hated the years he'd spent trying to find a replacement for Agostino Fattore.

Giving himself permission to close his heart off at seventeen had been the best decision he'd ever made.

So why are you here? You're nothing like him.

He needed to be sure. Agostino might no longer be alive, but he needed to look into the heart of Fattore's legacy and reassure himself that the lost little boy who'd thought his world would end because of another's rejection was obliterated completely.

Impatient with himself for prevaricating, Romeo smashed his foot on the accelerator and grunted in satisfaction as the tyres squealed on the asphalt road leading to the courtyard. Unfolding himself from the driver's seat, he stalked up to the iron-studded double doors and slammed them open.

Striding into the chequer-tiled hallway, he glared at the giant antique chandelier above his head. If he had cared whether this house stood or fell, that monstrosity would have been the first thing in the incinerator. But he wasn't here to ponder the ugly tastes of a dead man. He was here to finally slay ghosts.

Ghosts that had lingered at the back of his consciousness since he was a child but that had been resurrected one night five years ago, in the arms of a woman who'd made him lose control.

He turned as slow feet shuffled in his direction, followed by firmer footholds that drew a grim smile from Romeo. So, the old order hadn't changed. Or maybe the strength of Romeo's anger had somehow transmitted to Fattore's former second in command, prompting the old man who approached to seek the protection of his bodyguards.

Lorenzo Carmine threw out his hands in greeting, but Romeo glimpsed the wariness in the old man's eyes. 'Welcome, *mio figlio*. Come, I have lunch waiting for us.'

Romeo tensed. 'I'm not your son and this meeting will not last beyond five minutes, so I suggest you tell me what you withheld in your letter right now and stop wasting my time.' He didn't bother to hide the sneer in his voice.

Lorenzo's pale grey eyes flared with a temper Romeo had witnessed the last time he was here. But along with it came the recognition that Romeo was no longer a frightened little boy incapable of defending himself. Slowly, his expression altered into a placid smile.

'You have to pardon me. My constitution requires that I strictly regulate my mealtimes or I suffer for it.'

Romeo turned towards the door, again regretting his decision to come here. He was wasting his time looking for answers in stone and concrete. He was wasting his time, full stop.

'Then by all means go and look after your constitution. Enjoy the rest of your days and don't bother contacting me again.' He stepped towards the door, a note of relief spiking through him at the thought of leaving this place.

'Your father left something for you. Something you will want to see.'

Romeo stopped. 'He was not my father and there's nothing he possesses in this life or the next that could possibly interest me.'

Lorenzo sighed. 'And yet you came all this way at my request. Or was it just to stick out your middle finger at an old man?'

Romeo's jaw clenched, hating that the question he'd been asking himself fell from the lips of a man who'd spent his whole life being nothing but a vicious thug. 'Just spit it out, Carmine,' he gritted out.

Lorenzo glanced at the nearer bodyguard and nodded. The beefy minder headed down the long hallway and disappeared.

'For the sake of my friend, your father, the Almighty rest his soul, I will go against my doctor's wishes.' The remaining guard fell into step behind Lorenzo, who indicated a room to their left.

From memory, Romeo knew it was the holding room for visitors, a garishly decorated antechamber that led to the receiving room, where his father had loved to hold court.

The old man shuffled to a throne-like armchair and sank heavily into it. Romeo chose to remain standing and curbed the need to pace like a caged animal.

Although he'd come through the desolation of his ragged past, he didn't care for the brutal reminders everywhere he looked. The corner of this room was where he'd crouched when his father's loud lambasting of a minion had led to gunshots and horrific screams the first time he'd been brought here. The gilt-framed sofa was where his father had forced him to sit and watch as he'd instructed his lieutenants to beat Paolo Giordano into a pulp.

He didn't especially care for the reminder that it was possibly because of Fattore's blood running through his veins that he'd almost taken the same violent path when, tired of living on the streets, he'd almost joined a terror-loving gang feared for their ruthlessness.

Sì, he should've stayed far away, in the warmth of his newest and most lavish by-invitation-only Caribbean resort.

His eyes narrowed as the second bodyguard returned with a large ornately carved antique box and handed it to Lorenzo. 'It's a good thing your father chose to keep an eye on you, wasn't it?' Lorenzo said.

'Scusi?' Romeo rasped in astonishment.

Lorenzo waved his hand. 'Your mother, the Almighty rest *her* unfortunate soul, attempted to do her best, but we all knew she didn't have what it took, eh?'

Romeo barely stopped his lips from curling. The subject of his mother was one he'd sealed under strict lock and key, then thrown into a vault the night he'd buried her five years ago.

The same night he'd let his guard down spectacularly with a woman whose face continued to haunt him when he least expected it. A woman who had, for the first time in a long time, made him want to feel the warmth of human emotion.

A tremor went through him at the memory, its deep and disturbing effect as potent, if not more so, than it'd been that night when he'd realised that his emotions weren't as clinical and icy as he'd imagined them to be.

He shut down that line of thought.

Maisie O'Connell had had no place in his life then, save as a means of achieving a few hours of oblivion, and she most certainly didn't have one now, in this cursed place. Like the bush outside this miscreation of a mansion, she represented a time in his life he wanted banished for all time.

Because it makes you uncomfortable...vulnerable even? Basta!

'You seem to be under the misapprehension that I'll indulge you in fond trips down potholed memory lanes. Be assured that I will not. If I remember correctly, *you* helped to throw me out of the gates when I was a child. Your exact words, presumably passed down from my father, were—*I see you again, you leave in a body bag.*'

Lorenzo shrugged. 'Those were hot-headed days. Look at you now. You've done very well for yourself despite your less than salubrious beginning.' A touch of malice flared in his eyes. 'None of us imagined a boy conceived in the gutter would rise to such esteem.'

Romeo shoved his hands in his pockets so he wouldn't do the unthinkable and strangle the old man where he sat. 'Then I guess it's a good thing I was intelligent enough to realise early on that whether you were born in the gutter or with a dozen golden spoons clutched in your fist, our lives are what we make them. Otherwise, who knows where I'd be today? In a mental institution, perhaps? Bemoaning my fate while rocking back and forth in a straitjacket?'

The old man laughed, or he attempted to. When the sound veered into a bone-jarring coughing spell, his bodyguards exchanged wary glances before one stepped forward with a glass of water.

Lorenzo's violent refusal of help had the guard springing back into his designated position. When the coughing fit passed, Lorenzo opened the box and took out several papers.

'You were never going to go down without a fight. I saw that in you even when you were a boy. But you'll do well to remember where that intelligence comes from.'

'Are you really suggesting that I owe what I've made of myself to you or the pathetic band of thugs you call a family?' he asked, incredulous.

Lorenzo waved him away. 'We'll discuss what you owe in a bit. Your father meant to do this before he was tragically taken from us,' he muttered.

Romeo curbed the need to voice his suspicions that his father's departure from this life hadn't been tragic at all; that the boat explosion that had taken his life and those of his wife and the two half-sisters Romeo had never been allowed to meet hadn't been accidental, but the target of a carefully orchestrated assassination.

Instead, he watched Lorenzo pull out document after document and lay them on the desk.

'The first order of business is this house. It's yours free and clear from any financial obligations. All the lawyers need is your signature to take possession. It comes with the collection of cars, the horses and the three hundred acres of land, of course.'

Astonishment rendered Romeo speechless.

'Then there are the businesses. They're not doing as well as we'd hoped, and certainly not as well as your own businesses are doing. The Carmelo *famiglia* mistakenly believe this is an excuse for them to start making moves on Fattore business, but I suspect that will all turn around once our business has been brought under the umbrella of your company, Brunetti International—'

Romeo laughed. 'You must be out of your mind if you

think I want any part of this blood-soaked legacy. I'd rather
return to the gutter than claim a single brick of this house,
or associate myself in any way with the Fattore name and
everything it stands for.'

'You may despise the Fattore name, but do you think
Brunetti, son of a two-bit whore has a better ring?' Lorenzo sneered.

It didn't, but in the bleak, terrible hellhole of his childhood it had been the better of two evils. Especially since that
greater evil had warned him never to use the name *Fattore*.

'This is your legacy, no matter how much you try to deny
it,' Lorenzo insisted.

'You can sit there and rewrite history until the walls
crumble around you,' Romeo enunciated with a burning
intensity he suspected would erupt the longer he spent in
this house. 'But your five minutes have come and gone, old
man. And this meeting is well and truly over. Any problems
you have with your extortion business and territorial wars
with the Carmelo family are yours to deal with.'

He made it to the door before Lorenzo spoke.

'Your father suspected that when the time came you
would prove intransigent. So he asked me to give you this.'

For the second time, Romeo froze, his instincts screech-
ing at him to keep walking, but his brain warning that to do
as he so desperately wanted would be unwise.

Lorenzo held out a large manila envelope, which he slid
across the desk with a smug look.

'I told you I'm not interested in anything bearing the Fattore name. Whatever is in that envelope—'

'Is of a more…personal nature and will interest you, *mio
figlio*. I'm confident of it.'

Romeo abandoned the need to remind the old man not
to call him son. Lorenzo was enjoying needling him a little too much, and Romeo was fast reaching boiling point.

Striding across the room, he snatched up the envelope
and ripped it open. The first picture punched him in the

gut, expelling a harsh breath. It showed him standing at his mother's graveside, the only attendee besides the priest, as Ariana Brunetti was laid to rest.

He flung the picture on the desk, his mouth twisting as the next picture showed him in funereal black, sitting at his hotel bar, staring into a glass of cognac.

'So Fattore had me followed for an afternoon five years ago. Perhaps he would've better profited using that time to tend his businesses.'

Lorenzo tented his fingers. 'Keep going. The best is yet to come.'

Dark premonition crawled up Romeo's spine as he flipped to the next photo. It showed him walking out of his hotel and down the street that led to the trendy cafés near the waterfront.

He froze at the next picture and stared at the image of himself. And her.

Maisie O'Connell—the woman with the angelic face and the tempting, sinful body. The combination, although enthralling enough, wasn't what had made her linger in his mind long after he'd moved on to other women, and other experiences.

Something had happened with her in that hotel room, above and beyond mind-obliterating sex. He'd walked away from her feeling broken, fighting a yearning that had terrified him for a long time, until he'd finally forced it back under control.

He had no intention of resurrecting those brief, unsettling hours. He was in control of his life. In control of the fleeting moments of emotion he allowed himself these days.

He threw down the pictures, not caring when they fanned out in a careless arc on the desk. Eyes narrowed at Lorenzo, he snapped, 'It's almost laughable that you think documenting my sex life would cause me anything but acute irritation. Irritation that might just push me into having this house torn to the ground and the whole estate turned into a car park.'

The old man reached across, shuffled through the pictures, then sat back again.

Exhaling, Romeo looked down and saw more pictures of the woman he'd shared his most memorable one-night stand with. But these were different. Taken in another country, judging from the street signs. Dublin, most likely, where Maisie had said she was from during one of the brief times they'd conversed in that electric night they'd spent together.

Still caught up in riotous emotions, he nudged the picture impatiently with his fingernail.

Maisie O'Connell, striding down a busy street in a business suit and high heels, her thick, glorious hair caught up in an elaborate bun. A vision far removed from the sexy little sundress and flip-flops she'd been wearing the first time Romeo had seen her outside a waterfront café in Palermo. Her hair had been loose then, hanging to her waist in a ripple of dark fire.

Romeo unveiled the next picture.

Maisie, hailing a taxi outside a clinic, her features slightly pale and drawn, her normally bright blue eyes dark with worry.

Maisie, sitting on a park bench, her face turned up to the sun, her hand resting on her belly.

Her very distended belly.

Romeo swallowed hard and picked up the last picture, his body suspended in shock as he brought it up to his face.

Maisie, pushing a pram down a quiet Dublin street, her mouth tilted in a postcard-perfect picture of maternal bliss as she reached into the stroller.

'*Madre di Dio*, what is the meaning of this?' he breathed, his voice cold enough to chill the whole mausoleum of a mansion.

'I will not insult your deductive powers by spelling it out for you,' Lorenzo answered.

Romeo flung the photo down, but he could not look away from them. Spreading his fingers through the glossy images, he found further evidence of surveillance. Apparently his father had decided to stop following Romeo and focus instead on the woman he'd slept with on the day of his mother's funeral. A woman whose goodness had threatened to seep into him, to threaten the foundations of his carefully barricaded emotions.

'If these images are supposed to paint some sort of picture, then you've wasted your time. Sexually active individuals have brief encounters and go on to have relationships and families all the time. Or so I'm told.'

He'd never indulged in a relationship. In fact, he actively discouraged his lovers from even entertaining a glimmer of the idea. Romeo suppressed a grim smile. He knew his attitude to relationships had earned him the amusingly caustic label of *Weekend Lover*. Not that he cared. Hell, if it spelled out his intentions before he even asked a woman out, then all the better.

Affection was never on the table, the faintest idea of love strictly and actively forbidden. His interactions were about sex. Nothing more.

'So you don't care to know the time span during which these pictures were taken?'

'Fattore must have had his own warped reason, I'm sure.'

Lorenzo continued to stare at him. 'Then you won't want to know that the woman gave her child an Italian name?'

Romeo snorted in disbelief. He hadn't told Maisie his surname. He'd been very careful in that regard because he hadn't wanted any association with either his mother or his father discovered, as tenuous as the connection could've been, seeing that he hadn't set foot in Sicily in over fifteen years.

'You two must have been desperate to clutch at so many straws. My suggestion to you would be to leave this woman alone to raise her child. She means nothing to me other than a brief dalliance. Whatever leverage you seek through her has no teeth.'

Lorenzo shook his balding grey head. 'Once you have calmed down and learnt a little of our ways, you'll realise that we don't tend to leave stones unturned. Or facts unchecked. Your father certainly wouldn't pin the future of his organisation, of his *famiglia*, on a whim. No, *mio figlio*, we checked and double-checked our facts. Three DNA tests by three different doctors confirmed it.'

'How did you come by samples for these tests?'

'Contrary to what you think of us, we're not bumbling idiots. A strand of hair or a discarded juice cup is all we need, and quite easy to come by.'

The gross violation that deed would've entailed turned his stomach and primitive anger swelled through him. 'You set your thugs loose on a little boy?'

'He's not just any little boy. Your woman gave birth exactly nine months after your encounter. And your son is very much a Fattore.'

CHAPTER TWO

MAISIE O'CONNELL FLIPPED the Closed sign to Open and enjoyed the tingle of excitement that never failed to come with that little action.

It had been a long, hard slog, but *Maisie's* was finally ticking over very nicely, was making a steady profit, in fact. Putting her beloved restaurant in the hands of a professional chef while she'd taken the intensive course in gourmet Italian cooking had paid off. The added feature in one of Dublin's top newspapers had given *Maisie's* the extra boost that had seen her bookings go from half full to booked solid a month in advance.

Picking up the glass-topped menu stand, she pushed open the door and positioned it for maximum effect on the pavement.

As she turned to go back in, a stretch limo with blacked-out windows rolled by and stopped two doors down from where she'd paused. Maisie eyed the car. Although it wasn't strange for luxury cars to pass through the quiet little village of Ranelagh, seeing as they were close to Dublin city centre, the presence of this car caused a different sort of tingle. Telling herself she was being too fanciful, she swiped a dishcloth over the surface of the menu stand and went back in. She checked on her kitchen and waitstaff of twelve, made sure preparations were under way for their first booking at midday, then went into her office.

She had roughly half an hour to get to grips with the restaurant's accounts before she had to be back in the kitchen. As she sat down, her gaze fell on the picture propped up on her desk. The pulse of love that fired to her heart made her breath catch. Reaching out, she traced the contours of her son's face, her own face breaking into a smile at the toothy, wide-eyed happiness reflected in his eyes.

Gianlucca. The reason for her existence. The reason the hard decisions she'd made five years ago had been worth every moment of heartache. Turning her back on the career she'd trained so hard for had not been easy. Certainly her parents had piled on enough guilt to make walking away feel like the betrayal they'd accused her of committing. Her own guilt for confirming their fears that the apple didn't fall far from the tree was bone-deep and would probably always be. She hadn't planned on getting pregnant as her mother had at twenty-four but she refused to let the guilt prevent her from loving or caring for her child.

She'd known from a very young age that her parents, had they been given a choice, would've remained childless. As hard as it'd been, she'd tried to accept that not everyone was built to nurture a child. Her parents certainly had found raising her a challenge, one they hadn't deemed as worthy as the academic careers they'd pursued relentlessly. She'd always known she came an indifferent second to her parents' academic ambitions.

But she'd wanted Gianlucca the moment she'd found out he was growing inside her.

There had been nothing she wanted more than providing the very best for her son.

She had given him the very best.

The tiny niggle of ever-present guilt threatened to push its way through, but she smashed it down. She'd done everything she could when she'd found out she was pregnant. Even going against her parents' intense disapproval to make that daunting trip back to Sicily. She'd tried.

Yes, but did you try hard enough?

She dropped her hand from the picture and resolutely opened the account books. Indulging in *might have beens* wouldn't get the chequebook balanced or the staff paid. She was content enough. More important, her son was happy.

Her gaze drifted back to the almost-four-year-old face that was already taking the shape of the man he would one day be. To the deep hazel-gold eyes that looked so much like his father's. Eyes that could sometimes make her believe he could see straight into her soul, just as the older pair had done to her that long afternoon and longer night in Palermo five years ago.

Romeo.

A portentous name if there ever was one. While her life hadn't ended in fatal tragedy like the famous story, meeting Romeo had significantly altered it, her son being the only bright thing that had emerged from encountering that dangerously sexy, but deeply enigmatic Italian with eyes that had reflected enough conflict to last him several lifetimes.

Enough.

She switched on her computer and had just activated the payroll system when a knock sounded on her door.

'Come in.'

Lacey, her young reservations manager, poked her head around the door, her eyes wide and brimming with interest. 'There's someone here to see you,' she stage-whispered.

Maisie suppressed a smile. Her young employee had a flair for the dramatic and saw conspiracies and high drama in the simplest situations.

'If it's someone else looking for a job, please tell them I'm not hiring anyone. Not till the summer season really kicks off…' She stopped speaking as Lacey shook her head frantically.

'I don't think he's looking for a job. Actually, no offence, Maisie, but he looks like he could buy this place a hundred times over.' Her eyes widened and she blushed, then bit her lip. 'Sorry, but he looks really, really rich, and really, really, *intense*.' Lacey's eyes boggled some more. 'And he came in a *limo*,' she whispered again, looking over her shoulder into the restaurant.

The tingling Maisie had experienced earlier returned full force. 'Did he give you a name?'

'No, he just asked if you were in and ordered me to come and get you.' Lacey glanced furtively over her shoulder again, as if expecting their visitor to materialise behind her. 'He's very...*full-on*.'

Recalling her own line of thoughts moments ago and the intensity of Romeo's personality, she shivered. Shaking it off, Maisie stood up and brushed her hands down the practical black skirt and pink shirt she'd chosen to wear today.

She'd left all that dangerous intensity back in Palermo. Or *it* had left her, seeing as she'd woken up alone the morning after, with only rumpled sheets and the trace of her lover's scent on the pillow as evidence that she hadn't imagined the whole encounter.

She was in Ranelagh, the serene village she'd chosen to build a life for herself and her son in, not the sultry decadence of Palermo and its dangerous residents.

No danger or intensity whatsoever welcome here.

'Okay, Lacey. I'll take care of it.' Lacey's head bobbed before she disappeared from the doorway.

Sucking in a breath and telling herself she was being silly to feel so apprehensive, Maisie stepped out from behind her desk. In her short but successful stint as a criminal lawyer, she'd faced her share of unsavoury and even dangerous characters.

Whatever unknown quantity faced her out there in her beloved restaurant, she could face it.

Maisie knew just how wrong she was even before the tall, broad-shouldered figure clad from head to toe in black turned around from his brooding inspection of his surroundings.

Outwardly, her body froze a few steps into the restaurant. But inside, her heart kicked into her stomach. *Hard.*

'Romeo.'

She realised she'd said the name rattling through her brain aloud when he turned slowly and pinned her with those brooding hazel-gold eyes. That impossibly rugged jaw she'd thought she'd blown out of all proportion tightened as his gaze raked her from head to toe and back again. His prominent, cut-glass cheekbones were more pronounced than she remembered and his hair was longer, wavier than it had been five years ago. But the man who stood a dozen paces away was no less dynamic, no less captivating than the man who'd sat across from her in the café that memorable day.

If anything, he commanded a more overpowering presence. Perhaps it was because they were so far away from the place they'd first met, or because her mind was turning itself inside out to decipher exactly why he was here. All the same she found herself bunching a fist against her heart as if that would stop its fierce pounding.

'I'm not certain whether to celebrate this moment or to condemn it,' he rasped in a tense, dark voice.

'How did you… How did you find me?'

One eyebrow spiked upwards. 'That is what you wish to know? How did I find you? Were you attempting to stay hidden, perhaps?' he enquired silkily.

'What?' Her brain grew fuzzier, her heart racing even faster at the ice in his tone. 'I'm not hiding. Why would I want to hide from anyone?'

He approached slowly, his eyes not leaving her face, nor his hands the deep pockets of his overcoat. Even though it was early June, the weather remained cool enough to require a coat, and he wore his as a dark lord wore a cape, with a flourish that demanded attention. 'We haven't seen each other in five years and your first request is to know how I found you. Pardon me if I find that curious.'

'What would you have me say?' She licked lips gone

dry as he took another step closer until she had to crane her neck to see his eyes.

Mesmeric, hypnotising eyes.

So like his son's.

The blood drained from her face and thinking became difficult. She'd imagined this scene countless times. Had imagined how she would say the words. How he would take it. How she would protect her son from even the slightest hint of rejection, the way she'd done when her parents had transmitted that same indifference they'd shown Maisie all her life to her beloved son.

But words wouldn't form in her brain. So she stared at him, her thoughts twisting and turning.

'*Hello*, perhaps? Or, *how have you been, Romeo*?'

She caught his chillingly mocking tone and stiffened.

'Why would I? I seem to recall waking up to find myself alone in a hotel suite rented by an anonymous stranger. You didn't bother to say goodbye then, so why should I bother to say hello now?' she replied.

His nostrils flared then and a memory struck through her jumbled thoughts. They'd been caught up in one of the few short bursts of conversation in his suite. She'd unwittingly let slip the fraught state of her relationship with her parents, how lonely and inconvenient she felt to them, as if she were an unwanted visitor sharing a house with them.

His nostrils had flared then, too, as he'd admonished her to be grateful she had parents at all—strangers or otherwise. That observation had rendered her silent and a little ashamed, not because she'd hated being chastised, but because she'd seen the naked agony in his eyes when he'd said that. As if the subject of parents was one that terrorised him.

Maisie pushed the memory away and struggled to stay calm when he finally released her from his stare and looked around.

'What do you do here when you're not dabbling in being a restaurateur?' he asked.

She bristled. 'I'm not dabbling. I own this restaurant. It's my career.'

'Really? I thought you were a high-powered lawyer.'

She frowned. Had she told him that in Palermo? Back then she'd been newly qualified and working on exciting cases. Back then her parents had finally, grudgingly, accepted her career choice. She would even go as far as to consider that for the first time in her life she'd achieved something they were proud of, even if they hadn't quite been able to show it in the warm, loving way she'd seen her friends' parents exhibit.

Of course, they hadn't been thrilled that she'd announced soon after that she was taking a whole month off to travel Europe.

Despite her having the full support of her bosses to take the time off, her parents had advised her against the trip. Their utter conviction that stepping off the career ladder, even briefly, would ruin her life had finally confirmed how much they rued bringing a child, bringing *her*, into their lives.

And once she'd returned and told them she was pregnant...

Her heart caught at their bitter disappointment when she'd finally revealed her news. Roberta O'Connell hadn't needed to spell out that she thought Maisie had ruined her life for ever. It'd been clear to see. And knowing that by definition they thought having *her* had been a mistake had been an ache she hadn't been able to dispel.

Maisie shook her head to dispel the memory. 'No, not any longer. I gave up practising four years ago,' she answered Romeo.

He frowned. 'Why would you give up the job you trained so hard for?'

So she *had* told him more than she thought. Because how else would he know? And why was he questioning her like this, probing her for answers he already knew? Was he trying to trip her up somehow?

She swallowed. 'My priorities changed,' she replied crisply and stepped back. 'Now if you were just passing through and stopped to catch up, I really must get on. My first customers will be here shortly and I need to make sure the kitchen's ready to start the day.'

'You think I came all this way simply *to catch up*?' He looked around again, as if searching for something. Or someone.

Apprehension flowed like excess adrenaline through her blood, making her dizzy for a moment.

Romeo couldn't know about Gianlucca. Because *she'd* searched for him to no avail. No one else knew who the father of her child was. The only people who she would've confessed Romeo's identity to—her parents—hadn't wanted to know after she'd confessed to the one-night stand. Which was just as well because Maisie wouldn't have liked to confess that she hadn't known the surname of the man who'd impregnated her.

Maisie had a hard time accepting the fact that the only time her mother had initiated a heart-to-heart conversation had been to tell her to abandon her child's welfare to childminders and nannies. That her son, once he was born, should be left to others to raise, so Maisie could focus fully and solely on her career. There'd even been an offer of a fully paid boarding school once he was a toddler! Despite her knowing her parents' views on hands-on parenting, it'd still been harrowing to hear her mother's words, to know that had her parents had the choice when she was born, they'd have abandoned *her* to the same fate.

'I really don't know what you're doing here. But like I said, I need to be getting on—'

She gasped when he caught her upper arms in a firm, implacable hold.

'Where is he, Maisie? *Where is my son?*' he demanded, his voice a cold, deadly blade.

Several things happened at once. The door to the kitchen burst open and Lacey rushed through, just as the front door swung inward and a party of four walked in. The scene stopped in almost comical freeze-frame. No one moved except for Romeo, whose eyes narrowed as they went from the door to Lacey and then to Maisie's face.

When shock continued to hold her tongue prisoner, Romeo's lips compressed. Glancing at Lacey's name badge, he jerked his head imperiously. 'Lacey, you're in charge of reservations, yes?'

Lacey nodded, her wide-eyed look returning full force.

'Then see to the customers, *per favore.* Your boss and I will be in her office.'

Romeo marched her into the small room and shut the door behind him with a precise movement that suggested he was suppressing the need to slam it. Maisie was conquering equally intense emotions.

She put the width of her desk between them, then glared at him.

'I don't know who you think you are, but you can't walk in here and start bossing my employees about—'

'Deflecting won't help this situation. You know why I'm here. So let's dispense with trivialities. *Tell me where he is.*' That last remark was said with icy brevity that hammered a warning straight to her blood.

'Why?' she fired back, potent fear beginning to crawl up her spine.

Astonishment lit through his golden eyes. '*Why?* Are you completely insane? Because I want to see him.'

'Again, why?' A cloud descended on his face and Maisie held up her hand when he opened his mouth, no doubt to once again question her sanity. 'Let's stop for a moment and think about this rationally. We had a one-night stand.' She couldn't help the high colour that rushed into her face at the so very telling term. 'After which you walked away without so much as a thank-you-ma'am note. You used me, then disappeared into the night. A month later, I found out I was pregnant. Fast-forward five years later, you walk in the door and demand to see my son.' Maisie raised her hand and ticked off her fingers. 'I don't know your background. I don't know whether that aura of danger about you is just for show or the real thing. Hell, I don't even know your *last name*. And you think I should just expose you to my child?'

Several emotions flitted across his face—astonishment, anger, a touch of vulnerability that set her nape tingling, then grudging respect before settling into implacable determination.

He stared at her for a time, before he exhaled sharply. 'If the child is mine—'

She laughed in disbelief. 'Let me get this straight. You came here without even being sure that the child you're so desperate to see is yours?'

He folded his arms across his massive chest, the movement bunching his shoulders into even wider relief. Maisie became acutely aware of the room shrinking, and the very air being sucked up by his overwhelming presence. 'Since I've never met him, I cannot be one hundred per cent sure that he's mine, hence the request to see him. A man in my position has to verify allegations of fatherhood.'

Her eyes widened. 'Allegations? *Plural?* Are you saying this isn't the first time you've left a woman in a hotel room and found out there have been consequences to your actions?' Maisie wasn't sure why that stung so much. Had she imagined herself somehow unique? That a man who *looked* like him, kissed and made love as he had, would have limited the experience to her and only her? 'And what do you mean, a man in your position?'

Her barrage of questions caused his eyes to narrow further. 'You don't know who I am?'

'Would I be asking if I did?' she threw back. 'If you want

any semblance of cooperation from me, I demand to know your full name.'

His jaw flexed. 'My name is Romeo Brunetti.' The way he said it, the way he waited, as if the pronouncement should be accompanied by a round of trumpets and the clash of cymbals, set her spine tingling. When she didn't speak, a curious light entered his eyes. 'That means nothing to you?'

She shrugged. 'Should it?'

He continued to stare at her for another minute, before he shook his head and started to pace the small space in front of her desk. 'Not at all. So now we have our long-overdue introductions out of the way.'

Maisie cleared her throat. 'Mr Brunetti, I—' She froze as he let out a stunned breath.

Her gaze flew to his face to find his gaze transfixed on the photo on her desk. 'Is this… Is this him?' he asked in a tight, ragged whisper.

When she nodded, he reached forward in a jerky movement, then stopped. Apprehension slid over his face. He fisted and then flexed his hand, before he slowly plucked up the frame. In another person, she would've been certain he was borderline terrified of a mere picture.

Terrified or dreading?

The reminder of the cold indifference her parents had felt about their grandson, about her, made her itch to snatch the photo from him, protect her son's image the way she fought every day to keep him from the rejection she'd been forced to live with her whole life.

She glanced at the picture clutched in Romeo's large hand.

It had been taken at Ranelagh Gardens on the first day of spring. Dressed in a smart shirt, jeans and bright blue woollen jumper, Gianlucca had looked a perfect picture of health and happiness, and Maisie hadn't been able to resist capturing his image.

She watched now as Romeo brought the picture up close

to his face, his features drawn tight, his breathing slow and controlled. After almost a minute of staring at the photo without a hint of emotion, he raised his hand and brushed his fingers over Gianlucca's cheek, almost in direct imitation of what Maisie herself had done a mere half hour ago.

'*Mio figlio,*' he murmured.

'I don't know what that means,' Maisie replied in a matching whisper.

He blinked and sucked in a deep, chest-filling breath. 'My son. It means my son.' He looked up, his gaze deeply accusing. '*He's my son.* And you kept him from me,' he snarled, his voice still not quite as steady as it'd been moments ago.

Maisie stumbled backwards, bumping into the chair behind her. 'I did nothing of the kind. And if you stopped to think about it for a moment, you'd realise how ridiculous that allegation is.'

He shoved a hand through his thick dark hair, dislodging any semblance of order it'd been in. He began to pace again, the photo clutched in his large hand. 'How old is he?' he demanded when he paused for a moment.

'He's four in three weeks.'

He resumed pacing in tight circles. 'Four years… *Dio mio*, four years I've been in the dark,' he muttered to himself, slashing his hand through his hair again.

'How *exactly* were you enlightened?' It was a question he hadn't yet addressed.

He froze, as if her question had thrown him. 'We'll get to that in a moment. First, please tell me his name and where he is.'

The urgency in his voice bled through to Maisie. She wanted to refuse. Wanted to rewind time and have this meeting not happen. Not because being given the chance to reveal her son's existence to his father wasn't what she wanted.

From the moment she'd found out she was pregnant, she'd known she would give her child every opportunity to know his father. She'd gone to Palermo during her first trimester with that exact reason in mind and had given up after two weeks with no success in tracing Romeo.

No, the reason Maisie wanted to rewind time and take a different course was because she knew, deep in her bones, that Romeo's presence wasn't just about wanting to get to know his son. There was a quiet hint of danger about him that set her fear radar alight. And he hadn't yet shown her that the prospect of a son filled him with joy. All he'd done so far was put an alpha claim on a child he didn't know.

A child she would lay her life down to protect.

'Why are you really here?'

His brows clamped together. 'I believe we've tackled that particular question.'

She shook her head. Something was seriously, desperately wrong. Something to do with her precious son.

'No, we haven't. And I absolutely refuse to tell you anything about him until you tell me what's going on.'

CHAPTER THREE

ROMEO STARED DOWN at the picture one more time, his heart turning over as eyes the exact shade as his own stared back at him. The child...*his son*...was laughing, pure joy radiating from his face as he posed, chubby arms outstretched, for the camera. A deep shudder rattled up from his toes, engulfing him in a sense of peculiar bewilderment. And fear. Bone-deep fear.

He couldn't be a father. Not him, with the upbringing he'd had, the twisted, harrowing paths his life had taken before he'd wrestled control of it. He wasn't equipped to care for a dog, never mind a child. And with the blood flowing through his veins...the blood of a thug and a vicious criminal...

Dio mio.

Lorenzo hadn't been lying after all. A single wave of impotent rage blanketed him to know that the two men he despised most had known of the existence of the boy before he did. And while a part of him knew levelling accusations of subterfuge on the woman standing before him was unfair, Romeo couldn't help but feel bitter resentment for being kept in the dark, even while he continued to flounder at the reality stabbing him in the chest.

He pushed the emotion aside and concentrated on the reality he *could* deal with—her continued denial of access. Because whether he was equipped to handle the prospect of fatherhood or not, she was at this moment behaving like an irrational person...a mother bear—a concept acutely alien to him.

Inhaling deep to keep his emotions under control, he

rubbed his thumb over the face of his son. 'I have only just discovered I have a child.' He stopped when she raised her eyebrow again to remind him of her unanswered question. 'Through...business associates who wished to get my attention—'

She shook her head, her long ponytail swinging. 'What on earth does that mean? Why would business associates want to use your child to get your attention?' High colour had flown into her cheeks, reminding him of another time, another place when her emotions had run equally passionate. 'What type of business are you involved in?' she voiced suspiciously.

So she didn't know who he was. Something vaguely resembling relief speared through him. When his business partnership with Zaccheo Giordano had become public knowledge five years ago, his world had exploded with fawning acolytes and women falling over themselves to get his attention. That attention had increased a hundredfold when he'd opened his first super-luxury resort off the coast of Tahiti, a feat he'd repeated soon after with five more, seeing him skyrocket onto the World's Richest list.

It was curiously refreshing not to have to deal with the instant personality change that accompanied recognition of his name. But not refreshing enough to know his response had triggered suspicion that could keep him from his reason for being here. Even though her instinct might yet prove correct.

He needed to frame his words carefully.

'You have nothing to fear from me.' He'd managed to lock down his control after that gut punch he'd received on seeing her again. From here on in, he would be operating from a place of cold, hard intelligence.

She shook her head again. 'Sorry, that's not good enough. You'll have to do better than that.' Her gaze went to the picture frame he held on to, a fierce light of protection and possession burning in her striking blue eyes.

'Tell me the exact nature of your business or this conversation ends now.'

Romeo almost laughed. She was seriously deluded if she thought her heated threats would in any way dissuade him from seeing his son, from verifying for himself that the child truly belonged to him.

'I'm the CEO and owner of Brunetti International,' he replied.

She frowned for a moment, then her features morphed into astonishment. 'Brunetti…those resorts you need to sell an organ or a limb before you can afford a night there?'

He made a dismissive gesture. 'We cater to people from all walks of life.'

She snorted. 'As long as they've sold their grandmothers to be able to afford your billionaire rates.'

Romeo pursed his lips. His wealth wasn't the subject under discussion here.

The fact that she seemed to be a rare species, a mother who stood like a lioness in protection of her child, a child whom he'd yet to be certain without a shadow of a doubt shared his DNA, should take precedence.

'You know who I am now. You'll also know from your previous career that information can be discovered if one digs deep enough. My business associates dug deep enough and they found you and my son.'

'My son.'

The sudden urge to snarl *our child* took him by surprise. He stared down at the picture, clutching at the fraying edges of his control when he began to feel off balance again. '*Per favore*. Please. Tell me his name.'

Her gaze went to the picture and her features softened immediately.

The look was one he'd witnessed before, in that hotel room five years ago. It was a look that had set so many alarm bells ringing inside his head that he'd withdrawn swiftly and decisively from it. He looked away because just as he'd had no room to accommodate *feelings* then, he had no room for them now.

'His name is Gianlucca. Gianlucca O'Connell.'

An irrational surge of displeasure threatened to floor him. *'O'Connell?'*

Again that challenging arch of her eyebrow. Back in Palermo he'd seen her passion, her fire, but that had been directed to the bedroom, and what they'd done to each other in bed. Seeing it in a different light didn't make it any less sexy. Yet the punch of heat to his libido took him by surprise. He'd grown so jaded by the overabundance of willing women that lately he'd lost interest in the chase. For the past three months, work had become his mistress, the only thing that fired his blood in any meaningful way.

'That *is* my name. Or did you expect me to call him Gianlucca Romeo?'

He gritted his teeth. 'Did you even make an effort to find me when you knew you carried my child?'

A look crossed her face, a mixture of pride and anger, and she raised her chin. 'Did you want to be found?' she fired back.

Knowing how well he'd covered his tracks, a wave of heat crawled up his neck. He'd succeeded more than in his wildest dreams. He'd walked away, having effectively smashed down any residual feelings of rejection, or the idea that he could be worthy of something more than the brain and brawn that had seen him through his harrowing childhood into the man he was today.

The hours of imagined softness, of imagined affection, had been an illusion brought on by his mother's passing. An illusion he'd almost given in to. An emotion he'd vowed then never to entertain even the merest hint of again.

'We'll address the subject of his surname at another time. But now we've established who I am, I'd like to know more about him. Please,' he added when her stance remained intransigent.

'All I know is your surname. I don't even know how old you are, never mind what sort of man you are.'

Romeo rounded the desk and watched her back away, but looking into her eyes he saw no sign of fear. Only stubbornness. Satisfied that she didn't fear him, he moved closer, watched her pupils dilate as a different sort of chemistry filled the air. Her sudden erratic breathing told him everything he needed to know.

'I'm thirty-five. And five years ago, you gave yourself to me without knowing anything more about me besides my first name.' He watched a blush wash up her throat into her face with more than a little fascination. 'You were in a foreign place, with a strange man, and yet you trusted your instinct enough to enter my hotel suite and stay for a whole night. And right now, even though your heart is racing, you don't fear me. Or you would've screamed for help by now.' He reached out and touched the pulse beating at her throat. Her soft, silky skin glided beneath his fingertips and blazing heat lanced his groin again. Curbing the feeling, he dropped his hand and stepped back. 'I don't mean you or the boy harm. I just wish to see him. I deal in facts and figures. I need visual evidence that he exists, and as accommodating as I'm willing to be, I won't be giving you a choice in the matter.'

She swallowed, her eyes boldly meeting and staying on his. 'Just so you know, I don't respond well to threats.'

'It wasn't a threat, *gattina*.' They both froze at the term that had unwittingly dropped from his lips. From the look on her face, Romeo knew she was remembering the first time he'd said it. Her nails had been embedded in his back, her claws transmitting the depth of her arousal as he'd sunk deep inside her. His little wildcat had been as crazy for him as he'd been for her. But that was then, a moment in time never to be repeated. 'I'm merely stating a fact.'

She opened her mouth to reply, then stopped as voices filled the restaurant. 'I have to go. This is our busiest afternoon slot. I can't leave Lacey on her own.'

Romeo told himself to be calm. 'I need an answer, Maisie.'

She stared at him for a long moment before her gaze dropped to the picture he held. She looked as if she wanted to snatch it from him but he held on tight. She finally looked back up. 'He goes to playgroup from eleven to three o'clock. I take him to the park afterwards if the weather's good.'

'Did you have plans to do that today?'

She slowly nodded. 'Yes.'

Blood rushed into his ears, nearly deafening him. He forced himself to think, to plot the best way he knew how. Because rushing blood and racing hearts were for fools. Fools who let emotion rule their existence.

'What park?' he rasped.

'Ranelagh Gardens. It's—'

'I will find it.'

She paled and her hands flew out in a bracing stance. 'You can't… Don't you think we need to discuss this a little more?'

Romeo carefully set down the picture, then took out his phone and captured an image of it. He stared down at his son's face on his phone screen, and the decision concreted in his mind. 'No, Maisie. There's nothing more to discuss. If he's mine, truly mine, then I intend to claim him.'

Maisie slowly sank into the chair after Romeo made a dramatic exit, taking all the oxygen and bristling vitality of the day with him. She raised her hand to her face and realised her fingers were shaking. Whether it was from the shock of seeing him again after convincing herself she would never set eyes on him again, or the indomitability of that last statement, she wasn't certain.

She sat there, her hand on her clammy forehead, her gaze

in the middle distance as she played back every word, every gesture, on a loop in her mind.

The sound of laughter finally broke through her racing thoughts. She really needed to walk the floor, make sure her customers were all right. But she found herself clicking on her laptop, typing in his name on her search engine.

The images that confronted her made her breath catch all over again. Whereas she hadn't given herself permission to linger on anywhere but Romeo's face while they'd been in her office, she leaned in close and perused each image. And there were plenty, it seemed. Pictures of him dressed in impeccable handmade suits, posing for a profile piece in some glossy business magazine; pictures of him opening his world-renowned resorts in Dubai and Bali; and many, many pictures of him with different women, all drop-dead gorgeous, all smiling at him as if he was their world, their every dream come true.

But the ones that caught Maisie's attention, the ones that made her heart lurch wildly, were of Romeo on a yacht with another man—the caption named him as Zaccheo Giordano—and a woman with two children. The children were Gianlucca's age, possibly a little older, and the pictures were a little grainy, most likely taken with a telephoto lens from a long distance.

He sat apart from the family, his expression as remote as an arctic floe. That lone-wolf look, the one that said approach with caution, froze her heart as she saw it replicated in each rigid, brooding picture that followed. Even when he smiled at the children, there was a distance that spoke of his unease.

Trembling, Maisie sat back from the desk, the large part of her that had been agitated at the thought of agreeing to a meeting between Romeo and her son escalating to alarming proportions.

She might not know how he felt about children generally, but if the pictures could be believed, Romeo Brunetti wasn't the warm and cuddly type.

Maisie gulped in the breath she hadn't been able to fully access while Romeo had been in the room and tried to think rationally. She'd tried to find Romeo five years ago to tell him that they'd created a child together. It was true that at the time she'd been reeling from her parents' further disappointment in her, and in hindsight she'd probably been seeking some sort of connection with her life suddenly in chaotic free fall. But even then, deep down, she'd known she couldn't keep the news to herself or abandon her baby to the care of strangers as her parents had wanted.

So in a way, this meeting had always been on the cards, albeit to be scheduled at a time of her choosing and without so much…pulse-destroying drama.

Or being confronted with the evidence that made her mothering instincts screech with the possibility that the father of her child might want him for reasons other than to cement a love-at-first-sight bond that would last a lifetime.

She clicked back to the information page and was in the middle of Romeo's worryingly brief biography when a knock announced Lacey's entrance.

'I need you, Maisie! A group of five just walked in. They don't have a booking but I don't think they'll take no for an answer.'

Maisie suppressed a sigh and closed her laptop with a guilty sense of relief that she didn't have to deal with Romeo's last words just yet.

'Okay, let's go and see what we can do, shall we?'

She pinned a smile on her face that felt a mile from genuine and left her office. For the next three hours, she pushed the fast-approaching father-and-son meeting to the back of her mind and immersed herself in the smooth running of the lunchtime service.

* * *

The walk to Gianlucca's nursery took less than ten minutes, but with her mind free of work issues, her heart began to race again at the impending meeting.

Every cell in her body urged her to snatch her son and take him far away.

But she'd never been the type to run, or bury her head in the sand.

She'd give Romeo the chance to spell out what he wished for, and if his parting remarks were anything to go by he would be demanding a presence in her son's life. She would hear him out, but nothing would make her accommodate visitation with her son until she was absolutely sure he would be safe with Romeo.

Her heart lurched at the thought that she'd have to part from him for a few hours maybe once or twice a week. Maybe a full weekend when he grew older. Her breath shuddered out, and she shook her head. She was getting ahead of herself. For all she knew, Romeo would take one look at Lucca, satisfy himself that he was his and ring-fence himself with money-grubbing lawyers to prevent any imagined claims.

But then, if that was what he intended, would he have taken the time to seek them out?

Whatever happened, her priority would remain ensuring her son's happiness. She stopped before the nursery door, unclenched her agitated fists and blinked eyes prickling with tears.

From the moment he'd been born, it'd been just the two of them. After the search for Romeo had proved futile, she'd settled into the idea that it would always be just the two of them.

The threat to that twosome made her insides quiver.

She brushed her tears away. By the time she was buzzed in, Maisie had composed herself.

'Mummy!' Gianlucca raced towards her, an effervescent bundle of energy that pulled a laugh from Maisie.

Enfolding him in her arms, she breathed his warm, toddler scent until he wriggled impatiently.

'Are we going to the park to see the ducks?' he asked eagerly, his striking hazel eyes—so like his father's it was uncanny—widened expectantly.

'Yes, I even brought some food for them,' she replied and smiled wider when he whooped and dashed off towards the door.

She spotted the limo the moment they turned into the square. Black and ominous, it sat outside the north entrance in front of an equally ominous SUV, both engines idling. Beside the limo, two men dressed in black and wearing shades stood, their watchful stance evidence that they were bodyguards.

Maisie tried not to let her imagination careen out of control. Romeo Brunetti was a billionaire and she'd dealt with enough unscrupulous characters during her stint as a lawyer to know the rich were often targets for greedy, sometimes dangerous criminals.

All the same, she clutched Gianlucca's hand tighter as they passed the car and entered the park. Gianlucca darted off for the duck pond, his favourite feature in the park, as soon as she handed him the bread she'd taken from the restaurant.

He was no more than a dozen paces away when a tingle danced on her nape. She glanced over her shoulder and watched Romeo enter the park, his gaze passing cursorily over her before it swung to Gianlucca.

Maisie's heart lurched, then thundered at the emotions that washed over his face. Wonder. Shock. Anxiety. And a fierce possessiveness that sent a huge dart of alarm through her.

But the most important emotion—love—was missing.

It didn't matter that it was perhaps irrational for her to

demand it of him, but the absence of that powerful emotion terrified her.

Enough to galvanise her into action when he walked forward, reached her and carried on going.

'Romeo!' She caught his arm when she sensed his intention.

'What?' He paused, but his gaze didn't waver from Gianlucca's excited form.

'Wait. Please,' she whispered fiercely when he strained against her hold.

He whirled to her, his nostrils flaring as he fought to control himself. 'Maisie.' His tone held a note of barely leashed warning.

Swallowing, she stood her ground. 'I know you want to meet him, but you can't just barge in looking like...' She stopped and bit her lip.

'Looking like what?'

'Like a charging bull on steroids. You'll frighten him.'

His face hardened and he breathed deep before spiking a hand through his hair. After another long glance at Gianlucca, he faced her. '*Bene*, what do you suggest?'

Maisie reached into her bag. 'Here, I brought one of these for you.'

He eyed her offering and his eyebrows shot up. 'A bag of dried bread?'

'He's feeding the ducks. It's his favourite thing to do. I thought you could...approach him that way.'

Romeo's eyes darkened to a burnished gold. Slowly, he reached out and took the offering. '*Grazie,*' he muttered with tight aloofness.

She held on when he started to turn away, silently admonishing herself for experiencing a tiny thrill of pleasure when his arm flexed beneath her fingers. 'Also, I'd prefer it if you didn't tell him who you are. We can have a longer discussion about where we go from here before anything happens.'

A dark look gleamed in his eyes, but he nodded. 'If that is what you wish.'

'It is.'

He nodded, then tensed as a trio of kids flew by on their way to the pond. 'I agree, perhaps this isn't the most appropriate venue for an introduction.'

A tight knot eased in Maisie's stomach and she realised a part of her had feared Romeo would only want to see his son from afar and decide he didn't want to know him. She had yet to decipher his true motives, but she would allow this brief meeting.

'Thank you.'

He merely inclined his head before his gaze swung back to Gianlucca. Knowing she couldn't postpone the meeting any longer, she fell into step beside Romeo.

Gianlucca threw the last of his bread into the waiting melee of ducks and swans and broke into a delighted laugh as they fought over the scraps. His laughter turned into a pout when the ducks swam off to greet the bread-throwing trio of kids. 'Mummy, more bread!' When Maisie remained silent, he turned and raced towards them. 'Please?' he added.

She glanced at Romeo and watched the frozen fascination on his face as Gianlucca reached them. She caught him before he barrelled into her and crouched in front of him. 'Wait a moment, Lucca. There's someone I want you to meet. This…this is Romeo Brunetti.'

Lucca tilted his head up and eyed the towering man before him. 'Are you Mummy's friend?'

Romeo's head bobbed once. 'Yes. Nice to meet you, Gianlucca.'

Gianlucca immediately slipped his hand into Romeo's and pumped with all his might. A visible tremble went through Romeo's body, and he made a strangled sound. Gianlucca heard it and stilled, his eyes darting from the giant man to his mother.

The overprotective mother in her wanted to scoop him up and cuddle him close, but Maisie forced herself to remain still. Her breath caught as Romeo sank into a crouch, still holding his son's hand, his eyes glistening with questions.

'I look forward to getting to know you, Gianlucca.'

Lucca nodded, then gasped as he saw what Romeo held in his other hand. 'Did you come to feed the ducks, too?'

Romeo nodded. '*Sì*...yes,' he amended and started to rise. His body bristled with a restlessness that made Maisie's pulse jump. 'That was my intention, but I'm not an expert, like you.'

'It's easy! Come on.' He tugged at Romeo's hand, his excitement at having another go at his favourite pastime vibrating through his little body.

Maisie stayed crouched, the residual apprehension clinging to her despite the sudden, throat-clogging tears. As meetings between father and son went, it had gone much easier than she could've hoped for. And yet, she couldn't move from where she crouched. Because, she realised, through all the scenarios she'd played in her mind, she'd never really thought beyond this moment. Oh, she'd loftily imagined dictating visitation terms and having them readily agreed to, and then going about raising her son with minimal interference.

But looking at Romeo as he gazed down at his son with an intense proprietary light in his eyes, Maisie realised she really had no clue what the future held. Her breath shuddered out as Romeo's words once again flashed through her brain.

There's nothing more to discuss. If he's mine, truly mine, then I intend to claim him.

She slowly rose and looked over her shoulder. Sure enough, the two black-clad bodyguards prowled a short distance away. About to turn away, Maisie froze as she spotted two more by the south gate. Two more guarded the west side of the park.

Heart in her throat, she approached the duck pond, where Romeo was throwing a piece of bread under her son's strict instruction.

His head swung towards her and his expression altered at whatever he read on her face. 'Something wrong?'

'I think I should be asking you that,' she hissed so Gianlucca wouldn't overhear, but she placed a protective hand on his tiny shoulder, ready to lay down her life for him if she needed to. 'Do you want to tell me why you have *six* bodyguards watching this park?' Her voice vibrated with the sudden fear and anger she couldn't disguise.

His face hardened and the arm he'd raised to throw another bite into the pond slowly lowered to his side. 'I think it's time to continue this conversation elsewhere.'

CHAPTER FOUR

ROMEO WATCHED SEVERAL expressions chase over her face.

'What does that mean?' she asked, her blue eyes narrowing before she cast another alarmed glance at the burly men guarding the park.

He followed her apprehensive gaze and indicated sharply at his men when he saw that other parents were beginning to notice their presence. The men melted into the shadows, but the look didn't dissipate from Maisie's face. When her hand tightened imperceptibly on Gianlucca's shoulder, Romeo's insides tightened.

'My hotel is ten minutes away. We'll talk there.' He tried not to let the irony of his statement cloud the occasion. He'd said similar words to her five years ago, an invitation that had ended with him reeling from the encounter.

That invitation had now brought him to this place, to his son. He had no doubt in his mind that the child was his. Just as he had no doubt that he would claim him, and protect him from whatever schemes Lorenzo had up his sleeves. Beyond that, he had no clue what his next move was. He didn't doubt, though, that he would find a way to triumph. He'd dragged himself from the tough streets of Palermo to the man he was today. He didn't intend to let anything stand in the way of what he desired.

He focused to find her shaking her head. 'I can't.'

Romeo's eyes narrowed as a hitherto thought occurred to him. 'You can't? Why not?' He realised then how careless he'd been. Because Lorenzo's pictures had shown only Maisie with his son, Romeo had concluded that she was unattached. But those pictures were four years old. A lot could have happened in that time. She could've taken another lover, a man who had perhaps become important enough to see himself as Gianlucca's father.

The very idea made him see red for one instant. 'Is there someone in your life?' He searched her fingers. They were ringless. But that didn't mean anything these days. 'A *lover*, perhaps?' The word shot from his mouth like a bullet.

Her eyes widened and she glanced down at Gianlucca, but he was engrossed in feeding the last of the bread to the ducks. 'I don't have a lover or a husband, or whatever the *au fait* term is nowadays.'

Romeo attributed the relief that poured through him to not having to deal with another tangent in this already fraught, woefully ill-planned situation. 'In that case there shouldn't be a problem in discussing this further at my hotel.'

'That wasn't why I refused to come with you. I have a life to get on with, Romeo. And Lucca has a schedule that I try to keep to so his day isn't disrupted, otherwise he gets cranky. I need to fix his dinner in half an hour and put him to bed so I can get back to the restaurant.'

He stiffened. 'You go to work after he's asleep?'

Her mouth compressed. 'Not every night, but yes. I live above the restaurant and my assistant manager lives in the flat next door. She looks after him on the nights I work.'

'That is unacceptable.'

Her eyes widened with outrage. 'Excuse me?' she hissed.

'From now on you will not leave him in the care of strangers.'

Hurt indignation slid across her face. 'If you knew me at all, you'd know leaving my son with some faceless stranger is the last thing I'd do! Bronagh isn't a stranger. She's my friend as well as my assistant. And how dare you tell me how to raise my son?'

He caught her shoulders and tugged her close so they wouldn't be overheard. 'He is *our* son,' he rasped into her ear. 'His safety and well-being have now become my concern as much as yours, *gattina*.' The endearment slipped out again, but he deemed it appropriate, so he didn't allow the tingle that accompanied the term to disturb him too much. 'Put your claws away and let's take him back to your flat. You'll feed him and put him to bed and then we'll talk, *sì*?'

He pulled back and looked down at her, noting her hectic colour and experiencing that same punch to his libido that had occurred earlier.

Dio, he needed this added complication like a bullet in the head.

He dropped his hand once she gave a grudging nod.

'Lucca, it's time to go,' she called out.

'One more minute!' came his son's belligerent reply.

A tight, reluctant smile curved Maisie's lips, drawing Romeo's attention to their pink plumpness. 'He has zero concept of time and yet that's his stock answer every time you try to get him away from something he loves doing.'

'I'll bear that in mind,' he answered.

He glanced at his son and that sucker-punch feeling slammed into him again. It'd first happened when Gianlucca had slid his hand into his. Romeo had no term for it. But it was alive within him, and swelling by the minute.

Unthinking questions crowded his mind. Like when had Gianlucca taken his first step? What had been his first word?

What was his favourite thing to do besides feeding greedy ducks?

He stood, stock-still, as a plan began to formulate at the back of his mind. A plan that was uncharacteristically outlandish.

But wasn't this whole situation outlandish in the extreme?

And hadn't he learned that sometimes it was better to fight fire with fire?

The idea took firmer root, embedding itself as the only

viable course available to him if he was to thwart the schemes of Lorenzo Carmine and Agostino Fattore.

The more Romeo thought about the plans the old men, in their bid to hang on to their fast-crumbling empire, had dared to lay out for him, the more rage threatened to overcome him. He'd tempered that rage with caution, not forgetting that a wounded animal was a dangerous animal. Fattore's lieutenant might be old, and his power weakened, but Romeo knew that some power was better than no power to people like Lorenzo. And they would hang on to it by every ruthless means available.

Romeo didn't intend to lower his guard where Lorenzo's wily nature was concerned. His newly discovered son's safety was paramount. But even if Lorenzo and the shadows of Romeo's past hadn't been hanging over him, he would still proceed with the plan now fully formed in his mind.

He followed Maisie as she approached and caught up Gianlucca's hand. 'Time to go, precious.' The moment he started to protest, she continued, 'Which do you prefer for your tea, fish fingers or spaghetti and meatballs?'

'Spaghetti balls,' the boy responded immediately, his mind adeptly steered in the direction of food, just as his mother had intended. He danced between them until they reached the gate.

Romeo noticed his men had slipped into the security SUV parked behind his limo and nodded at the driver who held the door open. He turned to help his son into the car and saw Maisie's frown.

'Do you happen to have a car seat in there?' she asked.

Romeo cursed silently. 'No.'

'In that case, we'll meet you back at the restaurant.' She turned and started walking down the street.

He shut the door and fell into step beside her. 'I'll walk back with you.'

She opened her mouth to protest but stopped when he

took his son's hand. The feel of the small palm against his tilted Romeo's world.

He hadn't known or expected this reality-changing situation when he'd walked into that mansion in Palermo yesterday. But Romeo was nothing if not a quick study. His ability to harness a situation to his advantage had saved his life more times on the street than he could recount. He wasn't in a fight-to-the-death match right now, but he still intended to emerge a winner.

Maisie's first priority when she'd decorated her flat was homey comfort, with soft furnishings and pleasant colours to make the place a safe and snug home for her son. But as she opened the door and walked through the short hallway that connected to the living room she couldn't help but see it through Romeo's eyes. The carpet was a little worn, one cushion stained with Lucca's hand paint. And suddenly, the yellow polka-dot curtains seemed a little too bright, like something a *girlie* girl would choose, instead of the sophisticated women Romeo Brunetti probably dated.

What did it matter?

She turned, prepared to show her pride in her home, and found him frozen in front of the framed picture collage above her TV stand. Twelve pictures documented various key stages of Lucca's life so far, from his scrunched-up hours-old face to his first Easter egg hunt two months ago.

Romeo stared at each one with an intensity that bordered on the fanatic. Then he reached out and traced his fingers over Lucca's first picture, the tremor in his hand hard to miss.

'I have digital copies…if you'd like them,' she ventured.

He turned. The naked emotion in his eyes momentarily stopped her breath.

'*Grazie*, but I don't think that would be necessary.'

Her heart stopped as the fear she hadn't wanted to fully

explore bloomed before her eyes. 'What does that mean?' she asked, although she risked him further exploiting the rejection he'd just handed her.

'It means there are more important things to discuss than which pictures of my son I would like copies of.'

Lucca chose that moment to announce his hunger.

Maisie glanced at Romeo, questions warring with anger inside her.

She didn't want to leave her son now that she knew Romeo was preparing to back away. Especially since there was also the outside threat evidenced by the bodyguards in the SUV that had crawled behind them as they'd walked back. He travelled with too much security for a garden-variety billionaire.

That knowledge struck fear into her heart that she couldn't dismiss.

'Go and make his meal, Maisie,' Romeo said.

The taut command in his voice jerked her spine straight.

'I'd rather take him into the kitchen with me.'

'Is that your normal routine?' he queried with narrowed eyes.

'No, normally he likes to watch his favourite children's TV show while I cook.'

Romeo gave a brisk nod. 'Go, then. I'll find a way of entertaining him,' he replied.

'What do you know about entertaining children?' she demanded fiercely.

His jaw clenched. 'Even rocket science has been mastered. Besides, you'll be in the next room. What could go wrong?'

Everything.

The word blasted through her head. She opened her mouth to say as much but saw Lucca staring with keen interest at them. The last thing she wanted was for her son to pick up the dangerous undercurrents in the room.

Romeo watched her for a minute, clench-jawed. 'Are there any other exits in the flat, besides the front door?'

Maisie frowned. 'There's a fire escape outside my bedroom.'

'Is it locked?'

'Yes.'

'Okay.' He strode out and she followed him into the hallway. She watched him lock and take out the key and return to her. 'Now you can be assured that I won't run off with him while your back is turned. I'll also keep conversation to a minimum so I don't inadvertently verbally abuse him. Are you satisfied?'

Her fingers curled around the key, and she refused to be intimidated. 'That works. I won't be long. The meatballs are already done... I just need to cook the pasta.'

Romeo nodded and looked to where Lucca knelt on the floor surrounded by a sea of Lego. He shrugged off his overcoat and draped it over the sofa. Maisie watched him advance towards Lucca, his steps slow and non-threatening, to crouch next to him.

Lucca looked up, smiled and immediately scooped up a handful of Lego and held it out to him.

Maisie backed out, fighting the tearing emotions rampaging through her. Admonishing herself to get her emotions under control, she rushed into the kitchen and set about boiling water for the spaghetti, all the while trying to dissect what the presence of the bodyguards meant.

Surely if Romeo was in some sort of trouble the Internet search would've picked it out? Or was she blowing things out of proportion? Was she wrong about billionaires travelling with that much security? She frowned at the total excess of it. And what about Romeo's explanation that his business associates had found Lucca? From her time as a lawyer, Maisie knew deep background checks had become par for the course during business deals, but from Romeo's expression in the park, she couldn't help feeling there was more.

Her heart hammered as horrific possibilities tumbled through her mind. The world was a dangerous place. Even in a picturesque haven like Ranelagh, she couldn't guarantee that she would always be able to keep Lucca safe.

She froze at the sink. Had she invited danger in by letting Romeo Brunetti through her front door? Or had he been right when he'd told her she'd instinctively trusted him in Palermo or she'd never have gone up to his suite that day?

She must have on some level, surely, or she'd never have given him her virginity so easily.

Stop!

The only way to find out what was going on was to talk to Romeo. That wouldn't happen unless she stopped dawdling and got on with it.

She fixed Lucca's meal and set it up in the dining nook attached to her kitchen. Seeing Romeo sprawled on his side on the living-room floor stopped her in her tracks. Between father and son, they'd built a giant castle and were debating where to station the knights, with Lucca in favour of ground sentry duty and Romeo advocating turret guards.

He sensed her watching and looked up. Again Maisie was struck by the determination on his face.

And again, he shuttered the look and handed the knight to Lucca.

Maisie cleared her throat before she could speak. 'Lucca, your food's ready.'

'One more minute!'

Romeo lifted an eyebrow and gave a mock shudder. 'Do you enjoy cold spaghetti, Gianlucca?'

Lucca shook his head. 'No, it tastes yucky.'

'Then I think you should eat yours now before it turns yucky, *si*?'

'See what?' Lucca asked, his eyes wide and enquiring.

Romeo reached out and hesitantly touched his son's hair. '*Si* means yes in Italian,' he said gruffly.

'Are you Ita…Itayan? Mummy said I'm half Itayan.'

Romeo's eyes flicked to Maisie for a moment, then returned to his son. 'Yes, she's right. She's also waiting for you
to go eat your dinner.' A quiet, firm reminder that brought
Lucca to his feet.

He whizzed past her and climbed into his seat at the small
dining table. He barely waited for Maisie to tuck his bib into
place before he was tearing into his spaghetti.

Romeo leaned against the doorjamb, a peculiar look on
his face as he absorbed Lucca's every action.

Then he turned and looked at her, and her heart caught.
Nothing could keep down the geyser of apprehension that
exploded through her at what that absorbed look on Romeo's
face meant for her and her son.

In that moment, Maisie knew that nothing she said or did
would stop what was unravelling before her eyes. It didn't
matter whether Romeo loved his son or not, he would do
exactly as he'd said in her office this morning.

Romeo Brunetti had every intention of claiming his son.

Maisie entered the living room and paused to watch
Romeo's broad frame as he looked out of the window at the
street below. With the endless horrific thoughts that had
been tumbling through her mind for the past three hours,
she wondered if he was just pavement-watching or if there
was some unseen danger lurking out there.

He turned and her breath caught at the intensity in his
face, the dangerous vibe surrounding his body. Wanting to
get this over with quickly, she walked further into the living room.

'He's out like a light. When he's worn out like that, he
won't wake until morning.' Maisie wondered why she'd
been dropping little morsels like this all evening. Then she
realised it was because Romeo voraciously lapped up each
titbit about his son.

Because a part of her hoped that, by doing so, she could
get him to rethink whatever he was plotting for Lucca's fu-

ture? Did she really think she could turn Romeo's fascination with their son into love?

Love couldn't be forced. Either it was there or it wasn't. Her parents had been incapable of it. They'd cared only for their academic pursuits and peer accolades. None of that love had spilled to her.

She balled her fists. She would rather Romeo absented himself completely than dangle fatherhood in front of her son, only to reject him later. 'You wanted to talk?' she ventured. The earlier they laid things out in the open, the quicker she could get back to the status quo.

Romeo nodded in that solemn way he sometimes did, then remained silent and still, his hands thrust into his pockets. He continued to watch her, dark hazel eyes tracking her as she straightened the cushions and packed away the toys.

Too soon she was done. Silence filled the room and her breath emerged in short pants as she became painfully aware that they were alone, that zing of awareness spreading wider in the room.

She realised she was fidgeting with her fingers and resolutely pulled them apart. 'I don't mean to hurry this along, but can we just get it over—'

'Sit down, Maisie.'

She wanted to refuse. Just on principle because she wouldn't be ordered about in her own home, but something in his face warned her she needed to sit for what was coming.

Heart slamming into her ribcage, she perched on the edge of the sofa. He took the other end, his large body turned towards her so their knees almost touched. Again awareness of just how big, how powerfully built he was, crowded her senses. Her gaze dropped to his hands, large with sleek fingers. She recalled how they'd made her feel, how the light dusting of hair on the back had triggered delicious shivers in her once upon a time.

A different tremble powered up her spine.

Maisie gave herself a silent shake. This wasn't the time to be falling into a pool of lust. She'd been there, done that, with this man. And look where it had got her.

Look where she was now, about to be given news she instinctively knew would be life-changing.

She glanced up at him. His hazel eyes probed, then raked her face, and his nostrils flared slightly, as if he, too, was finding it difficult to be seated so close to her without remembering what they'd done to each other on a hot September night in Palermo five years ago. His gaze dropped to her throat, her breasts, and she heard his short intake of breath.

'Romeo…'

He balled his fists on top of his thighs and his chest expanded in a long inhalation. 'You're right about the bodyguards. I normally only travel with two members of my security team.'

Her stomach hollowed out. 'Why…why the increase?'

'It's just a precaution at this stage.'

'What does that mean?' she demanded. 'Precaution against what?'

'It means neither you nor Gianlucca are in danger at the moment.'

'But you're expecting us to be at some point?' Her voice had risen with her escalating fear and the shaking had taken on a firmer hold.

He shook his head. 'You don't need to panic—'

'Oh, really? You tell me my son could be in danger and then tell me not to panic?' she blurted, all the different scenarios she'd talked herself out of tumbling back again. She brushed her hands over her arms as cold dread drowned her.

'I meant, there was no need to panic because I'll ensure your safety,' he said.

'Safety from what?' When he remained silent, she jumped to her feet and paced the small living room. 'I think you should start from the beginning, Romeo. Who are these people and what do they want with you? With our son?'

She froze. 'Are you involved in…in criminal activity?' she whispered in horror.

His mouth compressed and his face set into harsh, determined lines. 'No, I am not.'

The scathing force of the words prompted her to believe him. But the fear didn't dissipate. 'Please tell me what's going on.'

He rose, too, and paced opposite her. When his fists clenched and unclenched a few times, she approached. At the touch of her hand on his arm, he jerked, as if he'd been elsewhere.

As he stared down at her, his mouth compressed. 'My past isn't what you'd call a white-picket-fence fairy tale,' he said obliquely.

Maisie attempted a smile. 'Only the books I read to Lucca contain those. Real life is rarely that way.'

A grim smile crossed his lips. 'Unfortunately, mine was a little more dire than that.'

She kept quiet, mostly because she didn't know how to respond.

'The man whose blood runs through my veins was the head of a Sicilian organised crime family.'

She gasped, then stepped back as the import of the words sank in. 'You're a member of a Mafia gang?'

'No, I'm not.' Again that scathing denial.

'But your…your father is?'

'He wasn't my father. We just share the same DNA,' he bit out in a harsh tone that spoke of anger, bitterness and harrowing pain.

Maisie's eyes widened. As if aware of how he'd sounded, Romeo breathed deeply and slid his fingers through his hair. 'The abbreviated story is that I met him twice. Both times ended…badly. What I didn't know until yesterday was that he'd kept tabs on me all my life.'

'Why?' she demanded.

Romeo shrugged. 'Since I didn't know the man, I can

only guess it was some sort of power-trip thing to watch whether I failed or succeeded. Or it may have been for other reasons. I care very little about what his motives were.'

Maisie frowned. 'You talked about him in the past tense…because…'

'He and his family died in a yacht explosion a year ago.'

The rush of blood from her head made her light-headed. 'Was it an accident?' she asked, her lips numb.

His mouth pursed for a few seconds before he answered, 'Officially. But probably not.'

Her gasp brought his head up. Cursing under his breath, he strode to her and grasped her arms. 'I'm only going by what my gut tells me, Maisie. I don't have hard evidence to the contrary.'

'And your gut tells you he was assassinated?'

He nodded.

A million more questions crowded her brain, but she forced a nod. 'Go on.'

His hands moved to her shoulders, a firm glide that left a trail of awareness over her skin. 'I received a letter from his lawyers a month ago, summoning me to Palermo, which I ignored. I received a few more after that. The last one told me he'd left me something I needed to collect in person.' His mouth twisted. 'My curiosity got the better of me.'

'What was it?'

'His monstrosity of a mansion. Along with his plans for my future.'

Ice slithered down her spine. 'What plans?'

One hand moved to her neck and cupped her nape. The familiarity of that gesture thawed the ice a little, replacing her terror with a wave of warm awareness.

'He never had a son…not a legitimate one anyway. I think somewhere along the line he intended to contact me, bring me into the *family business*. He just never got the chance to. But he told his second in command about it. He was the one who asked the lawyers to contact me.'

'What does he want from you?'

'The *famiglia* is falling apart. They need a new injection of young blood, and an even greater need for an injection of financial support.'

'You have both.'

'But I intend to give them neither.'

Maisie stared at his granite-hard face, the deep grooves bracketing his mouth and the dark gold of his eyes, and the pennies finally tumbled into place. 'But if you don't intend to... Oh, my God. You think they mean to use Lucca to make you do what they want?' she rasped in a terror-stricken voice.

His grip tightened and one finger caught her chin and raised her face to his spear-sharp gaze. Her stomach knotted at the savage determination on his face. 'They will *never* get their hands on you or our son. You have my word on this, Maisie.'

She shook her head, her insides growing colder by the second. 'But you can't guarantee that, can you? Or you wouldn't be here with *six* bodyguards in tow.'

'There's one way to ensure your safety,' he said, his gaze raking her face as if he wanted to pull the answer from her even before he'd asked the question.

'What's that?' she murmured.

'You will marry me. Then you and our son will know the protection of my name.'

CHAPTER FIVE

SHE WENT HOT, then cold, then colder. Until she felt as brittle as chilled glass. Dumbly, she stared into those burnished gold eyes, sure she'd misheard him.

'What did you say?'

'The *famiglia* isn't as powerful as it once was, but I'm not willing to dismiss them out of hand, either. Marrying me will grant you and Lucca protection, which you could be vulnerable without.'

'No way. I can't…I can't just *marry* you! We know next to nothing about each other.'

A look curled through his eyes. 'Our circumstances aren't commonplace. Besides, we've already done things a little out of sequence, don't you think?'

She laughed, but the sound was more painful than she wanted it to be. 'This is far from a quaint little romantic caper.'

He nodded. '*Sì*, which is why I want to ensure I have all the bases covered for your protection.'

'Oh, God!'

'Maisie—'

'No.' She pulled out of his hold and backed away. 'This is preposterous. You have to find another way to protect Lucca.'

Golden eyes bored into hers. 'There's no other way. There's an unspoken code, *gattina*. They may be thugs, but they respect family. Marrying me means you and Lucca become off limits.'

'But it still won't be a cast-iron guarantee, will it?'

He shrugged. 'Nothing in life is guaranteed. I have no

intention of involving myself in that life, but there may be resistance. A temporary marriage is our best option.'

The cold pronunciation chilled her to the bone. She kept backing away until her shoulders nudged the window. Unrelenting, he prowled towards her.

'No way. I can't do it, Romeo. I just… I can't just fold up my life and uproot my son to live goodness knows where, looking over my shoulder every day!'

'Look!' He reached her, grasped her shoulders and turned her around, directing her gaze to the street, where his men maintained a watchful guard. 'Is this how you want Lucca to live? Surrounded by men in black carrying guns? Can you honestly say that you'll experience a moment of peace in the park, knowing that his life could be in danger from unknown elements at each second of the day?'

She shuddered. 'That's not fair, Romeo.'

His bitter laugh scoured her skin. 'Life's *never* fair, *gattina*,' he whispered in her ear. 'Believe me, I have firsthand experience in just how unfair life can be. That's why I want this for our son. He will bear my name, legitimately, and my protection.'

'But you *cannot* guarantee that, can you? Can't you just go to the authorities and tell them about this?'

He levelled a deep sigh. '*Sì*, I can. My lawyers have been apprised of what's going on. But, technically, Lorenzo hasn't committed a crime yet, just issued veiled threats. Even when he does, the wheels of justice don't always move fast, Maisie. You of all people should know that.'

Sadly, she knew that all too well. Nevertheless, she couldn't give what he was suggesting any room to grow. That a part of her wanted to let it grow deeply unnerved her. 'We can still—'

'We can do a lot of things.' He reached for her again, pinning her arms to her sides. 'None would be as effective as what I'm proposing. At the very least, it'll buy time until I can find another solution.'

She pulled away. She thought of her parents, of the frosty existence she'd lived with. Her parents' lack of warmth hadn't just been directed at her. They'd been equally frosty to each other. As she'd grown up, she'd realised that the only reason they'd married and stayed married had been because of her. A shiver of horror raked her from head to toe at the thought of placing herself in a similar arrangement. Lucca was sharp. It would be a matter of time before he sensed that his parents didn't love one another. The thought of what it would do to him made her recoil.

'Maisie—'

'No!' she cried. The part of her that hadn't been freaking out completely threw up its arms and buckled beneath the part that was exploding with hysteria. 'I won't do it! I won't—'

She gasped as strong arms clamped around her and she was hauled into his body.

'*Basta!* There's no need to get hysterical.'

She fought to free herself, but his arms tightened their hold on her. 'I'm not getting hysterical,' she lied. Inside, she was going out of her mind with information overload. And being this close to Romeo, feeling his taut, warm body against hers, wasn't helping, either. Planting her hands on his chest, she pushed. 'Let me go, Romeo!'

'Calm down, then I will.'

She stilled, then made the mistake of glancing up at him.

His eyes were molten, his lips parted slightly as he stared down at her. The look on his face morphed to replicate the dangerous sensations climbing through her.

'No...' she whispered.

'No,' he agreed roughly. And yet his head started to descend, his arms gathering her even closer until her breasts were pressed against his chest.

A second later, his hot, sensual mouth slanted over hers, and she was tumbled headlong into a different quagmire.

Only, this one contained no fear, no horror. Only an electrifying sizzle that rocked her from head to toe.

His tongue breached her mouth, his teeth biting along the way. Maisie whimpered as sensation engulfed her. She opened her mouth wider, her tongue darting out to meet his.

He groaned and pulled her closer. One hand fisted her hair, angled her head for a deeper penetration, while the other slid down her back to cup her bottom. He squeezed and yanked her into his hardening groin. As if a torch paper had been lit between them, Maisie scoured her hands over him, trailing his shoulders, his back, the trim hardness of his waist before her fingers dug into the tightness of his buttocks.

A rough sound exploded from his lips as he rocked against her pelvis, imprinting his erection against her belly in a clear demand that made her moan. Hunger she'd taught herself to bury suddenly reared up, urgent and demanding. When his hand cupped her breast and toyed with her nipple, Maisie wanted to scream, *Take me!*

But even that sound would have taken too much effort, drugged as she was by the power of his kisses. Her fingers trailed back up, curled into his hair as she gave herself over to the sensation drowning her.

'*Gattina*...my little wildcat,' he groaned once he'd lifted his head to trail kisses along her jaw.

Maisie moaned as he bit her earlobe. 'Romeo.' Her speech was slurred and the secret place between her legs lit on fire from wanting him. From wanting her hunger assuaged.

He recaptured her mouth and Maisie was certain she would die just from the pleasure overload.

'Mummy!'

They exploded apart, their breaths erratic and ragged as they stared at each other across the space between them.

Romeo looked dazed, hectic colour scouring his cheekbones, his golden eyes hot and brooding and alive with arousal. She suspected she wore the same look, if not worse.

'Mummy!'

She lurched, still dazed, towards the door leading out into the hallway.

'Gattina.'

She didn't want to hear that term, didn't want to be reminded that she'd behaved like a horny little hellcat with her son asleep two doors away. But she turned anyway, met that torrid, golden gaze.

'Fix your shirt,' he rasped throatily.

Maisie looked down at the gaping shirt exposing her chest. The buttons had come undone without her having the vaguest idea when it'd happened. Flushing, she shakily secured them and hurried to her son's room.

He sat up in bed, rubbing his eyes, his lower lip pouting. She sat and scooped him into her lap and hugged him close.

'Hey, precious. Did you have a bad dream?'

'Yes. It was the bad goblins.' His lip trembled and he tucked his head into her shoulder.

'It's okay now, baby. Mummy's here. I'll slay the silly goblins so they can't get you.'

He gave a sleepy little giggle and wriggled deeper into her embrace.

She sat there, minutes ticking by as she crooned to him, until he fell back asleep. Planting a gentle kiss on his forehead, she caught movement from the corner of her eye and looked up to see Romeo framed in the doorway.

With her emotions nowhere near calm, Maisie couldn't form a coherent thought, never mind form actual words, so she watched in silence as he came and crouched at the side of the bed, his hand trailing gently down Lucca's back.

When his eyes met hers, her breath strangled at the fierce determination brimming in the hazel depths.

'You will slay his imaginary goblins. But what about his real ones?' he murmured, his voice low and intense.

'Romeo—'

'*I* will take care of those. All you have to do is accept my name.'

The implications of what he was asking was no less daunting, no less grave than it'd been half an hour ago when he'd dropped the bombshell. While she'd never given much thought to a future beyond being a mother and owner of a business she loved, she'd also not written it off. But what Romeo was asking... The idea was too huge to even comprehend.

'It's not as monumental an undertaking as you think,' he said, reading her thoughts with an accuracy that terrified her. 'Think of it as a time-buying exercise.'

His gaze fell to Lucca's sleeping form. His hand moved, as if to touch him, but he placed it back down on the bed.

The telling gesture made Maisie's breath strangle in her chest. 'You care about him, don't you?' she murmured.

A look crossed his face, which he quickly blanked. 'I didn't know he existed until twenty-four hours ago. But he's mine, and I take care of what's mine.'

He looked up, the clear, deadly promise blazing for her to see. It shook her to the soul, seeing the promise she'd made to her son the moment he'd drawn breath visible on another person's face.

She opened her mouth to say yes, then felt a cold finger of dread. As much as she wanted to protect her son, she couldn't live with herself if she risked swapping Lucca's physical well-being for his emotional one.

His eyes narrowed, and she was sure he was reading her thoughts again. He gently scooped up Lucca and placed him back in bed, pulling the Lego-themed coverlet over his little body before he straightened.

'Let's finish this talk. Now.' His voice vibrated with low, commanding intensity.

His heavy, dominating presence crowded her as they re-entered the living room. Knowing what she had to say, she turned to face him.

'What's the problem?' he asked.

She threw out her arms. 'Where do you want me to start? Even if I wanted to say yes to what you're proposing, what happens with us?'

A dark frown clamped his forehead. 'Us?'

'Yes, us. You and me. We're virtual strangers. What makes you think we'd last a day under the same roof?'

He shrugged. 'I'm inclined to think if we both know what's at stake, we can make it work.'

And what was at stake was her son's welfare. This was all for Lucca. She was merely the extra passenger along for the ride. The current situation had only made the claiming more urgent. The kiss that had happened was just residual hormones from their last time. Nothing more.

Lucca was the reason Romeo was here in the first place. She didn't think for a second that saying no would send Romeo packing. Regardless of the *Mafia code* or a marriage of convenience, the man in front of her would claim his son. She knew it with a bone-deep certainty.

'Maisie.' Another hard command. She was beginning to recognise how he'd risen to his powerful status so quickly. He packed more imperious presence in his little finger than most men packed in their whole bodies.

'I don't know what to say…'

He waited.

'Before I agree, I need your assurance that you'll resolve this as quickly as possible.'

His nostrils flared, but he nodded. *'Sì.'*

'That you'll tell me if anything changes where protecting Lucca is concerned.'

'You have my word.'

She sucked in a breath, but the enormity of what she was contemplating weighed on her with crushing force. 'Okay… then I'll marry you.'

A golden light flared in his eyes, and he nodded once.

'I'll take care of the details. You don't need to worry about anything.'

With that, he strode to where he'd draped his coat over the sofa and shrugged into it. Surprise scythed through her.

'You're leaving?'

'I have a few phone calls to make. I'll be back in the morning.'

Maisie was still reeling from his words and from what she'd committed herself to hours later when she realised that sleep would remain elusive.

She was still awake at 6:00 a.m. when firm knuckles hammered on her door.

'Is there a particular reason you feel inclined to break down my door at the crack of dawn?'

Romeo raised an eyebrow at the scowl that greeted him from beneath the cloud of auburn hair.

'I would've called, but I didn't want the phone to wake Lucca.' He also hadn't wanted to give her a chance to back out of what he'd convinced her to agree to yesterday.

Nothing would get in the way of him claiming his son. Attempting to give the child who was a part of himself the one thing that was denied him—a chance to choose his own path, free from the stain of illegitimacy.

Romeo might not know or even believe in love. But he could grant Gianlucca the acceptance and security that was never given him.

And Maisie O'Connell wouldn't stand in his way.

But she could, and continued to, glare at him. 'I suppose I should thank you for that consideration.'

'You're not a morning person, I see.'

'Great observation.' She eyed the coffee and croissants in his hand before slicing him with those bright blue eyes again. 'Is one of those for me?' she asked in a gruff, sleep-husky voice.

It was then he noticed the shadows under her eyes. Perhaps he should've waited a little while longer before arriving. But he'd grown tired of pacing his hotel suite. And he hadn't been certain that her *yes* had been from a place of belief that they were doing the right thing. The more he'd paced, the more he'd been sure she would change her mind given any more thinking room.

Romeo intended to give her none.

It had become clear very early on that her devotion to Lucca was absolute. It had been the only thing that had made him leave last night.

That and the need to push his investigators harder to find something concrete he could use against Lorenzo.

'Is that a no?'

He focused to see Maisie sliding a hairband from her wrist. She caught it in her teeth, then gathered her heavy silky hair into a bunch at the back of her head. The action drew up her nightshirt, showing off her shapely thighs and legs. Heat trickled through him as his gaze trailed up to linger on her heavy, pert breasts, thrown into relief by the act of securing her hair.

She seemed to notice the thick layer of awareness that had fired up, and her eyes darkened a touch.

Reining in his libido and burying the recollection of how those breasts had felt in his hands last night, he held out the coffee. There would be no repeat of last night's lust-fuelled encounter. Romeo had no intention of letting sex clutter up his plans.

He of all people knew one moment of madness could destroy a life. It was the reason he existed. It was the reason his mother had spent years blaming him for destroying her life.

It's the reason your son's here.

He accepted that sound analysis, just as he'd accepted that now he knew of Lucca's existence, he would safeguard his upbringing with everything he possessed. He'd witnessed too many people fall through the cracks to leave his son's fate to miracles and chance.

His own existence had been proof that miracles didn't exist.

'Thank you,' Maisie murmured huskily, taking the proffered beverage before stepping back to let him in. He handed her the pastry and followed her into the kitchen. She placed the croissants on a plate but didn't make a move to touch them. 'It's a little too early for me.'

Again he experienced a tiny bout of guilt, then told himself there would be plenty of time for her to rest once he got them away from here.

Her gaze flicked to him, then darted away. But in that look Romeo caught the hesitation he'd been dreading. He gritted his teeth.

He didn't want to resort to plan B, but he would if necessary. 'Second thoughts are natural. As long as you keep your eye on the big picture.'

She bit her lip. 'I can't believe this is happening.'

'It's happening, *gattina*. We'll tell Lucca when he wakes up. Is there anyone else you wish to inform? Your parents?' He vaguely recalled her mentioning them in the intermittent burst of chatter that had preceded him inviting her to his suite that night in Palermo.

Her expression shuttered and she took a large gulp of coffee. 'My parents are no longer in the picture.' A bleak note of hurt threaded her voice. 'And even if they were, this wouldn't be the ideal scenario to present to them, would it? Their only child marrying the father of her child because the Mafia were issuing threats?' Her mouth twisted in mocking bitterness.

His eyes narrowed at the odd note in her voice. 'They wouldn't want you to do what is necessary to safeguard their grandson?'

Her gaze remained lowered and she crossed her arms around her middle in a gesture of self-preservation. 'I wouldn't know. Besides the odd birthday and Christmas card, I haven't spoken to them in four years.'

Four years. The same length of time as his son had been alive. Certain there was more to the story, he opened his mouth to ask. But her head snapped up and she flashed him a pursed-lip smile.

'How much time do I have to get my things in order? I'll need a few days at least to talk to... You're shaking your head. Why?' she enquired curtly.

'We're leaving this morning.'

'That's impossible. I have to pack and make sure I get the right person to look after the restaurant until...' She stopped and frowned. 'Will I be able to return any time soon?' Wide blue eyes stared at him with a mixture of res- ignation and sadness.

'Not for a while.'

'How long is a while?'

'A few weeks, a few months? It's probably best that you forget about this place for the time being.'

The sadness was replaced with a flash of anger. 'That's easy for you to say. You haven't spent the better part of two years working night and day to get a business off the ground.'

He allowed himself a small smile. 'I know a little bit about the hard work it takes to establish a business.'

She grimaced. 'But you don't know how it feels to do it on your own with no support from anyone else. The fear that comes from knowing that one failure could mean you have nothing to help you look after your child.' She shook her head, as if realising how much she'd revealed.

Romeo chose not to enlighten her about his personal re- lationship with fear and failure—of the rough, terrifying nights he'd spent on the streets when he was barely into his teens; of the desperate need for acceptance that had led him to contemplate, for a blessedly brief moment, whether he was truly his father's son.

He'd rejected and stumbled away from the gang initiation rites and earned himself a bullseye on his back for a while. But it hadn't stopped the fermenting thought that perhaps the life of a *Mafioso* was blueprinted in his blood.

That was a part of him he intended would never see the light of day.

But it was a thought he had never been able to shake off.

He downed the espresso and watched her struggle to get her emotions under control. 'Tell me what you need to do to expedite things.' He had spent most of the night putting things in place to remove her and Lucca as quickly as possible, but he had the feeling telling her that right now wouldn't go down well.

'I have to speak to Bronagh about assuming a full-time managerial position for starters. Then make sure the staff are taken care of.' She started to slide her hands through her hair, realised she'd caught it in a ponytail and switched to sliding the long tail through her fingers. 'I can't just up and leave.'

The need to get her and Lucca away from here, as quickly as possible, smashed through the civilised barrier he'd placed on himself so far. 'A Michelin-star chef will be here at nine to take over the day-to-day running of the restaurant. Once Lucca is awake, I have a team of movers waiting outside to pack your things. You can keep the apartment or I can arrange for it to be sold, that's your choice. We'll stop over in London, where we will be married at four this afternoon. After that we'll fly straight from London to my island in Hawaii.'

She'd stilled as he spoke, her eyes growing wider with each plan he laid out. 'But…we can't get married that quickly,' she blurted. 'We need a special licence and that takes—'

'It's taken care of.'

She shook her head. 'This is going too fast, Romeo.'

He folded his arms. 'The sooner this layer of protection

is in place, the sooner I can concentrate on dealing with Lorenzo.'

Apprehension crept into her eyes and he cursed under his breath.

She abandoned her coffee and folded her arms. Romeo willed his gaze to remain above her neckline, not to watch the tail of hair trail across her breasts with each breath she took. 'Do we at least have time to discuss what sort of marriage we're going to have?'

He tensed. 'Excuse me?'

'Well, this isn't going to be a traditional marriage, is it? As you said, we're only doing this to ensure Lucca's safety, so I presume the physical side of things won't be part of the marriage.'

Despite having told himself precisely the same thing after his control slipped last night, something moved through his belly that felt very much like rejection. He gritted his teeth.

'If that is what you wish, then it will be so.'

Her lashes swept down. 'Yes, that's what I want. I think you'll agree, sex tends to cause unnecessary confusion.' A flush crept up her neck and Romeo was struck by how innocent she looked.

'Sì, Lucca is the most important thing in all this.' Why did the words feel so hard to get out?

She gave a brisk nod. 'I'll go and get changed. He'll be waking up any minute now.' She started to walk towards the door, then stopped and turned with a grace that hinted at balletic training.

Romeo frowned. He knew next to nothing about the mother of his child. All he had were the basic facts produced by his private investigators. He'd been so focused on his son that he'd only requested information from Maisie's pregnancy to date.

He hadn't really paid attention to their random conversations five years ago. He'd gone seeking oblivion of the carnal nature and had fallen head first into a maelstrom of emotions he still had a hard time reliving. He'd tried afterwards to explain it away as his grief talking, but that hadn't quite rung true.

The idea that he'd been burying a lonely yearning that had chosen his mother's death to emerge had shaken him to the core.

It wasn't a place he wanted to visit ever again.

He mentally shrugged. He didn't *need* to know any more about Maisie, other than that she would continue to remain devoted and invested in keeping their son safe.

'I'd like to keep Bronagh as assistant manager. She's been a huge support and I don't want this new manager tossing her out after I'm gone, okay?'

'If that's what you need to put your mind at rest, then it will be done.'

She opened her mouth, as if she wanted to say more, but nodded and left.

His phone vibrated in his pocket. He pulled it out before it started to ring. Anger throbbed to life when he saw the familiar area code. Strolling out of the kitchen, he answered it.

'You may be used to not taking no for an answer, but if you want to have any dealings with me, you'll listen when I say I'll be in touch when I'm good and ready.'

'You have the benefit of youth on your side, Brunetti, but I'm reduced to counting the minutes.'

'Perhaps you should remember that before you test me any further,' he grated out.

Lorenzo gave a barking laugh. 'You think I don't know what you're up to? You may secure your *figlio* a layer of protection, but your legacy will still need to be claimed.'

Romeo's rage built. 'My legacy doesn't involve indulging a handful of geriatric old men, desperate to hang on to the old ways. I'm better at this game than you give me credit for. Being forced to live in the gutter has a way of bringing out a man's survival instincts.'

For the first time, Lorenzo seemed to falter. 'Brunetti…'

'Do not call me again. I'll be in touch when I'm ready.'
He hung up and turned at the sound of his son's laughter.

The sound moved through him, and he froze in place for a second.

Gianlucca was his legacy. One he intended to guard with his life, if necessary.

He swallowed and got himself under control just as his son burst excitedly into the living room.

'Mummy says we're going on a plane today!'

'Yes, you're coming to live with me for a little while.'

'Do you have a big house?'

The corner of Romeo's mouth lifted. 'It's big enough for my needs, yes.'

Lucca's head tilted pensively. 'Does it have a duck pond?'

'Not yet,' he replied, then gave in to the compulsion to offer more; to make a little boy happy. 'But I will build one for you.'

His eyes rounded. 'My very own duck pond?' he whispered in awe.

A peculiar stone lodged in Romeo's throat, making it difficult to swallow. '*Sì*…yes. Your very own.'

A giant smile broke over his son's face. 'Wow! Can I also have a bouncy castle?'

Romeo opened his mouth, but Maisie shook her head. 'We'll discuss it later.'

Lucca continued to beam. 'It's going to be the best adventure ever!'

Unable to speak on account of all the tectonic plates of his reality shifting inside him, Romeo could only nod.

CHAPTER SIX

MAISIE FOUND OUT just how much of an adventure when she was ushered into an exclusive Mayfair boutique five hours later with a team of stylists. As per Romeo's imperious request, the shop had been shut so the attendants could focus solely on her. He sat in the large reception room, flipping through a document while keeping an eye on Lucca, who was getting his own special outfit for the wedding.

Wedding...

She was getting married. To the father of her child. The man she'd thought she'd never set eyes on again after waking up alone in a hotel room in Palermo. The dizzying turn of events threatened to flatten her. But as she'd taken to reminding herself in case any fanciful thoughts took over, all this was happening for the sake of her son.

This was a wedding in name only; it would *be* a marriage in name only. And once this whole business with Romeo's dark past was over with, she would resume her life.

All the same, she couldn't stop a bewildering shiver as the wedding dress she'd chosen was slipped over her head.

Made entirely of cream silk, the calf-length dress had the scoop-neck design both in the front and back, and lace sleeves covering her to the elbow. The material hugged her from bodice to thigh, with a slit at the back for ease of movement. It was simple, elegant and businesslike enough to not portray any of those fanciful thoughts that fleeted through her mind every time she so much as dropped her guard. Dress on, she slipped her feet into matching cream heels and moved to where a hair and make-up expert had been set up.

Maisie had lost the ability to keep up with how fast Romeo had moved once things were set in motion. There'd been no time to get sentimental once she'd summoned the staff, especially with Romeo's overwhelming presence at her side reassuring them that nothing would change in the running of the restaurant.

Her staff knew and respected Bronagh. It was that alone that had made temporarily stepping away from the place she'd poured her heart and muscle into bearable.

And then Romeo had floored her by inviting Bronagh to London to act as witness at their wedding.

The surprises had kept coming, with her first, brief trip in a private jet, hammering home to her just how powerful and influential the man she would be marrying shortly really was.

'There, I think you're set.'

Maisie refocused and examined the chic pinned-up hairstyle and subtle, immaculate make-up, and forced a smile. As much as she'd told herself this marriage wasn't real, she couldn't halt the horde of butterflies beating frantically in her belly. 'Thank you.'

'And I hope you don't mind, but we sent out for a bouquet. It seems a little wrong that a bride should get married without one, you know?' The owner of the boutique, an elegant, fortyish woman, said. 'Especially when you're marrying Romeo Brunetti.' The clear envy in her eyes and the awe in her voice echoed through Maisie.

She was saved from answering when the door opened and Bronagh entered holding a stunning cream-and-lilac rose arrangement bound with crystal-studded ribbon. 'I'd say this bouquet is the most gorgeous thing I've ever seen, but I think you take the prize for that, Maisie,' she said, her soft brown eyes widening as Maisie rose and she looked her over. 'You're going to knock that man of yours dead.' There was a faintly querying note in her voice, but the reason Maisie had become fast friends with Bronagh Davis was because she'd offered friendship without prying just when Maisie had needed that. And although the other woman had probably guessed that Romeo was Lucca's father—the similarities between them seemed to grow with each passing second—she hadn't questioned Maisie.

'You win all the points for flattery,' Maisie replied, surreptitiously rubbing her palms together to keep them from getting any more damp.

Bronagh smiled and handed over the bouquet. 'You can award me the points later. Your men are getting impatient, and from the way the older one is pacing, I wouldn't be surprised if he storms in here and claims you.'

The butterflies' wings flapped harder. Maisie swallowed down her absurd nervousness and any lingering sadness that indicated she wished this were real, that she were marrying a man she'd taken the time to meet, fall in love and ultimately join her life with.

That was a pipe dream she'd long ago abandoned, even before she'd been faced with an unplanned pregnancy and the sheer dedication she'd needed to take care of her child. She'd been exposed too many times to the ruthless indifference inherent in loveless relationships to believe that she would be the exception to the rule. The love she'd felt for Lucca the moment he was born had been a miraculous gift she intended to guard with everything she held dear. So she'd driven her energy into providing a home for her child, despite her parents' icy disapproval.

Maisie reminded herself that this situation wasn't in her control, that even in this she was putting Lucca's needs first.

Her needs didn't matter.

That particular thought took a steep dive when she emerged from the changing room and was confronted with Romeo Brunetti in a three-piece suit. Immaculate, imposingly masculine and utterly breathtaking, he was impossible to ignore. From the top of his neatly combed, wavy black hair, to the polished toes of his handmade shoes, he reeked irrefutable power and enough sexual magnetism to make kings quake and women swoon in his presence. And that look in his eyes…that brooding, almost formidable intensity that had made her tingle from head to toe the first time she'd seen him…

Yes. Maisie was reminded then how very needful she could be. And how some needs were impossible to suppress even with an iron will. She stared. Tried to pull her gaze away. Failed. And stared some more. At the back of her mind, a tiny voice said it was okay to stare because he was doing the same to her.

The look in his eyes was riveting, as if he were seeing her for the first time. A part of her thrilled at that look, the way it made her feel sexy and desirable…until she reminded herself that nothing would come of it. Nothing could.

Her attention was mercifully pulled away when Lucca rushed towards her. 'You look beautiful, Mummy!'

Her smile wobbled when she saw his own attire—a miniature one of his father's, right down to the buttoned-up waistcoat. 'So do you, my precious.'

Romeo seemed to unfreeze then from his stance. 'Come, the car's waiting.'

Everyone snapped to attention. Two guards appeared at the shop door and nodded. They exited and slid into the back of the limo and were driving the short distance to the register office at Marylebone when he reached into his jacket, pulled out a long, velvet box and handed it to her.

'What's this?' she blurted.

One corner of his mouth lifted. 'I thought your absence of jewellery should be addressed.'

Her hand went to her bare throat. 'I…I didn't think it was necessary.' Which, in hindsight, sounded a little foolish. She was marrying one of the world's richest men. Whether the marriage was real or not, she was about to be thrust into the limelight the proportions of which she was too afraid to imagine. The women Romeo had dated before were all raving beauties compared to her.

A flush rose in her face when his eyebrow quirked. 'You may not, but we don't wish to attract unnecessary gossip,' he murmured, his voice deep but low enough to keep Bronagh and Lucca, who sat on the far side of the limo, from over-hearing. 'Open it.'

Fingers shaking, she prised the box open and gasped. The three-layered collar necklace contained over two dozen diamonds in different cuts and sizes, the largest, teardrop gem placed in the middle. The stunning jewels, along with a pair of equally breathtaking earrings, sparkled in her trembling hand. Maisie realised her mouth was still open when Romeo plucked the necklace off its velvet bed and held it out.

'Turn around.'

Still stunned, she complied and suppressed a tremble when his warm fingers brushed her nape. She turned towards him to thank him and froze when he leaned forward to adjust the necklace so the large stone was resting just above her cleavage. The touch of those fingers...there... sent her blood pounding through her veins. She looked up and met dark hazel eyes. The knowing and hungry look reflecting back at her stopped whatever breath she'd been about to take. They stared at each other, that intense connection that seemed to fuse them together whenever they were close sizzling between them.

'Wow, that's stunning.'

Maisie jerked guiltily at Bronagh's awed compliment. Another blush crept into her face when she realised she'd momentarily forgotten that her friend and son were in the car. To cover up her embarrassment, she hastily reached for the earrings and clipped them on. Then exhaled in a rush when Romeo produced another ominous-sized box.

'Romeo...'

His eyes flashed a warning and she swallowed her objection. This time he opened it. The large diamond-and-

ruby engagement ring defied description. And probably
defied any attempt to place a value on it. Silently, Maisie
held out her left hand, absurdly bemused to take in the fact
that between one heartbeat and the next she'd been draped
in jewels that cost more than she would earn in a lifetime.

She smiled through further gasps from Bronagh and just
willed herself to breathe. She might not have fully absorbed
what she was letting herself in for publicly by agreeing to
marry Romeo Brunetti the billionaire, instead of Romeo
Brunetti, father of her child, but she'd faced tougher challenges and triumphed. She could do this.

The marriage ceremony itself was shockingly brief.

Whatever strings Romeo had pulled to secure a special licence had pressed home his importance. They were
ushered into an oak-panelled room that reeked history and
brevity. The registrar read out their commitments in a deep
but hushed voice and announced that they were man and
wife within twenty minutes of their arrival.

Romeo's kiss on her lips was swift and chaste, his hands
dropping from her shoulders almost immediately. She told
herself the wrench in her stomach was nerves as she followed him to the desk where their signatures formalised
their union.

As she signed her name, Maisie reaffirmed that she
was taking the necessary steps to keep her son safe. It was
what kept her going through the lavish Mayfair meal with
Bronagh, after which Bronagh was driven to the airport to
catch a flight back to Dublin, and they were driven straight
to a private airport south of London.

Unable to stand the thick silence in the car now that
Lucca had fallen asleep, she cleared her throat.

'I didn't know Italians could marry in London without
jumping through bureaucratic hoops.'

Romeo switched from looking out of the window. The
brooding glance he sent her made her wish for a moment

she'd let the silence continue. 'I've lived in London for over ten years. Other than two days ago, the last time I was in Italy was when you and I met.'

Surprise lifted her brows. 'I thought you were a resident. You seemed to know your way about where...where you were staying.'

His mouth twisted. 'I was, once upon a time. But in a much more inhospitable part.'

'Inhospitable?' she echoed.

That brooding gaze intensified. 'I wasn't always affluent, *gattina*. I can probably go as far as to say I'm the definition of *nouveau riche*. I know the streets where we met well because I used to walk there at night in the hope that I would find leftover food in bins or a tourist who was willing to part with a few euros for a quick shoe shine. Barring that, I would find an alleyway to sleep in for a night, but only for a night because inevitably I would be sent packing by the *polizia* and threatened with jail should I return.'

Maisie wasn't sure which was more unnerving—the harrowing account of his childhood or the cold, unfeeling way in which he recounted it. Either way, the stone-cold horror that had wedged in her stomach grew, until she was sure her insides were frozen with pain at imagining what he'd been through.

'You said you only met your father twice,' she murmured, unable to erase the bleak picture he drew in her mind, 'but what about your mother?'

Lucca stirred in his sleep, and Romeo's eyes shifted to his son before returning to hers. 'My mother is a subject I don't wish to discuss, especially on my wedding day.' His smile mocked the significance of the day.

But Maisie couldn't dismiss the subject as easily. 'And child services? Surely there was some support you could've sought?'

He blinked, his nostrils flaring slightly before he shrugged. 'The support is the same in Italy as it is in England. Some fall through the cracks. And if one tried hard enough to evade the clutches of a system that was inherently flawed, one could succeed.'

Despite catching his meaning, Maisie couldn't fathom why he would choose to live on the streets. 'How long did you sleep rough for?' she asked, her heart bleeding at the thought.

His mouth compressed in a cruel line. 'Two years until the authorities got fed up with hauling me away every other night. A do-gooder policewoman thought I would be better off in the foster system.' He gave a harsh, self-deprecating laugh. 'Unfortunately, she couldn't have been more wrong. Because then it was really driven home that my kind wouldn't be welcome in a normal, well-adjusted home.'

'Your kind?'

'The bastard children of violent criminals.'

Her hand flew to her mouth. 'Oh, God!'

Romeo's eyes once again flicked to his sleeping son and he shook his head. 'Don't worry, *gattina*. I got out the second I could. Now look at me.' He spread his hands in mock preen. And although his voice was even, Maisie saw the shadows of dark memory that blanketed his eyes and hardened his mouth. 'According to the media, I'm every woman's dream and every parent's ideal suitor for their wholesome daughter. Consider yourself lucky for bagging me.' His teeth barred in a mirthless smile.

'Romeo—'

He lunged close so quickly, filled every inch of her vision so spectacularly, her breath snagged in her chest. His fingers pressed against her mouth, forcibly rejecting any words she'd been about to utter. 'No, *gattina*. Save your warm-hearted sympathy and soft words for our son,' he rasped jaggedly. 'You be there for him when he scrapes his knee and when the goblins frighten him at night. I require no sympathy. I learnt to do without it long before I could walk.'

He sat back and for a full minute remained frozen. Then

his chest rose and fell in a single deep exhalation before he pressed a button next to his armrest. A laptop slid from a side compartment and flickered on. Strong fingers tapped the keys, flicking through pages of data with calm efficiency.

As if he hadn't just torn open his chest and shown her the raw wounds scarring his heart.

Romeo tapped another random key, stared unseeing at the stream of words and numbers filling the screen.

What in the name of heaven had he been thinking?

Had he not sworn only last night to keep his past locked in the vault where it belonged? Through all the voracious media attention that had exploded in his life once his first resort had achieved platinum-star status, he'd kept his past safely under wraps. Besides Zaccheo Giordano, the only man he considered a friend, and his wife, Eva, no one else knew about the desperately traumatising childhood he'd suffered. Many had tried to dig, only to accept the illusion that his secret past made him alluringly mysterious, and left it at that. Romeo had been more than glad to leave things at that.

So why had he just spilled his guts to Maisie O'Connell? And not only spilled his guts, but ripped off the emotion-free bandage he'd bound his memories with in the process?

He tried to think through it rationally; to decipher just what it was about this woman who let all the volatile, raw emotions overrun him.

Their meeting hadn't been accompanied by thunder and lightning. There'd been nothing remotely spectacular about it. To the contrary, he'd walked past her that night at the waterfront café in Palermo with every intention of continuing his solitary walk.

Lost in thoughts of bewildering grief and hoping the night air would clear his head, he'd walked for miles from the cemetery where Ariana Brunetti had found her last resting place. He'd barely taken in where he was headed, the need to put distance between the mother whose only interest had been for herself and how much she could get for selling her body, a visceral need.

When he'd finally reached the stone wall overlooking the water, he'd stood lost and seriously contemplated scaling the wall and swimming away from the city that bore only harrowing memories. The sound of tourists drinking away the night had finally impinged, and he'd had the brilliant idea of drowning his sorrows with whisky.

He'd walked past her, barely noticing her.

It was only as he'd ordered his third whisky that he'd caught her staring. Even then, he'd dismissed her. He was used to women staring at him. Women coming onto him since he'd been old enough to shave.

But he'd caught her furtive glances, those bright blue eyes darting his way when she thought he wasn't looking. Romeo wasn't sure why he'd talked to her that night. Perhaps it'd been that lost look she'd been trying so hard to disguise. Or the fact that a group of male tourists had noticed her and were placing bets on who would buy her the next drink. Or the fact that his mother's last words to him had left him raw, feeling as if his very skin had been peeled off.

You're just like him...just like him...

In the hours and days that had followed, he'd been able to stop those words ringing in his head.

Having that drink in that café had been a last, desperate attempt to drown out the words.

He'd raised his glass to her in a silent toast. She'd smiled shyly and asked what he was toasting. He'd made some smart remark or other he couldn't recall. He'd kicked out the seat opposite in brusque invitation and she'd joined him.

Midnight had arrived and they'd walked to his hotel, both of them very much aware of what would happen next.

He'd walked away the next day, even more exposed than he'd ever been in his life.

But he'd pulled himself together, refusing to be the needy

shadow of a man who'd yearned for a kind word from the mother who'd rejected him all his life. And he'd succeeded.

Nothing should've prompted this puzzling and clever way Maisie had managed to slip under his guard not once, but twice. It was a weakness he couldn't, *wouldn't* abide.

He stole a glance from the corner of his eye and saw that she was gazing at the passing scenery, her fingers toying with her new rings.

He breathed a little easier, confident that moment of madness was behind him. That she was taking his advice and letting the temporary aberration pass.

'I'm sorry I dredged up bad memories for you,' she said suddenly.

Romeo shut the laptop with studied care, resisting the urge to rip the gadget out of its housing and throw it out of the window.

'Maisie—' he growled warningly.

'I know you don't want to talk about it now and I respect that. But I just wanted you to know, should you ever feel the need to talk, I'm here.'

For one shocking, ground-shaking moment, his black soul lifted at those words. He allowed himself to glimpse a day when he would unburden himself and feel whole, clean. The picture was so laughable, he shook his head in wonder at his own gall.

He was the son of a whore and a vicious thug. He'd contemplated hurting another human being just so he could join a gang…to gain respect through violence. Walking away, sick to his stomach, hadn't absolved him of the three days he'd worn the probation leathers and trawled the dark streets of Palermo, looking for a victim. He would never be clean, never be washed free of that stain. He hadn't bothered to try up until now. He never would.

'*Grazie*, but I can assure you that day will never come.'

CHAPTER SEVEN

THE BRUNETTI INTERNATIONAL RESORT MAUI was a tropical oasis that had been created with heaven itself in mind. Or at least that was what the brochure stated.

Maisie had silently rolled her eyes when she read the claim.

Looking around her as they alighted from the seaplane, she accepted the statement hadn't been an exaggeration. A long, sugar-sanded beach stretched for a half mile before it curved around an outcrop of rock that looked perfect for diving.

From the beach, the land rose gently, swaying palm trees blending with the increasingly denser vegetation Maisie had spotted from the plane before they'd landed.

She knew the resort housed six koa-wood-and-stone mansions, each large and luxurious enough to cater to the most demanding guest, with the largest, a twelve-bedroom sprawling architect's dream, sitting on top of a hill in the centre of the island.

From the brochure she'd read she also knew that the mansion had been booked for the next three years and that guests paid a king's ransom for the privilege.

She had been admiring the stunning architecture of the resort when her eyes had grown heavy. Jerking awake, she'd found her shoes had been taken off, her seat reclined and a pillow tucked under her head. She'd looked up from the soft cashmere throw keeping her warm to find Lucca and Romeo at the dining table, tucking into a meal. Or rather, Lucca had been eating and chattering away, with his father watching him with that silent intensity and awe that had struck a peculiar ache in Maisie's chest.

Romeo had looked up then, locked gazes with her before being diverted by their son. Unlike in the car when his emotions had bubbled just beneath his skin, he'd looked cool and remote, very much the powerful, in-control billionaire. He'd looked untouchable, and Maisie believed he meant for the moment in the car never to happen again. Whatever had prompted him to reveal a horrific chapter of his past had been resealed in an impenetrable fortress, never to be revisited again.

She'd berated herself for feeling mournful, for experiencing his pain as acutely as if it were her own. She had no right to it, no right to pry or feel strangely bereft when he'd shut her out and refocused his attention on Lucca.

Her parents had tried to drill into her that her brain was her most valuable asset, but Maisie had known that wasn't true. With the birth of her child, she'd known love was the greatest gift she could give, and receive. Same as she knew that Romeo, like her parents, didn't have a need for it. He believed in protecting his son, much as her own parents had provided a roof over her head and put clothes on her back. But, like them, he had nothing more to give.

And while she couldn't turn her compassion off at will, she needed to guard against overexposure of the emotion that had drawn her to Romeo in the first place. His grief and misery that night had been like a beacon. She'd wanted to comfort him, grant him reprieve from the shackles that bound him.

The result had been waking up alone, and returning home weeks later, pregnant. She would do well to remember that.

'Are you coming?'

She jumped at Romeo's prompt and realised she'd stopped at the bottom of the stone steps leading up from the beach.

'Yes, of course.' She smiled at the six white-uniformed staff ready to unload their luggage and followed Romeo up to the buggy parked on the pavement. He lowered an excited Lucca onto the seat and fastened his seat belt before turning to her.

'Would you like a quick tour now or later?' he asked coolly.

'Now would be great, thanks.'

He nodded and started the buggy. When Lucca wriggled excitedly, Romeo slowed down and touched his son's arm. 'Sit still, *bambino*, or you'll have to walk all the way back to the house.'

Lucca looked round. 'Where's the house?' he asked.

Romeo pointed up the hill to a large villa whose glass cathedral-like dome dominated the hilltop. 'All the way up there.'

Lucca immediately stilled, his eyes rounding as he stared up at Romeo. 'I'll be still.'

Romeo looked over at her, a small smile playing on his lips before he tentatively ruffled Lucca's hair. '*Bene*…that means good in Italian.'

'*Bene,*' Lucca repeated, intoning the syllables in near perfect match of his father's accent.

Maisie looked around and realised two things. That the brochure hadn't done enough justice to the description of Hana Island. And also that only two of the mansions that Romeo drove past looked occupied.

'But I thought this place was fully booked for years in advance?'

'It was…until yesterday when I cancelled half of the bookings.'

'Why?'

'Because I wanted to guarantee our privacy. The two families who are staying here have been fully vetted and have signed confidentiality agreements. The others were a little more testy, so I compensated them for their trouble and sent them to another resort. Complimentary, of course.'

Maisie looked around as they headed up the hill. The whole place was the very epitome of paradise. But then paradise had contained a poisonous snake.

'Surely you don't think...'

He sent her a warning look. She bit her lip and waited until he'd stopped the buggy in front of a large set of double doors made of polished koa wood and released Lucca's seat belt. When Lucca scampered off towards the house, he turned to her.

'No, I don't think we'll have any trouble here, but I took the necessary precautions nevertheless.'

She looked around the lush paradise. 'But we can't stay here for ever, Romeo.'

His jaw flexed. 'We'll remain here until I find a way to fix this. Besides, the world thinks we're on our honeymoon, so why not enjoy the time off?' He glanced over to where Lucca was examining a spray of giant bright orange flowers. 'I can't imagine you've had any downtime since he was born.'

Maisie smiled reluctantly. 'I don't imagine I'll be getting any until he's at least eighteen.'

He watched her with a quizzical look. 'But it will be a relief not to be burdened with him 24/7, *si*?' There was a hard bite to his tone that set her nerves on edge.

She frowned. 'I don't consider him a burden,' she retorted.

'Was he the reason you switched careers?' he enquired.

'Well...yes, but—'

'Pursuing a career in criminal law to operating a restaurant in a quaint little village is quite a change.'

'It was a choice I made both for Lucca and myself.'

He nodded. 'You've proved you're capable of adapting. So adjusting to our new situation shouldn't be a big problem.'

She looked around. 'I'm not built to lie about sipping cocktails. I need a challenge, even with Lucca around.'

'Then we will find other challenges for you.'

'Thank you. Now, is this interview of my mothering skills and commitment over? I'd like to get out of these travelling clothes.'

He continued to stare at her in that direct, invasive way of his, as if trying to see beneath her words to any truth she was hiding.

After several minutes he nodded and alighted from the buggy.

Double doors swung open and two women came forward, one an older Tongan native and a younger girl who approached Lucca with a smile. Maisie noticed she walked with a slight limp.

'This is Emily. She'll be helping you look after Lucca. And Mahina is our housekeeper.

Maisie managed to keep a smile on her face throughout the introductions and the tour of Romeo's mansion. She even managed to make the right noises when she saw the Olympic-sized pool and the hot tub, and the man-made cave that opened up into a private waterfall complete with pool at the back of the property.

She smiled through giving Lucca a quick wash, with a helpful Emily unpacking his clothes. When the girl offered to take him away for a glass of juice, Maisie forced a nod, welcoming the opportunity to find Romeo and give him a piece of her mind.

After searching fruitlessly upstairs and knocking on over a dozen doors, she finally found him in a large, airy room converted to a study, with rows of books covering one wall, and an imposing desk and chair fronting a floor-to-ceiling glass window.

She shut the door behind her after his imperious directive to come in and stalked to where he sat, master and commander of his empire.

'How dare you hire a nanny without consulting me,' she fired at him when he looked up from the document he was perusing.

His brows clamped for a second before he rose and rounded the desk. Maisie forced herself not to step back from the broad-shouldered magnificence of his physique. He'd also changed from the suit he wore to travel, into a turquoise polo shirt and a pair of white linen trousers, into which he shoved his hands. 'I didn't think you would object.'

'Why? Because I'm so eager to be lightened of the *burden* of caring for my son?'

'Because I'm told every mother needs a break every now and then.'

'And who, pray tell, enlightened you of this fact? It can't have been your mother, since I'm guessing she wasn't a contender for mother of the year?'

His cold tensing confirmed she'd gone too far. 'We seem to be straying away from the issue under discussion. You slept for less than an hour on the plane and I'm sure you didn't have much sleep the night before. The jet lag will kick in very hard shortly.' He shrugged. 'I thought you would welcome the help.'

She told herself not to soften at his consideration. 'Is that all she is—temporary help?' she pressed.

'No. She helps around the resort when needed, but she's the only one with childcare training.'

She shook her head. 'Romeo—'

Narrowed eyes studied her closely. 'What exactly is the problem here?'

'The problem is you made a decision about Lucca's care without consulting me.'

He exhaled with a rush of irritation. 'This is an adjustment for all of us, Lucca included. Some decisions will have to be made with or without your input.'

'No, I don't accept that. Not when it comes to my son.'

He shrugged. 'Okay, you can use Emily when you see

fit, or not at all. I'll leave that decision up to you. But you can't control every moment of his life, Maisie.'

Cold anger robbed her of breath for a moment. Then the words came tumbling out. 'You've known him for what, two days? And you dare to say that to me?'

His eyes turned a burnished gold. 'Is it my fault that I didn't know of his existence before then?'

'Well, it's not mine! Had you bothered to stick around the morning after—'

'For what purpose? Exchange false promises of hooking up again? Or perhaps you wanted compliments on what a great night we shared?'

An angry flush replaced the cold rage. 'I don't know why you're being so vile! And pardon me if I didn't know the right etiquette for the morning after one-night stands. That was my first and last experience. But I certainly didn't think I'd wake up alone with no trace of the man I'd spent the night with. Or that you'd instruct the concierge not to divulge any information as to your identity. If you want to be angry at anyone, be angry at yourself, because despite that deplorable behaviour, despite you leaving me there to do the walk of shame on my own, I still went back to look for you when I found out I was pregnant.'

His face froze in a mask of surprise. 'You did what?'

'I went back. I used savings I would've been better off investing for my unborn child to pay for a two-week stay in that exorbitant hotel. I walked the streets of Palermo every day and visited every café I could find for a fortnight.' She laughed. 'I drank enough decaf lattes to float a cruise ship, all in the hope that I might find you. Do you know how many hits there are for *Romeo of Palermo* on the Internet?'

He shook his head slowly, as if in a daze.

'Well, I won't bore you with figures. Let's just say tracking every one of them down would've taken me years. I didn't speak the language, so either I was laughed off or every enquiry was met with a blank look. So, yes, I gave up after two weeks and decided my time would be better spent planning a safe and comfortable future for my son. So don't you dare tell me I won't be consulted about each and every decision where he's concerned. And don't you dare make me feel bad about the consequences of something that we both did *consensually*.'

A red flush scoured his cheekbones before he inhaled deeply. Whirling about, he strode to the window and gazed out at the spectacular view.

When she was convinced the silence would stretch for ever, she approached and stood next to him. 'Are you going to say something?' she ventured in a quieter voice once several more minutes had passed.

He slanted a glance at her. 'It is not often I'm surprised. But you have surprised me, *gattina*,' he rasped.

'Because I've shown that underneath that auburn hair I have a temper?' she half joked.

A flicker of a smile ghosted over his lips. 'That wasn't a surprise. I'm very much aware of the depths of your passion.'

She reddened and glanced away before she was tempted to read a different meaning to his words. 'What, then?'

'What you did…' He paused and shook his head. 'No other person I know would've done that. And you're right. After the way I left, you had every right to write me off. And I did make sure that I would not be easy to find.'

'That's an understatement. Do you do that often? Erase your presence so thoroughly your conquests can never find you?' she asked before she could stop herself.

'Not in such direct terms. There is usually an understanding of the transient nature of my liaisons.'

'Oh…right.' That told her.

'That night was different for me, too, in many ways.'

She wanted to ask, but that bleak, haunted look was back in his eyes again, along with that do-not-disturb force field that told her she would risk emotional electrocution if she so much as raised an eyebrow in inquiry. To her surprise, he continued.

'It had been a trying day, one I didn't wish to face even though I knew it was coming.'

'Yeah, we all have days like that.'

He looked at her, his gaze brushing her face, her throat, her body, before turning his attention to the window again. 'But you came back, despite feeling the sting of rejection and perhaps a lot aggrieved?' he asked.

'I put myself in my child's shoes and knew that I needed to give him a chance to know his father. But I guess a part of me was terrified that I couldn't do this on my own and was in some way looking for support.' She shrugged. 'The moment I got back to Dublin, I accepted that I was in this alone. Then Lucca was born, and with each day that passed the fear receded. I was no longer alone. I had him.'

His stare returned, stayed longer this time. 'You're no longer alone where his care is concerned.'

She raised her eyebrows. 'But you don't agree that I should be consulted on all things?'

A steely look entered his eyes. 'I'll grant you a healthy debate about the major issues that concern him. And you can attempt to tear me to pieces on the minor ones.'

'So in other words, we'll argue about everything?'

The corner of his mouth lifted. 'Only because you seem to thrive on arguments.'

Her mouth curved in answer. 'Be warned, I never stop until I get my way.'

His eyes dropped to her mouth, and a heated channel forged between them. Her breath shallowed, her heart racing as she read the look loud and clear.

Desire thickened in her veins, her core throbbing until she yearned to squeeze her thighs together to alleviate the ache.

'Perhaps I will let you win on occasion,' he murmured,

his voice husky and deep. When his gaze dropped to linger on her breasts, a light tremble went through her.

She was thinking it was wise to move away before she did something foolish, like rise on tiptoe and taste his mouth, when a knock sounded on the door.

'Yes?' he answered, his eyes still on her.

Emily entered with Lucca, who smiled broadly when he saw her. 'Lucca wants to go for a swim. I wanted to check with you that it was all right to take him,' Emily said.

Romeo eyed Maisie with one brow quirked.

She lifted her chin. 'I'll take him,' she answered. When his eyes narrowed, she sighed. 'We'll *both* take him?' she amended.

The corner of his mouth twitched. *'Grazie,'* he murmured.

Maisie nodded. 'Okay. I'll go and change.'

Romeo strode forward and caught Lucca up in his arms. 'We'll meet you by the pool.'

In her room, Maisie fingered her sensible one-piece suit, replaying the conversation with Romeo in her mind. He'd been surprised that she'd returned to look for him, more than surprised, in fact. Stunned. That she would want to do the right thing.

Again she found herself wondering just how damaging his relationship with his mother had been. He'd called her a whore in the car. Had he meant that *literally*? She shuddered. Why else would a child call his mother by such a derogatory term?

It was clear that Romeo Brunetti had huge skeletons in his closet. And she was treading on dangerous ground in being so interested in uncovering them. That he'd taken such drastic steps to disconnect himself from her after their single night together should warn her that he didn't want any entanglements that didn't involve his son. She would do well to remember that. Along with remembering that theirs would in no way be a physical merger. No matter how heatedly he looked at her. No matter how much her blood thrilled to insane sexual possibilities each time he was within touching distance.

There would come a time when she'd have to walk away with her son after all this was done.

She would be better off if she made sure to walk away with her heart intact.

Romeo noticed her cooler demeanour the moment she came down the terrace steps and walked through the leafy archway dividing the extensive barbecue and entertainment area from the pool. And it had nothing to do with the military-issue swimming suit she wore, or the tight knot she'd pulled her hair into at the top of her head.

Her gaze, when it skated over him, was wary. As if between the time they'd spoken in his study and her changing, she'd withdrawn into herself.

Had she somehow guessed at his true intention towards his son when this problem with Lorenzo was over?

No, there was no way she could know. He quashed the voice in his head that prompted him to recall Maisie's uncanny intuitiveness. She'd known just how to delve beneath his skin and burrow to the heart of his need that night five years ago.

She'd given him passion and compassion in abundance, two emotions that had been seriously lacking in his life up till then. She'd made him *believe* and *hope*, for a few blissful hours, until dawn and reality had come crashing in. For a while he'd resented her for those feelings. Until he'd realised the fault wasn't hers. It was him, daring to believe in mirages and miracles.

He watched her drop her sunglasses on the table and walk to the edge of the pool, her smile guarded as she observed Lucca's antics. For the first time in his life, Romeo experienced the need to enquire as to a woman's feelings. The unsettled feelings that had slashed through him in the car returned and grew as he watched her swim to the other end of the pool and stay there.

Normally, when the women he dated began exhibiting contrary attitudes, it was a prelude to them asking for *more*. Of his time. Of a commitment. It was the reason he'd drastically reduced his dating span from a few weeks to the odd weekend.

He had nothing more to offer a woman besides a good time in bed and a very generous parting gift come Monday morning.

So what did Maisie's attitude mean?

She had his ring on her finger. Albeit temporarily, and for the sake of their son. But she also had him here, far from civilisation should they choose, and as exclusive as resorts came. And if and when she chose to alter the terms of their non-physical relationship to a physical one, he was more than willing to negotiate.

So what was wrong?

'Faster, faster!' Lucca urged as he rode on Romeo's back. 'Mummy, let's race.' He held out his arms to his mother. Maisie smiled and swam towards them, but she still avoided Romeo's gaze. And kept a conspicuous distance between them as they splashed from one end of the pool to the other.

Eventually, he took a tired and protesting Lucca out of the water. Maisie followed them out and dried him, before taking him indoors. When she returned and perched on her lounger with that same air of withdrawal, he narrowed his eyes.

'I don't like mixed signals,' he snapped.

Her head jerked towards him. 'What?'

'You were fine when you left the study. Something has obviously happened between then and now. What is it?'

'Nothing. I just took a little time to think, that's all.'

Something tightened in his chest, but he forced out the question. 'And what did thinking produce?'

She flashed a bright, false smile. 'I concluded that you're

right. Lucca and I have never had a holiday. This will be good for him…for all of us. As long as I can find something to keep me busy at times, I won't stand in your way about the small things.'

He heard the words and processed them as the half-truth they were. Then sat back and formulated how to get the full truth out of her.

CHAPTER EIGHT

'WE'RE HEADING OUT to choose a venue for a duck pond. You said you'd join us.' Romeo used a tone that made it clear his request wasn't up for debate. His annoyance the past few days had grown into a simmering anger. Albeit that anger was directed more at himself for the unaccustomed feeling of *caring* so much.

But some of it was directed at the woman who raised her head from her video conversation with her friend in Dublin and looked at him with a blank stare.

He'd been on the receiving end of that stare every time he walked into a room, just as every time he came within touching distance she found a way to move away. He'd thought she would be happy when he'd arranged for her to work with the chef at the resort restaurant a few hours each day to keep her skills sharp. She'd been pleased and his chef had sung her praises, but Maisie continued to be aloof.

Enough was enough. He wanted that distance gone.

The voice that suggested he might live to regret closing that distance was ruthlessly suppressed. He strolled further into the room and stopped in front of her, arms folded. 'Our son is waiting.'

Satisfaction burst through him when her eyes lit up with rebellious fire.

'Um…sorry, Bronagh, I have to go. I'll be in touch again at the end of the week.' She smiled and signed off, then glared up at him. 'Was there any need to be so rude?'

'Perhaps you should ask yourself the same question.'

A frown marred the light, golden hue of her skin, the result of enjoying the Hawaiian sun. 'What on earth are you talking about?'

'You've called your friend three times since we got here. You don't think she'd be offended that you're micromanaging her from a distance?'

Her eyes widened. 'Of course not, we discussed me calling her before I left Dublin.'

'Every other day?'

'Maybe not, but—'

'What percentage of your call involved discussing the restaurant?'

She bit her lip and flushed bright red. 'That still doesn't excuse your rudely interrupting me.'

'I'm only doing what you asked, *gattina*, and reminding you that you said you'd come with us to view the site. If you've changed your mind, all you have to do is say so. Lucca would be disappointed, of course, but…' Romeo shrugged.

She frowned and checked the clock on the laptop. 'I haven't changed my mind. I just didn't realise what the time was, that's all.' She looked at him and her gaze swung away almost immediately. 'I…I'll be right there.'

He narrowed his eyes when she remained seated. 'Is there a problem I should know about?' he grated, realising he was reaching the end of a hitherto unknown rope of patience.

'No.' Her lower lip protruded in an annoyed action so reminiscent of their son that he almost laughed. But his annoyance was far greater than his mirth. And it grew the longer she remained seated.

'Do I need to eject you from that chair?' he asked softly.

Her loose, waist-length hair slid over her shoulders as she swivelled her chair sideways. 'I only meant that I'd meet you outside after I get changed.'

He assessed her blue vest top. 'There's nothing wrong with what you're wearing.'

Her colour rose higher. 'Not the top maybe, but the shorts aren't appropriate for going outside.'

Romeo's legs moved of their own accord, skirting the desk to where she sat. 'Stand up.'

She threw him another of those highly annoyed looks but reluctantly stood.

He nearly swallowed his tongue.

The bright pink hot pants moulded her hips like a second skin and ended a scant inch below where the material met between her thighs. Instant arousal like nothing he'd ever experienced before battered him so hard, he was sure his insides had been rearranged in the process.

'Che diavolo,' he managed to squeeze out when he dragged his gaze from that triangle of temptation between her thighs and the silky smooth length of her shapely legs to her bare feet and up again.

'Don't blame me,' she muttered with husky accusation. 'It's not my fault your personal shoppers got my size wrong. If you'd let me go with them like I suggested, none of this would've happened.'

He met her impossibly blue eyes with a stunned exhalation. 'Are you telling me *all* your clothes are too small?'

He'd had a new wardrobe organised for Maisie and Lucca when it had become apparent that she'd packed clothes suitable for an Irish summer, not the tropical Hawaiian heat. And he for one had been tired of Maisie's ugly swimsuit after seeing it a second time.

She lifted her hand to fiddle with her hair and a glimpse of her toned midriff sent his temperature soaring another thousand degrees. 'They're a size smaller than I'd normally prefer.'

'And you didn't say something because?' He was aware his voice was uneven, hell, *strangled*, and that continuing to stand this close to her while she was dressed like a naughty cheerleader was an immensely bad idea, but his feet refused to move anywhere but closer, the need to slide his fingers between her legs, test the heat of those hot pants, almost overpowering.

'Would I have sounded anything but a diva if I'd demanded they send everything back?'

Since he knew every single one of the women he'd dated before would've made exactly that demand, and more, he allowed himself a smile. 'You're my wife. You're well within your rights to demand anything you want, as often as you want.'

She seemed to grow unsteady, her hand reaching out blindly for the sturdiness of the desk. But her gaze didn't move from his, an action for which he felt almost elated. Romeo couldn't take in how much he'd missed looking into her eyes until that moment. Which was absurd, but unshakeably true.

'It's okay, it's not a big deal. I can get away with most of the tops and dresses, and I'd planned to only wear the shorts indoors.' She licked her lips and laughed a touch nervously. 'Besides, I can stand to lose a pound or ten.'

'*Nothing* about your body requires adjustment,' he growled.

She was perfect. And she was blushing in the full-bodied way again that was pure combustion to his libido.

His eyes dropped to where she was winding one leg around the other, her toes brushing her opposite insole. Hunger clawed through him.

Madre di Dio!

'Go. Change if you must. We'll be waiting out front,' he forced out before the unbearable need pounding through him overcame his better judgement and he bent her over the desk.

She nodded and backed away, turning to hurry out of the door. When he was sure she was out of earshot, he let out a thick, frustrated groan, the sight of her delicious backside seeming to tattoo itself in his mind.

He was nowhere near calm when she emerged in a strapless lilac sundress and flip-flops. Luckily for him, his son's presence served as enough of a deterrent for his out-of-control libido.

Ten minutes later, it became clear she'd gone back to not fully engaging with him, busying herself with fussing over Lucca and avoiding his eyes when he looked her way.

Gritting his teeth, he focused on delivering them to the first duck-pond scouting location.

They toured three sites before arriving at the perfect place for a duck pond. Well within sight of the villa, the area was flat and clear of trees, within full view of the beach. Not that Lucca would ever be alone, but Romeo was satisfied the security posted at various points around the island would have a perfect view of where Maisie and his son were at all times.

The head of the three-man construction crew he'd hired spread out the blueprint on a portable table and began discussing design and schedules, with Lucca merrily pointing out where he wanted his rocks and fountain situated.

Leaving them to it, Romeo strolled to where Maisie stood several feet away, her gaze on the beach a quarter of a mile below.

Her head jerked up as he neared, and she inhaled sharply at the force of his stare, her eyes widening before she attempted to avert her head. He caught her chin and held her still.

'You want to tell me what's going on?'

That blank stare again. 'Sorry, I don't know what you mean.'

'I thought we agreed to make this work,' he rasped.

'We are.'

'You call *this* making it work?' he blazed under his breath.

'Romeo, why are you annoyed with me?'

His low mocking laughter grated. 'I suppose I should be gratified that you've noticed that I am annoyed.'

She pulled her chin from his hand. 'If it's about me forgetting about the time of the duck-pond visit—'

'Don't do that, *gattina*. It's beneath you,' he cut across her.

'I don't know what you want me to do. I'm here for Lucca. Isn't that what we both ultimately want?' Her voice pulsed with something he couldn't put his finger on.

No, he wanted to say. *I want you to stop shutting me out.*

He stepped closer and her delicate apple shampoo and sunflower perfume washed over his senses. 'What he needs is parents who exchange more than a greeting and a "pass the salt" when they're in the same room. I may not know enough about little boys yet, but I know he'll pick up the tension between us if we don't clear the air.'

She shook her head. 'But there *is* nothing to clear.'

He begged to differ. About to demand the truth, he looked deeper into her eyes and finally got *why* the atmosphere between them had altered so drastically.

'*Dio*, how could I have missed this?' he muttered almost to himself.

Panic flared in her eyes, darkening the striking blue to an alluring navy. He allowed himself a smile, a little less unsettled now he knew the root cause of her frostiness.

'We'll take this up again tonight, when Lucca is in bed.'

'I have nothing to take up with you,' she blurted.

'Then you can enjoy your meal and listen to me talk.'

Enjoying the heated suspicion in her eyes, he turned and strode back to join the group. The final design of the pond was agreed, an ecstatic Lucca skipping back to the buggy.

Back at the villa, he watched Maisie rush away with an excuse of rustling up a snack for their son. Romeo curbed a smile, satisfied now that he knew what the problem was of fixing it. He was pussyfooting his way through the unfamiliar landscape of being a father. The tension between him and Maisie stood to jeopardise that. The unnecessary argument in his study this afternoon had proved that. It needed to be resolved. And by midnight, the situation between them *would* be rectified, with results he was sure would please them both.

He picked up his son and hurled him in the air, his heart tumbling over when he received a shriek of delight in return.

'Again!' Lucca urged.

Romeo's smile widened and he complied.

He'd never relied on luck to achieve his goals, but with a tiny bit of luck he'd get his son's mother shrieking those same words to him by the time he was done with her.

Maisie inspected the multitude of new dresses in her wardrobe and finally selected a bronze-coloured cotton shift with a crossover bodice tie. She knew she was risking being late, but ever since her conversation with Romeo earlier she'd been dreading the seven-thirty dinner he'd asked Mahina to prepare.

To say she was terrified of that sudden light that had dawned in his eyes after he'd demanded to know what was going on would be an understatement. And that self-assured smile he'd worn from then on had been an even more ominous sign that whatever he intended to discuss with her tonight would be something she might not be able to deny him.

She tied the knot beneath the bodice of the dress and shakily clipped her hair into a loose knot at her nape. The sleeveless design of the dress would ensure she remained cool in the sometimes sultry evening heat.

And if all hell broke loose, there was also the swimming pool to jump into. She gave a short hysterical giggle and slipped her feet into open-toed platform heels.

Knowing she couldn't linger any longer, she hurried to Lucca's room and checked on him, smiling at Emily, who was folding laundry in the walk-in closet, before making her way to the terrace.

The light from fat candles giving off evocative scents blended with solar lamps dotted around the garden and pool.

Next to the table set out for two, a tall silver ice bucket held a bottle of champagne. Romeo was nowhere in sight.

Before she could breathe a sigh of relief from the nerves churning her stomach, she sensed him behind her and turned.

He was dressed in black trousers and a fitted black shirt, his sleeves rolled back to reveal bronzed forearms and a sleek watch. With a few buttons opened at his throat, it was impossible to miss the light wisps of hair or the strong neck and the rugged jaw thrown into relief by all that black. That image of a dark lord, master of all he surveyed, sprang into her mind again.

Maisie swallowed and willed her hormones to stop careening through her bloodstream. But even at this early stage in the night, she knew it would be an uphill battle to continue fighting the need that whistled through her with the ominous sound of a pressure cooker reaching explosion point.

'There you are,' he murmured in a deep, hypnotic voice. 'I was beginning to think I'd been stood up.'

'I wasn't aware this was a date,' she replied feebly. The setting sun, the soft Hawaiian music playing from hidden speakers…the way he looked at her, all pointed to this being all about the two of them and nothing to do with their son.

She took a tiny step back as he came towards her, all dark and brooding. His eyes told her he knew what she was fighting. And the calculating gleam told her he intended to make sure she would lose.

'Come, sit down.'

He walked past her, trailing an earthy scent of spicy sandalwood and his own potent musk that drew her like a supercharged bee to pollen, and pulled out a chair.

With a feeling of walking towards her doom, Maisie approached and took her seat, then gasped when his fingers trailed the back of her neck.

'You must be more careful in the sun, *gattina*. You have mild sunburn right here.'

She shivered and touched the slightly sore spot, berating herself for being disappointed because his touch had been for an impersonal reason. 'September in Palermo was the hottest weather I'd encountered before Hawaii. I think I might need a stronger sunscreen.'

He sat opposite her, his gaze thoughtful as it rested on her face.

As Mahina served their first course, she held her breath, knowing questions were coming from Romeo.

As soon as the housekeeper left, he asked, 'You never took holidays abroad when you were younger?'

She shook her head. 'There was never time for holidays. Or any free time for that matter. Dedication to my studies seven days a week from kindergarten till I graduated from law school saw to that.'

His eyes narrowed. 'Your parents demanded this of you?'

'Yes.'

When she didn't elaborate further, he pressed. 'Tell me about them.'

'I thought our pasts were out of bounds?'

Reaching for the chilling bottle, he poured her a drink before serving himself. 'They are, but I seem to have shared a lot of mine with you without meaning to. I think it's time we address the imbalance.'

Looking away from him for a moment, she contemplated the last of the lingering orange-and-purple sunset and the stars already beginning to make an appearance.

She didn't want to talk about her parents, or the single-minded ambition that drove them and had made her child-hood an endless drudge of trying, and failing, to please them.

And yet, she found herself nodding.

CHAPTER NINE

SHE PICKED UP her fork and tasted the exotic fruit and prawn salad, and busied herself with chewing while pushing her food around on her plate as she struggled to find the right words.

'My parents knew very early on that I wasn't academically gifted as they were—they're both Fulbright scholars and prize academic excellence above everything else.'

'Including you?' he asked astutely.

She swallowed and answered without looking up. 'Including me. I was an accident, who turned even more burdensome when I was unable to fulfil my full potential in their eyes.' When he didn't respond, she risked a glance.

His face was set in a carefully blank expression, but she glimpsed a look in his eyes, a *kinship*, that made her throat clog.

Clearing it, she continued. 'To say they were stunned their genius hadn't been replicated in me was an understatement. I was five when they made me take my first IQ test. They refused to believe the result. I took one every year until I was fifteen, when they finally accepted that I wouldn't be anything more than slightly above average.'

She sipped her champagne, let it wash away the bitter knowledge that she would always be a disappointment in her parents' eyes.

'Did they stop pushing you at this point?' he enquired sharply after helping himself to the last morsel on his plate.

Her mouth twisted. 'On the contrary. They pushed me harder with the belief that as long as they continued to polish me I would turn into the diamond they wanted instead of the unacceptable cubic zirconia.'

'I disagree with that description of yourself, and the assessment that you're average, but go on,' he encouraged, lounging back, all drop-dead-gorgeous danger, to nurse his drink as their first course was cleared away.

She shrugged. 'There's nothing much to add to that. They were indifferent to everything in my life besides my academic achievements, such as they were. When I told them I wanted to be a lawyer, they grudgingly accepted my decision, then immediately started pulling strings for me to be hired by one of the Magic Circle law firms in the country. When I told them I was taking three months off and then returning to take a position at a firm in Dublin, our relationship strained even more.'

'But you didn't back down?'

She laughed bitterly. 'It's hard being an average child of two geniuses, who hadn't wanted a child in the first place. I guess I'd reached a point where I'd had enough.' She'd wanted to lash out, rebel against the oppressive weight of her parents' indifference. Palermo had been her moment of rebellion. And while she would never regret having Lucca, she was beginning to be afraid that the one man she'd rebelled with had set a benchmark for all other men to come. And that each and every one of them would be found wanting.

She drank some more, felt the bubbles buzz through her veins and loosen her tongue. She even managed a less strained smile when Mahina delivered their second course.

'I presume that three-month vacation included your stop in Palermo?' he asked when they were alone again.

With the unburdening of her past came an unexpected increase in appetite. Or it could've been the alcohol.

Shrugging inwardly, Maisie tucked into the grilled mahi mahi and gave an appreciative moan. 'Yes. I'd always been fascinated with all things Italian.' She paused, glanced at him and saw the mildly mocking brow he lifted in her direction. Flushing, she returned her attention to her plate. 'I had some money saved from when I worked part-time at uni, and toured the whole of Italy. Palermo was my third stop.'

'And did your relationship improve once you resumed your career?' he asked. His questions weren't prying, as she supposed hers had been. He seemed to be interested in her life, her past, and not just as a means of passing time at the dinner table.

So she found herself recounting the one painful event in her life she'd sworn never to revisit again. 'Not once they found out I was pregnant by a man whose last name I didn't even know. Both my mother and father came from broken homes. They were estranged from their parents by the time I grew up. I know they hadn't planned on getting married, but they did because my mother fell pregnant with me. When I in turn got pregnant, the confirmation that the apple truly didn't fall far from the tree was too much for them to stomach.' The words fell from her lips in sharp bursts, the pain she'd smothered away in her heart rising to stab her once again.

She chanced a glance at Romeo and saw that he had frozen, his face a taut, forbidding mask.

'So they severed ties with you?' he asked in a chilling voice.

'Not exactly. But they had views on how to bring up Lucca that I didn't welcome.'

'What views?'

'They wanted me to put him in the care of nannies to start, and then boarding school when he was four—'

Romeo's curse stemmed the flow of her narrative. 'So he wouldn't get in the way of your career?' he bit out.

'Yes,' she replied, her throat painful with the admission that no matter what she achieved, she wouldn't be worthy in her parents' eyes.

His breath hissed out in pure rage. '*Madonna mia,*' he sliced out, his nostrils flaring as he struggled to control himself. 'Did you consider it?' he asked with a narrow-eyed stare.

'No. I gave up my job, enrolled in a gourmet cooking course, then moved to Ranelagh to open the restaurant.'

A morose silence fell over the table, their half-eaten meal growing cold as the sharp cries of cicadas pierced the night.

'This wasn't how I planned this evening unfolding,' Romeo said several minutes later after he'd refilled her glass.

Maisie laughed self-deprecatingly, that buzz in her veins somehow making the pain throbbing in her chest sharper. She was sure it was light-headedness that made her enquire breezily, 'So how had you planned this evening going, then?'

He didn't answer for a long time. Then he stood, tall, imposing, breathtaking. 'Come, we'll walk on the beach for a while.' He grabbed his glass and the half-finished bottle in one hand and held out his other. 'Let the night air wash away unpalatable memories.'

Maisie knew she ought to refuse, that the alcohol swirling through her bloodstream would inhibit any rational decisions she needed to make.

And yet she found herself sliding her hand into his, rising to her feet and discarding her shoes when he instructed her to.

The walk to the beach was lazy, the sultry night air and soft ukulele-threaded music emerging from hidden speakers seeming to slow everything down to a heavy, sensual, irresistible tempo.

He let go of her hand when they reached the sand, filled their glasses with the last of the champagne, then walked a few feet away to dispose of the bottle.

Toes curling in the warm sand, she strolled to the water's edge, laughing softly when the cool water splashed over her feet.

For a single moment, Maisie dared to wonder how it

would be to be in this place with the man of her dreams under different circumstances; if she'd been on a real honeymoon, not a desperate attempt to thwart a wizened old thug's threats.

The path her parents had set her on as a child hadn't left much room for dreaming. She'd been too busy trying to earn their love, to make herself worthy of their acceptance, to entertain such flights of fancy.

But she was a grown woman now, and surely there was nothing wrong with letting her imagination run wild for a few minutes, in letting her senses be overwhelmed by this beautiful place, this breathtaking man beside her?

She drained her second glass and didn't protest when Romeo took it away, then returned to stand behind her. Her breath shuddered out when he slid his hands over her shoulders and started a gentle massage of the tension-knotted muscles.

'What are you doing, Romeo?' she asked shakily after several minutes, when she started to melt beneath the warm kneading.

'You're tense. Why?'

'Probably because you're touching me.'

'You were tense before I touched you. Did I do something to make you this way?'

She released a single bark of laughter. 'The whole world doesn't revolve around you, Romeo.'

'Perhaps not, but if there's a problem going on with you it needs to be addressed, do you not agree?' He turned her around, looked into her face and frowned. 'Are you bored? Do you require more challenges?'

'No, I'm finding the lessons with Chef Sylvain illuminating and Mahina is teaching me a few Tongan recipes that will come in handy when I return to Ranelagh.'

His mouth compressed but he nodded. 'But you're not happy. Don't deny it.'

She tried to step out of his hypnotising sphere, but he held her by the elbows.

'This afternoon you thought you knew what ailed me.'

His gaze sharpened, then he gave a wry smile. 'Maybe it was my own need talking.'

'What…what need?'

'The need that claws beneath my skin, threatens to eat me alive…'

She made a barely audible sound when he pulled the clip from her hair and the heavy knot tumbled over her shoulders. Strong fingers slid through her hair in slow, sensual caresses. Maisie realised her dream was sliding dangerously into a yearning for reality that would be hard to push back in a bottle should she set it free.

But still she stayed, moaning softly when his mouth brushed the sensitive and tender spot below her ear. Light kisses traced along her jaw, down her neck to the pulse hammering at her throat. Desire pounded her, making her limbs heavy and the need to maintain that distance she'd been struggling to achieve melt away.

He spun her into his arms, and she gasped at the voracious hunger stamped on his face.

'Romeo…'

His kiss stopped whatever feeble attempt she'd been scrambling for to save herself from the unstoppable freight train of sexual fury that hurtled towards her. But as he took control of her mouth, control of her body, Maisie knew she would welcome being taken over, being flattened by the sheer force of his hunger, as long as it satisfied hers.

And it would.

From searing memory, she knew Romeo was an unselfish lover. If anything, he achieved a deeper level of arousal by piling on her pleasure, taking her to the very brink of sexual release and burning with her as they both fell.

He would give her everything her body desperately craved. And more.

But what happened next? What of tomorrow?

The questions began like small, icy kernels at the back of her mind. Then loomed, snowballed, until she pushed at his chest, desperate to free herself of this illusion.

'Stop!'

He raised his head immediately but didn't release her. 'You want me. Don't bother denying it,' he lashed out at her, his body vibrating with the tension that would surely explode at any moment.

His gaze dropped to her lips when she licked them, savouring the taste of him to pathetically add to her collection of memories.

'Yes, I do. But I won't let you use me to scratch an itch that only stems out of being thrown together more than anything else.'

He cursed under his breath. 'What's that supposed to mean?'

'It means we have a thing for each other, I won't deny that. But it's meaningless. Just a brand of chemistry that will probably go away if we ignore it. I'm not going to experiment on something cheap and tawdry just because we both happen to have time on our hands. I have more self-worth than that.'

He dropped his hands and took a single step back, but his dark gold eyes stayed on her. Accusing. Condemning. 'We took marriage vows. I think that elevates anything that happens between us well above cheap and tawdry.'

'Please don't do that. Don't rewrite the script on what the end goal is here. We only got married because of Lucca. And we agreed there would be no physical manifestation of those vows. Don't change the terms now.'

He laughed mockingly. 'You talk to me about changing the terms when you can't be in the same room as me or have a simple conversation without your pulse jumping all over the place?'

Heat suffused her face, along with anger. 'So you thought

you'd take pity on your sexually frustrated wife and do something about it?' she threw at him. 'How very stoic of you.'

'If I recall, leaving the physical side out of the marriage was your decision. I merely agreed because you seemed strongly wedded to the idea, pun intended. There's no shame in requesting a renegotiation.'

'I'm not requesting anything! All this…' she waved her hand at the sandy beach, the jaw-droppingly gorgeous moonlight and the discarded champagne bottle and glasses '…was your doing. Some sort of attempt at seduction, perhaps?'

He fisted his hair and then released it with a Latin flourish that made her belly quiver against her will.

'Only because I thought it wise to tackle the situation before one of us exploded,' he growled, his cheekbones hollowing out as he glared at her.

'Well, consider it tackled. I'll endeavour to keep my *desires* under better control from now on.'

The tension in his body was so palpable, she could almost reach out and touch it.

'You do realise there are millions of married couples who actually have sex with each other? Why not us?'

A shiver went through her, but she still managed to lift her chin and face that challenge head-on. 'Because I'm not built to have emotionless sex,' she flamed at him, at the end of her tether. 'And I'm damn sure you know that, Romeo. So stop. Please…just stop!'

Burnished gold eyes gleamed with such intensity, Maisie feared she might have poked the lion one too many times. For several seconds he just stared at her, hands on hips, his gaze probing to her very soul.

A heavy sigh depressed his chest, then he nodded solemnly. 'I will stop if you want me to. But I think we both know it won't be that easy, *gattina*. Come and find me when you change your mind.'

CHAPTER TEN

SHE MADE IT through the next seven days. Even went as far as to pat herself on the back for her stellar performance. Even when her body threatened resistance and advocated surrender at every turn, Maisie ground her teeth and sallied forth.

She looked into Romeo's eyes when he addressed her; didn't move away when he approached to discuss whatever was on his mind, or dance away as she normally would've when they took turns teaching Lucca to swim.

Even when she began to suspect that Romeo was deliberately testing her resolve by standing too close when they watched a particularly stunning sunset, or when his fingers lingered a touch too long when he passed her a plate of fruit at the breakfast table.

In those times she forced herself to remember how transient this situation was. And that the end might come sooner rather than later. He'd opened up when she'd heard him having a heated phone call two nights after their escapade on the beach.

Lorenzo had finally come out and demanded a cash settlement to restore the *famiglia's* dwindling power. Romeo had flatly refused.

The old man had retreated.

Whether that was merely a distraction tactic was something Romeo was investigating, but so far they had nothing concrete to indict him with. But if it proved not to be, then Lucca could be well out of danger before his fourth birthday next week. They hadn't discussed what would happen afterwards and she'd presumed Romeo would want access to his son, but Maisie couldn't see the man who'd been la-belled the Weekend Lover, the same man who'd walked away from her so definitely five years ago, wanting to re-main tied down through a marriage licence.

Her heart lurched painfully and she turned from watch-ing Romeo and Lucca splashing on the other side of the pool. She thought of her little flat in Ranelagh and im-mediately hated herself for thinking it would be dull and dreary compared to this brilliant paradise. Compared to living under the same roof as Romeo.

Ranelagh was her home. One she was proud of.

She'd survived putting Romeo behind her five years ago. As painful as it'd been, she'd survived walking away from parents who would never love her the way she knew par-ents should love their child.

She would get through this when the time came.

'Is this your new way of attempting to tune me out? Staring out to sea and hoping you'll be turned into a mer-maid?' His low voice seared along her nerve endings, start-ing that infernal flame that would only build the longer he stayed close.

She looked around and saw Emily walking off with a tired Lucca. Once they'd settled into a routine, Maisie had come round to the idea of letting Emily help with Lucca. They got on well, and Maisie could indulge in honing her culinary skills without guilt.

Bracing herself, she met Romeo's dark hazel eyes, the blazing sexual fire he no longer attempted to hide evident in his return stare.

'How very arrogant of you to assume my every thought revolves around you,' she replied coolly, although cool was the last thing she felt when he was this close, his arms braced on either side of the pool wall, caging her in.

'When I'm with you, like this, I guarantee that every one of mine revolves around you,' he supplied in a whis-pered breath.

Maisie suppressed a shiver. 'If you're trying to get me to crawl into your bed like a pathetic little sex slave, forget it.'

'There's nothing remotely pathetic about you, *gattina*. When you *do* crawl into my bed, I imagine you'll be a fierce little warrior woman.' He moved closer, his warm, chiselled torso sliding against her back in the water. 'Don't make me wait too long, though.'

Her fingers clung to the edge of the pool, her knuckles turning white with the effort. 'Or what?' she whispered fiercely. Daringly.

'Or your wildcat ways will be met with a much more predatory force than would be wise for either of us,' he breathed.

'Romeo, don't.'

It was then she felt the barely leashed dominance of his whole body. His powerful erection nudged her bottom, its hard and thick promise making her shut her eyes and bite back the helpless, hungry moan that rose to her lips.

'You think sex between us will be emotionless?' he queried in a harsh whisper.

She shook her head. 'What else can it be?'

'It wasn't five years ago. You had enough passion for both of us, and more. And I gave you what you needed. This time, we're husband and wife. You can let it count for something or you can let the transient nature of our situation stop you from demanding what you want. What we both want. Think about that, Maisie.'

The next second, he was swimming away, hauling himself out of the water like an arrogant god. He didn't look her way again as he towelled off and entered the villa.

Maisie stayed put, fighting the need to surrender with every last atom in her body, fiercely resisting the knowledge that the uphill battle with herself where Romeo was concerned was only just starting. And that this time, she risked losing more than just her dignity.

* * *

As Romeo had instructed all week, they dined outside, between sunset and when the stars came out. She kept the conversation on safe topics, determined to stay away from the bombshell he'd placed between them at the pool.

We're husband and wife.

The yearning those words triggered in her was something she didn't want to dwell on.

'The builders assure me the work will be done by the weekend. Which is just as well because I think our son has reached the point where we'll wake up one morning and find him down there finishing the pond with his own two hands.' The words were delivered with a bracing amount of amused dread.

Maisie laughed. 'I think poor Emily's at her wits' end, too, with reassuring him the pond will be ready by his birthday. If he decides to finish it on his own, I think she might help him, just for the sake of achieving some peace.'

Romeo smiled, and his face was transformed from brooding sexiness to heart-stopping so fast her heart took a dizzy dive. 'I suppose it's a blessing then he's managed to twist her around his fingers so soon. I can foresee a time when she adores him as much as we do.'

He froze suddenly and his breath caught. The eyes that met hers held stunned shock and when he reached for his red wine, she saw how his hand trembled.

She laid her hand over his as a lump rose in her throat. 'It's okay to admit you love your son, Romeo,' she said gently. 'In fact, I think it's time you told him as much, and that you're his father.'

The shock dissipated, replaced by the customary brooding. He eyed her with a mildly disparaging look. 'So was this some sort of test?'

She jerked her hand away. 'Excuse me?'

'To see how I fared in the fatherhood stakes before offering your permission to let him know I'm his father?' he tagged on.

'Of course not,' she replied, the barb stinging deep and painfully. 'You really think so little of me? Or of yourself?' she added, because she sensed some of that pointed remark was directed at himself.

A fleeting expression flashed across his face, almost like regret. Then his features tightened. 'Why would you think any more of me or my fathering skills? You know enough about my background to know I have no experience in this. That my own childhood has left scars I'll never be able to erase. Scars that could manifest in unpredictable ways somewhere down the line.'

She frowned. 'What do you mean?'

His mouth pursed for so long she thought he wouldn't answer. 'You know I lived on the streets. What you don't know is that I joined a gang a few years after that. One that even the authorities feared to tackle.'

Unease climbed into her throat. 'Why?'

'Because I wanted to fit in, *somewhere*.'

The raw vulnerability caught at her heart. 'And did you?'

He exhaled harshly. 'Not after I refused to perform the initiation rites.'

'Which were?'

Her heart froze as he enunciated what he'd been asked to do. Silence settled over their table, until he raised his head.

'You see why fatherhood isn't a job I'm to be trusted to settle into easily.'

Maisie's heart squeezed at the pain in his voice. 'But you walked away. You chose to walk away instead of hurting another human being.'

'That doesn't mean I'm equipped to handle this!'

'You're fighting Lorenzo instead of giving in to threats and extortion. You swore to protect Lucca within hours of meeting him. You've done nothing but care for him since we got here. Doesn't that tell you something? Love makes you vulnerable sometimes, but it doesn't make you weak.'

His mouth twisted, but the pain in his eyes dissipated a little. 'I wouldn't know. Lucca's young now, adorable and easy to handle. Who's to say what will come later, and how well we'll handle it?' His voice was thin and a touch bleak, holding echoes of his past.

Her hands clenched on the pristine white tablecloth. 'Stop borrowing trouble, Romeo. You've done well so far. Let's just take it one day at a time. And if you're not ready to tell Lucca that you're his father, then we'll wait.'

A muscle flexed in this jaw. 'I wanted to tell him who I was the first moment I knew he was mine.'

The touch of frost inside her melted. 'Fine. Tomorrow, then, or the day after. Whenever you're ready.'

His mouth compressed for several seconds. Then he nodded. *'Bene.'*

Maisie swallowed and nodded in return. She started to reach for her water glass, but he caught her hand in his.

'I'm sorry for not handling this better.'

The remaining frost was replaced by dizzying warmth. 'It's okay. I muddle through motherhood every day.' She smiled.

He raised her hand to his lips and kissed the soft skin. 'You've done an admirable job, *gattina.*'

Heat unfurled in her stomach, wending its way through her body when he continued to caress her with his mouth.

She cleared her throat and forced herself to say something before she crumbled beneath the smouldering onslaught. 'And you've had more experience than I think you're letting on.'

His eyebrows rose.

'There was a picture of you in the paper, on a yacht with two little boys,' she pried gently.

A look crossed his face, a facsimile of the one he wore whenever he interacted with his son. 'Rafa and Carlo are

Zaccheo's twin sons, and my godsons.' He shrugged. 'At least that's what it says on paper. I don't really have much interaction with them.'

'Zaccheo is your ex-business partner?'

He hesitated for a moment, then nodded. '*Sì*, but he is more than that.'

'In what way?'

Hazel eyes darkened a touch. 'Our pasts were intertwined for a brief time during which we formed an unlikely bond.' His tone suggested he wouldn't elaborate, but as she had before, Maisie couldn't help but pry, her need to know this man inside and out a yearning that wouldn't go away.

'Before or after you lived on the streets?'

'Before. Zaccheo's parents took me in for a while, but that situation could never be anything but temporary because my presence in their lives was not their choice.'

He turned her hand over, his fingers tracing her palm in slow, lazy circles. It wasn't a sensual move, even though there was plenty of that arcing between them. It was a grounding touch that sought, and received, a connection.

'Are you ever going to tell me what happened with your mother?' she murmured.

He froze immediately. 'I don't consider the subject suitable dinner conversation.'

She sighed. 'Then I guess, since dinner is over, I should retire to bed.'

'So you can tuck yourself into your cool sheets and congratulate yourself for escaping this needless torture you insist on putting us both through?' he grated at her, a different, more dangerous brooding taking over his face. She also detected a vulnerability that made her wonder whether there was something more going on here than she was aware of.

She slowly pulled her hand away. 'It's not needless.'

His mouth twisted. 'I suppose it's something that you don't deny it's torturous.' He caught up his glass and drained the last of his wine. The precision with which he set down the exquisite crystal made her think he would very much like to launch it across the terrace floor and watch it shatter in a million pieces.

He shoved his chair back and stood. 'Perhaps I'll take a leaf out of your book and live in denial for a while. I'm sure there's an urgent business decision I need to make somewhere in my company. Sleep well, *gattina*,' he said mockingly, before striding off in the direction of his study.

She knew the mocking command would have the opposite effect even before she undressed and slid into bed two hours later after giving up the pretence of reading.

Tossing and turning, Maisie tried rationalising and reaffirming her decisions. When by the thousandth time her own reasoning sounded mockingly hollow, she gave up. Frustrated, she yanked back the sheets and sat up. The hot-pink silk negligee she wore felt sticky on her skin, but the warm night air was inviting, a great way to empty her thoughts of the disturbing feeling that her resistance was crumbling.

Tugging the silk over her head, she went into her dressing room and rummaged through the drawer containing her new selection of swimwear. When her fingers closed over an as-yet-unworn set, she pulled out the string bikini she'd looked at and immediately discarded when her wardrobe had arrived. Of all the swimwear that had been delivered, this was the most daring. The cups of the top part of the black-and-orange set barely covered half her breasts and the matching panties were made of nothing more than three pieces of string, leaving very little to the imagination.

Making a face, she set it aside. Then glanced back at it. The little thrill of naughtiness surged higher the longer she eyed the garment.

She was tired of being sensible. Especially at one o'clock in the morning. Deciding to add a little bit of spice to her illicit swim, she quickly donned the bikini and threw a white linen tunic over it.

The villa was quiet, and she breathed a sigh of relief as she passed Romeo's empty study.

The path to the waterfall was softly lit by garden lamps. Snagging a towel from the stack near the swimming pool, she skirted the villa and hurried through the short tunnel and cave that opened into the stunning rock pool. Disrobing, Maisie dived into the pool, submerging for several seconds, hoping the heavenly cool water would wash away her turbulent thoughts.

The strong compulsion to make the most of what she had *now* before it was taken away from her wouldn't dissipate. On the contrary it grew stronger the harder she willed it away, the harder she swam from one end of the pool to the other.

Finally, wrung out emotionally and physically, she perched on the rock beneath the waterfall, leaning her head back to catch the edge of the cascading water, and sighed at the delicious sting of the warm water on her face.

'You insist you have no illusions of pursuing a life as a mermaid, and yet here you are again.'

She jerked at the sound of Romeo's voice and nearly fell into the water. Righting herself, she stared at his imposing, braced-legged stance at the opposite end of the pool. And swallowed hard.

He was dressed, like her, for swimming, his trunks hugging thick, hair-dusted thighs. But whereas she'd worn a tunic, he only wore a towel around his neck. Her breath strangled and died in her lungs, her pulse racing at the sheer magnificence of him.

She was doomed.

She knew it even before he dropped into the pool and swam lazily towards her. Halfway, he ducked under the water, struck out in a powerful crawl and emerged at her feet. Hands braced on either side of her thighs, he stared wordlessly at her, his gaze intense, broodingly ravenous. Maisie stared down at his breathtaking face, the droplets of water glistening on his skin in the moonlight like tiny diamonds.

Raw sexual energy leapt where their skin connected, firing arousal so strong she could almost touch it.

'Did sleep elude you, as it did me, *gattina*?' he enquired with a husky rasp after an endless throb of silence.

She nodded dumbly, her fingers reaching out of their own accord to trace his eyebrow, his cheekbones. His jaw.

'Have you grown tired of fighting the inevitable?' he pressed.

Her blood roared in her ears, drowning out her every resistant thought. 'I've grown tired of fighting you.'

The gleam in his eyes dimmed for a moment. 'It's not me you've been fighting, but yourself. If nothing else, be true to yourself about that, before this goes any further,' he growled, his stare telling her he wouldn't accept anything but her agreement.

And he was right.

She had been fighting this purely for her own self-preservation. How could she not? The consequences should he reject her a second time would be even more devastating than before. She knew it deep in her soul. With the passage of time her feelings towards him were changing, morphing into something deeper, stronger, that she couldn't seem to control.

The movement of the water jerked him a tiny fraction. The result was a slide of her fingers across his hot, beautiful skin, bringing her to the here and now, to the almighty need pounding through her blood.

'I'm tired of fighting,' she whispered raggedly.

'Then surrender,' he urged thickly. 'Just let this be.' His hands moved, sliding over her thighs to capture her knees. Tugging them open, he surged closer, his eyes so fierce and intense they seemed aflame from within. 'I can't stand another night of wanting you and being denied. Of imagining the many ways of having you, without going out of my mind. Surrender, *gattina*. Surrender now.'

Desire, wild and unfettered, wrenched through her, rendering the last of her resistance useless. Her fingers speared into his wet hair, using her hold to tilt his face up to hers.

Bending, she took his mouth in a greedy kiss, intent on gorging herself on a feast she'd stalwartly denied herself but couldn't resist another moment longer.

Somewhere down the line the devastation would be great. When she was back in her role of single mother far away in Ranelagh, her shredded emotions would have time to mourn, to berate her for her choices.

But here…now, in this heavenly place with this man who put the very gods to shame, she would live in the moment. She would just…*live*. As she had that night in Palermo, she would give as much of herself as she could and take what Romeo offered.

She groaned when he moved her closer to the edge of the rock and deepened the kiss, taking over her surrender with the terrifyingly intoxicating thrust of his tongue and the thrilling power of his body.

The waterfall pounded with elemental force behind her, but it was nothing compared to the demanding power of Romeo's kiss. He kissed her as if he'd hungered for her for aeons. As if he couldn't get enough of her.

Being wanted like that was like a drug to her senses. After years of bleak, icy indifference, it was a drug she craved more of with each passing second.

So she protested with a loud whimper when he pulled away. Before she could reach for him, he planted a hand on her belly, pressed her back till she was flat on the rock. He picked up her legs and swung them onto the rock before surging out of the water to join her.

For a long, taut moment, he stared down at her, his gaze

sizzling over her from top to toe. Then he prowled over her, his hands braced on either side of her head.

'I've often imagined you like this, spread over this rock like a pagan sacrifice for me to feast on, to pleasure until neither of us can move. Now here you are, wearing this wisp of clothing meant to tempt even the holiest of saints,' he breathed, triumph blazing through his golden eyes.

'It's a good thing you're not a saint, then, isn't it?' she managed, then watched a wicked smile curl his lips.

'*Sì*, it's a very good thing. Because no saint should be allowed to see you like this. Or allowed to do this.' He flicked his tongue over the wet material of her bikini top, then, with a deep groan, he shoved the material aside with his teeth and repeated the action several times, before pulling her nipple into his mouth.

Her back arched off the rock with a cry that was indeed pagan, thick arousal firing straight between her legs. He suckled long and hard, his groans matching hers as sensation cascaded through her.

'*Dio mio,*' he muttered when he lifted his head. He speared her with an almost shocked expression before he looked down at her exposed breasts. '*Dio mio, gattina,* you're intoxicating. I want to devour every inch of you.' Impatiently, he tugged at the bikini strings, pulling them away to bare her body to him.

A drop of water splashed onto her neglected nipple. With another wicked smile, he licked at it, then trailed his hot mouth down her torso to the line of her bikini bottom. Unable to keep her hands at her sides, Maisie speared her fingers in his hair, holding him to her quivering belly when he nipped her flesh in tiny, erotic bites.

By the time he released the ties and pulled away her meagre covering, she'd skated into pure delirium, compelled by a force beyond her control. She raised her head and met his gaze a second before he tasted the centre of her.

'Oh, God!' The force of her need jerked through her, then

set in motion a series of undulations he was only too glad to follow. When her eyes started to roll shut, he pulled away.

'No, watch me, *gattina*. Watch me enjoy you the way I've been dying to do.'

The eroticism of the request pushed her closer to the edge. Panting, she nodded and kept her gaze on him as he lapped at her, his tongue executing wicked circles that cracked open a previously untapped well of pleasure.

'Romeo,' she groaned raggedly, the rush of feeling almost too much to bear. 'Please…I can't take any more.'

'You can.' Opening her wider, he altered the pressure of his tongue, his hypnotic gaze telling her she was under his control, to do with as he pleased.

When she began to thrash, he simply laid a hand on her belly and continued his assault. And with each kiss, he grew just as possessed with the red-hot fire consuming them.

'Now, Maisie,' he growled against her swollen flesh an eternity later.

With an agonised cry, she let go, her whole body convulsing with a release so powerful, she lost all sense of space and time.

CHAPTER ELEVEN

SHE OPENED HER EYES to find him sprawled next to her, his fingers tracing her mouth as he stared down at her, a peculiar expression simmering in his eyes.

'What?'

He kissed her, her earthy taste on his lips and the reason for it making her blush. When he raised his head, that look still lingered.

'You returned home from Palermo pregnant.' His hand trailed from her neck to her belly and stayed there while his eyes held her prisoner.

'Is there a pointed question in there somewhere?' she murmured, her heartbeat still thundering loud enough to compete with the sound of the waterfall. 'I'm on the Pill now if that's what you're asking. It helps regulate my period.'

'It's not, but that's good to know.' His hand continued to wreak havoc on her. 'You changed careers and forged another life for yourself all alone. Did you at any point seek another man's bed to alleviate your loneliness?' he asked thickly.

She knew how weak and pathetic responding in the positive would make her look. But she couldn't lie. Not when she'd just experienced an incredible earth-moving event.

She threaded her fingers through his wet hair. 'I was alone, not lonely. But no, Romeo. You were the last man I slept with.'

His chest moved in a deep inhalation and his eyes filled once again with that primitive, razor-sharp hunger that threatened to obliterate her.

The hand on her belly trailed to her thighs, his fingers

digging into her skin in an urgent caress as his head dropped to hers once more. Falling into the kiss, Maisie gladly let sensation take over again, moaning when her hand trailed over taut muscle and bone to finally close on his steely length.

She caressed him as he'd once hoarsely instructed her to, a thrill coursing through her when he groaned brokenly against her lips.

All too soon, he was rolling on the condom he'd plucked from his trunks. Bearing her back, he parted her thighs and hooked his arms under her knees.

He stared deep into her eyes and thrust home in one smooth lunge.

'Oh!'

His growl of male satisfaction reverberated to her very soul. Her fingers speared into his hair as he began to pleasure her with long, slow strokes, each one pulling a groan from her that only seemed to turn him on harder.

He kissed her mouth, her throat, her nipples, with a hunger that grew with each penetration, until she was sure he wouldn't stop until she was completely ravished.

'You're mine. Say it,' he demanded gutturally, when her world began to fracture.

'Romeo…'

'I want to hear it, Maisie.' He slid deep and stopped, the harsh, primitive request demanding a response.

Something shifted inside her, a deep and profound knowledge sliding home that once she admitted this there would be no going back. That she would be giving herself over to him completely, body and soul.

He angled his hips, the move a blatant demonstration that he had all the power, that he controlled every fibre of her being.

'I…' She groaned when he moved again, delivering that subtle thrust that sent her to the very edge of consciousness.

'Tell me!'

'I'm yours…yours. Please…' Her nails dug into his back, and she surged up to take his mouth with hers. 'Please, Romeo. I'm yours…take me,' she whispered brokenly.

Romeo moved, his senses roaring from the words, from her tight and wet heat, from the touch of her hands on his skin. He couldn't get enough. He wanted more. All of her, holding absolutely nothing back. He reared back so he could look into her eyes, to see for himself that she meant it, that she belonged to him completely.

Her eyes met his, the raw pleasure coursing through her shining in the stunning blue depths. There was no fight, no holding back, just a beautiful surrender that cracked something hard and heavy in his chest, bringing in the light and abating the tortured, weighted-down bitterness for the first time in his life.

The sense that he could fly free, that he could find even deeper and truer oblivion in her arms than he had their first time in Palermo, slashed across his consciousness, making his thrusts less measured, the need to achieve that transcendental plane a call to his very soul.

He looked down at her, saw her eyes grow dazed and dark as her bliss encroached. Letting go of her legs, he speared his fingers into her hair and kissed her.

'Now, *gattina mia*,' he croaked, knowing he was at the edge of surrender himself.

'Yes, oh, yes,' she replied. Then she was thrashing beneath him, her sex clamping around his in a series of convulsions that sent him over the edge.

With a loud roar, Romeo flew, barely able to keep from crushing her as he found a release so powerful, had he believed in heaven he would've been certain he'd truly found it in that moment.

He came back down to the touch of her hands trailing up and down his back, her mouth moving against his throat in a benediction of soft kisses.

Again another blaze of memory slashed across his mind,

a sense of déjà vu throwing him back five years, to his hotel suite in Palermo. The feeling that he was raw and exposed, that the woman beneath him wasn't one he could bed and discard, pounding through him. Romeo was certain it was why he'd left as he had the next morning, ensuring he left no trace of himself behind.

Because after mere hours with her, he'd instinctively known that Maisie O'Connell had the power to burrow under his skin, unearth tortured truths and hidden desires he wanted no man or woman to unveil. He'd listened abstractedly as she'd spilled her hopes and dreams and had wanted nothing more than to tell her he'd arrived in Palermo the week before, hoping that for once in his life the woman who'd given birth to him would look at him with any feeling other than hate. That he'd spent a week by his mother's bedside, hoping for a morsel of affection, or regret for the way she'd callously discarded him.

He'd somehow managed to keep his tortured thoughts to himself, but he could tell she'd sensed them, and she'd soothed his soul with the same soft kisses and caresses she gifted him with now.

Then, as now, she'd given herself completely, despite not knowing any more than his first name.

The need to unburden completely powered through him now, but he held himself back. She knew about his father partly through the need to furnish her with information about Lorenzo's plans and partly because he'd let down his guard. But his mother was a different story.

The secret shame that clawed through him had never abated, despite the years he'd spent in bitterness. After he'd buried his mother, he'd bricked away the pain, secure in the knowledge that she no longer had the power to hurt him with her rejection. He'd only ever felt those foundations crumble with Maisie. And her power over him wasn't one he felt comfortable with. It spoke to a weakness he wasn't ready to face.

Shoving his unsettling thoughts back in the vault, he stared down and allowed himself to bask in her soft smile. The sex he could more than deal with, even if it came with a brief exposure of his soul. The benefits were worth it. More rewarding than securing the best business deal.

'Should I be afraid of that smug smile you're wearing right now?' she asked, her voice slightly dazed and heavy with spent bliss.

Arousal spiked again, the magic of her body transporting him into pleasure with blinding speed. Replacing the condom, he expertly reversed their positions, lying back to take in her goddess-like beauty.

With her long, wet hair plastered to her golden skin, she truly looked like a wanton mermaid.

'*Sì*, you're about to make another of my fantasies come true.' He cupped her heavy breasts, played his thumbs over the stiff peaks and felt her body quicken to his touch. He grew harder, need lashing through him as he watched her accept, then revel in, her new position.

She tested the rhythm, quickly found one pleasing to them both and commenced a dance that had them gasping and groaning within minutes.

He reached between them and found her heated centre. Playing his fingers expertly over her, he watched her throw back her head, her nails digging into his chest as she screamed her release.

He followed gladly, eager to experience that piece of heaven again. Eager to leave behind hopes and yearnings that would never be fulfilled. He'd refused to wish after seeing each fragile desire turn to dust before his eyes as a child.

But Maisie in his arms, in his bed, was an achievable goal. One he intended to hang on to for as long as he could.

Maisie awoke slowly, her senses grappling with the strange bed she slept in and the warm, solid body tangled around hers. Vague memories of being carried from the waterfall slid through her mind. She stirred and the heaviness of satiation moved through her limbs, bringing back wild and more vivid memories of last night.

Opening her eyes to brilliant sunshine, she forced herself not to panic as the full realisation of what had happened reared up like a giant billboard in front of her.

She'd given herself to Romeo. Not just her body, but her heart, her soul. She'd known right from the start that giving herself to him this time round would be her undoing. Heck, she'd told him as much!

Just as she'd suspected when she'd promised she was his, she'd been making a declaration that went beyond sex. Each decision she'd taken when it came to her child and his father had been made from her heart. She just hadn't been brave enough to admit it to herself. But now she knew.

She was in love with Romeo Brunetti.

Had probably fallen in love with him the moment she'd sat down across from him that day in Palermo.

Her stomach clenched even as her heart accepted the deep, abiding truth. He was the reason she'd never paid another man any attention, had embraced motherhood without much of a thought for finding a father figure for her son. Deep down she'd known no one could come close to Romeo so she hadn't even tried to replace him.

And now… She breathed deep as her eyes fell on her wedding rings. Now, she could do nothing but brace herself for the agony to come. And it would come. Loving Romeo was her greatest risk and would bring the greatest consequence. Of that, she was certain.

'*Buon giorno, gattina.*' Strong fingers brushed her hair from her face and drew her back against the warm sheets. 'What troubles you so much that you wake me with the power of your thoughts?' he asked, his eyes probing hers with the sharpness of a scalpel.

'Everything and nothing,' she replied obliquely, desperately hoping to buy more time to compose herself.

'An answer guaranteed to send a man into fits of puzzlement. Or the nearest jewellery store.'

'Is that how you usually placate your other women?' she asked, a sensation moving through her that she deciphered as deep jealousy.

Intense eyes narrowed. 'I wasn't aware you needed placating. Perhaps you should tell me where I've misstepped?'

She glanced away. 'I don't. You haven't. Sorry, I was prying again.'

Warm fingers captured her chin, a thoughtful look in his eyes. 'I guess it's only fair, since I questioned you about past liaisons.'

She shook her head, perversely wanting to know, but also desperate to live in denial. If only for a while longer. She chose the latter. 'I don't need a biography of your past conquests. I know enough to get that you have a healthy sexual appetite.' A blush suffused her face and he slanted her a wicked grin.

'Is that what concerns you?'

She shook her head, but she couldn't tell him, of course. Because that would be tantamount to shoving her heart underneath the wheels of a Sherman tank. So she went for the next best thing. 'Why did you bring me to your bedroom? I wasn't expecting to wake up here.'

The smile left his face and that dark brooding look returned. 'Why do you think?' His voice pulsed with an emotion she couldn't name.

She pulled her lower lip into her mouth. 'I thought last night was just…' She paused. 'I meant it when I said I don't want this to get complicated.'

Too late.

But that didn't mean she couldn't salvage a little bit of dignity from the dire situation. Guard her heart from more pulverising down the road.

'So *your* itch has been scratched and you're ready to put

it all behind you?' he queried in a dark, dangerous voice, throwing her own words back in her face.

'I didn't expect it to last beyond last night. Isn't that your record?'

'I see we're back to past conquests again.'

'Romeo—'

'No, you listen. Last night barely dented the depth of my need. And if you're truthful, you'll admit the same. I brought you to my bed because this is where you belong. You can protest as much as you want and we can go back to circling each other until we drive each other insane, or you can choose to admit your feelings and take what you want.'

She opened her mouth, intent on denying everything he'd said. On doing *the right thing*. Getting up, walking back to her own room. To her painfully lonely bed. And more nights filled with the vicious ache of wanting him.

But the words died in her throat. Denying herself suddenly felt like the opposite of *the right thing*. As if saying the words out loud would be like slicing a knife into her arms and opening her veins. Sure, there was a life of desolation waiting for her once she walked away from him, but there was no need to start the torture *now*.

She stared up at him, at the vitality of the body caging hers, the need blazing in his eyes, and resolved to just *be* for now.

'Will you stay?' he pressed.

Slowly, she nodded. 'Yes, I will.'

He proceeded to show her the true meaning of good morning. And she gave herself over to the incandescent sensation.

She was still smiling four mornings later, even as she studiously ignored the tiny voice that called her ten kinds of a fool.

They rose, showered together, their hands and lips revelling in the newness of just being together without tension. Oh, the sexual tension was ever-present. It barely left them alone and Maisie was beginning to doubt it ever would. But there was an ease between them that tugged at her heart when Romeo smiled at her and walked her to her room so she could get dressed.

He lounged in the doorway of her dressing room, his eyes wickedly intent on her body as she pulled on panties and a bra, and slid her white shift dress over her head.

After slipping her feet into heeled sandals, she took his outstretched hand and they left the room.

'Are you sure?' she asked him.

He nodded, although his throat moved in a hard swallow. 'Yes, it's time to tell him.'

As they reached the stairs, she glanced at him and was shocked to see that, for the first time since she'd known him, Romeo looked nervous. Vulnerable.

'Are you okay?' she asked as they descended the stairs and headed towards the kitchen, where Lucca could be heard chattering away to Mahina and Emily.

Romeo gave a strangled laugh. 'It's not every day I tell an almost-four-year-old boy I'm his *papà*.'

Her hand closed on his and drew him to a stop. Standing on tiptoe, she offered what she'd intended to be a supportive kiss.

His hands locked on her hips, and he slammed her back against the wall to deepen the kiss. He kissed her as if trying to draw sustenance from her. By the time they pulled apart several minutes later, they were both breathing hard. His eyes were needy pools, searching and a little lost.

She placed her hand on his cheek, her heart melting when he cupped it and pressed it deeper into his skin. 'You'll be fine. He adores you as much as you do him.'

His head dipped as if he wasn't quite sure how to deal with the alien feeling of being the object of a child's adoration. *'Grazie,'* he finally murmured. When he raised his head, the confident, virile man had slid back. 'Let's do this.'

He tugged her after him, and they entered the kitchen together.

Ten minutes later, in the privacy of Romeo's study, Lucca stared at his father from the safety of his perch on his mother's lap. Then his gaze moved to her face and back to Romeo's, his eyes wide, hazel saucers. 'You're my daddy?' he asked in hushed awe.

Romeo's throat moved several times before he could speak. '*Sì*, I am your *papà*,' he intoned in a deep, moving voice.

Lucca tilted his head to one side, then shook his head. 'Not *papà*...*daddy*. I want you to be a *daddy*.'

A telltale sheen covered Romeo's eyes and he blinked rapidly before he nodded. '*Va bene*, I will be a daddy.'

Lucca launched himself off her lap and threw his arms around his father. Romeo's strong arms gathered the chubby body to him, his eyes closing on a depth of feeling that made Maisie's eyes fill with helpless tears. Father and son stayed locked for an eternity. Or as much as a toddler could stand until impatience set in.

When he was lowered to his feet, Lucca stared up at his father. 'Can I tell Emily?'

Romeo nodded. 'You can tell whomever you wish.'

Lucca started to race out of the door but then stopped suddenly. 'I wished very, very hard for a daddy,' he said solemnly. 'And it came true!'

Romeo looked stricken for several long seconds. Then he shook his head, as if denying whatever thought had crossed his mind. 'I'm glad for you, *bel bambino*.'

After watching Lucca run off, Romeo turned to her and pulled her to her feet. Seeing her tears, he gently wiped them away and planted a soft kiss on her lips. '*Grazie, il mio dolce.*'

Swallowing the lump in her throat, she smiled. 'I told you it'd be a piece of cake,' she said.

His blinding answering smile lit her up from the inside,

starting a shaky weakness that made her lower her gaze in case he read the depth of emotions moving through her. 'Perhaps I should listen to you more,' he suggested with a quirked brow.

'Perhaps I should get that in writing,' she answered.

He was still chuckling when they trailed their son. The announcement turned into an impromptu celebration with pancakes and juice, after which they got down to the urgent business of planning Lucca's heavily duck-pond-themed birthday party.

Finding out that the Giordano family would be joining them on the island in two days, along with the guests staying at the villas, and that Romeo was expected to host a dinner party, Maisie felt a rush of panic.

The only party she'd thrown so far had involved a cake, sandwiches and screaming kids in a playgroup's ball pit.

She was nowhere near sophisticated enough to handle a houseful of billionaires. She tried to pin a smile on her face as Romeo's eyes narrowed at her from across the kitchen island.

'What's wrong?' he asked as soon as they were alone.

'Nothing…' she started to say, then blurted, 'I've never thrown a dinner party before. Or a birthday party for a billionaire's son for that matter.'

He frowned. 'He's still the son you raised from birth. As for the party, everything's taken care of. I have caterers flying in from Honolulu to assist the chefs who cater for the island guests.'

Somehow her anxiety only escalated. 'Oh, so you don't really need me at all, do you?'

His frown deepened. 'Of course I need you. What's this really about?'

On some level, Maisie knew she was reacting to a deeper anxiety, one that stemmed from the knowledge that Romeo's life was so smoothly coordinated, aside from her role in his bed, he didn't need her for much else. Even Lucca would be extremely well taken care of by Emily and Mahina, should Maisie suddenly find herself rubbed out of the picture.

'Maisie?' he growled warningly.

She shrugged. 'I guess I'm feeling a little surplus to requirements.' Not to mention suddenly aware of her precarious position of temporary wife. 'I barely do anything for Lucca any more besides eat breakfast and sometimes lunch with him. Other times, he'd rather play with Emily or hang out with you.'

He took her by the arms. 'You've had him to yourself for almost four years. It's understandable the small separation on occasion would feel strange. And that separation was probably more pronounced because you were avoiding *me*,' he pointed out. 'But if you want me to prove that you're not surplus to requirements, just say the word, and I'll oblige you.'

She looked into eyes darkening into burnished gold and a blaze sparked through her. But alongside it rose a wave of desolation. Sex with Romeo was out of this world. Each experience felt as if she were touching the stars. But it was *just sex* for him. It would never be anything more.

So when he gathered her close and kissed her, she responded with a lingering taste of sadness that made tears brim behind her closed eyes.

His phone rang just when she thought the tears would spill and betray her, and she breathed a sigh of relief. He pulled it from his pocket and checked the screen. Frowning, he looked at her. 'Sorry, it's Zaccheo. I have to take it.'

Waving him away, she hurriedly escaped the sunlit living room. Her first thought was to find Lucca. She found him in the playroom and pulled him into a close embrace. When he demanded she read his favourite story, she obliged.

She was on the fifth read when Romeo entered the room.

She jerked upright at the volcanic fury on his face. 'What's wrong?'

'Zaccheo and Eva are arriving tomorrow.'

A day earlier than planned. 'Why?'

'Because they've been pulled into this insane situation in Palermo. It's time to end this before it gets out of hand.'

CHAPTER TWELVE

HER FIRST IMPRESSION of Zaccheo Giordano drove home the understanding of why the two powerful men were friends.

He carried himself with the same ruthless energy as Romeo, albeit with a little less brooding intensity. That energy was exhibited clearly when he stepped from the buggy and clasped Romeo's hand in an unsmiling, yet moving greeting.

His intensity lessened dramatically when he helped his heavily pregnant wife up the short steps into the wide villa entranceway.

Eva Giordano was gorgeous in a pocket-Venus, burst-of-energy way that drew interested eyes to her wild tumble of blonde hair and sharply contrasting dark eyebrows and darkly ringed green eyes.

Despite the strong evidence of love between them, Maisie sensed a tension between her and Zaccheo, which was explained once introductions had been made and Romeo was hugging Eva.

'I'm sorry we had to descend on you prematurely, but it was either *we all* came here or *we all* went to Palermo.' She cast an irritated look at her husband. 'The vote was eventually unanimous that we come here, since I refused to be left behind while Caveman over here went off to tackle Carmelo and Lorenzo on his own.'

Zaccheo muttered under his breath about intransigent women and helped corral his twin sons when they escaped their nanny and started fighting over who was better suited to drive the buggy.

Eva turned from greeting Romeo and her gaze fell on

Lucca. 'Oh, hello there, beautiful boy.' Her wide smile seemed to enchant her husband, who lost his growly look and came to stand beside her, one hand gently caressing her swollen belly.

The look of pure, blazing love that passed between them caused Maisie's heart to drop in misery into her belly. But she managed a smile and coaxed a shy Lucca from behind her. Within minutes he and the Giordano boys were exploring the new toy room Romeo had installed for him.

Mahina served drinks on the terrace and the tension mounted again the moment she left.

'What exactly did Carmelo want from you?' Romeo asked tersely, once Zaccheo had apprised them of the threat from Palermo's other crime lord.

'His ridiculous demands are the same as Lorenzo's to you. They're both terrified one would attain more power than the other. But he had the nerve to threaten my family. I cannot allow that to stand.'

Eva rolled her eyes. 'You realise how much like a bad gangster movie actor you sound?' When his eyes narrowed, she continued, completely unfazed. 'You have a veritable army guarding me and the boys when you're not around, and Carmelo's claims of you owing him allegiance because your father was a one-time lieutenant of his before he switched sides to Romeo's father is flimsy at best. How do we even know that's true?' She looked at Romeo. 'Besides, I know you two have enough dirt on the man to send him to jail for a long time.'

Romeo shook his head. 'I've talked to the lawyers about it. It's all circumstantial without hard evidence. I only witnessed Zaccheo's father being beaten.' He sent his friend a look of grim-faced sympathy, to which Zaccheo nodded. 'He was still alive when I was thrown out of Fattore's mansion. We need irrefutable evidence of blood on Lorenzo's hands.'

'So, what's the alternative?' Eva exclaimed. 'A duel at dawn beneath Mount Etna?'

Romeo's jaw clenched but he didn't refute Eva's outlandish claim. Maisie's stomach hollowed out, both at the news Romeo had just delivered and his intent expression.

'You're not thinking of going back to Palermo, are you?' she demanded in a shocked whisper.

His eyes when they met hers were hard, implacable, with no trace of the gentleness they'd held yesterday before Zaccheo's phone call. 'It's the only option. I won't entertain the idea of my son living in fear.'

Zaccheo nodded in grim agreement and captured his wife's hand when she began to protest.

Maisie struggled not to feel excluded and even more miserable as Romeo proceeded to converse to the couple, switching to Italian when the debate got heated.

Once or twice, she spotted Eva's probing glance and fixed a smile on her face, answering her questions about the island and the villa when she switched back to English.

When Eva yawned loudly and started to droop, Zaccheo stood and ushered her inside.

Knowing she wouldn't be able to sit and make small talk while her insides were shredding with the knowledge that Romeo had room in his heart only for his son, and not her, she jumped to her feet.

'I'll go see if the boys are okay.'

He caught her hand and stopped her. 'You're upset because I intend to confront Lorenzo?'

'Does my opinion matter enough for you to change your mind? I thought you were pursuing a different route other than direct confrontation.'

His jaw flexed. 'I suspected his mellowed stance was all a bluff. Just as I suspect, this is nothing more than an extortion scheme, probably concocted between him and Carmelo. The timing is a little too synchronised. Whatever it is, I need to end it once and for all.'

She tried to pull away but he held on. 'Since your mind's made up, there's no need for my opinion, is there?'

'*Gattina*—'

'Don't call me that.' The blurted plea rushed out before she could stop it.

He gave a hiss of frustration. 'You suddenly have a problem with the name?'

'No, only your use of it when you're trying to put me back in your little box marked *Handled*.'

His mouth twisted. 'Even if such a box existed, the physical and psychological scratch marks you leave on me would point to an abject failure in my task.'

She tugged at her hand again until he freed her. 'And you'll continue to fail. Because I won't be put in a box and labelled as to what I need to be. Never again.'

A new tension stilled his body. 'You think that's what I've been doing to you?'

'What have you been doing, if not knocking down my every objection in a bid to get your way since you found out about Lucca?' she threw back.

'He's my son. There was never a doubt that I would claim him. You knew that. Did you think I wouldn't do everything in my power to give him everything that had been denied me?' he demanded.

'No, but what sort of mother would I have been if I'd wilfully turned my back on the one thing you led me to believe would save our son.'

His nostrils flared. 'You believe that's no longer true?'

'I went along with this marriage because it would protect us while you found a *business* solution to this problem. Now you tell me you're planning some sort of vendetta-settling and I'm left asking myself whether this marriage was worth the aggravation I put myself through in the first place if the outcome is going to be a different one! Would I not have been better off in Ranelagh, alone with my son while you carelessly diced with death?'

A searing wave of shock washed over his face before his eyes, mouth and jaw hardened in a look of pure bitterness.

'So you regret this marriage?' he demanded in a low, icy voice.

'Tell me the truth, Romeo. Was marrying me really necessary?'

His jaw clenched for a long time before he bit out, 'Yes.'

'To save Lucca from Lorenzo or to give him your name?'

Her heart threatened to beat itself out of existence, and her limbs felt frozen and useless as she stared at him.

'At the time, the two weren't mutually exclusive.'

'So you didn't exaggerate one to get the other?'

He jerked upright and strode to the edge of the terrace, his movements erratic. For several minutes he said nothing, and slowly his balled fists loosened.

Then he turned. 'You're right. I should've thought this through a little longer, given myself better options.'

Maisie's agonised gasp was barely audible, but it seemed to open a new set of floodgates, bringing fresh waves of pain. She knew she was a fool then for expecting him to tell her their marriage wasn't a mistake. That it was more than just a means to ensure Lucca's safety. That however it'd started out, it was worth holding on to, worth salvaging.

Hearing his words brought home to her just how foolish she'd been to hope. Just like five years ago, Romeo had made a mistake with her. One he regretted. Only this time, he'd told her so to her face rather than let his absence speak for him.

Footsteps preceded Zaccheo's reappearance on the terrace and brought a jagged but final end to the conversation. Catching the other man's narrow-eyed, assessing glance, she pinned a smile on her face. 'I'm going to check on the boys.'

She stumbled blindly indoors, operating on automatic rather than with any sense of purpose, as she headed for the toy room. Reaching the doorway, she saw that Emily and the Giordano nanny had readied the boys for bed.

Forcing her feet to move, she went to her son and brushed her fingers over his hair. He looked up for a moment, his deep hazel eyes connecting with hers in a wide, loving look before he was distracted by one of his new best friends.

Feeling lost, cast adrift in a merciless ocean, Maisie wandered back out, trying hard not to buckle under the realisation that she'd sped up her exit from Romeo's life with that last tirade. Because surely telling the man who'd married you for the sake of his son that you'd rather not be married to him was a request to be freed the moment the necessity became obsolete?

Pain ripped through her heart as she entered her bedroom. How could it look so bleak and lonely after just a few short nights spent away from it? How could her heart shred so badly at the thought that she wouldn't spend another night in Romeo's bed?

A broken moan, much like a manifestation of grief, poured out of her throat as she sank onto the side of her bed.

Her shame at the knowledge that she would shed her dignity for another night in Romeo's bed bit deep as she lay back and sobbed into her pillow. She would go back on her word, on the promise she'd made after distancing herself from her parents' continued disapproval never to contort herself into another's expectations of her. She would put herself in a box labelled *desperate and willing to beg for Romeo's love* if she had the faintest glimpse that he returned a sliver of what she felt for him.

The sickening feeling of how far she would go triggered harder sobs, until her head throbbed and her body was wrung out. Still the pain came, washing over her in waves as the sun slid low and she knew she had to get up and dress for dinner.

Over and over as she showered, she saw his face, felt his silence like a final, doomed slash across her heart and wondered how she would face him across the dinner table. For a moment she wished for the man who had brushed her feelings aside and taken control. But she shook her head.

They'd gone past that this afternoon. There was no hiding from the glaring knowledge that Romeo didn't love her and never would. That his only interest was for his son.

Her only choice was to muddle through the next few days, and leave the island when Romeo did. If he was intent on having his son guarded by a security detail, he could do so in Ranelagh. She wouldn't be able to bear staying here, cocooned in a fool's paradise. She would confront reality head-on, put one foot in front of the other until she learned to live with the pain.

Shutting off the shower, she dressed in an ensemble appropriate for entertainment, applied enough make-up to disguise the puffiness under her eyes and left her room.

She encountered Eva emerging from her own suite and pinned a smile on her face.

'Oh, good, were you going to check on Lucca? We can share story time and be done in half the time,' Eva said with an engaging grin.

They entered the large guest suite where the children had been relocated after Lucca refused to be parted from his new friends and took turns reading until all three fell asleep.

In the living room, they found the men sipping whiskies. Romeo crossed to the drinks cabinet and returned with a mineral water for Eva and a glass of champagne for her, which he handed over with a rigidly blank look on his face.

Her breath caught painfully and she looked away as Eva smiled and patted the bump covered by her stunning jade-green gown. 'Sorry I conked out on you earlier. These two kept me up during the flight with their incessant kicking.'

Maisie's eyes widened. 'You're having another set of twins?'

Eva grinned. 'Turns out twins run in both our families. My great-grandmother was a twin, and Zaccheo's mother told him his grandfather was a twin, too. Something to be thankful for, since he's determined to not stop knocking me up until he has a full football team. That means I get to do this *only* half a dozen times.'

Zaccheo broke off his muffled conversation with Romeo and strolled over to his wife. 'You know you love carrying my children, *dolcezza*.'

'Yeah, keep telling yourself that, champ. After these two I'm taking an extended leave of absence from getting pregnant.'

Zaccheo lifted a brow. 'As long as it's merely a leave and not a resignation.'

Eva rolled her eyes but curled into his side when he sat down next to her.

The conversation turned to children. Romeo maintained brooding silence throughout, and only offered brusque opinions when Eva forced him into the conversation. Zaccheo seemed perfectly at ease with Romeo's mood, but Maisie couldn't help her breath catching whenever Romeo slid her an icy glance.

The tense atmosphere continued through dinner, the men chatting about business and Eva attempting to engage Maisie in general conversation. She couldn't remember because she was concentrating on keeping the sob at the back of her throat whenever she looked at Romeo.

And how pathetic was that? To know she'd been nothing more than a plaything in his bed while he got to know his son, and yet still feel as if her world were caving in on itself every time she remembered that in a handful of days she would walk away from him for ever.

'Oh, for goodness' sake. Can we sort this thing out once and for all? Can't you see how distressed this is all making Maisie?'

Her head jerked up at Eva's sharp retort to find the other woman glaring at her husband.

Zaccheo turned to her with one brow tilted. 'Don't get yourself worked up, *dolcezza*. Everything's under control.'

Eva snorted. 'God, you men can be so blind at times! Can't you see we're tearing ourselves apart here? Tell them, Maisie.'

Both sets of male eyes turned towards her, one grimly amused and the other as icily brooding as they'd been all evening.

Painfully pulling her gaze from Romeo's, she pursed her lips. 'Sorry, it seems I no longer have a vote.' Not that she ever did. Or ever would.

Eva sighed heavily and pulled her fingers through her wild, curly blonde hair. 'What do we have to do to get through to you two?' she demanded, exasperated.

'Eva, *mia*, I won't have you this distressed,' Zaccheo all but growled.

'Then stop this stupid cavemen course of action.' She threw her napkin down, winced when her babies also made their thoughts known about the effect her distress was having on them. Zaccheo started to rise, but she waved him away. 'I'm fine. I think Maisie and I will go for a walk, leave you two to ponder the wisdom of your ideas.'

The excuse to be out of Romeo's oppressive presence was too great to turn down. Rising, she took the arm Eva held out after kicking off her shoes. Following her, Maisie kicked off her shoes, too, and they headed outside.

'I hear there's a stunning waterfall here somewhere. I'd love to see it.'

Maisie stumbled to a halt. 'Um…do you mind if we don't?' she pleaded raggedly, unable to bear the thought of returning to where she and Romeo had made love. She knew she'd given herself away when Eva's eyes widened.

'Of course,' she murmured softly. 'We'll go down to the beach instead.'

They walked in silence for a while, taking in the lush vegetation gleaming under strung-out lights, and the view of a night-lit Maui in the distance, before Eva glanced at her. 'You'll have to take the bull by the horns at some point, you know. Men are obtusely blind sometimes—even the cleverest, billion-dollar-empire-commanding ones can fail to see what's right in front of their faces.'

Maisie shook her head. 'It's not like that between Romeo and me,' she painfully explained.

'Maybe not, but the pain you are feeling right now, I've been there. It took weeks before I came to my senses, and I didn't have a toddler to contend with during that time. You and Romeo—there's something there.' She stopped Maisie when she opened her mouth to deny it. 'You had his child four years ago, and he married you within two days of seeing you again.'

'Because of Lucca.'

Eva pursed her lips. 'I married Zaccheo because I thought I didn't have a choice. But deep down, I knew I did. Things happen for a reason, but it's the endgame that matters. Fighting for what you want even when you think everything's hopeless.'

'I don't *think* it's hopeless. I know it is,' she stressed.

Eva looked as if she wanted to argue the point, but her lashes swept over her lovely green eyes and she nodded. 'Okay. I'm sorry for prying. I'll let the matter drop, except to say I've never seen Romeo like this before. Sure, he has that sexy brooding thing going on most of the time, but never like this, not even five years ago, when his mo—' She stopped, visibly pursing her lips to prevent her indiscretion.

Maisie's chest tightened. 'Something bad happened to bring him to Palermo then, didn't it?' It went to show how much she didn't know about Romeo.

'I can only say a bad chapter of his life came to an end. But he wasn't as affected as he is now.'

Maisie shook her head. 'This is all about Lucca,' she insisted as they reached the beach.

Eva nodded, a sage smile curving her lips, before she pulled up the skirt to her elegant gown. 'Okay. Now I'm probably going to ruin my dress, but since my husband refuses to allow me to swim in the ocean until our sons are born, but he happens to be annoying me a lot right now, I'm damn well going for a quick dip.'

Maisie gave a smile that barely lifted the corners of her mouth. 'You know he can see you from the villa, right?'

Eva gave a stubborn, cheeky smile. 'I'll be out before he gets here.'

Maisie didn't think it was wise to stand in her way. The waters weren't especially deep for half a mile or so, but she kept an eye on her, trying not to think about what Eva had said.

Because it wasn't a subject worth pursuing. Romeo had made himself more than clear. And if he'd looked shocked, it was because he probably hadn't thought she would confront him about it.

After a few minutes, tired of the agony replaying through her soul, Maisie adjusted her clothing and waded into the warm, inviting water.

CHAPTER THIRTEEN

ROMEO DIDN'T LOOK UP from the fireplace when his friend joined him, but he accepted the glass containing a double shot of whisky Zaccheo held out to him.

'Tell me your wife drives you half as crazy as mine does me,' Zaccheo growled.

Romeo downed half the glass's content and stared into the remaining amber liquid. 'She's not my wife,' he growled.

'That ring on your finger and the misery on your face tell a different story, *mio fratello*,' Zaccheo challenged with a grim chuckle.

Romeo's chest squeezed at the term. Although he'd only connected with Zaccheo for a brief month when they were children, he'd never forgotten the boy whose life had touched his. Rediscovering that bond of brotherhood as an adult had made Romeo believe he wasn't truly alone in this world. But lately, he'd discovered there were various forms of loneliness.

A loneliness of the heart, for instance…

Zaccheo's hand of friendship might have conquered a small part of his soul, but he was finding out, much to his emerging horror, that it would never be enough. Not like what he'd been secretly hoping for a few weeks.

'The ring is meaningless. She doesn't want to be married to me,' he snapped and downed the rest of the drink. A replacement arrived seconds later, and he took it, his fingers tightening around the cold glass. The platinum-and-gold wedding ring in question caught the light, winking mockingly, and a deep urge to smash the glass moved through him.

Before he could give in to it, Zaccheo replied, 'Before you tear the place to pieces, perhaps you should listen to what your woman has to say.'

'She's already said her piece. And I heard her loud and clear.' Although he wished he hadn't. He wished he hadn't stopped her on the terrace in the first place, that he'd postponed the moment of complete rejection for a while longer.

Why? So he could continue to live in this fool's paradise?

'I've learned to my cost that there's a difference between listening and hearing.'

Romeo's mouth twisted. 'You sound like a damn agony-aunt talk-show host. A very bad one.'

'Mock all you want. You'll learn the difference soon enough.'

Used to Zaccheo providing solid, formidable opinions when needed, Romeo wondered whether his friend was going soft in the head. A glance at him as he strolled to the window to look down at the beach where his wife and Maisie had headed proved otherwise. The ruthless man was behind those strong features.

Zaccheo turned towards him. 'What are we going to do about Palermo? We need to resolve it soon before my wife decides she doesn't want to be married to me any more, either.' The mocking tone belied the brutal intent in his face.

Romeo shook his head. 'Fattore's absurd demands started all of this. Eva's right. You need to be with her and the boys in New York. I'll handle Lorenzo and Carmelo.'

The old man was what had set all this in motion. And while he was grateful for having his son in his life, he couldn't let the nuisance carry on any longer.

The need to teach Fattore's ex-lieutenant a salutary lesson charged through him and he rolled his tense shoulders. 'I should've gone with my instincts and cut Lorenzo off at the knees much sooner, instead of entertaining his foolishness.'

'You needed time to find out what he was capable of.'

'And now I have.'

His phone buzzed and he looked at the screen. Speak of the devil.

'Lorenzo.' His blood boiled as he put his phone on speaker. 'You've saved me the trouble of a phone call.'

'*Bene.* You have good news for me, I hope.'

'I don't deal in hope, old man. Never have,' Romeo snarled.

Zaccheo gave a grim smile and sipped his whisky.

'Whether you like it or not, you have blood ties to this family. Your father left it to you. You can't just turn your back on it.'

Romeo exhaled through the need to punch something. He managed to suppress his rage and frustration and glanced at Zaccheo.

The man he considered his only friend also wore an expression of quiet rage. Romeo knew Zaccheo had learned a thing or two about seeking retribution from his wrongful imprisonment several years ago. Just as he knew the threat against his sons would need to be answered.

But he also knew getting dragged into a Mafia war wasn't what either of them wanted. What he wanted was to be done with this in a single, definitive way.

He hardened his voice so there would be no mistaking his intent.

'You've insisted on shoving my parentage down my throat every chance you got to suit your needs. Well, you got your wish. I'll be in Palermo in seventy-two hours. I promise, you won't like the news I deliver.'

He ended the call and threw the phone on the sofa. About to down his drink, he noticed Zaccheo's rising tension as he stared at the beach far below. In a split second, his friend's disbelieving expression turned into bewilderment. '*Madre di Dio*, is that…? Are they…?'

Romeo followed his gaze, and horror swept through him. 'Yes, they're swimming in the ocean,' he supplied grimly.

And Maisie was further out, almost at the point where the ocean floor dipped dangerously.

'*Porca miseria*, only my wife would decide to swim in the Pacific Ocean fully clothed and at five months pregnant with twins.' He sprinted towards the door with Romeo fast on his heels.

They reached the beach in minutes, with Zaccheo a few feet ahead of him, just as Eva waded ashore. Romeo didn't have to guess that she was exhausted, despite the sheer exhilaration on her face.

Exhilaration that turned into wary apprehension when she spotted her husband's thunderous look. She put out her hands. 'Zaccheo—'

'Not a single word, *dolcezza*, if you know what's good for you,' he sliced at her, before scooping her into his arms and striding off the beach.

Romeo rushed past them, toeing off his socks and shoes. He'd discarded his jacket and shirt as they raced from the villa. He dived into the water, striking out for the lone figure a quarter of a mile away.

He reached Maisie in minutes. And she had the audacity to look at him with a puzzled expression.

'What are you doing out here? Is Eva all right?' she asked.

'What the hell do you think you're doing?' he snapped.

'I thought it was obvious.' She searched the beach, her face turning anxious. 'Is—'

'*Sì*, Eva is fine,' he reassured impatiently. 'Although I've no idea what she was thinking, going for a swim in her condition.'

'She's a strong swimmer, and I was right beside her until she decided to head back. Then I made sure I kept an eye on her.'

'From here, close to where the currents swirl dangerously?' he accused. He couldn't see below the water, but he could see the neckline of her gown and knew how long her dress was, and how hopelessly inept she would've been at saving herself had she been caught in a rip current.

Her mouth twisted as she treaded water. 'Did I not mention I was regional champion swimmer? It was one of the many *almost* talents my parents tried and failed to turn me into. Sadly, I never made it to nationals. One of my many, *many* failures, I guess.' The bitterness in her voice caught him in the raw, threatened to rip open a place he didn't want touched. Especially not since her declaration this afternoon.

'So you thought you'd add one more tick to this imaginary quota by wearing a dress that adds at least twenty pounds to your body weight when it's soaking wet?' he snarled, all the alien feelings that had been bubbling through him since their conversation on the terrace this afternoon rising to the edge.

She looked away from him, and he could've sworn she blushed before her face tightened with deep unhappiness. 'Not exactly.'

He caught hold of her shoulders and pointed her towards the beach. 'Swim back now.'

Her chin rose mutinously. 'Or what?'

Despite the dark emotions swirling through him...the searing agony of knowing that ultimately this woman didn't want him, the knife-edge of arousal lanced him at the fire in her eyes. 'You swim back under your own steam or I drag you back. Those are the only two choices available to you.'

'Romeo—'

'Now,' he interrupted her, unable to believe how like heaven and how very much like hell it felt to hear his name on her lips. 'You may be in a hurry to end this marriage, but it won't be through you carelessly drowning yourself.'

Her mouth dropped open in stunned shock, and he wanted to believe tears filled her eyes, but she turned abruptly and struck out towards shore before he could be certain, her strokes surprisingly swift and strong considering what she wore. He waited until she was a few dozen feet away before he followed.

She was wading waist deep by the time he passed her a few metres from shore. Heading for the cabana where fresh supplies of towels were stocked, he grabbed two and stalked back.

'You had no right to say that to me!'

Romeo looked up and stopped dead. 'What the hell are you wearing? Where's the rest of your dress? And I had no right to say what?' he tagged on abstractedly, unable to tear his eyes away from her body.

'To say that I'd deliberately drown myself.'

'I didn't say you'd do it deliberately, but I didn't think you'd be that careless, either. Although from the look of you, I was wrong in my assumption.'

The bottom part of her dress was missing, leaving her clad in a scrap of wet white lace that brought a growl straining from his chest. And with the top part wet and plastered to her skin, Romeo wondered how long he would last on his own two feet before the strength of need pounding through him buckled his knees.

Under the lights strung out between the palm trees, he watched heat crawl up her face. Although it was a fraction of the fire lighting through his veins. 'Care to tell me what happened to the rest of your dress?' he asked, his voice thick and alien to his own ears.

She waved at the sand near the steps. 'The skirt's over there. The top and bottom are joined by a zip,' she supplied. 'See, I wasn't as stupid as you imagined,' she added bitterly. 'Nor did I plan on risking drowning, either accidentally or deliberately. Amongst other things, I love my son too much to do that.'

Romeo wanted to ask what those other things were, whether it could include him, but for the first time in his life he stepped back from the need to know, his mind clasping on the fact that she hadn't corrected him on the need to end their marriage. Weariness moved through him, parts of him he didn't want to acknowledge feeling brutalised, as if he'd gone ten rounds with an unseen opponent and emerged the loser.

'Are you going to stand there all night or will you hand me one of those towels?' she asked in a low, tense voice.

He started to hand it to her, then stopped. Moving closer, he stared into her eyes, darker now with whatever emotions swirled through her. 'You're not a failure.'

'What?' she croaked, her face raised to his.

'In the water, you said you'd failed at many things.'

'Oh.' Her eyes darkened further and tears brimmed her eyes. 'I have. I failed to get my parents to love me, for instance.'

Her naked pain slashed him hard, despite thinking he'd steeled himself adequately against further unsettling emotion. 'That is *their* fault, not yours. I've learned the hard way that, with the best will in the world, you can't get someone to love you if they're incapable of it.'

Her eyes widened, questions swimming in her eyes. Questions he felt too raw to answer right then. He shook his head and briskly rubbed the towel in her hair. 'You're a huge success at the things you're passionate about.'

Her eyelids swept down, hiding her expression from him. Her laugh was hollow as she tried to take the towel from him. 'I wish I could agree, but sadly the evidence states otherwise. For one thing, you insist on calling what we have a marriage, but has it really been? Or have I just been the body to warm your bed while you burrow your way into your son's life? The woman you didn't trust enough to let her know how much legitimising your son means to you.'

His arms dropped. 'Maisie—'

'Don't, Romeo. I don't want to hear your slick excuses. The moment you found out about Lucca, you wanted him, regardless of who stood in your way. You scooped me up for the ride because that was the easiest option for you.'

He stepped behind her, and his gaze was dragged helplessly over her body, down the enticing line of her spine to
the twin dimples at the top of her buttocks, and the alluring globes below, perfectly framed by the wet lace caressing her skin.

'Easy? You think any of this has been easy?' He shook
his head in self-disgust. 'I'm stumbling round in the dark,
pretending I've got my head screwed on straight when the
reality is that I'm terrified I'll irrevocably mess up a four-
year-old boy's life. And, believe me, I'm perfectly equipped
to do it. Whereas you know the answer to every question
he asks. You know what he wants before he does. So yes, I
exploited your devotion to him to help me get to know my
flesh and blood. Condemn me for that, but believe me, *none*
of this has been easy for me,' he rasped.

Her head fell forward with a defeated sigh. He told himself to remember that she intended to walk away, take away
the only thing resembling a true family he'd ever known.
She was the reason he couldn't take a full breath without
wondering if his organs were functioning properly. Somehow, she'd taught him to hope again, to dare to dream. And
she'd smashed that dream with a handful of words.

Romeo *tried* to remember that.

But he couldn't help it. He lowered his head and brushed
his lips against the top of her spine, where the wet hair had
parted to reveal her creamy skin.

She made a sound, part arousal, part wary animal, but
he was too far gone to heed the latter. The thought of her
leaving, of never being able to do this again, scattered his
thoughts to a million pieces, until only one thing mattered.

Here and now.

'Maisie.' He heard the rough plea in his voice. He
dropped the towel and trailed his mouth over her shoulders, down her back, anxiety hurrying his movements. She
shuddered under his touch.

'Romeo, please…'

He dropped to his knees and spun her around. '*Tesoro mio*, don't deny me this. Don't deny *us* this.' He wanted to say more, bare himself with words that were locked deep, but it was as if the language he needed to express himself was suddenly alien to him. But he could show her. He *would* show her.

He held her hips and kissed her soft belly, where his son had nestled, warm and loved. She gave a soft moan. Empowered, he deepened the caress, his tongue tasting her intoxicating skin. When she swayed and her hands clutched his shoulders, he groaned.

Roughly pulling her panties to one side, he fastened his mouth to her sex, caressing her with his tongue as he lapped at her.

'Romeo!'

He drowned beneath the heady sensation, of his wildcat digging her fingers into his skin. He dared to entertain the thought that there might be a way through this landmine that threatened to destabilise his world. He went harder, desperate to bring her pleasure, unashamed to hope it brought him something *more*, something lasting.

She gave another cry and shattered in his arms, her head dropping forward as she shuddered. Rising, he caught her in his arms, saw the dazed but almost resigned look in her eyes, and his stomach hollowed.

Ignoring the look, he carried her to the steps and helped her with the skirt. Then, covering her top half with the towel, he swung her into his arms and headed for the villa.

'I can walk, Romeo,' she said in a small, tight voice.

'I believe I'm living up to my caveman reputation.'

'You're performing to the wrong audience. You don't need to prove anything to me.'

He glanced down at her tear-stained face and his chest tightened. 'Do I not?'

She shook her head, but her eyes refused to meet his. 'I think we understand each other perfectly.'

He wanted to rail at her that he didn't understand; that he'd thought their moment at the waterfall, *before* they'd made love, had started something they could build on. Her mutinous expression stopped him.

Besides, he was beginning to think they communicated much better using a different language.

Entering the villa, he headed for the stairs and his bedroom. The moment she raised her head and looked around, she scrambled from his arms.

Romeo set her down and shut the door.

'Why have you brought me here?' she demanded.

The accusation in her eyes ripped through him but he forced himself not to react to it. Reaching for the towel, he tugged it from her, then he pulled her close.

'Answer me, Romeo…'

'Shh, *gattina*, just let this be.' Another rough plea he was unashamed of, even though it threw him back to another time, another place, pleading in a much younger but equally desperate voice.

It was the night his mother had packed his meagre belongings in a tattered bag and told him she was sending him to his thug of a father.

Disturbed by the memories that seemed intent on flooding in, he sealed his mouth to Maisie's, searching for her unique balm that soothed his soul.

His heart leapt when she didn't push him away, but then she wasn't responding, either. Groaning in frustration, he pushed his fingers into her hair, desperate to stem the alarm rising through him that he was fighting a losing battle.

Eventually, she tore her mouth away. 'Please stop. I don't want this.'

He raised his head, the landmine seeming to spread like an ocean before him. 'This?' he intoned starkly.

Her eyes slid past his, to a point beyond his shoulder. 'You. I don't want you.'

Acrid bitterness filled him, along with the sharp barbs

of memory, but still he pushed. 'That's a lie. I proved it once, I can prove it again and as many times as you need to face the truth.'

She shook her head wearily. 'That was just the sex talking. Nothing more.'

'So you mean you don't want me, the man?' Why did that feel so damn agonising to say?

Her gaze remained averted for another minute before meeting his eyes. 'You're an amazing father, and I'm sure you'll offer Lucca support and opportunities in life I can only dream of. But I can't stay with you. After our guests leave, I'm returning to Ireland with Lucca. I'm sorry, but this…this was a mistake.'

She started to take her rings off. He lunged for her hands, stopped the action before he fully realised he'd moved. 'You will not take off your ring!' The snarled command stemmed from deep within his soul.

Her blue eyes reflected pain, enough to hammer home just how much being here, being with him, was costing her. How could he not have seen that? How could he have entertained the idea that they could attempt a proper marriage?

'I can't…'

'I know my opinion matters very little to you, but think of our son. It's his birthday tomorrow. Are you this determined to throw a shadow over the occasion?'

Her face lost a trace of colour. 'Of course not.'

'Then wait. For his sake.'

Her head dipped and she pushed the rings slowly back on her finger. He forced himself to drop her hands, move away.

'I'll see you in the morning,' she murmured.

He didn't respond. He was struggling to find even the simplest explanation of what was going on inside him. He heard the door shut and paced to the window. In the reflection behind him, he saw the bed they'd risen from this morning and wondered at how much he hated the idea of sleeping in it now.

Undressing, he entered the shower and let the water beat over his head. It wouldn't drown out her words, her face.

I can't stay with you.

His bitter laughter rose above the pounding cascade.

At least those words had been less harsh than the ones his mother had thrown at him before she'd left him on Agostino Fattore's doorstep.

At least this time he wouldn't starve. Or live rough.

And yet he found himself bypassing the bed when he left the bathroom, and collapsing onto the sofa in his private living room. And when he was still awake when the orange streaked the horizon, he'd almost convinced himself the pain ripping through him wasn't worse than it'd been when he was a child.

The performance Maisie gave the next day was award-worthy. At some point while she was smiling and taking pictures of her son at what had been dubbed *The Best Birthday Party Ever*, she half hysterically toyed with contacting her parents and telling them they should've tried enrolling her into acting school.

Because she was able to stand next to Romeo as he helped an ecstatic Lucca cut the ribbon that officially unveiled his duck pond. Then look into his eyes and smile as they helped their son release the fifty balloons tied to the sturdy bridge in the middle of the pond. She even managed a laugh as two necking swans were immediately named Maisie and Romeo. She didn't crumble into a pain-ravaged heap when Lucca insisted his father kiss his mother to celebrate the naming.

And she certainly aced the small talk with the grown-ups while the kids took turns at the duck-feed dispenser.

Once the birthday-cake candles had been blown, the cake devoured, the children tucked in bed, she retired to her suite, showered and got ready for the dinner party.

She stood by Romeo's side as they greeted the two couples Romeo had trusted to remain on the island. Then calling on her skills as a restaurant owner, she supervised the caterers, made sure each guest was looked after, while avoiding being too close to Romeo for longer than a few minutes.

Luckily, Eva, and the phenomenon of carrying a second set of twins, quickly became the centre of attention and, seeming to have made up with her husband, engaged everyone with her effervescent personality.

As soon as the last guest left, Maisie headed for the door.

Romeo blocked her path. She stopped, her heart pounding.

'Well done on the dinner party,' he muttered.

She tried to avert her gaze, to stop absorbing every expression and contour of his face. But she couldn't look away.

'Thank you,' she replied.

He stared at her for another long moment, then he stepped away. 'Goodnight.'

She couldn't respond because her heart had lodged itself in her throat. Hurrying away, she gave in to the insane urge to glance over her shoulder. Romeo was watching her.

She tried to tell herself she didn't yearn for him to follow. By the time she got to her room and shut the door behind her, she knew she was lying to herself.

CHAPTER FOURTEEN

THEY LEFT THE ISLAND two days later, with a distraught Lucca heartbroken at having to leave his beloved ducks. Although he was slightly appeased at the thought of returning to his old pond at Ranelagh Gardens, Maisie knew there would be more tears when he found out his father wouldn't be staying.

The thought troubled her as she played with Lucca during the long flight. A couple of times, she'd attempted to start a conversation with Romeo about scheduling visits, but he'd given her a stony look and a crisp, 'We'll discuss it later,' after which he'd promptly returned to his endless phone calls.

That he was returning to Palermo had become clear during a particularly heated conversation.

Her heart flipped over hard at the thought of him returning to the place that had given him such a rough start in life.

He looked up then, and their eyes connected. For a moment, she thought she saw a flare of pain mingled with hope. But his expression hardened and his gaze veered away. This time, her heart bypassed the somersault stage and went straight for cracking right down the middle.

She was still trying to hold herself together when he took a break to eat and play with Lucca. He stopped by her armchair on the way back to where he'd set up his office and looked down at her.

'I have a team childproofing my London apartment and another scouting for a place in Dublin. Emily will be flying out to help take care of Lucca when he's with me. Is that acceptable to you?'

As she stared up at his grim face, her heart broke all over

again. Slowly, she nodded. 'I won't keep him away from you. I just need a reasonable heads-up when you're coming to see him, so I can arrange it with the playgroup.'

His mouth compressed and he nodded. '*Bene,* it will be done.' He walked away to the far side of the plane and didn't speak to her again until they landed.

As predicted, Lucca turned hysterical at the idea of his father leaving. Maisie watched, a stone lodged in her throat, as Romeo hugged him on the tarmac and reassured him that his absence wouldn't be a long one. After several minutes, Lucca calmed down and Romeo strode to where she stood.

He handed Lucca over, his hand lingering on his son before his jaw clenched. 'I'll be in touch in the next few days, a week at the most, to arrange a time to see him. And I'll call him tonight.'

'Um…sure.'

With another look at his son, Romeo turned and walked back into his plane.

Maisie stood frozen, her mind reeling at the thought that her marriage was ending right then and there, on a painfully bright summer's day in Dublin.

She clutched Lucca closer as he whimpered at his departing father. Romeo disappeared, and Lucca began to weep.

Forcing herself to move, she strapped him into his seat in the sleek car waiting for them, then buckled herself in next to him.

The sun was still shining when they pulled up outside her restaurant despite it being evening. Unable to face going in, she waved at a gawping Lacey and went straight up to her apartment. Her heart sank when a knock came at the door less than an hour later.

She opened it to Bronagh, who was trying hard to pretend she wasn't shocked to see her.

'I've just put Lucca down for the night. Do you want to come in for a cup of tea?' Maisie offered.

'Tea is great, but *you* look like you need something stron-

ger.' Bronagh held out a bottle of red wine, the concern she
was trying to hide finally breaking through.

By her third glass, Maisie had broken down and spilled
every last pathetically needy feeling.

'So...what are you going to do?' Bronagh asked when
Maisie stopped to toss back another fortifying gulp of wine.

Maisie looked up. 'Oh, please don't worry that I'm going
to take over again at the restaurant. To be honest, I could
do with the break.'

Bronagh shook her head. 'That wasn't what I meant.
What are you going to do about Romeo?'

Maisie frowned. 'What do you mean? It's over.'

'You really think so? From what you said he didn't *have*
to marry you. This is the twenty-first century and he's rich
enough to afford a dozen armies to protect you and Lucca
if he wanted to without putting a ring on your finger.' She
nodded to Maisie's hand. 'And you're still wearing your
wedding rings. Is he still wearing his?'

Maisie nodded abstractedly and frowned at the sparkling
rings. 'What are you saying?'

Bronagh shrugged. 'That things seem awfully *unresolved* for two people hell-bent on chucking in the towel
so quickly.'

'I'm not...I wasn't... He only wants sex.' She blushed
and drank some more wine.

'Of course he does. Sex is the easiest way to hide deeper
emotion, that's why it's called angry sex, rebound sex,
make-up sex...need I go on?'

Miserably, Maisie shook her head.

Bronagh laid a gentle hand on her arm. 'You haven't
known a lot of love in your life, but then neither has he.
One of you has to be brave enough to scratch beneath the
surface.'

'Why do I have to do the scratching?' Maisie blurted.
'Just because he thinks I'm a wildcat in bed doesn't mean...
God! I can't believe I just said that.'

Bronagh laughed and rose. 'I think the jet lag and wine are doing their job. Get some sleep. I'll take the monitor with me when I go downstairs in case Lucca wakes up.'

Maisie hugged her friend, her thoughts rioting as she prepared for bed. When she lay wide awake three hours later, she wasn't surprised.

Bronagh's words raced through her mind.

While she didn't think she'd misinterpreted her conversations with Romeo, was it possible she'd blinded herself to a different possibility?

Could she guide Romeo into loving her? He might have been devoid of love before he'd arrived on her doorstep three weeks ago, but Maisie had seen what he felt for his son. And Romeo hadn't rejected the love that poured from Lucca. Surely he couldn't rule it out of his life for ever?

Turning over, she exhaled slowly, careful not to let too much hope take root.

When Romeo arrived on Saturday, she would try to broach the subject, see if there was a glimmer of anything worth pursuing.

Except Romeo didn't come on Saturday. He sent Emily and a team of bodyguards after calling with his apologies. He'd established a routine with Lucca where they videocalled for half an hour in the morning and half an hour in the evening. His greetings to Maisie when she connected his calls were cool and courteous. Any attempt at a conversation was quickly curbed with a demand for his son.

By the time he cancelled on Saturday, she knew, once again, she'd been foolish to hope. Yet she couldn't bring herself to take off her wedding rings. Nor could she find the strength to tell Lucca that, no, Mummy and Daddy would never live together again.

Admitting to herself that she was burying her head in the sand didn't stop her from doing exactly that. She helped out in the restaurant when she could, but even there she knew she wasn't on her full game, so she kept her presence to a minimum.

And then Romeo stopped calling.

For the first two days, she didn't have time to worry because she had her hands full controlling Lucca's misery-fuelled tantrums.

By the third day she was debating whether to call him. She talked herself out of it for half a day before dialling his number. It went straight to voicemail. Leaving a garbled message guaranteed to make her sound like a lunatic, she sat back, her stomach churning.

When he hadn't called by evening, she marched downstairs and strode across the road to where one of his guards was stationed.

'Have you heard from your boss?'

The thickset man frowned. 'My boss is across the road.' He indicated another heavily muscled man wearing wraparound shades.

She sighed, exasperated. 'I mean your boss's boss. Mr Brunetti.'

'Oh. Sorry, miss, I don't have his number.'

'It's not miss, it's Mrs…Brunetti.' She waved her rings, unnecessarily, then cringed inside. 'I need to speak to Mr Brunetti.'

The man snapped to attention, then quickly strode over to his boss. The hushed conversation ensued and Wraparound Shades approached.

'I'm sorry, Mrs Brunetti, but Mr Brunetti requested that his whereabouts not be disclosed.'

Panic flared through her belly. 'Why?'

A shrug. 'He didn't say. I'm sorry.'

Maisie raced back upstairs, her heart crashing wildly against her ribs. She tried Emily's number and got a message to say she was on sabbatical in Hawaii.

She spent the night pacing her living room, alternating

between leaving a message and hitting Romeo's video-call button. Both went unanswered.

By mid-morning she was frantic. And angry. And miserable. For herself and for her son. But mostly, she was angry with Romeo.

Yanking her front door open, she faced the head bodyguard, arms folded. 'I'm about to buy a round-the-world plane ticket and drag my four-year-old to go and look for his missing father. I'm assuming your job includes accompanying us on trips abroad?'

He nodded warily.

'Good, then consider this your heads-up. We're leaving in an hour. I intend on starting in…oh, I don't know… Outer Mongolia?'

His eyes widened.

'Or perhaps you can save us all a wasted journey and tell me what country I should start in.'

The man swallowed, shifted from foot to foot. Maisie glared harder. 'You should start in Italy.'

The relief she'd expected never materialised. If Romeo was in Italy, then… 'Specifically in Palermo?'

Another wary nod.

She raced back to her flat and opened her laptop. The restaurant was closed today, and Bronagh had issued a standing babysitting assistance.

After debating whether to take Lucca with her, she decided against it, called Bronagh to tell her to pick up Lucca from nursery and booked a solo ticket.

Until she knew where Romeo was and the reason for his silence, she wasn't risking taking their son to Palermo.

After flying in Romeo's private jet, her cramped economy seat felt like torture. She emerged from the flight hot, sweaty and filled with even more panic when she realised she had no idea where to start looking for Romeo.

The last time she'd done this she hadn't been in possession of a last name.

This time the last name was one that held such power and prestige that, in her state of dishevelled hair and worn jeans, she would probably achieve the same results as last time. Laughter and ridicule.

Hailing a taxi to a three-star hotel, she quickly texted Bronagh to say she'd arrived, then showered, changed into a blue cotton dress and clipped her hair at her nape. Smoothing on lip gloss, she froze for a second when she realised it was the same dress she'd worn the night she'd met Romeo.

Hand shaking, she capped the tube and grabbed her bag.

The weather was much hotter in July than it had been the last time she was here, and a sheen of sweat covered her arms by the time she made it to Giuseppe's.

Heart thumping, she sat at a table and ordered a *limoncello*. Sipping the cool drink more for something to do than anything else, she tried to think through what she'd say to the only person who could give her answers as to Romeo's whereabouts—Lorenzo Carmine.

Whether the old man would actually answer her questions was a bridge she'd cross when she came to it. According to the article she'd found online, Lorenzo lived in a mansion once belonging to Agostino Fattore, a man whose picture bore a strong resemblance to Romeo, once you dragged your gaze from the skin-crawling cruelty in his eyes.

Her fingers curled around her glass, her stomach churning in horror at what the man she loved had suffered. Was probably still suffering…

Shutting her eyes, she dropped her head into her hands and breathed in deep. She wouldn't think the worst. She would get her chance to tell Romeo exactly how she felt.

All of it. With nothing held back.

Firming her jaw, she opened her eyes and jerked upright in shock.

He was pulling back the chair at the adjacent table. Sunglasses obscured his eyes and the direction of his gaze suggested he wasn't looking at her, but Maisie knew Romeo had seen her.

Her body's sizzling awareness was too strong to be anything but a reaction to his direct scrutiny.

A judder shook its way up from her toes as she stared at him, relief pounding through her to see him in one piece. Hungrily her eyes roved over him. His cheekbones looked a little more prominent, and his mouth a lot grimmer, but there was no mistaking the powerful aura emanating from him or his masculine grace when he curled elegant fingers around the tiny espresso cup the waiter slid onto his table a few minutes later.

He picked up the beverage, knocked it back in one greedy gulp, then stood, extracted a ten-euro note from his pocket and placed it on the table.

She sat poised in her chair unable to believe he would just leave without speaking to her.

Then his arrogant head turned her way. Heat sizzled over her skin, far hotter than the sun's rays as she stared back at him. His hands clenched into fists, then released.

Without a word, he strode onto the pavement leading away from the waterfront.

Maisie grabbed her handbag and raced after him. Everything about his quick strides and tense shoulders suggested he didn't want to be disturbed. But she hadn't come all this way to be turned away.

He turned into a vaguely familiar street five minutes later. When she recognised it, she froze, her pulse tripling its beat as she read the name of the hotel.

She jerked into motion when Romeo disappeared inside. By the time she entered the jaw-dropping interior of the marble-floored atrium, he was gone. She bit her lip and looked around the plush surroundings, wondering whether she would receive the same humiliating reception as she had last time.

'Signora Brunetti!' A sharply dressed man hurried towards her, his hand proffered in greeting.

'Um, yes?'

'I was asked this morning to look out for you and inform you that the room you seek is Penthouse One.'

'Ah...thank you.'

'*Prego.* If you'll come with me, I'll personally access the private lift for you.'

He escorted her to the lift, inserted the key and pressed the button, before stepping back with a respectful bow.

Clutching her bag against her chest, Maisie willed her pulse to stop racing. But it was no use. Now that she'd seen that Romeo was unharmed, every ounce of adrenaline was churning towards the emotional undertaking she was about to perform.

Should that fail...

Her knees buckled and she sagged against the gilt-edged mirrored walls as the lift doors opened. Sucking in a deep breath, she forced one foot in front of the other. The pristine white doors and gold-encrusted knobs loomed large and imposing in front of her.

Lifting a hand, she knocked.

CHAPTER FIFTEEN

HE OPENED THE DOOR after the third round of knocking. And said nothing. Bleak hazel eyes drilled into hers, seething emotions vibrating in the thick silence.

Maisie cleared her throat.

'You haven't called in four d-days. Our son is miserable without you,' she stammered when she eventually found her brain.

Romeo's face twisted with agonised bitterness and regret, before it resettled into stark blankness. 'I'll make it up to him. My business in Palermo took longer than I thought. I have a month-long business commitment in London starting next week. Once I'm settled, Emily will resume coordinating with you on visiting schedules. I'll also have my team provide you with useful numbers including my pilot's so you don't have to rely on commercial travel. There's a car waiting for you downstairs right now. My plane will take you back home. Have a safe trip back. *Arrivederci.*'

He shut the door in her face.

Her mouth dropped open in shock for several seconds before, temper flaring, she slapped her open palm repeatedly on the door. When he yanked it open, his face was a mask that covered a multitude of emotions. Emotions he was hell-bent on keeping from her.

'I came all this way and that's all you have to say to me?'

He shoved his hands deep into his pockets. 'What more is there to say? You've made it more than clear our son is the only subject on the table when it comes to you and me.'

'That's not true,' she replied.

His jaw worked. 'Dammit, what the hell do you want from me, Maisie?' he demanded gutturally.

'For starters, why did you tell the concierge my name with the instructions to let me up when I arrived?'

'Because you're the mother of my child, and still my wife—at least until one of us decides to do something about it. And also because I have security watching over you and Lucca twenty-four hours a day. I was told the moment you bought a plane ticket to Sicily. I thought I'd save you the trouble of an awkward enquiry at the front desk when you eventually got here.' The thinly veiled mockery made her skin sting.

Nervously, she shifted on her feet. 'Well…okay. I'm here. So are you going to let me in?' she asked with a fast-dwindling bravado.

He raised an eyebrow. 'Are you sure you want to come in? Surely this room holds bad memories for you.'

She looked over his shoulder and caught sight of the mixture of opulent and beautiful antique and modern furniture, some of which they'd appreciated up close and personal with their naked bodies. 'They weren't all bad,' she murmured huskily. 'In fact, the night before the morning after was quite spectacular. One of the best nights of my life.'

He froze, his hazel eyes flaring a bright gold before a cloud descended on his face. 'What a shame it is then that your worst was finding yourself married to me.' His voice leaked a gravel roughness coated with pain and her heart squeezed.

'Don't put words in my mouth, Romeo. I said I didn't want to be married to you. I didn't say it was because I hated the idea. Or you.'

Tension filled his body. 'What did you mean?' he asked raggedly.

'Are you going to let me in?'

He jerked backwards, his hand rigid around the door-knob. His warmth seemed to reach out to her as she passed him, his scent filling her starving senses so headily, she almost broke down and plastered herself against him.

The suite was just as she remembered. The luxurious gold-and-cream-striped sofa stood in the same place she'd first made love with Romeo. She dropped her handbag on it, her fingers helplessly trailing over the exquisite design as memories flooded her.

Unable to resist, she touched the glass-topped console table set between two floor-to-ceiling windows, then the entertainment centre, where Romeo had played *Pagliacci's* mournful theme tunes while he'd feasted on her.

'Do you wish me to leave you alone to reminisce?' he enquired tightly.

She turned to find him frozen against the closed door, his arms folded. He wasn't as calm as he appeared, a muscle flicking in his jaw as he watched her.

'Why are you standing over there, Romeo? Are you afraid of me?' she challenged, even though her heart banged hard against her ribs.

A harsh laugh barked from him, then his face seemed to crumple before he sliced his fingers through his hair. '*Sì*, I'm afraid. I'm terrified of what I feel when I'm around you. And even more terrified of my emotions when I'm not.'

The naked vulnerability in that announcement strangled her breath. The room took on a brightness that made her blink hard. Then she realised the brightness was her heart lifting from the gloom, hope rising fast and hard, against her will.

'What are you saying, Romeo?' She couldn't allow room for misinterpretation. The stakes were higher than ever this time.

He exhaled. Deep and long and shakily, his massive chest quaking beneath his black shirt. 'I mean, I love you, Maisie. Of course, I could be mistaken because I really don't know what love is. But I feel a ravaging emptiness every second of every day that I have to survive without you. I thought I knew what it felt to contemplate a hopeless future until the day you told me you regretted marrying me.' He shook his head and surged away from the door.

Striding to the window, he stared down into the street. 'I haven't been able to function since that moment. You're all I think about, all I crave...' Another juddering breath. 'Is that love? This feeling of desperate hopelessness?' he intoned bleakly.

Maisie moved until she was a few feet from him, desperate to touch him. 'I don't know, Romeo. Do you feel the same ache when you imagine us being together instead of apart? Or is it different, better?' she whispered.

His head dropped forward, his forehead resting against the cool glass as a tremble moved through his body. '*Per favore*...please, *gattina*, why are you doing this?' he groaned roughly. 'Why are you here?'

Maisie swallowed. 'I needed to see that you're all right. That Lorenzo—'

'Lorenzo is no longer an issue. The *famiglia* are abandoning his sinking ship. We have a witness who'll testify to what happened to Zaccheo's father after my father threw me out that night. Lorenzo is now facing a murder charge. Our combined testimony will put him away for good.'

She gasped. 'Why did he attack Zaccheo's father?'

'Paolo Giordano had the task of disposing of me after my mother left me on my father's doorstep. My father didn't want me, so Paolo took me home. Unfortunately, his wife was less than enthusiastic about having another mouth to feed. Paolo had the audacity to offend my father by trying to return me to him after a month. My father set Lorenzo on him.' He stopped, distant memories glazing his eyes before he shook them off. 'I made a statement to the chief of police two days ago. He issued warrants for Lorenzo's arrest. The case may collapse or it may not. Either way, Lorenzo is going to spend some time in prison before the case goes to trial. He'll know better than to come after me or mine again.'

'So, that was how you ended up on the streets? Because your mother didn't want you?'

'She was a high-class prostitute. Getting pregnant with me put a huge obstacle in her chosen career. When I became too much for her, she drove me to a house I'd never visited before, told me it was my father's house and drove away.'

'Did you see her again?'

He closed his eyes for a split second. 'Not until I stayed with her for a week, here in Palermo, five years ago.'

'The week we met?'

He nodded. 'She called, finally. After years of silence, she called me. I'd kept tabs on her over the years and knew when she fell on particularly hard times. I found ways to send her money without her knowing it came from me. I didn't want her contacting me because I was rich. I wanted her to do it because I was her son and she wanted to see me.' He shook his head, bitterness and pain warring over his face. 'The week before she died, she finally called. I was elated.'

'What happened?'

'She wanted the use of my credit card. She wasn't interested in who I was or whether I could afford it. She had a fast-growing brain tumour and didn't have long to live. She wanted to die in style. I checked her into the presidential suite at the Four Seasons. And I stayed with her, hoping that she'd show me, in some small way, that she'd regretted giving me away. She didn't. I held her hand until she passed away and all she did was curse me for looking like my father.

'So, you see, I don't know if this living, breathing thing inside me is love, or if it's a twisted need to cling to something that's damaged because I've touched it.'

The words wrenched at her soul. 'Please don't say that.'

He turned to face her, and his eyes were deep dark pools of pain. 'That day we met was the first time I accepted that hope was a useless emotion. That love didn't exist. Not for people like me.'

'Romeo...'

'It's okay, *gattina*. I know you don't love me.' His shoulders drooped in weary, agonised defeat. 'I'll make sure the divorce is fast and the settlement more than generous.'

Her breath shook. 'I don't want a divorce or your money, Romeo.'

A sound of a wounded animal seared from his throat. She took the final step and placed her left hand on his chest. 'If I did, I would've taken off my wedding ring the moment we left Hawaii.'

His gaze fell on her ring and his eyes flared bright, and then dimmed almost immediately. As if a light had gone off inside.

'We can't stay married simply for the sake of Lucca. I won't be responsible for bringing unhappiness to your life.'

'Then bring happiness. Love me. Be with me.'

His eyes slowly rose, connected with hers. 'But on the island, you said—'

'I said I didn't want to be married because I couldn't bear the thought of loving you and not having you love me back.'

His eyes widened and he jerked upright, his strong arms closing on her shoulders. *'Che cosa?'*

Tears brimmed her eyes. 'I love you, Romeo. I've loved you since the night we spent in this room. I've been miserable without you and I really don't want a divorce, if you don't mind,' she pleaded in a wobbly voice.

'I don't mind,' he responded, his face and voice dazed. 'If you let me, I intend to not mind for at least a dozen lifetimes.'

That bright light ripped through her senses once again. This time she embraced it. Revelled in its warmth. 'Good, because that's how long it'll take for me to show you how much you mean to me, too.'

'*Dio mio, gattina...*' His voice held humble worship, a touching vulnerability that made her cup his face.

'Hold me, Romeo. Kiss me. I've missed you so much.'

With a groan, he sealed his lips to hers.

Three hours later, she dragged her head from his chest and the soothing sound of his heartbeat. 'Are you ready to video-call with Lucca?'

Romeo raised his head and kissed her mouth. 'Hmm, I think I've finally come up with something that'll make him forgive me for not being in touch these past few days.'

'Oh, what's that?'

'A promise of a brother or sister.'

Maisie's heart leapt. She planted a kiss of her own on his willing lips. 'I think you just elevated yourself to *Best Father Ever* status.'

Romeo laughed and set up his laptop after Maisie alerted Bronagh to the incoming call.

Seconds later, the screen filled with their son's beautiful face. 'Mummy! Daddy, when are you coming home?' he demanded plaintively.

Romeo exchanged glances with her. 'We will be there by the time you wake up tomorrow, *bel raggazo.*'

'Okay! I've been learning some Itayan words, Daddy.' He gazed keenly into the screen.

Romeo's hand found hers, and he pressed it to his chest. 'Tell me,' he invited softly.

'*Ti amo, Papà,*' he said haltingly, then his face widened in a proud smile. 'It means, I love you, Daddy.'

Beneath her hand, Romeo's heart lurched, then raced wildly. His throat worked for several moments, before he spoke. 'That is exactly right, and I...' His eyes connected with hers, and tears brimming in hers, she nodded in encouragement. 'I love you, too.'

They rang off several minutes later, and Romeo took her in his arms and just held her. Somewhere in the suite, a mournful opera started.

'Why do you listen to those things? They're so sad.'

He hugged her closer. 'It was a reminder that hope was a futile emotion, that everything dies in the end. But now it'll be a reminder that even in the bleakest moments, the voices of heaven can still be heard.'

She raised her head and stared deep into his soul, her heart turning over. 'I love you, Romeo.'

He kissed her, accepting her love.

He hadn't said he loved her after that first time. But she didn't mind, because she felt it in every touch, every look, and knew he would get around to saying it again eventually, when their world grew less shaky with the depth of emotion rocking them.

When he raised his head, his eyes shone with a brightness that seared her with happiness, right to her very fingertips.

'I see you got away with not being taken to task by Lucca.'

He laughed. 'But I still intend to keep my promise to him and provide him with a brother or sister. Soon,' he stated with serious intent.

She traced his mouth with her fingers. 'Soon. I can think of nothing I want more than another baby with you.'

He gently turned her around and caressed her belly with both hands. Then his strong arms slid around her, swaying her to the sound of angels' voices.

'You're my beginning and my end, *il mio cuore*. My everything.'

EPILOGUE

Three years later

'WHO CAME UP with the brilliant idea that it'd be fun to pack seven hyperactive kids and two overachieving fathers onto a yacht for a vacation?' Eva grumbled as she chased after her ten-month-old daughter crawling at top speed towards the boat's chrome railing. Baby Donatella Giordano immediately screeched in protest at her thwarted bid for freedom.

Maisie grinned, raising her face to the dazzling Mediterranean sunshine. 'You think there would've been any stopping Romeo or Zaccheo once they co-bought the super-yacht they'd been drooling over for a year?'

Eva walked across the wide marble-tiled second-floor deck of the stunning vessel to join Maisie, her white bikini accentuating her tanned skin beautifully. Sitting down, she bounced Donatella on her lap until she quieted. 'It's a beautiful boat, but I haven't been able to sleep a wink from worrying that one of the boys will throw themselves overboard just for the sheer hell of it.'

'Romeo assures me that's impossible. Trust me, I grilled him for hours on that very subject before I agreed to bring Lucca and Marcelo.'

Two-year-old Marcelo glanced up at the mention of his name and grinned from where he splashed in the shallow pool with the second set of Giordano twins, Gianni and Angelo.

Eva kissed the top of her baby's head and sighed happily.

'It's good to see them relax, though, isn't it? I just wish they wouldn't relax so...*vigorously*.'

Maisie laughed and glanced to the side as two power-ful Jet Skis whizzed by, trailed by excited cheers and urges to *go faster*.

Romeo's jet carried Lucca and Zaccheo's his oldest sons.

As they made a final turn past the boat, Romeo's gaze met hers. The contact was brief, but the love blazing in his eyes snagged Maisie's breath. Her heart raced as the over-whelming love, which incredibly grew stronger every day, pounded through her blood. She reached up and touched lips that still tingled from when they'd made love hours ago. Then her hand drifted down to her flat belly, and the surprise that would bring another smile of joy to her hus-band's face.

'Since Romeo hasn't crowed about it, I'm guessing he doesn't know yet?' Eva asked, glancing pointedly at Maisie's stomach.

Maisie gasped. 'No, he doesn't, but how...?'

'Please. You've been positively glowing since you stepped aboard the *Dolcezza Gattina* yesterday. I'm guess-ing you didn't get a chance to tell him because Zaccheo mo-nopolised his attention until the early hours?'

Maisie snorted. 'He didn't come to bed until five this morning.' Whereupon he'd woken her and made love to her until she'd been too exhausted to move. By the time she'd woken again, he'd been up with their children. 'I'll tell him tonight.'

'Tell me what, *amore mio*?'

Maisie jumped guiltily at the deep voice that heralded her husband's arrival.

Romeo climbed the last step and headed straight for her. This close, his tight, lean physique, damp from the ocean's spray, was even more arresting. 'If I told you now, it wouldn't be a surprise, would it?' she finally said when she could speak past the wondrous reality that this gorgeous, incredible man belonged to her.

After kissing his younger son, he lowered his body onto her lounger and braced his hands on either side of her hips, caging her in. Outside the unique cocoon that wrapped itself around them whenever they were this close, Maisie peripherally saw Zaccheo greet his wife with a kiss; heard the staff attend to the children.

But she only had eyes for the man who stared down at her with an intensity that hadn't abated since the first moment they'd set eyes on each other.

'Is there any reason it needs to wait till tonight?' he asked with a thick rasp that spoke of other urgent desires.

She scrambled for a sound reason, but in the end couldn't find one. 'No.'

'Bene.' He stood and held out his hand. 'Come.'

Her excitement ratcheted another notch, but she paused as she stood. 'The children…'

His fingers tightened around hers. 'Emily has everything in hand.'

Romeo led his wife to the master suite and shut the door behind them.

Surprise or not, he would've found a way to bring her here at the first opportunity. Because he couldn't get enough of her. Of her love, her devotion to him, to their family. Of everything.

He pulled her bikini-clad body close now and exhaled with happiness when her arms slid around his neck.

'I love you.' She sighed against him.

He shuddered hard, those three words never ceasing to move him. *'Ti amo anch'io,'* he replied gruffly. 'I'm so thankful you made that journey to Palermo three years ago.'

'So am I, but I'd like to think you would've found your way to me sooner or later. You just needed to put your ghosts to rest.'

He nodded. The ghosts *had* finally been slain. Lorenzo Carmine had been found guilty of murder and jailed, never to breathe free air again. The rest of the *famiglia* had scattered to the wind, bringing an end to Agostino Fattore's poisoned legacy.

Romeo had resisted the urge to raze the Fattore mansion to the ground, instead renovating it with Maisie's help and donating it to the local orphanage.

From the trauma of his childhood and the bleak landscape he'd anticipated his future being, he was now submerged in love and happiness so profound, it scared him sometimes. Not enough that he would fail to hang on to it with both hands.

He pulled his wife closer. 'So, about my surprise?' he pressed as he tugged at the strings of her bikini.

Breathtaking blue eyes met his as she captured his hand, kissed his palm, then laid it gently over her stomach.

His heart stopped, then raced with pure bliss. 'Another baby?' he murmured in awe.

Maisie nodded, tears filling her eyes.

Dropping to his knees, he kissed her belly, and the miracle nestled within. *'Ciao, bella bambina,'* he whispered.

She smiled. 'You're so sure it's a girl this time?'

'I'm certain. She'll be as beautiful as her mother. And she will go a little way to balancing out the testosterone you find so challenging.'

She laughed as he scooped her up and tumbled her into bed.

Laughter ceased, and desire took over. They expressed their love in the gentle kisses and furnace-hot lovemaking.

A few hours later, they dressed and joined their children and the Giordanos around the large dinner table.

Their news was greeted with hugs and kisses, after which Zaccheo raised his glass.

'To family,' he toasted, glancing at every face around the table until finally resting lovingly on his wife. 'And to love.'

'*Sì*, to family,' Romeo echoed. Then his gaze found Maisie's. 'To my for ever,' he murmured for her ears alone.

* * * * *

FALLING FOR
HER ARMY DOC

DIANNE DRAKE

I dedicate this book to Mr Kahawaii,
who took me into his amazing world for a little while.

CHAPTER ONE

SHE LOOKED BEAUTIFUL, standing outside in the garden, catching the morning light. He watched her every day about this time. She'd take her walk, sit for a few minutes on the stone retaining wall surrounding the sculpted flowers, then return to the building.

Once, he'd wondered what weighed her down so heavily. She had that look—the one he remembered from many of his patients, and probably even more he didn't remember. She—Lizzie, she'd told him her name was—always smiled and greeted him politely. But there was something behind that smile.

Of course, who was he to analyze? It had taken a photo he'd found among his things to remind him that he'd been engaged. Funny how his memory of her prior to his accident was blurred. Nancy was a barely recognizable face in a world he didn't remember much of. And, truthfully, he couldn't even recall how or why he'd become engaged to her. She didn't seem his type—too flighty, too intrusive. Too greedy.

Yet Lizzie, out there in the garden, seemed perfect. Beautiful. Smart. In tune with everything around her.

So what wasn't he getting here? Had he changed so much that the type of woman who'd used to attract him didn't now? And taking her place was someone…more like Lizzie?

Dr. Mateo Sanchez watched from the hospital window until Lizzie left the garden, then he drew the blinds and went back to bed. He didn't have a lot of options here, as a patient. Rest, watch the TV, rest some more. Go to therapy. Which somehow he never quite seemed to do.

This was his fourth facility since he'd been shipped from the battlefield to Germany, and nothing was working. Not the therapy. Not his attitude. Not his life. What he wanted to know they wouldn't tell him. And what he didn't want to know just seemed to flood back in when he didn't want it to.

The docs were telling him to be patient, that some memory would return while some would not. But he wanted a timeline, a calendar on his wall where he could tick off the days until he was normal again.

He reached up and felt the tiny scar on his head. Whatever normal was. Right now, he didn't know. There was nothing for him to hold on to. No one there to ground him. Even Nancy hadn't stayed around long after she'd discovered he didn't really know her.

In fact, his first thought had been that she was a nurse, tending him at his bedside. She'd been good when he'd asked for a drink of water, even when he'd asked for another pillow, and she'd taken his criticism when she'd told him she couldn't give him a pain pill.

This had gone on for a week before she'd finally confessed that she wasn't his nurse, but his fiancée. And then, in another week, she'd been gone. She wasn't the type to do nursing care in the long term, she'd said. And unfortunately, all she could see ahead of her was nursing care, a surgeon who could no longer operate, when what she'd wanted was a surgeon who could provide a big home, fancy cars, and everything else he'd promised he'd give her.

So, he knew the what and the when of his accident. What he *didn't* know was the annoying part. As a surgeon he needed to know all aspects of his patients' conditions, even the things that didn't seem to matter. It was called being thorough. But for him…

"Giving you the answers to your life could imprint false memories," his neurologist Randy always said, when he asked. And he was right, of course. That was something he did remember. Along with so many of his basic medical skills—the ones he'd learned early on in his career.

The more specific skills, though… Some of them were still there. Probably most of them. But in pulling them out of his memory he hesitated sometimes. Thought he remembered but wasn't sure of himself.

Wait a minute. Let me consult a textbook before I remove your gall bladder.

Yeah, right. Like *that* was going to work in surgery.

He looked up and saw Lizzie standing in his doorway, simply observing him. Probably trying to figure out what to do with him.

"Hello," he said, not sure what to make of this.

She was the house primary care physician—not his doctor, not even a neurologist. Meaning she had no real reason to be here unless he needed a vaccination or something.

"I've seen you watch me out in the garden. I was wondering if you'd like to come out with me for a while later…breathe some fresh air, take a walk?"

"Who's prescribing that?" he asked suspiciously.

"You are—if that's what you want to do. You're not a

prisoner here, you know. And your doctor said it might be a good idea…that it could help your…" She paused.

"Go ahead and say it. My disposition."

"I understand from morning staff meetings that you're quite a handful."

"Nothing else to do around here," he said. "So, I might as well improve upon my obnoxious level. It's getting better. In fact, I think I'll soon be counted amongst the masters."

"To what outcome?"

He shrugged. "See, that's the thing. For me, there *are* no outcomes."

"If that's how you want it. But I'm not your doctor and you're not my problem. So, take that walk with me or not."

"And tomorrow? What happens to me tomorrow?"

"Honestly? I'm a one-day-at-a-time girl. Nothing's ever guaranteed, Mateo. If I get through the day, tomorrow will take care of itself."

"Well, I like seeing ahead. And now, even behind."

"To each his own," she said nonchalantly.

"Which implies what?" he asked, feeling a smile slowly crossing his face. Lizzie was…*fun*. Straight to the point. And challenging.

"You know exactly what it implies, Mateo. In your effort to see 'behind,' as you're calling it, you're driving the staff crazy. They're afraid of you. Not sure what to do with you. And that false smile of yours is beginning to wear thin."

"Does it annoy you?" he asked.

"It's beginning to."

"Then my work here is done," he said, folding his arms across his chest.

He wanted clothes—real clothes. Not these blue and

green things that were passed off as hospital gowns. Those were for sick people. He wasn't sick. Just damaged. A blood clot on his brain, which had been removed, and a lingering pest called retrograde amnesia. That kind of damage deserved surfer shorts and a Hawaiian shirt, seeing as how he was in Hawaii now.

"And my work has nothing to do with you. I was just trying to be friendly, but you're too much of a challenge to deal with. And, unfortunately, what should have been a simple yes or no is now preventing me from seeing my patients."

She sure was pretty.

It was something he'd thought over and over about Lizzie. Long, tarnished copper hair. Curly. Soft too, he imagined. Brown eyes that could be as mischievous as a kitten or shoot daggers, depending on the circumstance. And her smile… It didn't happen too often, he'd noticed. And when it did, it didn't light up the proverbial room. But it sure did light up his day.

"And how would I be doing that? I'm here, wearing these lovely clothes, eating your gourmet green slime food, putting up with your hospital's inane therapy."

"And by 'putting up with,' you mean not showing up for?" She took a few more steps into the room, then went to open the blinds.

"In the scheme of my future life, what will it do for me?"

"Maybe nothing. Maybe everything."

"No vagaries here, Lizzie. Be as specific as I have to be every time I answer someone's orientation questions. 'Do you remember your name?' 'Where are you?' 'What's the date?' 'Who's the current President?'"

"Standard protocol, Mateo. You know that." She

turned back to face him. "But you make everything more difficult than it has to be."

She brightened his day in a way he'd never expected. "So why me? You're not my doctor, but you've obviously chosen me for some special attention."

"My dad was a military surgeon, like you were. Let's just say I'm giving back a little."

"Did he see combat?"

"Too many times."

"And it changed him," Mateo said, suddenly serious.

"It might have—but if it did it was something he never let me see. And he never talked about it."

"It's a horrible thing to talk about. The injuries. The ones you can fix…the ones you can't. In my unit they were rushed in and out so quickly I never really saw anything but whatever it was I had to fix. Maybe that was a blessing."

He shut his eyes to the endless parade of casualties who were now marching by him. This was a memory he didn't want, but he was stuck with it. And it was so vivid.

"Were you an only child?" he asked.

Lizzie nodded. "My mom couldn't stand the military life. She said it was too lonely. So, by the time I was five she was gone, and then it was just my dad and me."

"Couldn't have been easy being a single parent under his circumstances. I know *I* wouldn't have wanted to drag a kid around with me when I was active. Wouldn't have been fair to the kid."

"He never complained. At least, not to me. And what I had…it seemed normal."

"I complain to everybody."

In Germany, after his first surgery, it hadn't occurred to him that his memory loss might be permanent. He'd been too busy dealing with the actual surgery itself to get any more involved than that. That had happened after he'd been transferred to Boston for brain rehab. Then he'd got involved. Only it hadn't really sunk in the way it should have. But once they'd got him to a facility in California, where the patients had every sort of war-related brain injury, that was when it had occurred to him that he was just another one of the bunch.

How could that be? That was the question he kept asking himself over and over. He had become one of the poor unfortunates he usually treated. A surgeon without his memory. A man without his past.

"You're a survivor who uses what he has at his disposal to regain the bits and pieces of himself he's lost. Or at least that's what you could be if you weren't such a quitter."

"A quitter?"

Maybe he was, since going on was so difficult. But did Lizzie understand what it was like to reach for a memory you assumed would be there and come up with nothing? And he was one of the lucky ones. Physically, he was fine, and his surgery had gone well. He'd healed well, too. But he couldn't get past that one thing that held him back…who was he, *really*?

Suddenly Mateo was tired. It wasn't even noon yet and he needed a nap. Or an escape.

"That walk this evening…maybe. If you can get me some real clothes."

Lizzie chuckled. "I *should* say you'll have to wear your hospital pajamas, but I'll see what I can do."

"No promises, Lizzie. I don't make promises I can't keep, and who knows what side of the pendulum my mood will be swinging on later."

"Whatever suits you," she said, then left the room.

Even though he hated to see her go, what he needed

was to be left alone—something he'd told them over and over. He needed time to figure out just how big a failure he was, medically speaking. And what kind of disappointment he was to his mother, who'd worked long and hard to get him through medical school. The arthritis now crippling her hands showed that.

There was probably a long list of other people he'd let down, too, but thankfully he couldn't remember it. Except his own name—right there at the top. He was Dr. Mateo Sanchez—a doctor with retrograde amnesia. And right now that was all he cared to know. Everything else—it didn't matter.

She was not getting involved. It didn't usually work. Didn't make you happy, either. Didn't do a thing. At least in her case it never had.

Lizzie's mom had walked out when she was barely five, so no involvement there. And her dad… Well, he'd loved her. But her father had been a military surgeon, and that had taken up most of his time. While he'd always said he wanted to spend more time with her, it hadn't happened. So no involvement with him, either, for a good part of her life.

Then there had been her husband. Another doctor, but one who wouldn't accept that she didn't want to be a surgeon like him. He was a neurosurgeon and, to him, being a primary care physician meant being…*lesser*. He did surgeries while she did cuts and bruises, he'd always say. Brad had never failed to show his disappointment in her, so she'd failed there, too. Meaning, what was the point?

None, that Lizzie could think of. But that was OK. She got along, designed her life the way she wanted it to be, and lived happily in the middle of it. Living in the middle was good, she decided. It didn't take you far, but it didn't let you down, either.

She wondered about Mateo, though. She knew he watched her in the garden every morning. Knew he'd asked questions about her. But the look on his face… there was no confidence there. Something more like fear. Which was why she'd asked him out for a walk this evening. He needed more than the four walls of his hospital room, the same way her father had needed more.

But her father had been on a downward spiral with Alzheimer's. Mateo was young, healthy, had a lot of years of life ahead of him—except he was getting into the habit of throwing away the days. It was hard seeing that, after watching the way her father had deteriorated.

But to get involved…? They weren't friends. Weren't even doctor-patient. Weren't anything. But she'd been watching the watcher for weeks now, and since she'd be going on holiday shortly what would it hurt to get involved for once? Or, in this case, to take a simple evening walk?

Watching Mateo walk toward her now, she thought he struck her as a man who would have taken charge. His gait was strong, purposeful. And he was a large man—massive muscles on a well-defined body. He'd taken care of himself. You didn't get that physique by chance. Yet now he was stalled, and that didn't fit. To look at him was to think he had his life together—it was in the way he carried himself. But there was nothing together about him, not one little piece. And he was sabotaging himself by not trying.

Many of the staff's morning meetings lately had opened with: *"What should we do about Mateo?"*

The majority wanted him out of there. Even his own doctor didn't care. But Lizzie was his advocate because he deserved this chance. Like her dad had, all those times someone had tried to convince her to put him away. That was exactly what they wanted to do with Mateo, and while neurology wasn't her specialty, she did know that some types of brain trauma took a long time to sort themselves out.

But beds here were at a premium. The waiting list was long, and military veterans always went to the top of the list. There was no guarantee they'd stay there, though, especially if they acted the way Mateo did.

He was never mean. Never outright rude, even though he was always on the edge of it. In fact, he smiled more than anybody she'd ever seen. But he refused to try, and that was ultimately going to get in the way, since there were other veterans who could have his bed and display more cooperation.

The waiting line for each and every bed was eight deep, Janis always reminded her, when she was so often the only one at the meeting table who defended him. His bed could be filled with the snap of her fingers, and that was what she had to impress upon Mateo or he'd be out.

Truthfully, Lizzie was worried about Mateo's progress. Or rather his lack of it. His time was indeed running out, and there was serious talk of transferring him elsewhere. He knew that, and it didn't faze him. Not one little bit. Or if it did, he hid it well. Making her wonder why she tried so hard to advocate for a man who didn't advocate for himself.

"Well, you look good in real clothes," she said as he walked up to the reception hub where she'd been waiting.

He spun around the way a model on a runway would, then took a bow as a couple of passing nurses applauded him. "It's good to feel human again."

"You're allowed out in the garden any time, Mateo.

All you have to do is ask and someone will walk along with you."

"But today I scored you." He leaned in toward her and whispered, "Who happens to be the prettiest doctor in this hospital."

"Save the flattery for someone else, Mateo. All I'm doing is trying to chart a doctor's note saying you were cooperative for once. So far there aren't any of those on record."

Staff were tired of sugar-coating what they said about him and had started opting for snarky comments instead. In their defense, they were a highly dedicated lot who were bound to their jobs by the need to make improvements in patients' lives—physically and emotionally. And, while Mateo might make them smile, he also frustrated them by pushing them to the limit.

Lizzie nudged a wheelchair in his direction.

"You know I can walk," he said.

"Of course, you can, but…hospital policy. If I take a patient outside, they must go by wheelchair or else I'll be in trouble. In other words, comply, or give back the clothes and go to bed."

"Comply? Easier said than done," he said, not budging from where he was standing at the nurses' hub. "Especially when you're treating me like an invalid."

In truth, he'd prefer not to step outside—or in his case, be wheeled. There were too many things reminding him of how much he'd forgotten. Most days he wasn't in the mood to deal with it. Staying in bed, watching TV, playing video games, sleeping…that was about the extent of his life now.

Except Lizzie. She was the bright spot. And she was asking him out…no way he could turn that down.

"Isn't that how you're treating yourself?" she asked. "We've designed a beautiful program for you here—took days going over it and tweaking it. It's a nice balance for what you've got going on, yet have you ever, just once, referred to it? Daily walks in the garden, for instance? It's on there, Mateo. And workouts in the gym. But I'll bet you tossed the program in the trash as soon as you received it.

"Might have. Don't remember."

"Saying you've forgotten has become an easy excuse because retrograde amnesia is about forgetting things in the past. Not in the future, or even now. What you're not retaining right now is left over from your brain surgery, but that will improve in time. With some effort. If you let it. Also, if you don't care about your past you can walk out of here right now—a new man with a clean slate. You're healthy, and with some caution you're basically healed. Your destiny at this point is up to you. You can go, if that's what you want. But I don't think it is, because I believe you still want help with your memory loss, as well as trying to recall as much as you can about your life."

"Oh, you mean I want to remember things like how to repair a hernia?"

"It's all in there," she said, tapping her own head. "Like you've been told. Unless you missed your session that day, procedural things aren't normally lost. Life things are. And, as you already know, you do still have a little bit of head-banging going on after the surgery. But that's not even significant at this point. Your attitude is, though."

"Head-banging would be your professional diagnosis?"

Why the hell did he do this? He didn't like it, but sometimes the belligerence just slipped out anyway. And

Lizzie was only trying to help. He'd heard it whispered that she was the only one standing between him and being sent elsewhere.

"It would be the way *you* described your headaches when you were first admitted. But you remember that, Mateo. Which means you're in one of your moods now. You think you can smile your way through it and maybe the staff won't notice that you're not working toward a better recovery? Well, I notice. Every little detail." She smiled back at him. "I'd be remiss in my duties if I didn't."

"So, I'm part of your duty?"

"You're one of the patients here. That's all. Whatever I choose to do, like go for a walk with you, is because I understand where you are right now."

"*Do* you, Lizzie?" he asked, his voice turning dark. "Do you really? I mean, even if I do retain knowledge of the procedural side of the surgeries I used to perform, would you honestly want a surgeon who comes to do your appendectomy and doesn't even remember what kind of suture he prefers?"

Lizzie laughed, giving the wheelchair one more push toward him. This time it bumped his knees, so he could no longer ignore it.

"Sometimes I wonder if someone should change your diagnosis to retrograde amnesia with a secondary symptom of being overly dramatic. You're a challenge, Mateo, that's for sure. And, just between us, an open appendectomy skin closure works best with an absorbable intradermic stitch. Although if you're doing the procedure laparoscopically, all it takes is a couple of dissolvable stitches on the inside and skin glue on the outside."

"And you know this because…?"

"I've done a few stitches in my time. That's part of

being a PCP. So quit being so dramatic. It doesn't score points with me, if that's what you're trying to do."

Well, he might have gaps in his memory, including the kind of women he'd been drawn to, but Lizzie certainly held his attention now. Petite, bouncy. Smart. Serious as hell. And that was the part that didn't escape him. Lizzie Peterson was a great big bundle of formidable perfection all tied up in a small package.

Maybe that was what intrigued him the most. He couldn't picture himself with someone like her. Of course, in his recent spotty memory he couldn't picture himself with anybody, including his former fiancée.

"Not overly dramatic. I'm allergic to flowers, which is why I don't want to go to the garden."

"Says who?"

"Says me."

"Then why, just a few minutes ago, did you want to go out?"

"Maybe I wasn't allergic a few minutes ago. Maybe it was a sudden onset aversion."

"Well, it's your choice, Mateo. Your life is out there somewhere. Maybe it's not the one you want, but it's the one you're going to be stuck with. You can make your own choices with it, but what you do now will affect what you do later on. And there is a 'later on' coming up. You can't keep postponing it indefinitely."

She started to walk away but turned back for a final word. She smiled when she saw that he was in the wheelchair, ready to go. Why not? he thought. Nothing else was happening in his life. So why not take a stroll in the garden? Or, in his case, a roll.

He gave Lizzie a deliberate scowl, which turned so quickly into a smile it almost caught her off-guard. "Is there any way I can talk you out of the wheelchair?"

"Nope. I play by the hospital rules and you play by my rules. So, here's the deal. You cooperate."

"Or what?"

"That's all there is to it. You cooperate."

"Isn't a deal supposed to be two-sided?"

"Maybe your deals are, but mine aren't. I like getting my way, Mateo. And when I don't, I'm the one who gets grumpy. Trust me—my grumpy out-grumpys yours any day of the week, so don't try me."

He liked Lizzie. Trusted her. Wanted to impress her even though that was a long way from happening. "OK. Well…if that's all you're offering."

"A walk is a walk, Mateo. Nothing else. So don't go getting ideas."

"You mean this is a pity walk?"

"Something like that. You cooperate and I'll do my best to help you. If you don't cooperate…" She smiled. "I'm sure you can guess the rest."

He could, and he didn't like it. This was a good facility, and as a doctor he recognized that. But as a patient he didn't even recognize himself—and that was the problem. When he looked in the mirror, he didn't know the face that looked back. The eyes, nose and mouth were the same, but there was nothing in his eyes. No sign of who he was or used to be.

And he was just plain scared.

"Big date? You wish," she said on her way out through the door, pushing Mateo in front of her.

Today was Lizzie's thirteenth day on without a break. But she had her nights to herself and found that if she worked hard enough during the day she could sleep through her nighttime demons. So, she worked until she was ready to drop, often stopped by The Shack for something tall and tropical, then went home and slept. So far it was working. Thoughts of her dad's death weren't invading every empty moment as much as they'd used to.

Leaning back to the wall, just outside the door, Mateo extricated himself from his wheelchair—which was totally against the rules.

"Is he getting to you?" Janis Lawton asked, stopping to hand Lizzie a bottle of water.

Janis was chief of surgery at Makalapua Pointe Hospital. The one in charge. The one who made the rules and made sure they weren't broken. And the one who was about to send Mateo to another facility on the mainland if he wasn't careful.

"I know the nurses are having problems with him." Janis leaned against the wall next to Lizzie and fixed her attention on Mateo, who'd rolled his chair off the walkway and seemed to be heading for the reflecting pond. "But the thing is, he's so darned engaging and nice most of the time. Then when he's not cooperative, or when he's refusing therapy… It's hard justifying why he's here when my waiting list is so long."

"Because he needs help. Think about what you'd do if you suddenly couldn't be a surgeon anymore."

"I do, Lizzie. All the time. And that's why Mateo keeps getting the benefit of the doubt. I understand exactly what's happening. The rug is being pulled out from under him." She held up her right hand, showing Lizzie a massive scar. "That was almost me. It took me a year of rehab to get back to operating and in the early days… Let's just say that I was more like Mateo than anyone could probably imagine. But as director of the hospital I have some lines I must draw. And Mateo isn't taking that seriously. Maybe you could…?"

Lizzie held up her hand to stop the older woman. "It's

an evening walk. That's all. No agenda. No hospital talk, if I can avoid it."

Like the walks she used to take with her dad, even in the days when he hadn't remembered who she was. It had been cathartic anyway. Had let her breathe all the way down to her soul.

"The way Mateo is happens when you don't know who you are." The way her dad had gotten. The less he'd remembered, the more uncooperative he'd become—and, while Alzheimer's was nothing like amnesia, she was reminded of the look she'd seen so often on her dad's face when she looked at Mateo. The look that said *lost*. And for Mateo, such an esteemed surgeon, to have this happen to him...

"You're not getting him mixed up with your dad, are you?" Janis asked.

Lizzie laughed outright at the suggestion. "No transference going on here! My dad was who he was, Mateo is who he is. And I do know the difference. My dad was lost in his mind. Mateo is lost in his world." She looked out at Mateo, who was now sitting on the stone wall, waiting for her.

"You do realize he's supposed to be in a wheelchair, don't you?" said Janis.

"But do *you* realize how much he doesn't like being treated like an invalid? Why force him across that line with something so trivial as a wheelchair?"

"Well, just so you know, your *friend* isn't on steady footing and he might be best served in another facility."

"This is his fourth facility, Janis. He's running out of options."

"So am I," she said, pushing herself off the wall, her eyes still fixed on Mateo, whose eyes were fixed right back on Janis. "And with you about to take leave for a while…"

That *was* a problem. She'd signed herself off duty for a couple of weeks. There were things in her own life she needed to figure out.

Was this where she wanted to stay, with so many sad memories still fighting their way through? And hospital work—it wasn't what she'd planned to do. She liked the idea of a small local clinic somewhere. Treating patients who might not have the best medical services available to them. Could she actually have something like that? Or was she already where she was meant to be?

Sure, it was an identity crisis mixed in with a professional crisis, but working herself as hard as she did there was no time left to weigh both sides—stay or go? In these two weeks of vacation there would be plenty of time for that—time to clear her mind, time to relax, time to be objective about her own life. It was a lot to sort out, but she was looking forward to it.

Everybody had choices to make, and so far, all her choices had been about other people. What did her husband want? What did her dad need? But the question was: What did Elizabeth Peterson want and need? And what would have happened if she'd chosen differently a year ago?

Well, for starters, her dad might still be alive. That was the obstacle she could never get past. But maybe now, after the tide had washed it all out to sea, that was something she could work on, too. Guilt—the big flashing light that always shone on the fact that her life wasn't in balance. And she had no idea how to restore that balance.

"I thought we were going to walk?" Mateo said, approaching her after Janis had gone inside.

"Did you *have* to break the rule about the wheelchair

in front of Janis?" Lizzie asked, taking the hand Mateo offered her when she started to stand up.

"Does it matter? I'm already branded, so does it matter what I do when decisions are being made without my input?"

The soft skin of his hand against hers... It was enough to cause a slight shiver up her spine—and, worse, the realization that maybe she was ready for that aspect of her life to resume. The attraction. The shivers. Everything that came after.

She'd never had that with Brad. Their marriage had turned cold within the first month. Making love in the five spare minutes he had every other Thursday night and no PDA—even though she would have loved holding hands with him in public. Separate bedrooms half the time, because he'd said her sleeping distracted him from working in bed.

But here was Mateo, drop-dead gorgeous, kind, and friendly, even though he tried to hide it. All in all, he was very distracting. How would he be in a relationship? Not like Brad, she supposed. Brad was always in his own space, doing everything on his own terms, and she had become his afterthought. There was certainly no happily-ever-after in being overlooked by the man who was supposed to love you.

Not that it had made much of a difference, as by the time she'd discovered her place in their marriage she'd already been part-way out the door, vowing never to make that mistake again.

But was that what she really wanted? To spend her life alone? Devote herself to her work? Why was it that one mistake should dictate the rest of her life?

This was another thing to think about during her time off. The unexpected question. Could she do it again if the right man came along? And how could she tell who was right?

Perhaps by trusting her heart? With Brad, it had been more of a practical matter. But now maybe it was time to rethink what she really wanted and how to open herself up to it if it happened along.

Shutting her eyes and rubbing her forehead against the dull headache setting in, it wasn't blackness Lizzie saw. It was Mateo. Which made her head throb a little harder. But also caused her heart to beat a little faster.

CHAPTER TWO

"I'D CLAIM AMNESIA, but I really don't know the names of most flowers. The purple and white ones...

"Orchids," Lizzie filled in.

"I know what orchids are." Mateo reached over the stone wall and picked one, then handed it to Lizzie. "There's probably a rule against picking the flowers, but you need an...*orchid* in your hair."

She took it and tucked it behind her right ear. "Right ear means you're available. Left means you're taken."

"How could someone like you not be taken?" he asked, sitting down next to her on the stone wall surrounding the garden.

Behind them were beautiful flowers in every color imaginable, with a long reflecting pond in the background. One that stretched toward the ocean.

"Because I don't want to be taken. It's one of those been-there-done-that situations, and I can still feel the sting from it, so I don't want to make the wound any worse.

"That bad?"

"Let's just say that on a rating of one through ten, I'd need a few more numbers to describe it. So, you haven't been...?"

"I was engaged briefly—apparently. Don't really have

any memory of it other than a few flashes, and those aren't very flattering. Definitely not my type, from the little I recall."

"Maybe with your head injury your type changed. That can happen with brain damage. People are known to come out the other side very different from what they were when they went in. Could be the Fates giving you a second chance."

"You can't just have a normal conversation, can you? You turn everything into work."

"Because that's what I *do*."

"That's *all* you do, Lizzie. You come in early, leave late, and probably sandwich some sleep in there somewhere. I lived that schedule in Afghanistan too often, and it catches up to you."

"But this isn't about me, Mateo."

"First-year Med School. 'Treating a patient is as much about you as it is the patient.' Even though some of my patients came in and out so fast they never even saw me, I worked hard to make every one of them feel that they were in good hands, even if those hands were exhausted. But you... There's a deep-down tiredness behind the facade you put on, and it shows in your eyes. And I don't think it's physical so much as something else."

"It's just an accumulation of things. Tough decisions. My dad's death. Things I've wanted I haven't had. Things I've had I haven't wanted." She gave him a weak smile. "You're very perceptive for a man who claims amnesia at the drop of a hat."

"Straightforward talk, honesty...that's what I was all about, Lizzie. Have to be when you're out on the battlefield making quick decisions and performing life-changing procedures." He sighed. "In the end, when you're all they've got, the only real thing that counts is your word."

"Was it difficult…practicing like that?"

"Isn't it what your dad did?"

She shook her head. "He had rank, which got him assigned to a base hospital. He was the one who took the casualties that people like you had fixed after you sent them on."

"Wouldn't it be crazy if our paths had crossed somewhere? Yours and mine?"

"He kept me pretty isolated from that part of his life. If our paths had crossed it would have been somewhere like that little *bäckerei* on Robsonstrasse in Rhineland-Palatinate. We lived in a little flat about a block from there, and I loved getting up early and going for a Danish, or even a raspberry-filled braid."

"The plum cake there was always my favorite. A little bit sweet, a little bit tart."

"So, you've been there?" Lizzie asked, smiling over the shared memory.

"When I had time. My trips in and out were pretty quick, but I started getting a taste for the plum cake about the same time I stepped on the plane to go there, so that was always my first stop."

"Small world," Lizzie said. "Almost like a fairy tale… where the Princess meets the Prince in the most improbable way, then they have battles to fight to get to each other. You know—the love-conquers-all thing, starting with a fruit Danish and plum cake."

"And the rest of the story in your little world?" he asked. "Do they ever get to their happily-ever-after, or do they eat their cakes alone forever?"

"Let's see…" she said. "So, their paths crossed at the bakery… His eyes met hers—love at first sight, of course.

It always happens that way in a nice romantic story. But since the hero of my story was a soldier prince, their time was fleeting. Passionate, but brief. And the kisses…?"

"Were they good?"

"The best she'd ever known. But she was young, and very inexperienced. Oh, and she'd never kissed a real man before. He was her first. Her other kisses had come from boys in the village…no comparison to the kisses of a man."

It was nice, putting herself in the place of a young village maiden. Yes, Mateo's kisses would definitely be those of a real man. She could almost imagine how they would taste on her own lips.

"Was he her first true love?"

Lizzie nodded. "Of course he was. But, the way as many war stories end, they were separated. He was sent somewhere else and her heart was broken."

"Badly, or would she eventually heal?"

"I don't think you ever heal when you've lost the love of your life. But she went after him. She was strong that way."

"*Then* true love prevailed?"

"In my story, yes."

"And they lived happily ever after?"

"As happily-ever-after as any two lovers could with six children. A house in the country. Maybe a few dairy cows."

"Or just a couple of children, a house on a beach in Hawaii, no cows allowed?"

"Nice dream," she said on a sigh. "And I'd kill for a blueberry Danish right now."

Mateo started to slide his hand across the ledge on which they were seated—not so much to hold her hand, but just to brush against it. But either she saw it coming and didn't want it, or she was still caught up in her fairy tale, because just as he made his approach she stood, then turned toward the beach.

"We used to come here when I was a child. It's grown up a lot. Not much tourism back then."

"Is there any one place you call home, Lizzie?"

She shook her head. "Not really. Home was where we were or where we were going. And you?"

"A small village near Guadalajara, originally. Then wherever my mother could get work after we came to the States."

"Is she…?"

"She's got some health problems…can't travel anymore. But we chat almost every day, and someone at the facility is helping her learn how to video chat."

"Does she know about your injury?"

Mateo shook his head. "Her life was hard enough because of me. Why add to it if I don't have to?"

"After what my dad went through with his Alzheimer's, I think you're doing the right thing."

"Now, about that walk…"

He would have been good doctor. She was sure of that. And she was touched by his caring attitude toward his mother. Even toward *her*. This wasn't the Mateo who refused his treatments or walled himself into his room like a recluse. This was someone entirely different. Someone she hadn't expected but was glad she'd found.

"Well, if we go one way we'll run into a shaved ice concession, and if we go the other way it's The Shack."

"And The Shack is…?"

"Fun, loud, dancing, music, watered-down drinks for the tourists… Pretty much a place I shouldn't be taking you."

"Which is exactly why I'm taking *you*."

"Two-drink limit, Mateo. Beer, preferably. You're not on any prohibitive meds, but…"

"I was wondering when the doctor would return."

"The doctor never left."

"Oh, yes, she did," he said, smiling. "And I was the one who got to see it happen."

It was well into the evening—"her time," as she called it. She really needed to go home and rest. But now that he was out here, she wanted to keep him here. Because while he was here he wasn't inside the hospital, getting into trouble. Even his good looks—which everybody noticed—weren't enough to change their minds, and right now the mindset was not in Mateo's favor. Presently she was too exhausted to deal with it, so this little time out was badly needed. Probably for both of them.

Lizzie took a quick appraisal, even though she knew what he looked like. But she liked his dark look. The muscles. The smooth chest. And his hands…large, but gentle—the hands of a surgeon. How would they be as the hands of a lover? she wondered, as he spotted her amongst the crowd, then came her direction.

"I saw you staring at me," he said, as a couple of young women from the bar watched him with obvious open invitation.

Who could blame them? Lizzie thought. He was the best-looking man there.

"Not staring. Just watching to make sure you weren't doing something that would embarrass you and cost me my job."

"But you're off duty."

"And you're still a patient of the hospital."

"But not your patient, Lizzie. And therein lies the distinction." He grabbed a cold beer from a passing server and handed it to Lizzie. "Do you ever allow yourself to have fun?"

"Do you ever allow yourself to *not* have fun?" she asked, wondering if, in his previous life, he'd been a party boy.

He held up his bottle to clink with hers, but she stepped back before that could happen.

"You're a beautiful woman, Lizzie. Prettier than anyone else here. And you're smart. But if I were your doctor I'd prescribe more fun in your life—because even when you're standing in the middle of it, you can't see it."

"Then it's a good thing you're not my doctor, isn't it?"

Mateo reached over and took Lizzie's beer, then took a swig of it.

"That's your limit," she warned him.

"Actually, it's one over—but who's counting?"

Lizzie shook her head, caught between smiling and frowning. "I shouldn't have to count. Somewhere in the manual on being adult there's a chapter on responsibility. Maybe you should go back and re-read it."

"You really can't let go, can you?"

"It's not about letting go, Mateo. It's about all the things that are expected of me—not least of which is taking care of you, since I'm the one who brought you here."

He reached over and brushed a stray strand of hair from her face. The feel of his hand was so startling and smooth she caught herself on the verge of recoiling, but stopped when she realized it was an empty gesture. Still, the shivers his touch left behind rattled her.

"I'm not going to let anything hurt you or your reputation," he said, his voice so low it was almost drowned out by the noise level coming from the rest of the people at The Shack. "I know how hard it is to get what you want and keep it, and I wouldn't jeopardize that for you, Lizzie."

This serious side of him…she hadn't seen it before. But she knew, deep down, this was the real Mateo coming through. Not the one who refused treatment, not even the one who partied hard on the beach. Those might be different sides to his personality, but she'd just been touched by the real Mateo Sanchez, and she liked it. Maybe for the first time liked *him*. If only she could see more of him, now.

"I appreciate that," she said.

She toyed with the idea of telling him that her job here might not be everything she wanted, that she was rethinking staying. But he didn't want to hear that. It was her dilemma to solve.

"Just keep it reasonable and we'll both be fine."

"Everything in my life has been reasonable, Lizzie. I may not remember all about that life, but I do recall who I was in the part I remember, and I was you—always too serious, always too involved."

"And now?" she asked.

"That is the question, isn't it? I have so many different pieces of me rattling around my brain, and I'm not able to put them in order yet."

And she suspected he was afraid of what he might find when he did put them into place. She understood that. Understood Mateo more now than she had.

"Sometimes they don't always come together the way you want or expect."

"Then I'll have a lifetime to adjust to what I'm missing, or what got away from me. And that's not me being pragmatic. That's me trying to deal with *me*, and I'm not easy. I know that."

He reached out and brushed her cheek, this time without the pretense of brushing back her hair. It was simply a stroke of affection or friendship. Maybe an old habit returning. And she didn't mind so much.

Affection had never really been part of her life. Not from her dad, not from her husband. Even if this little gesture from Mateo meant nothing to him, it meant something to her. But she wouldn't allow herself to think beyond that. What was the point? He was a man without a memory; she a woman without clear direction. It wasn't a good combination, no matter how you looked at it.

Still, his touch gave her the shivers again.

"So, moving on to something less philosophical, you wouldn't happen to know if I can swim, would you? I mean, being in the Army, I'm assuming I have basic skills. But enough to get me out there on one of those surfboards?"

"I could always throw you in to find out."

"You're not a very sympathetic doctor, Dr. Peterson."

She laughed. "Well, you're finally catching on."

"What I'm catching on to is that you're a fraud. I know there's a side of Lizzie Peterson she doesn't let out. That's the side I want to see."

"Good luck with that," she said, giving his shoulder a squeeze. "Because what you see with me is what you get."

"Under different circumstances that might not be so bad. But with what I'm going through..." Mateo shrugged. "As they say: timing is everything. Too bad that's the way it's working out."

Which meant what? Was he really interested, or was this only one small aspect of Mateo that had been damaged?

"In my experience, it's not so much about the timing as it is the luck of the draw. Things happen when they happen, and the only thing dictating that is what you're doing in the moment. If I'm the one paddling around in the surf after I've been warned there's a rip current, it should come as no surprise to me that I'm also the one who gets carried out to sea. Things happen because we make them happen—or we choose to ignore what could happen in their place."

"Like my amnesia. It happened because... Well, if I knew the answer to that, I'd tell you. But my doc prefers I make the discovery on my own. 'Vulnerable mind syndrome,' he calls it. Which means my mind is open and susceptible to anything."

"Except doing the things you're supposed to in order to help yourself improve."

"Claiming amnesia on that one," he said, smiling.

"As long as you're just claiming and not believing. And as for swimming... I don't know. But at some point, after I return from my holiday, if you're still here..."

"Ah, the veiled threat."

"Not a threat. An offer to take you out and see how you do in the water."

"That could motivate me to be on my best behavior."

"Or you could motivate yourself. Your choice, Mateo. So, are you up for a wade?" she asked.

"Didn't you just say something about throwing me in?"

"Maybe I did...maybe I didn't," she teased.

Mateo laughed, then suddenly turned serious. "What happens if the real me comes back, Lizzie—all of me—and I don't like who I am?"

"You haven't given yourself enough time. And maybe you underestimate yourself. Whatever the case, you're aware of changes and that's the first step. Always be mindful of that and you'll be fine. I mean, we all lose track of ourselves at one time or another, with or without amnesia. I really believe you're more in touch with who you are than you're ready to admit. So, like I said, there's no rush. Now, if you go in the water with me, it's ankle-deep or nothing."

"I could have been a Navy SEAL…which means I'm an expert swimmer." He kicked off his flip-flops and waded out in the water with her.

"Except you were an Army surgeon, stationed in a field hospital in Afghanistan. No swimming there."

"In my mind I was doing something more glamorous and heroic."

"You *were* doing something heroic. Patching, stitching, amputating…" She took hold of his hand, even though he was in perfect physical condition, and they waded in up to their knees. "Might not have been glamorous, but you were saving lives."

"Only some of which I remember," he said, taking the lead and then pulling Lizzie along until they were in halfway to their hips.

They stood there together for a few minutes, simply looking out over the water. In the distance, a freighter was making its slow way across the horizon—not destined for Oahu, where they were, but perhaps one of the other islands.

Faraway places, she thought, as she reluctantly turned back toward shore. She'd spent her life in faraway places, but she'd never taken the time to notice as she'd been too young, or too involved in trying to get along in yet another new place.

A big pity, that. So many opportunities wasted. Maybe someday she'd go back and have a do-over. Or maybe she wouldn't. Maybe she'd put the past behind her, find her roots, and venture out to see if a little happiness might go with that. Right now, she didn't know what she'd do. Her life was a toss-up.

"You're drunk," Lizzie said, not happy about this at all. Well, maybe not downright drunk so much as a little tipsy. But it would be the same once Janis found out.

After their wade in the ocean Mateo had decided to go back and join the partiers.

"That's why I'm taking you in the back door of Makalapua. Because if we go in the front, I'll lose my job."

Actually, she wouldn't. She was the primary care physician there and that brought some clout with it. And the patients weren't prisoners. Doing what Mateo had done, while not advisable, wasn't illegal, and in the hospital not even punishable. His condition wasn't physical. He was on no medications that had any bearing on the beers he'd consumed. So nothing precluded alcohol.

Lizzie recalled the evenings when her dad had been a patient here, and she'd taken him to The Shack for tropical drink. He'd loved that. When he was lucid, he'd claimed it made him feel normal. But he hadn't been on the verge of being sent elsewhere, the way Mateo was.

Still, there was no reason for Mateo to make a spectacle of himself—which he had done after three craft beers. He'd danced. On a table. With a waitress.

She'd turned her back to order herself another lemonade, and when she'd turned around there he'd been, doing everything a head trauma patient shouldn't do. And he'd refused to stop when she'd asked him to get off the table. It was almost like he was trying to get himself kicked out of his spot at the hospital.

It had taken two strong *wahines he'e nalu*—surfer women—to pull him down for her, and by that time he'd been so unsteady he hadn't even been able to take ten steps back without zigging and zagging. And there she'd been, looking like a total idiot, trying to get the man who'd become the life of the party to quit.

Well, in another day she'd have two whole weeks to sleep, swim, and forget about her patients, her obligations…and Mateo. Except he worried her. After having such a nice chat with him… Well, she wasn't sure what she'd hoped for, but this wasn't it.

"Not drunk. Just pleasantly mellow. And I'll take responsibility for my actions," he said, slumping in the wheelchair one of The Shack patrons had run back to the hospital and retrieved for her.

"You bet you will—because what you did is way out of line and I'm not going to get myself into trouble because you can't control yourself."

"Meaning you're going to report me?"

"Meaning I'm going to make a note in your chart. You're already close to the edge, Mateo, and you know that. Depending on what kind of mood Janis is in when she reads what I'm about to write, there's a strong likelihood she'll have you transferred. You know the policy."

"Yeah…one month to show I'm working, eight weeks to show progress. Well, isn't dancing progress?"

"I was trying to be nice by giving you a little time away from the hospital, but you turned it into a mess. And while dancing may show *some* sort of progress… on a table? With a waitress?"

"You're sounding a little jealous, Lizzie. I'd have asked you to dance, but, well…all work, no play. You'd have turned me down."

Yes, she would have. But was he right about her jealousy? Not over the other woman, but over taking the chance to have a little fun. She was all work, wasn't she?

Maybe all these years of no play had caught up to her and she didn't know how to have fun. Or maybe "Daddy's little soldier," as he'd used to call her, had never known what fun was.

Lizzie pushed Mateo's wheelchair up a side hall, through the corridor behind the kitchen, then through the physical therapy storage area. Finally, when they came to the hall that led to his room, Lizzie stopped, looked around, then gave his chair a shove and stood there watching him roll away while she did nothing to stop him.

It took Mateo several seconds to realize she wasn't controlling him, and by the time he'd taken hold of the chair wheels he was sitting in the middle of the hall, too woozy to push himself past the two rooms before his.

"Why are you doing this to me?" he asked, managing to move himself along, but very slowly.

"That's the same question I was asking just a little while ago," she said, walking behind him. "Why are you putting me in this position?"

"Maybe there's something wrong with my amygdala or even my anterior cingulate cortex. You know—the areas that affect impulse control and decision-making."

"Your brain is fine. I've seen enough CTs of it to know there's nothing wrong. The blood clot was removed successfully. No other bruising or swelling present. No tumors. No unexplained shadows. So you've got no physical excuse for the way you act."

When they came to the door to his room Mateo maneuvered to turn in, didn't make it, backed away, and tried again, this time scraping the frame as he entered.

"I wasn't aware I was putting you in any kind of bad position," he said, stopping short of the bed and not trying to get out of his chair.

"Seriously? You don't work, you don't cooperate with the nurses, you refuse to go to your cognitive therapy sessions most of the time, and when you do go you don't stay long. You've recovered from a traumatic brain injury and you're battling retrograde amnesia, Mateo, in case you've forgotten. Then you get drunk and dance on a table. All that puts me in a very difficult position."

She had no idea if he was even listening to her. His eyes were staring out of the window and there was no expression on his face to tell her anything.

"Look, I like you. And I know you're in a tough spot— you look normal, but you're not normal enough to get back to your old life."

"My old life?" he said finally, and his voice was starting to fill with anger. "You mean the one where I was a surgeon one minute and then, in the blink of an eye, a surgeon's patient? Is that what you're calling 'a tough spot?' And don't tell me how I'm working my way through the five stages of grief and I'm stuck on anger, because I damn well *know* that. What I don't know is what happened to me, or why, or what I was doing prior to the accident, or anything I did last year. And I'd say that's a hell of a lot more than *a tough spot*."

He shook his head, but still didn't turn to face her.

"I'm sorry if I got you in trouble. That wasn't my intention. Being a bad patient isn't my intention either. But when you don't know…" He swallowed hard. "When you don't know who you are anymore, strange things happen in your mind. Maybe you were this…maybe you were that. Maybe you're not even close to who you were. I have a lot of memories, Lizzie, and I'm thankful for that. But sometimes, when I'm confronted with something I should know, and it's not there…"

"It scares you?"

"To death."

"My dad… I lived for three years with him, watching him go through that same tough spot and never returning from it. His life was taken from him in bits and pieces until there were more gaps than memories—and he knew that. At least until he didn't know anything anymore. He didn't have the option of moving on, starting over in a life that, while it wasn't his, was still a good life. There's going to come a time when you must move on with whatever you have left and be glad you have that option. Some people don't."

She walked over to him, laid a reassuring hand on his shoulder, and gave him a squeeze.

"You've got to cooperate with your doctors, Mateo, instead of working against them. Right now, working against them is all you do, and I'm willing to bet that's not the way you were before the accident."

"I'd tell you if I knew," he said, his voice more sad now than angry. "I'm sorry about your dad, Lizzie. He deserved better. Anyway, my head is spinning and all I want to do is sleep. But I think I'll need some help out of the chair."

Immediately alert, Lizzie pulled a penlight from her pocket and bent over him to look into his eyes, in case there was something else going on with him other than the beginnings of a hangover.

"Look up," she said. "Now, down…to the right…to the left."

When she saw nothing of note, she tucked away her light, then offered Mateo a hand to help him get up. Which he did—but too fast. He wavered for a moment, then pitched forward into Lizzie's arms.

"Care to dance *now*?" he asked, not even trying to push himself away.

Admittedly, he felt good. And she could smell a faint trace of aftershave, even though he typically sported a three-day-old stubble. Had he splashed on a dash of scent for their walk?

"I think you've already done enough of that," she said, guiding him to the bed.

Once he was sitting, she helped him lift his legs, then removed his flip-flops when he was stretched out on the bed.

"I'll have one of the nurses come in and help you change into your…"

There was no point in continuing. Mateo was already out. Dead to the world. Sleeping like a baby.

And she—well…time to face Janis.

This wasn't how this part of her day was supposed to have gone. Taking a patient out for a walk…him getting drunk…

Thank heavens she had two blissful weeks of sitting on the beach, reading, and swimming coming up. She needed the rest. Needed to be away from her responsibilities. Needed to put her own life in order in so many ways.

CHAPTER THREE

"No, IT'S NOT your fault," Janis said, handing Lizzie a tiki cup filled with a Hawaiian Twist—a drink made of banana, pineapple, and coconut milk. And, yes, she'd even put a paper umbrella in it—not that Lizzie needed a tiki cup, a paper umbrella, or even a Hawaiian Twist. But Janis loved to make island favorites for anybody who came to her office, and today this was the favorite.

So Lizzie took a drink and, amazingly, it made her feel a little bit better. It didn't ease the headache, but it gave her a mental boost.

"It's not like I haven't taken a patient out for a walk before."

"Well, that's why we built the hospital here," Janis said, sitting down in a wicker chair across from Lizzie.

They were on the lanai outside Janis's office, as a perfect tropical breeze swept in around them.

"I know—to take advantage of the location. And the gardens. Because we want our patients to experience paradise. And I do truly believe there are curative powers in simply sitting and enjoying the view. And, in the case of some of our patients, when the memory is gone, they can still find beauty in the moment."

"Sometimes you're too soft," Janis said. "It's not necessarily a bad thing, considering most of the patients we treat, but for Mateo I'm not sure it's a good thing. He's a strong man, with a strong will, and right now that will isn't working to his advantage. I think he's trying to find his way around it. Get a foothold somewhere. Honestly, there's something in Mateo that just isn't clicking."

"Do you think he's trying to take advantage of me? Hoping I can do something for him?"

"He could be. It's always a consideration with some of our patients."

"Well, he seems harmless enough to me. And it's not like anything is going to happen between us."

"Just be careful of Mateo. I haven't figured him out yet."

"Nothing's going on," Lizzie stated. "We've crossed paths for weeks, and this evening I just… It was a *walk*, Janis. That's all. Except for the drinking, everything was fine."

"Everything except you gave in to your sentimental side and he used it against you. Be careful, Lizzie. I've seen it happen before and it never turns out well. And you're better than that."

Janis was right. She *was* better than that. But it wasn't showing right now. Yet she wasn't sure that she wouldn't take another walk with Mateo if he suggested it. Why? Because he was attractive? Because when the real man shone through she liked him? Because she was in the middle of her own crisis and Mateo was a distraction?

"Why don't you go ahead and start your holiday early? Get away from here. Forget us, forget your patients, and most of all, forget Mateo."

"There's no one to cover for me."

"The locum arrives in the morning. We'll put him straight to work while you sleep in or sip a mimosa on your lanai. However you choose to spend your days off,

Lizzie, they start tomorrow. I need you back at your best and, while I have no complaints about your work, you seem so distant lately. Take the time…get it sorted."

Forget Mateo? Easier said than done. But with any luck, and two weeks of rest ahead of her, she'd get much more sorted than Mateo. Her dad. Her life. Putting things into perspective.

Now, that was something she was looking forward to.

In her life she worked, she slept, and every Saturday morning she went surfing, if conditions were right. That was it. All of it. And even though she owned her house she'd never really settled in, because she had been so up in the air about her dad.

Was this the place for him? Did he have the best caregiver? Did he need more? Should she enroll him in a day program a few times a week even though he wouldn't have a clue what it was about?

She'd taken care of her dad for five years before he died, and all her energies outside work had been devoted to him.

Of course, she'd been contacted about great facilities all over the country that would have taken him in and made his last days meaningful. But what would have been "meaningful" to him? Her voice? The familiarity of his old trinkets and clothes? The chicken and rice she'd fixed him every Saturday night that he'd seemed to enjoy, when his enjoyment of other foods had gone away?

He'd had so little left, and there had been nothing any of these facilities could have done to make him better, so why deprive him of things he might remember?

Which was why she was here. He'd always wanted to retire to Hawaii and spend his days sitting on the beach, or planting flowers. That was what she'd given him when they'd moved here...the last thing she could recall that he'd ever asked for.

Now, here she still was, not sure whether to stay and live with the memories or go and start over someplace else. She really didn't have a life here. All her time had been taken up by work or her dad. Then, after he'd died, she'd filled in the empty hours with more work. Now it was all she could see for herself, and she wasn't sure she liked what she saw.

So maybe it was finally time to settle down, turn her house into a home, and start working on some of those plans she'd made when she'd moved here.

"I'll call you in a few days and let you know how it's going," she said to Janis as she headed out the door. "And maybe I'll have a party. A vegetarian luau."

"With lots of rum punch, since they won't be getting roast pig?"

Lizzie laughed. "Sounds like a plan. And if you get swamped, let me know. I'll come back."

"I know you will—which is why I'm going to ban you from the hospital until you're back to work full-time. Understand?"

Janis could be hard. In her position she had to be. But, as her former med school professor, and now her friend, she was the best. In fact, she'd been the one who'd offered to take her dad, when his Alzheimer's had been on the verge of becoming unmanageable at home. She'd even come to the mainland to help her make the move.

"Then how about we meet up at The Shack every few days and you can tell me all the gossip?" Lizzie suggested.

"Or maybe you could hang around there by yourself... meet a man...preferably a nice blond surf bum. How long's it been since...?"

"*Too* long," Lizzie said. "For anything. No details necessary."

"Then definitely find yourself a surf bum. A nice one with an older brother for me."

Lizzie was thirty-four, and Janis had twenty years on her, but with her blonde hair, and her teeny-bikini-worthy body, Janis was the one the men looked at while Lizzie was hiding in the shadows, taking mental notes on how to be outgoing.

"I thought you liked them younger these days?" Lizzie teased.

"I like them any way I can have them." She smiled at Lizzie. "Seriously, take care of yourself. And keep in touch."

"OK and OK," she said, then waved backward as she walked away, intending to head back to her office, tidy up, then leave.

But before she got there she took a detour and headed down the wrong hall. Or the right one, if her destination was Mateo's room. Which, this evening, it was.

"Well, the good news is I get to start my holiday early," she said to Matteo, who was sitting in a chair next to the window, simply looking out over the evening shadows of the garden, and not sound asleep in bed, as she'd expected. "So, this is me telling you goodbye and good luck."

"What? No more dates at The Shack?"

"First one was a total bust. With me it's one strike and you're out."

"But you haven't seen the real me. When that Mateo Sanchez emerges, do I get another chance?"

Lizzie laughed. "I'm betting you were a real charmer with the ladies. One look into those dark eyes and…"

"Do *you* like my eyes?" he interrupted.

She did—more than she should—and she'd almost slipped up there.

"Eyes are eyes. They're nice to use to get a clear picture of when you're being played."

"I'm not playing you, Lizzie."

"It doesn't matter if you are or you aren't. I'm off on holiday now, and once I'm outside the hospital door everything here will be forgotten for two whole weeks."

"Including me, Lizzie?"

"Especially you, Mateo. So, if you're not here when I return…have a good life."

He stood, then crossed the room to her before she could get out the door. He pulled her into his arms. He nudged her chin up with his thumb and simply stared into her eyes for a moment. But then sense and logic overtook him and he broke his hold on her and stepped away.

"We can't do this," he whispered. "I want to so badly, but I never should have started this, and I'm sorry."

"So am I," she said, backing all the way out through the door, and trying to walk to the hospital exit without showing off her wobbly knees.

Whatever had just happened couldn't happen again. She wasn't ready. Her life was in a mess. But it was one more thing to be sorted in her time off.

Was she really beginning to develop feelings for Mateo?

Or was Janis right?

Was he looking for a foothold? Someone to use?

Was he playing her?

She didn't want to believe that, but the thought was there. And so was the idea that she had to shore up her reserves to resist him, because he wasn't going to make it easy.

* * *

He wasn't sure what to think. Didn't even know if he cared. Still, what he'd done was stupid. Going against hospital policy. Drinking a little too much, dancing to prove…well, he wasn't sure what he had been trying to prove.

Had he been the doctor of a patient like himself he'd have taken it much worse than Janis and Randy had. In fact, all things considered, they'd been very calm. Or was it the calm before the storm?

Lizzie wasn't here to defend him now, and he missed her. Not just because she'd seemed to take his side, but because he genuinely liked her. Maybe even missed her already. Right now, he didn't have any friends, and she'd turned out to be not only a friend but someone he trusted.

Except she wasn't in the picture now. He was on his own and trying to figure out what would come next in his life.

"None of this is what I planned," he said aloud to himself as he looked out the window.

Five years in the military, then find a good surgical practice somewhere in a mountainous area. Or maybe near canyons or desert. He wasn't quite sure what he'd wanted, to be honest, but those were the areas that were tugging on his mind, so maybe that was what he'd wanted pre-amnesia. Not that it mattered now.

"You haven't been to your cognitive therapy group," Randy Jenkins said from the doorway.

He was a short man with thick glasses, who wore dress pants and a blue shirt, a tie and a white lab coat. He didn't look like he'd seen the inside of a smile in a decade.

"Haven't even left your room. You're way past the point where your meals should be served to you on a tray in your room. But you're refusing to come to the dining room."

Because he didn't want to. Because nothing here was helping him. Because he wanted his old life back, whatever that was, and he was pretty sure it didn't involve sitting in a group with nine other memory loss patients talking about things they didn't remember.

"And what, exactly, will those prescribed things do for me?" he asked, turning to face the man.

"Give you a sense of where you are now, since you can't go back to where you were before."

"Where I am now is looking out a window at a life that isn't mine."

"Do you *want* to get better, Doctor?"

Mateo shook his head angrily. "What I want is what I can't have. And that's something you can't fix."

"But there are other things you can do besides be a surgeon."

"And how do you think I should address the obvious in my curriculum vitae? *Unemployed surgeon with amnesia looking for work*?"

It wasn't Randy's fault. He knew that. It wasn't anybody's fault. But he was so empty right now. Empty, and afraid to face the future without all his memories of the past.

"Look, sit in on a therapy session this afternoon. Then come for your private session with me. I'll have my assistant look for some training programs that might interest you and—"

"Training programs? Don't you understand? I'm a surgeon."

"No, you're not. Not anymore. I've had to report you to the medical licensing board and—"

"You couldn't have waited until we were a little farther along in this?"

"You're not *in* this, Mateo. And that's the problem. Your license as a surgeon will be provisionally suspended, pending review and recommendations if and when you recover. I had to do it or risk my own medical license."

He'd worked so hard to get that. Spent years and more money than he'd had. Even if he couldn't operate, at least he had the license that proved he'd achieved his lifelong goal. He'd been somebody. But now he didn't even have that.

"I guess we all do what we have to do, don't we?" he said.

"It's nothing personal. And, for what it's worth, you'll probably still have your general license to practice, because at the end of all this there's every likelihood you'll be able to find a place in medicine, somewhere. But you've got to cooperate *now*."

But if he cooperated that meant all this was real. And he wasn't ready for that yet. Which was why he fought so hard against everything. Once he admitted it was real, he was done. Over. Nothing to hope for. Nothing left to hold on to. Not even that thin scrap of resistance.

Two days had gone by and she was already feeling better. She'd boxed up a few of her dad's belongings, which she'd been putting off for too long. Read a book on the history of Kamehameha, which had been sitting dusty on her shelf for two years. Done a bit of surfing and swimming.

Even just two days had done her a world of good, and as she headed off to the little stretch of beach at the front of her house, a guava and passionfruit drink in her hand, she was looking forward to more relaxation, more time to figure out if she should stay here or go somewhere else and start over.

Her plan had always been to go back home to upstate New York, but little by little this tiny patch of land she owned on Oahu had drawn her in. Her house was all glass on the side with the ocean view. It was large, but not too large...comfortable. Her dad had planted flowers that still bloomed in the garden and would for years to come, and the thought of leaving those brought a lump to her throat because he'd loved them so much in the last good days of his memory.

Her job... Well, that was one of those things she needed to rethink. It was good, but she wasn't sure it was where she belonged. She liked working there, loved working with Janis, but the whole fit seemed...*off.* Maybe because her dad was gone now. Maybe because she was alone. Or maybe those thoughts were simply her fatigue taking over. And, since she wasn't one to make rash decisions, she was going to let the job situation ride. Work through to the end of her contract, then see how she was feeling.

Stretching out on a lounger, Lizzie sat her drink on a little table topped with a mosaic of beach shells that her dad had collected and let her gaze drift to the waves lapping her small beach. She owned a *beach.* An honest-to-goodness beach. Even the sound of it impressed her a little, when very little else did these days.

"It's a nice view," came a familiar voice from behind her.

"How did you know where to find me?" she asked, turning to see Mateo standing just a few feet away with a duffle bag slung casually over his shoulder.

"Went to The Shack. Asked. They knew you and pointed me in the right direction."

"So, I'm assuming that since you've got your duffel you're no longer a patient?"

"Randy Jenkins made the recommendation this morning that I be transferred and your friend Janis dropped the axe." He shrugged. "So here I am."

"Then you're on your way to another facility?"

Mateo shook his head. "My transfer is back to California, where I was before I came here. It didn't do me any good then, and nothing's changed so it's not going to do me any good now."

This wasn't good. Too many soldiers returned home with PTSD and other problems and ended up on the street. Suddenly, she feared that for Mateo.

"What are your plans?" she asked, not sure she wanted to hear them.

"Don't have any. When they said they'd arrange a transfer in a couple of days I arranged my own."

"Meaning you're homeless? Or do you have a home somewhere?"

She didn't want to get involved. Shouldn't get involved. But he didn't deserve this, and it wasn't his fault that he'd lost the life he'd known.

"No home. Sold it when I went into the Army and used the proceeds to buy a house for my mother. It's in Mexico, and I'm not a citizen there. To get my veterans' medical benefits I have to live in the States. Meaning until I leave Hawaii I'm a beach bum. But before I take off to…let's call it to 'discover myself,' I wanted to thank you for being so kind to me and trying to help. I appreciate your efforts, Dr. Elizabeth Peterson, even if they were wasted."

"And what now? You walk off into the sunset? Because that's not where you're going to find yourself, Mateo."

He shrugged. "Do you really think I'll find myself if I'm admitted to an eight-bed ward and assigned to therapy to which I won't go, until I'm deemed so uncooperative they put me away in a home, give me drugs, and let me spend the rest of my life shuffling through the halls wearing bedroom slippers and existing in some kind of a stupor?"

"It's not that bad," she argued, even though she knew that in some cases it could be.

But for Mateo…she didn't know. He wanted something he wouldn't get back and he was stuck in the whole denial process. For how long, she had no clue. She was a personal care physician, not a psychiatrist.

"Could you go stay with your mother for a while?"

"I could, but she still doesn't know what happened to me and I'd rather keep it that way as long as I can."

"Well, I admire the reason, but how long do you intend on keeping up the charade?"

"To be honest, I don't know. Haven't thought it through that far, yet."

Everything inside Lizzie was screaming not to get involved, that Mateo wasn't her problem. But she felt involvement creeping up, pulling her toward the edge.

She thought of that day her dad had wandered off, just a year ago. If only someone had found him in time… And while Mateo wasn't at all in the same condition there could be just as many bad consequences for him as well. So, swallowing hard as she pushed aside all the reasons why she shouldn't do it, she did it anyway.

"Look, there's an *ohana* unit on the other side of the house. It's small, but no one's using it, and you're welcome to stay there a couple of days until you get things sorted."

"This is where me and my bad attitude would usually

take offense or say something to make you angry or hurt your feelings, but I'm not going to do that. I didn't come here looking for help, but I'm grateful you're offering. So, yes, I'd appreciate staying in your *ohana*. Because I don't want to be out there wandering alone, trying to find something I might not even recognize. I don't like being this way, Lizzie. Don't like being uncooperative… don't like hearing half the things I'm saying. But if I do get to be too much for you to handle, kick me out. You deserve better than what I know I'm capable of doing."

"I don't suppose you can cook?" she asked.

He chuckled. "No clue. But if you're willing to take a chance with an amnesiac surgeon in your kitchen…"

For the past two days there had been nothing incoming, meaning nothing outgoing either. No imposed time limit on life or death. One less death to record, one less chopped-up body to send back was always good.

Passing the time playing cards with his best buddy Freddy wasn't necessarily what he wanted to be doing, but there wasn't anything else. And it was always interesting to see the many ways Freddy cheated at cards. Some Mateo caught. Many he did not. He could see it— Freddy palming one card and trading it for another.

"Cheat," he accused his friend. All in fun, though.

"Prove it," Freddy always said. "Prove it, and when we get back I'll buy you the best steak dinner you'll ever eat."

Problem was Mateo couldn't prove it. Freddy was just as slick in his card-playing skills as he was at being a medic. The plan was that after they returned home Freddy would finish medical school and eventually end up as Mateo's partner.

But tonight, there was no plan, and Freddy was pacing

the hall the way he did when he got notice that someone was on their way in. In those tense minutes just before everything changed. Activity doubled. The less injured soldiers stepped aside for the more injured.

Sometimes they lined up in tribute, saluting as the medical team rushed through the door, pushing a gurney carrying the latest casualty.

"Stop it!" Mateo shouted at his friend. "Don't do that! Because if you do they'll come. Stop it. Do you hear me? Stop it!"

But Freddy kept on pacing, waiting...

No, not tonight. Mateo wanted to make it three nights in a row without a casualty.

"One more night. Just one more night..."

Outside in the back garden, on her way to take fresh towels and linens to the *ohana*, Lizzie stood quietly at his door, listening. He'd excused himself to take a nap while she'd stayed on the beach to read. Now this.

It hadn't happened in the rehab center, but something here was triggering it. Perhaps getting close to someone again? Close to her?

She thought about going in and waking him up. Then decided against it. If he was working out his demons in his sleep, he needed to. Besides, he was here as a friend, not a patient, and she had to take off her doctor persona or this would never work.

But it worried her. Because she knew the end of the story. Mateo's best friend had been killed in the raid that had injured him. Mateo had been pulled from the carnage and taken to the hospital, resisting help because he'd wanted to go back to save his friend. Except his best friend couldn't be saved.

While she wasn't a neurologist, she wondered if some

deep, buried grief over that was contributing to his condition. Certainly the head injury was. But not being able to save his friend…? She understood that profoundly. Because in the end she hadn't been able to save her father. It was a guilt that consumed her every day.

"Sleep well?" she asked, watching Mateo come through the door. Cargo shorts, T-shirt, mussed hair. She liked dark hair. Actually, she had never really thought about what she liked in terms of the physical aspects of a man, but she knew she liked the physical aspects of Mateo. Strong, muscled…

"Bed's comfortable, but I don't feel rested. Guess I've got more sleep to catch up on than I thought."

Sleep without nightmares, she thought.

"Well, the folks at Makalapua weren't happy to find out where you are. Apparently, you got out of their transportation at the end of the circular drive, when the driver stopped to enter the main road, and then disappeared."

"Transportation? Is that what they call it?"

"Makalapua owns a limo for transporting patients and families when necessary."

"And it also owns an ambulance, Lizzie. *That* was my transportation. Ordered by my doctor. They came in with a gurney, strapped me down to it, and shoved me in the back of the ambulance. I was leaving as a *patient*. Not a guest. And I'm tired of being a patient."

Lizzie sat down on the rattan armchair in her living room and gripped the armrests. "An ambulance? I don't believe—"

"I may have amnesia," he interrupted, "but I still remember what a gurney and an ambulance are. Oh, and in case you didn't hear, I was to be escorted straight onto a military medical plane and met at the airport in

California—probably with a gurney and an ambulance there, too."

"Did you get violent? Is that why they did it?"

"Mad as hell, but not violent." He sat down on the two-cushion sofa across from her but kept to the edge of it. "I'm guessing a couple of them are mad as hell right now."

"They only want to help you, Mateo."

They only want to help you.

We only want to help you.

I only want to help you.

Words she'd said over and over for years. Before, they'd sounded perfectly fine. Now, they sounded deceitful.

"Well, restraining me rather than giving me a sedative was preferable, but they were sending me to the place I specifically asked not to be sent."

"You're still Army, Mateo. On inactive duty. That means your commanders make the call and—"

"It's out of my hands." He shook his head in frustration. "I'm theirs until they cut me loose."

"Something like that. And you knew that's how it would be when you went in. When the military and veterans' hospitals didn't work for you, you were given a chance to recover outside the normal system. So, from what I'm seeing, they really were trying to help."

And now he was in no system but, instead in her *ohana.*

"Look, let me see if I can work something out with Janis. Maybe we can get you transferred somewhere else. Maybe another private hospital."

"Or maybe I should just go grab my things and wander on down the beach. The weather's nice. A lot of people move from their homes to the beaches during the hottest weather. Maybe someone will take pity on me and give me a meal every now and then."

"You're not going to live on the beach, Mateo. And I'm not sending you off on some journey to search for something you might not even remember when you find it."

Visions of her dad getting out and wandering around alone were the essence of her nightmares. And she'd even had a live-in caregiver who hadn't always been able to keep track of him.

"So for now you stay here, and we'll see what we can figure out."

"But the military…they know where I am?" he asked.

"Of course they do. I called them because you're not free of your obligation and they had to know. Like I've told you before, I play by the rules. But they're not going to come and take you away from here, Mateo. At least not yet. All they wanted was to know where you were and what you were doing. I told them you were going into outpatient care in a few days."

"That's what you think I'm going to do?"

"That's what I *know* you're going to do if you want to stay here. Janis approved it and, for the record, it's your last chance. After this the Army takes you back, and they'll be the only ones with a say in what happens."

Finally, he relaxed back into the sofa. "These last weeks it's like someone's always doing something to me, and most of the time not even consulting me before they do it. You're the first one who's ever told me beforehand what would happen, and I appreciate that."

"So…you mentioned your mother doesn't know about your current condition? Why is that? Is there some way she could take over medical responsibility for you until you're through this?"

He shook his head adamantly. "She has advanced diabetes. Arthritis. Partially blind. The less she knows, the better off she is. Like I said before, I do call her every day, and as soon as I'm free to travel I'll go to see her. But I don't want the stress of knowing what I'm going through anywhere near her. She deserves a better life than she's ever had before and I'm not going to deprive her of that."

"Which makes you a very good son."

She recalled how, in her dad's decline, she'd tried to keep so many things away from him—things that would cause him stress. So she certainly understood what Mateo was doing, and even admired him for that. It wasn't easy. She knew that.

"I remember when my mother became a citizen in the US. She'd studied for weeks, worked hard to learn the history, the language, and I think the day she was sworn in was one of the proudest days of her life. Making a new life isn't easy, and she did it for me."

"And you?"

"I was too young to realize all the sacrifices she was making to give me a better life. I don't think I appreciated it the way I should. And my mother... I don't want her worrying about me. It's the least I can do. And she's happy back in Mexico, living near her sister, proud of her son the...the doctor." He nearly choked on the words.

She thought about the life her dad had made for her. That had never been easy either, but it had always been good. And he'd put aside many opportunities because he'd chosen to be a father first.

"Anyway, what's next, Mateo? What do you want to happen or expect to happen?"

He chuckled, but bitterly. "Look, Lizzie. I don't know what I'm doing, and I'm sure that's obvious. But I'm not going to impose, and I'm not going to expect you to be my doctor while I'm here."

"Like I *could* be your doctor," she said. "That would require ethical considerations I don't want to think about. Doctor brings patient home for special treatment? Nope, not me. I can be your friend, even a medical colleague, but not your doctor. So, my friend, I want to take a walk down to The Shack and ask them why they thought it was appropriate to tell someone where I live."

"Then what?" he asked.

"Then guilt them into free shrimp burgers. They're *so* good. But no beer. And no dancing on the table."

"In my defense, it was only a couple feet off the ground."

"You have no defense, Mateo. Absolutely none. And if I catch you up on a table, and I don't care how high it is…" She pointed to the chaise on the lanai. "*That's* as far as you'll go. I might toss you a pillow and a plate of food every now and then, but if you dance on a table I'm done."

Mateo laughed. "You know, from the first moment I saw you walk by my hospital room I knew you were a real softie. Your threats don't scare me, Lizzie. You haven't got it in you to make me sleep out there."

Unfortunately, that was true. Something about Mateo caused her usual resolve to simply melt away.

It wasn't like him to think only in the moment. At least, he didn't *think* it was like him. He'd looked at his calendar and seen that he'd made notes about plans well into the future. Some things still months away. That was certainly a personality trait he didn't remember—especially now, when he was basically on the edge of living rough and not particularly worried about it.

Was that because he knew he could count on Lizzie as his backup?

Mateo looked at his half-eaten shrimp burger and wondered if he even liked shrimp. Had he been allergic his throat would have swollen shut by now. He might even be dead. But he wasn't, and his throat was fine.

Subconsciously, he raised his hand to his throat and rubbed it.

"You OK?" Lizzie asked him.

She was sitting across from him at a high-top for two, looking like an Irish lassie who simply fitted in here. Red hair wild. Brown eyes sparkling with gold flecks that were highlighted by the glow of the citronella candle on their table. The brightest, widest smile he'd ever seen.

"Just wondering if I have allergies."

"According to your military records, you don't."

"You really know more about me than I know about myself, don't you?" he asked. Realizing she had access to his life while he didn't felt strange.

"You do understand why I don't just tell you everything I know, don't you?"

"So you won't fill my impressionable mind with fake notions of who I am. I know it would be easy…false memories and all that. But sitting here with a stranger who knows me inside and out, while only a couple of hours ago I was homeless without a plan is…disconcerting."

Lizzie reached across the table and squeezed his hand. "I'll bet it is. But if you ever settle down you'll work through some of it. Maybe even more than you expect."

He studied her hand for a moment—porcelain-smooth skin, a little on the pale side compared to most of the people at The Shack. Nice hand. Gentle.

"Now that you're not restricted by any kind of medical ethics with me, tell me how much I can expect to return. Or how much will never return. Can you do that much for me?"

She pulled her hand back. "There's no formula for

that, Mateo. No way to predict. I'd like to be able to give you a definitive answer, but the brain can't be predicted. You may be where you're always going to be now, or you may improve. Losing pieces of yourself—or, as I call it, living in a fog—has got to be difficult. I see it, and I understand it, but I can't relate to it."

He smiled. "Wish I couldn't relate to it either. Look, I appreciate you taking me in for a couple of days. I really do need some time to figure out what comes next. But you're not responsible for me, Lizzie. Just be patient for a little while, and on my end of it I promise no more dancing on the table or anything else. I'll be cooperative. Tell me what to do and I'll do it."

He meant it, too. It was time to figure out his life, and it was nice having a friend on his side to help him. A friend who was patient and caring the way Lizzie was.

"Why didn't you do that at the hospital?"

"Four walls, a bed, and a window to the world. That's all it was, and it scared me, Lizzie. Still does when I think that's all my life might be about."

"So you refuse traditional help, do everything you can to distance yourself from it, in order to—what? I want to know, Mateo. If I hadn't lived within walking distance of the hospital, or if a couple of the people who work here hadn't known where I live, what would you have done? Because so far all you've done is walk away. From Germany, from the veterans' facility in Boston, then in California, and from the hospital here. From—"

She shut up and took a bite of her burger.

"From *everything*, Mateo," she said, once she'd swallowed. "And it all adds up to you walking away from yourself."

"You were going to say fiancée, weren't you?"

"You remember her?"

"Vaguely. Must have been a short relationship, because she didn't leave much behind in my head. Except, maybe… She didn't want to live with someone in my condition, did she?"

"Actually, I don't know the whole story. It was in your chart, but since you weren't my patient I didn't read it. The only things I know about you are what I heard at the weekly patient review meetings."

"That's right. By the book, Lizzie."

"You think that's a problem?"

"I think in today's medical world it's an asset. There are too many people getting involved in aspects of a patient's care who shouldn't."

Suddenly he could feel the tiredness coming on. And the headache. Dull to blinding in sixty seconds. So, rather than pursuing this conversation, he stood abruptly, tossed a few dollars on the table—enough to cover both meals and a tip—then walked away. He wanted to get out of there before the full force of the headache made him queasy, caused him to stagger.

Once away from The Shack, Mateo headed toward the beach, then sat down on the sand, shut his eyes, and tried to clear his head.

Right now, he didn't care about what Lizzie was holding back. All he cared about was the pain level rising in him and how to control it.

And that didn't come easy these days. Not easy at all.

She wasn't going to interrupt him, sitting alone out there on the sand. Mateo was entitled to his moods and his mood swings and it wasn't her place to hover over him. If he needed her help, he'd ask. Or not.

It was almost an hour later when he returned to the house. When she looked in Mateo's eyes she saw how lost he was, but she also saw the depth of the man. He was in there—just locked away.

"Look, I'm going out for a night swim, then I'm going to sit on the lanai for a while to relax. You're welcome to come, or you're welcome to stay here and read a book, watch a movie—whatever you want to do."

"You don't have to feel responsible for me, Lizzie. I can take care of myself."

"I was just being polite. You look tired, and I thought a swim might make you feel better."

He looked more than tired. He looked weary. Beaten down. He looked like a man who was fighting with everything he had to get back on the right path. It worried her, even though she had no right to be worried. Still, she couldn't help herself. There was something about Mateo that simply pulled at her.

"And I was just being honest. I don't want you disrupting your life for me."

She smiled. "To be honest, I hadn't intended on doing that. I just thought it would be a nice way to end the evening."

With that she went upstairs, changed into her swimsuit—a modest one-piece, black, no frills, nothing revealing—and went straight to the beach alone, leaving Mateo watching some blathering documentary on her TV.

Too bad, she thought as she dipped her toe in the surf. He might have enjoyed this. And she might have enjoyed doing this with him.

She was stunning, even though she was trying to hide it in that swimsuit. But her kind of beauty couldn't be hidden. Not the outside beauty, and not the inside beauty.

This was a huge imposition, him living in her home.

He knew that. But so much of him wanted to get to know her and, while ending up here really hadn't been his intention, when good fortune had smiled on him he hadn't had it in him to turn his back on it.

He moved along the beach from where Lizzie had entered the water. He wanted to join her, but he didn't want to impose. Yet he'd wandered down here, not sure what he was hoping for. Another invitation? Perhaps nothing?

In all honesty he had no right to think anything or want anything, in his condition. But watching Lizzie... It gave him hope he hadn't felt before. Maybe something in him would change. Or something would reset and at least allow him to look forward.

Unfortunately, Lizzie coming into his life now was too soon. He could see himself with her, but not yet.

Sighing, Mateo shut his eyes. All he could see was Lizzie. Her face. The way she looked at him. Sadness. Compassion. She had the power to change a man. The power to change *him*. And maybe that was good. He didn't know, but it felt right. Felt like he was ready.

She'd been on his mind constantly, and he'd thought of little else other than Lizzie from that first moment in the hospital, when she'd walked into his room, sat down in the chair opposite him and hadn't said a word. Not one single word. She had smiled as she'd watched him, but she hadn't talked, and it had got to the point that it had been so distracting, even annoying, that he'd been the one to break the silence.

"Why are you doing that?" he'd asked her.

"Sometimes you learn more from observing than talking," she'd told him.

"And what did you learn from observing me?" he'd asked.

"That you're not going to be easy for your doctors."

Mateo chuckled. Prophetic words. He hadn't been. Still wasn't. And she'd known that simply by observing him.

"There's a shorter way back to the house," Lizzie said, sitting down beside him on the rock where he'd been sitting for the past half hour.

"I didn't hear you coming." He scooted over to give her room.

"But I saw you sitting here. I used to sit here back when my dad was getting bad. I was looking for answers, and even though there were none I always went away with a sense of calm. Back then, calm was good."

"This whole area is nice. Not sure I found any calm here, but the view is amazing." He slid his hand across the rock until it was just skimming hers. "The only places I've ever lived were congested...loud."

"Sounds like a tough way to live life," Lizzie commented.

"There are a lot of tough ways to live life, Lizzie. Some we choose, some we don't." He stood. "Anyway, it's been a long, unexpected day, and I'm ready to see if I can get some more sleep. So..." He looked at her, then shrugged. "Care to have me walk you home?"

Lizzie smiled, then stood and took his arm. "I always did love a gallant man. Just never knew they existed outside of fairy-tale books."

"Well, consider me a poor and humble prince who's at your beck and call." He gave her a low-sweeping bow then extended his arm to her.

"Poor?" she asked, as they made their way along the path. "I saw your financials when you were admitted. You're not wealthy, but you're certainly not poor."

"Then maybe poor of spirit?"

Lizzie laughed. "Somehow I doubt that. I think you're a man with an abundance of spirit. It's just that your spirit is in hiding right now."

Mateo was testing her like he'd done in the hospital with everyone else he'd encountered. It was the same, but different, because now he was living in the real world, which called for real coping skills instead of avoidance.

He'd get the hang of it. She was sure of that. But what he *wouldn't* get the hang of was using her as his enabler. Once she'd enabled her dad too much for too long. In doing that she'd denied the obvious—that the next corner he turned would be worse than the one before. And the one after that worse again.

Well, not with Mateo. He was testing new legs, so to speak. Taking new steps. Learning new things to fill in the gaps. As much as she wanted to make it her battle, it wasn't. For Mateo to get better, find his new direction, he had to take those steps by himself, fight his way through to something that fit.

She could be on the sidelines, watching, maybe holding out a supporting hand. But it was his destiny to control. She had to keep telling herself that. His destiny, not hers.

But it wasn't easy walking into her house by herself, going up the steps to bed alone. No, none of it was easy. In the morning, though, depending on what Mateo did or didn't do tonight, she'd decide what she would do. Or would not do.

CHAPTER FOUR

THE SMELL WAS HEAVENLY. Coffee and… Was something baking? Lizzie wanted to bask in bed a while longer, simply to enjoy the rich variety of aromas drifting up to her, and she could do that. Nothing was stopping her. She was on holiday, after all. She could bask, lounge, sleep, do anything she wanted.

But the clock on her phone showed it was just a few minutes until eleven, which meant she'd spent most of the morning doing that already. It was amazing how good it felt—especially with her bad sleeping habits. Never more than an hour or two at a time. Sometimes missing sleep altogether for a day or more.

Also, she wanted to see Mateo. No particular reason. She simply wanted to see him and ask what he planned for the day.

So a quick shower and Lizzie was on her way downstairs, where he was waiting for her at the bottom, holding out a coffee mug.

"There was no cream, and you don't strike me as the type who'd go in for gratuitous sugar, so it's black. But I did find a papaya tree outside and I picked a ripe one, juiced it, and added a bit to your coffee."

"You remember what a papaya is?" She was not only pleased, she was surprised.

"My mother used to make them into a salsa to use on fish tacos. And papaya cake. That was the best."

"I'll bet it was," she said, taking a sip and letting it glide down her throat. "What else can you cook?"

He smiled. "Well, those fish tacos I just mentioned. Although I try to eat on the healthy side. Tacos, enchiladas, tamales, burritos…they might be food for the gods, but when you work out every day the way I used to do they're also food for the waistline, and it's never been my desire to see mine grow." He patted his belly. "So far, so good. Oh, and I baked muffins, if you're interested. Healthy ones. No sugar, no butter."

"Then you really *are* a cook."

"Let's just say that I'm pretty sure I know my way around a kitchen. Not sure about anything gourmet, but the muffins were easy enough and the coffee was self-defense. One of the nurses in Afghanistan made coffee and it was horrible. I'd been there three days when I decided to take it over myself. Either that or no coffee, because it was eating away my stomach lining."

Lizzie laughed. "Was she that bad or were you just that gullible?"

Chuckling, he shook his head. "I may have known the answer to that at one time. But, since I don't now, I'd like to say she was bad and leave it at that."

Did he know how much he'd just revealed to her? It had come so easily now, after she'd spent so much time asking him questions he wouldn't or couldn't answer. Then suddenly…*this*. She wasn't going to get too excited, but she did hope it was a step forward. Hoped in a non-medical way, of course.

"So, what's on your agenda for today?' she asked, fully expecting him to draw a blank on that.

But the bright look coming over his face told her otherwise.

"Clothes. What I have on…that's it. Hand-me-downs left behind at the hospital. And shoes."

"Then we go shopping," she said, smiling.

He chuckled. "I think I'm one of those men who hates shopping."

"Amnesia doesn't cut it with me, Mateo. You need clothes—we get you clothes. And I love to shop, so prepare yourself. I could turn this into an all-day outing."

Mateo moaned. "My mother loves shopping and when I was young, I was forced to walk behind her, carrying her handbag. It was humiliating, especially to a little boy who was bullied and called a mama's boy, but it worked out because I worked out and got strong, which scared away the bullies." He smiled. "I wasn't really a fighter, but nobody ever knew that."

"Well, I won't ask you to carry my handbag unless you really want to."

Mateo moaned again. "Can't we just do it online?"

"What? And miss the fun of it?" Lizzie took another sip of the coffee and arched her eyebrows in surprise. "This is really good. I'm glad you remembered, because you can make it every morning you're here."

"Actually, I didn't remember the coffee. I remembered my mom and her love of everything papaya. This was just a lucky guess."

"So, Dr. Mateo Sanchez, skilled general surgeon…"

"*Former* general surgeon."

"I'll get on to that later. Maybe ask Janis to sit down hard on Dr. Jenkins and come up with a better treatment plan for you. Anyway, surgeon, chef, devoted son…what else?

"Not much technology sense."

"With the technology sense of a *nene*."

"What's a *nene*?" he asked.

"A goose."

She didn't know if a few memories really were slipping back or if these were things he'd simply kept to himself. Maybe to maintain some control? But she wasn't a shrink and, whatever the case was, she wouldn't ask.

"The official Hawaiian bird, actually."

"Seriously, with all the pretty little colorful birds everywhere, Hawaii chose a goose?"

She turned and strolled out to the lanai, where one of those "colorful birds"—a beautiful yellow-green *amakihi*—was sipping nectar from one of the nectar stations her dad had built. He'd had such a way with the birds, and with flowers. It was all still there—the colors, the care he'd taken... It was the first thing she went to look at every single morning of her life.

"The goose is a worthy bird," she said, stepping away from where the *amakihi* was feeding, so as not to disturb it. "They've been here half a million years, and they don't damage their habitat, so they've earned their place." She studied the muffin he was holding out for her. "I'm assuming papaya?"

"I was taught to take advantage of what you're given and be grateful for it."

"As long as you didn't climb the tree to get it, I'm good. But if you did..."

Mateo chuckled. "It was on the ground. Trust me. I may not remember a lot of things, but I do remember that head injuries and climbing up papaya trees don't mix. So, about my clothes..."

The headache wasn't bad, but it was too early to feel this tired. All he wanted to do was sit out on the lanai and doze, even though he'd been the one to suggest clothes-shopping. Too much, too soon. Making the coffee hadn't been bad, but baking the muffins had done him in.

He had to show her he was better, because if he didn't she'd pack him off to a hospital somewhere. There was nothing in him that wanted to go. In fact, even though he'd worked in a hospital, being turned into a hospital patient filled him with a fear that, when he thought about it, nearly paralyzed him.

He wanted to know why, but the answer didn't come to him when he tried to find that piece of himself. In fact, the more he visualized himself as a patient, the more he sweated and came close to an anxiety attack.

There were so many mysteries to his life still locked away that when he let it happen the frustration of it all led to a bad temper. But bad temper didn't solve his problems. So why go there? Why not detour around that roadblock? Because perhaps, at the end of the road, something better might be waiting for him.

It made sense. Now all he had to do was convince his logical mind to follow through. And that was the tough part. Because the other part of his mind still wanted to kick and rebel.

But not so much since Lizzie.

"It's not too far. If you're up for a walk, it's about a mile."

She was dressed in a Hawaiian wrap-skirt, midi-length, yellow with a white floral print. Her shirt was a strappy white tank top that left a bit of her belly exposed. No bra. Hair tucked into a floppy straw hat with a few wild tendrils escaping, oversize sunglasses, and sandals.

Normally when she wasn't on duty she slouched around in terry shorts and an oversize T-shirt—*with* a bra. Going out with Mateo, for some uncharted reason, she wanted to look better. Funny how looking better made her feel better. Today she was feeling great. Something that hadn't happened very much recently.

"In fact, there are several shops, so you'll have a choice of clothing."

He stood, gave her an appreciative stare, and slipped into his sandals. "So what kind of clothing are we talking about?" he asked, as his gaze stopped on her exposed belly.

"Whatever you like. Do you remember the way you used to dress?"

She did like the three-day stubble on him, and hoped it wouldn't go once he'd fixed himself up.

"I remember scrubs. A couple of suits... Don't know if I used to hate them then, but the thought of wearing a suit now..." He faked a gigantic cringe. "Pretty sure I slept in the buff."

"Too much information," Lizzie said, fighting back a grin—and a vision of Mateo in the buff.

As a doctor, she'd seen a lot of him, but not all. As a woman, her fantasies went well beyond—and that was dangerous.

Mateo and her on the beach. On a blanket. Him rubbing sunscreen on her back, her shoulders, her thighs...

Definitely dangerous territory, since she hadn't sorted out what kind of man, if any, she wanted in her future. "You've been in the Army for a while. You weren't sleeping in the buff there."

He laughed. "Well, maybe if I didn't in the past, it's something I might start doing in the future."

"Beach shorts. Tropical print, lightweight, somewhat baggy, stopping just at the tops of your knees. And a sleeveless T-shirt. Maybe some cargo shorts and a few cotton floral print button-up shirts. Also a pair of long khaki pants, with a white, breezy cotton shirt."

"And here I was, picturing myself more as a surf bum."

"Do you surf?" she asked, her mind still stuck on beach shorts and sleeveless T-shirts.

"Don't have a clue. Do you want to teach me?"

"Your last doctor advised you to stay away from activities like that for at least four months. It hasn't been four months."

"Then it's a good thing my last doctor no longer has a say, and my new friend just might be willing to show me some basic, non-threatening surfing moves. *If* she surfs."

"She does—and she's very good at it." She hadn't done nearly as much of it as she would have liked, owing to her dad's condition, alongside her hyper zest for work. But the thought of surfing with Mateo—well, at least bodyboarding—caused a little flush of excitement. "And if she decides to take you out, she's in complete control."

"I never thought she wouldn't be." He smiled. "Anyway, my look is your decision. Except red. I won't wear red."

"Why not? With your dark skin color…"

He shook his head. "Too much like blood. I've seen more of that than I care to. Worn too much of that on me. No red."

"Red's overdone," she said, hiking her oversize canvas bag up to her shoulder. "But blue…*that's* a color."

"So is yellow," he said, smiling. "On you."

"Then you're the type of guy who notices these things about a woman, because in my experience—"

"What experience?" he interrupted.

"Well, in my case not much lately."

Not for years, to be honest. But Mateo didn't need to

be burdened with her problems when he had enough of his own to wrestle with.

"You know what they say about all work and no play?" he quipped lightly.

"You're right about that," she returned.

"No, seriously. What *is* it they say?" His eyebrows knit into a frown.

"You don't remember?" she asked, highly suspicious of the twinkle in his eyes.

Was this the real Mateo coming out, or one he was inventing just for her? She'd seen that in patients before—turning into the person they believed she wanted to see. The patient with excruciating headaches who refused to admit to them just to maintain a certain image. The patient with Parkinson's disease who denied his symptoms as a way of denying the disease.

People showed what they wanted—either to deny to themselves or put on a brave front for someone else—and she couldn't help but wonder if that was what Mateo was doing…showing her a side of himself he believed she wanted or needed to see. Maybe to maintain the roof over his head for a while? Maybe because he wanted to impress her?

Whatever was going on, she liked that spark, and hoped it was genuine.

He chuckled. "Of course I do. I was just wondering if you did, since you practically admitted you don't play. But you're not dull, Lizzie. Maybe not bursting with as much *joie de vivre* as you could be, or maybe should be, but definitely not dull."

"Well, dull is in the eye of the beholder, I suppose. I've never thought of myself as particularly effervescent, though."

That was the truth. She was hard-working, serious,

dedicated, and passionate about her career, but when it came to the personal aspects of her life, there'd never been much there. Not enough time. Or real interest.

"Then maybe you're not seeing what I'm seeing."

"Or maybe you don't know what you're seeing because you've forgotten what effervescence looks like in a person."

She motioned him to follow her off the lanai and then to the road in the front of the house. The hospital, and her home, were just a little way outside La'ie, on the north end of the island. It was out of the way, but bursting with life.

A lot of people at the hospital commuted up from Honolulu, or one of the larger cities to the south, like Kane'ohe, but she liked this area—liked the relative smallness of it, loved the people. Even though she'd left huge and disproportionate New York City for this, she couldn't imagine living anywhere else now.

Could she return to big city living? If she had to. Would she want to, though? Not a chance. Living in paradise had spoiled her.

"So, what we're going to see will be surf shops for the most part. There are a couple of shops that specialize in other things—clothes that are more traditional, shoes, those sorts of things. And then there are the food vendors. All I can say is…*heaven*."

"Where every day is a holiday?"

"It can be, if that's what you want. Oh, and just so you know, I need to run into the hospital and sign some papers. You're welcome to come in with me, or wait outside if the old familiar surroundings make you uncomfortable."

"Snakes make me uncomfortable. And bullets. And

I don't think I'm especially fond of clingy women, but I could be wrong about that one. Oh, and cats."

"You don't like cats?" she asked.

"Actually, I love cats. Love their independence and attitude. But I'm allergic."

"I've always wanted a cat. Or a dog. But we moved around too much, and my dad didn't think it would be practical, taking an animal with us. I had a goldfish once. His name was Gus. Had to give him to a friend when we moved from Virginia to Germany."

"Because your dad was a surgeon. Career Army?"

"Yep—I was seeing the world at a very young age."

"And enjoying it?"

"Most of the time. Unless he had to leave me behind when he was in a combat zone. Even so, he gave me everything I needed and wanted."

Except a mother. Somewhere along the way her dad had decided he didn't have enough time or energy for another marriage, and Lizzie had often wondered if, in the end, having someone with him besides her might have helped him hang on to reality a little longer.

"It must have been tough on your dad, raising a daughter and maintaining his military career."

"It was what it was, and we managed," Lizzie said, as they walked along the narrow road, while people on bikes and scooters passed by on both sides of them. "When you never have a person in your life—like I didn't have my mother—you get used to it and make it work. My dad and I did."

"What happened to your mother?"

"She lost interest in the life we lived, then in my dad, and left us when I was about five. Died a couple years after that."

"So she never had a chance to make amends?"

"She could have. But she didn't want to."

"And your dad...?"

"He wasn't interested in trying before Alzheimer's hit. Then afterwards he didn't remember her at all."

"It couldn't have been easy on you, taking care of your dad the way you did."

"It wasn't—but I gave him the care he gave me when I was a child. I couldn't just...send him away somewhere."

"He isn't the reason you're here?"

"Actually, he is. They have an excellent treatment program at the hospital and I think it gave him more than anybody might have expected. But he lived at home because he loved it there, and I didn't have the heart to take that away from him. Especially his garden. When he was losing so many things in his life, his flowers still made him happy. It's nice, looking out every day, seeing a little bit of my dad still there. Somehow it makes the end seem easier. But don't get me wrong. I miss him. We had a tough life together, which was no one's fault, but he always tried. He just wasn't single father material, I suppose you could say. And...and now I look at his flowers and wonder if we both could have tried a little harder. Of course, Alzheimer's stepped in before we had much of a chance to do anything."

"How long has he been gone?"

As they walked down the path to the hospital Mateo took hold of her hand and she didn't pull away. It was nice feeling his touch. Having someone there who cared...at least for a little while. His hand was soft, and she could almost imagine it caressing her skin, giving her goosebumps.

Maybe she'd give *him* a few goosebumps as she ran her hand over his tight six-pack abs...

Nice dream.

"A year, now. One less brilliant surgeon in the world."

She noticed Mateo was starting to lag behind, so she slowed her pace to match his, but when she did he slowed down even more. This doctor clearly wasn't comfortable returning to the hospital, even if he was no longer a patient there.

"Do you need to take a break?" she asked, coming to a stop on the narrow road that led to the hospital's front door. It was lined with a rainbow of flowers and green, with draping wisps of vine hanging from the trees.

She'd always loved this path. It had welcomed her the day she'd first arrived, and every day since then. And this was part of her dilemma. To stay or to leave? Admittedly, she wasn't as restless as she'd been only a few weeks before, but her choice still wasn't clear. In other words, she didn't know what she wanted. She'd spent a lifetime living the life her dad had wanted for her, and now it was her turn to choose. But what?

Truly, she didn't know.

"No," Mateo said. "I'm fine. Just not excited to be back here." He took his place against a large lava rock, leaned casually back on it, and folded his arms across his chest. "You go do what you need to do, and I'll wait here."

He pointed to the little shop just down the road. The front was totally open to the air, and several clothing racks spilled out onto the walkway.

"Or wander down there and pick out the most hideous clothes you can imagine."

"I'll be about ten minutes," she said, heading to the front door, walking along the path and crossing over the circular drive that led straight to the welcome sign: *Welina*. Greetings to you. It was a friendly place to some. But to some, not so much.

"I didn't know you'd be stopping by," Janis said, approaching the entrance to greet Lizzie.

"In the neighborhood." She glanced back over her shoulder to make sure Mateo was still there. "Looking for clothes for my...whatever he is."

"Speaking of which—how's he doing? We were worried until you called. But the thing that really concerns me is that he's living with you, Lizzie. That's not a good idea. Dependencies form. It may be difficult to get rid of him when the time comes."

"It was either that or the beach. And he was totally emphatic about not coming back here or going to the veterans' facility in California. So..." She shrugged. "What was I supposed to do? He's not exactly ready to be out in the world on his own, yet."

She took another hasty glance and saw Mateo talking to a handful of strangers who were huddled around him. He did have that kind of personality—the kind that drew people in. He was making good use of that now.

"He's not supposed to be living with one of his doctors," Randy Jenkins said, approaching Lizzie and Janis.

"I'm not his doctor—never have been, never will be. And, not that it's any of your business, he's in the *ohana*, not in the house," Lizzie said, almost defensively.

"Do what you want," Randy said. "He's not a patient here, and right now he's on his own. So be his friend. I'm sure he needs that."

"Randy's right. It's your choice, Lizzie. But don't get too involved. I don't want to see you getting hurt."

"Hurt?"

"You know...feelings that aren't reciprocated. You're vulnerable right now, just like he is, and I don't want that playing against you."

"He's not like you think he is," she insisted.

"Or maybe he's not like *you* think he is," Janis countered. "Just be careful. That's all I'm saying. That, and put a leash on his desire to practice medicine. Because if people associate the two of you as medical partners and he makes a mistake, or forgets something..."

"What?" Lizzie spun around and, sure enough, Mateo was examining the wrist of a young boy who couldn't have been more than seven or eight. "Look, courier those papers over later and I'll sign them. Right now I think I've got to stop a doctor from practicing medicine."

"Easier said than done," Janis warned. "It's in his blood."

That was going to be a huge problem—teaching an old dog new tricks. Or completely rewiring the old dog until he was an entirely new one. Also, staying detached. That, perhaps, was going to be the hardest part, because Mateo was charming and she was not above being charmed, no matter how much she denied it to herself.

Why? Because she was lonely. Because he was attractive. Especially because he was attractive. Oh, and the charm that just oozed from his pores. She didn't know if that was really him, or a new Mateo he was trying on for size. But she liked it. Too much.

CHAPTER FIVE

IT WASN'T LIKE he'd *meant* to practice medicine on a street corner, but he hadn't been able to help himself. The memory of the career that had been taken away from him kept poking at him, reminding him of who he'd used to be as opposed to who he was now. Nothing. That was who he was. Nothing. No one. A man without a memory living with a woman he barely knew.

"It's not broken," he told the little boy's mother. "Just sprained. It wouldn't hurt to go get an X-ray, but you could save yourself time and money by making a sling and keeping it immobile for a couple of weeks."

He was referring to a child who'd fallen and hurt his wrist. There was enough of the surgeon in him left that he could tell the difference between a sprain and a break. And while he shouldn't have been making the diagnosis, it had just happened. Child in pain, mother worried sick, him reaching out to help. It was not only the life he wanted, but the life he needed. If he wasn't a doctor, then who was he?

Someone from his own past, he decided as he rose to greet Lizzie—who, judging by the expression on her face, wasn't too happy with what he'd just done.

Lizzie.

He liked her.

She leaned a little too heavily toward the no-nonsense side, but he'd caught a few fleeting smiles and laughs, which only emphasized just how much she kept hidden.

"I suppose you're going to tell me I shouldn't be practicing medicine," he said, even before she'd reached him.

"You shouldn't. And without medical supplies?" she asked.

"With a hospital only a few feet away I assumed I was safe. And you know what they say: once a doctor, always a doctor."

"Well, don't tempt Fate, Mateo. You're standing on hospital property and you're lucky Janis is feeling tolerant. Just watch where you're dispensing bandages. OK?"

"Much ado about nothing," he said, grinning at her as he purposely moved to the middle of the street.

"Why did you join the military?" she asked as they headed down the road to a little shop with a rack of brightly floral shirts on display. Typical casual wear that never failed to draw the tourists.

"Honestly? I don't know. Something drew me. Just don't know what it was." Mateo sighed as they stopped to look through the floral shirts. "Like so many other things. It's trapped in my mind. I can almost feel it there. But it won't surface."

"Give it time," Lizzie said, pulling out a blue floral print, then holding it up for Mateo.

"Well, time is something I certainly have a lot of, isn't it?" He shook his head at the print and she put it back. "I think my tastes run more toward T-shirts. At least I can't picture myself in something like that."

"How about you try it on, then decide?" Lizzie suggested, pulling down another one. This time it was a seafoam-green with white hibiscus flowers.

This wasn't working. Whatever the cause, he was getting anxious. Too many colors, too much stimulation. Too many people watching. At least it felt like they were. All eyes on him. Wounds. Blood. Expectations. So many of them. And he was supposed to save them all. But he couldn't. And they kept coming and coming...

"Mateo?" Lizzie said, giving his arm a gentle shake. "Where did you go?"

He blinked hard, then looked at her, not quite sure at first what was going on. Then it came back to him. It was simply another one of those bad recalls. They happened when he was awake. The nightmares came when he slept.

"To a place I'd rather not visit again."

He was wiped out. No activity for so long and now even the little things bothered him. Maybe it was emotional fatigue? Whatever the case, he wanted to be left alone. Wanted time to himself to think, to see if he could bring anything back. To forget there were so many things he no longer remembered.

"Do you mind if I go take a walk on the beach?"

"Are you OK going by yourself?" she asked.

"I'm perfectly capable of taking a walk by myself," he snapped, then instantly regretted it. "Look, things build up in me. Sometimes it feels like I'm a tea kettle just ready to go off. I didn't mean to..."

She laid a comforting hand on his arm and it sent chills all the way up and down his spine. "Pressure relief," she said. "It's common."

"How do you do it, Lizzie? How do you work with people like me, day in and day out, and not get burned out? Because from what I'm seeing there may never be a satisfying result in my future. Multiply that by all the patients you've cared for who are just like me, or worse... I'm surprised you don't have your own pressure relief to deal with."

"I do, actually."

She took hold of his arm and they headed off down the road toward the beach, strolling casually, like longtime lovers who knew each other's moves intimately.

"Some doctors find it in tobacco, drugs or alcohol. But I'm a little more passive. I like to watch the sunset. Or swim. And if I'm really angsty… I surf. I grew up—well…pretty much alone. Had to learn at a very young age to take care of myself. Because if I didn't, no one else would. Don't get me wrong. My dad did his best. It's just that so much of the time there wasn't enough left of him to *be* my dad. So my pressure relief? A lot depends on where I am. We lived in a snowy part of Germany for a while and I learned to ski. We spent time in Texas and I learned to ride a horse with the best of them. On Okinawa I learned to cook seafood. It all worked out."

They stopped just short of the beach, where she let go of him.

"And medical school?" he asked.

"It seemed like a good choice. And I was ready to get out on my own. See a different world than the one he gave me…do something different than what I'd always done, which was to make the best of any situation I landed in."

"Had to be tough."

"Not all the time. I like working at Makalapua Pointe Hospital."

"But you don't love it?"

"To be honest, I'm not sure what I love. Most days it's my work, but some days it's just being lazy on the beach."

"Am I hearing mixed emotions?"

"Not mixed so much as changing. I love being a doctor. That's the easy part. But the rest of it… Well, that's to be determined later."

"It happens a lot. It's called career burnout."

"I'm just tired right now. Once I've been away a little while I'll be anxious to go back."

"What if you're not?' he asked.

"Then I'll figure it out when the time comes. My dad burned out before his Alzheimer's. Just decided one day he was done. He'd already served a full career in the Army and he was in general surgical practice. It bothered him for a while, but he was happy in his new life. I'm tired, but not burnt out the way he was."

"And my being here isn't helping you rest, is it?"

"Actually, it's nice having someone around. I'm glad you're staying with me for a while. It makes my day... interesting."

Mateo chuckled. "I've been told I've done a lot of things, but making someone's day interesting...can't say I've ever heard that one. But seriously, Lizzie. If I get in the way tell me to go, and I will."

She stepped away from Mateo. "I'll see you later," she said, reaching out, giving his hand a squeeze. "Unless you decide to go somewhere else."

"Why would you say that?" he asked, wondering if she really wanted to get rid of him and if her hospitality had been offered on little more than a frayed thread.

Maybe he should go. Find a little place to call his own. Open a surf shop. Forget that he'd ever been a surgeon and content himself with whatever life brought his way.

Except...that wasn't him. He wasn't sure exactly who he was. But he was sure who he *wasn't*.

"Do you want me to leave, Lizzie? Be honest with me. Should I go?"

Lizzie shook her head. "When I invited you I meant it. Besides, where would you go?"

"That's a question for the ages, isn't it?"

He had enough money to get him through for a while.

Or he could strike out on his own and hope that something good came of it. But truth be told the appeal of being alone was overrated—much the way Lizzie had claimed. And facing the world with only part of you intact was a scary proposition. He wasn't ready to try that. Not just yet.

"One day at a time," his mother used to tell him, because that was the way they'd been forced to live. If she'd had dreams beyond that he'd never known what they were.

Did he have dreams beyond his stint in the military? Surely he must have. Or maybe he was like his mother— one day at a time. And now one day at a time with Lizzie.

He liked that. Probably more than he should and more than he had a right to. For now, though, it offered him something he no longer had—an identity. From that he would grow.

But in what direction?

It wasn't like she didn't trust him to find his way back. That part of Mateo was perfectly fine, and if he wanted to return here he would. Simple as that. She was distracted, though. And worried. It had been several hours and there was still no sign of him. Naturally that had made her think of her dad—that day he'd wandered away and hadn't been found.

That was the nightmare that still caused her to wake up sweating and shaking, thinking of him out there alone, sitting in the underbrush near Kapu Falls, waiting for death to take him. Maybe it had been his choice—maybe that had simply been the way it ended for him. And now she was worried about Mateo. Probably needlessly. But all the same she couldn't settle until he was back.

"It's a nice offer," she said now to Kahawai, one of the wealthy property owners in the area.

He was a proper old man, with polished manners and a politeness that far exceeded anything she'd ever seen in another person. He'd come over to her house and brought cake. It was the way of the people here when one of their own was in trouble, and somehow he'd found out about Mateo. So they were eating cake and discussing business to keep her distracted—which wasn't working. Also, Kahawai had been trying to make her a serious offer for weeks.

"But I like where I am, and doing what I'm doing."

Even to her own ears her words didn't sound convincing.

Kahawai was offering to set up a small medical clinic for her to run. Something the immediate area lacked.

"It would be a good opportunity," he said, slicing her a second, huge piece of cake. "For the community and for you."

They were sipping banana coladas on her lanai—non-alcoholic drinks made from bananas, pineapples, and a splash of Hawaiian fruit syrup. She'd done this with her dad in the beginning, until being sedentary had made him nervous. Then they'd strolled the beach, gone wading, or picked up seashells.

"But I've never practiced general medicine in a small clinic," she said. "I've always had a hospital and hospital resources to fall back on."

That was her excuse for turning down his offer, her reason for not moving on. And, while this was something she and her dad had talked about doing someday, the thought of doing it on her own was daunting. She wasn't sure she trusted herself enough. Not now, anyway.

"Well, I'd never been a property owner," said Kahawai. "But look at what I have now. Good fortune and my uncle's wealth smiled on me."

Lizzie glanced down the beach to see if she could spot Mateo, but it was practically deserted, as it always was at this time of the day. The locals had all gone home, and tourists tended not to know about this spot. That and the fact that it was all privately owned, which meant no trespassing.

"He'll be back in his own time," Kahawai said. "Maybe he wanders the beach like you do, night after night, trying to find yourself. This doctor with no memory...does he mean something to you?"

"He has a memory," she defended, almost too quickly. "He just doesn't have... Let's just say that he's suffered some trauma and now he's trying to come to terms with it."

"And he's living with you until he's cured?"

"He's staying in my *ohana* until he knows what he wants to do. Big difference."

Kahawai grinned as he stood, preparing to leave. "Well, whatever the case. My offer stands. And if your roommate would like to work with you I'll have a place for him as well. I understand he was a great surgeon in his day."

"Good news travels fast around here, doesn't it?" Lizzie said, trying not to give in to the anxiousness awakening in her.

"We're like family, Lizzie. When you decide you want to be part of that family there'll be a place for you."

He carried his glass into the kitchen and exited through the front door, leaving Lizzie alone on the lanai, watching for Mateo.

What if he had decided to move on? Had he taken his things? What few things he had?

Suddenly the impulse hit her to head off to the beach and look for him. But, racing past the *ohana*, she found him standing on the doorstep, simply watching the night drop down on the beach.

"Looks like you're in a hurry to get somewhere," he commented, moving over to allow her room enough to stand there with him.

She squeezed in next to him, determined not to tell him what she was up to. She was his landlord, not his keeper, and she had to keep reminding herself of that.

"Just out for a walk," she said, enjoying the feel of being pressed next to him.

"A walk with a vengeance. You looked like a lady with a purpose." He slid his arm around her waist, and she readjusted to allow it.

"Just in a hurry."

"You and nobody else. That's what I've been observing—the way people take things at their own pace. They don't seem so caught up in modern life here."

"That's all I'm *ever* caught up in," she said.

"Did you learn that from your dad?"

"Maybe. I was always trying to keep up with him."

"Did you ever succeed…before his illness?"

Lizzie shook her head. "He was a tough man. When he had time for me, if I didn't take it he'd move on in the blink of an eye."

"And that's how you want to be? Like your dad?"

Lizzie laughed. "To be honest, I want to be just the opposite of what he was. I want to have a life *around* my work. He wanted nothing *but* work. Sometimes, if I catch myself doing or saying something he might have, I pull back…do just the opposite."

"And that's your problem now. You want to walk totally away from him and you don't know how."

"You should have been a shrink, Mateo." She leaned her head against his shoulder. "You have...depth."

"That surprises you?"

"Well, you haven't exactly been forthcoming about who you really are, have you?"

"It's easier to stay safe that way. I learned that when I was young, trying to make it through school with good grades rather than a bad reputation. Then again in medical school, where brown skin wasn't exactly the norm."

"Did that bother you much?" she asked.

"When I was young, yes. But most kids suffer at the hands of other kids one way or another. When I started discovering who I was..." He chuckled. "Well, let's just say that I know who I am, but in totally different terms now."

"It's almost funny how a man with amnesia may know more about himself than I know about myself."

She should leave now. Get away from him while she could. Because as intimacy wove around them she was becoming fully aware that Mateo was the man who might make a difference in her life—if she allowed it. But her legs were too weak to support her body and too shaky to move her away from there. And the humid night, even with the cool spritz coming from the air-conditioning in the *ohana*, surrounded her, held her in place...which allowed his kiss in.

Just like the way Lizzie felt, Mateo's kiss was unsteady at first. Tentative, with a masterful edge just waiting to break through. But he held back. Allowed time to pull her into his arms, tight enough so he could smell the faint scent of gardenias in her hair but loose enough to let her respond to his touch. Her arm, caressed by his, burned, and yet she shivered.

"Are you cold?" he asked, his breath warm on her neck.

Lizzie instinctively tilted her head to look up at him. He was tall, much taller than her, and his shoulders were broad...something she'd tried hard not to observe at the hospital in anything other than a professional way. But now her profession didn't stand between them, and she admired what she saw the way any woman would admire a beautiful man.

"Just...unaccustomed..." she replied, her voice barely above a whisper.

She thought briefly about the colors of the evening sky—the golds and oranges, all the colors that took on a different meaning tonight, other than simply being the colors of another night alone on the beach. Stars by the thousands were twinkling. And she was gazing out on the empty sea, her empty life, her empty world.

All full now—if only for a moment.

Mateo shifted just enough to catch her off-balance and push her against the door frame. In a heartbeat he grabbed her and held her tighter, his dark eyes staring intently into hers. Just a breath between them with no place to hide.

"To what?" he asked. "What are you unaccustomed to?"

"You...me...us. All of this. I've held myself back from it."

"Why?"

"Because there was nothing I wanted to become accustomed to. Nothing...no one who mattered. And being like that has become a habit. I'm always too tied up with...other things."

"Maybe this will break your habit," he said.

His voice was deep and intense. So much so, his meaning was clear. And when their lips met his hold on her tightened even more. He was pulling her into him, pressing himself into her.

It wasn't like she wanted to be somewhere else. She didn't. This moment—right here, right now—that was all there was. *Her* moment. And as her eager mouth fused to his she forgot who they were, where they were, or why they were. None of that mattered now. Nothing mattered but the tip of his tongue brushing her lips and the way she welcomed the urgent thrusting that sent even more shivers racing through her body.

Mateo had expected some heat just from being so close to her. Something mildly pleasant from almost touching. Then actually touching. But the sizzle, the pure magnetic draw of her—that was what caught him off guard. And not just the way she responded to him, but the way he responded to her. Like he'd never kissed a woman before.

The moment his lips touched hers, ever so briefly, and he cupped her neck with his hand, she arched backward, allowing him more of her. And as his thumb caressed the silken flesh of her throat, and she quivered hard against him, he pulled her even tighter to him, to close the gap, to feel the contours of her.

Damn, but her lips were soft. Too soft. And he fought to call back every bit of reason that was escaping him.

But before reason took over, he pressed his lips hard to hers, and felt the twining of her leg with his calf. A tiny, pleading sound was liberated from her throat—and that was when he lost his control. His cool. His will to keep this impersonal. That was when Mateo bent his head and seized that sound, drawing it between his lips and holding it there, for fear that once he backed away it would be gone, and they would return to normal.

His emotions were too close to the surface now. Too

naked. Too close to revealing parts of him he didn't even know in himself. Which scared him.

So rather than thinking about it, rather than letting his pure, raw emotions take over, he kissed her with everything inside him—fear for the future, desire for someone he didn't know, desperation for what would become of him once Lizzie was out of his life.

Because she *would* be out of his life. There may have been mere millimeters between them now, but those millimeters would soon turn into worlds. And those different worlds would separate them.

The thought of that pulled him back.

"Well, that's one thing you certainly haven't forgotten," Lizzie said, brushing her fingers across her red swollen lips.

"It's a natural response to you, Lizzie. Surely you've seen it building?"

"Sometimes I miss the obvious. Partly because I want to and partly because I don't put myself out there."

"How is it with me?"

She raised her fingertips to her lips. "Nice. Very, very nice."

He'd almost hoped she would say something like they couldn't do it again, or it had been terrible. But the smile on her face told him otherwise. Which wasn't good because already he wanted more, when there was no more to give. Or to have.

He was sitting on the lanai, sipping a fruit juice, watching the darkness surround him. It was a good place for him to be, because she was too confused to make much sense of their situation. In fact, broiling a *mahi-mahi*, a simple task, was proving to be almost more than she could handle right now.

"So, reason it out," she said aloud as she chopped the mangoes, cilantro, green onions, and bell peppers to top the fish. "He kissed you, or you kissed him. Either way, it was a kiss."

Perhaps the only kiss she'd ever had that was worth remembering.

"He enjoyed it…you enjoyed it."

Truer words never spoken. But was there anything beyond what they had already? She didn't know, and she was pretty sure he didn't either.

Lizzie drew in a heavy sigh. Her last relationship, which had been her marriage to Brad, was a disaster of epic proportions, and even though it was so far in the past, she wasn't sure she was ready for something else. She'd been played—expecting everything, getting nothing. Maybe she'd even let herself be played, believing what she wanted to believe, seeing what she wanted to see.

Because in the end their collapse had come as no real surprise to her. There'd been hints. His self-imposed curfew. The texts he'd sent when he'd thought she wouldn't notice. Other women. Another life.

"Mateo isn't married," she argued with herself.

But even if she were to get involved, the one thing that frightened her was his lack of memory. Would she always have to be on guard for him, like she'd been for her dad? Always nervous when he was late getting home? Or when she couldn't find him in the house?

She'd lived that life once and honestly didn't know if she had it in her to do it again. The circumstances might be different, but she saw so much sameness. Or maybe that was what she wanted to see. Something to keep her at a safe distance, because she honestly didn't know where she was going.

What would happen if he found himself again and he wasn't the man she thought he was? She'd certainly been in the dark about her husband, and perhaps that was what scared her most. She was falling for this Mateo, but there might be another one waiting to emerge. Having fallen in love with one man who'd turned out to be someone else…she wasn't going near that again.

"And the moral of that story," she said to her salsa, "is don't get involved."

She glanced out the sliding glass door, only to catch herself wondering how much that kiss had changed things. Or if it had changed things between them at all. They were, quite simply, house-owner and houseguest. End of story. At least, she hoped so.

"Doc Lizzie!" someone yelled into her kitchen window. "Come quick. I think he's dead."

That snapped Lizzie from her doldrums and she grabbed her medical bag, clicked on her outside flood-lights, and ran out the lanai door to follow the college-age man down to the beach, where one of his buddies, who'd had a little too much to drink, was lying uncon-scious in the sand.

Immediately she dropped to her knees on the left side of him, and saw Mateo drop to his knees on the right and lay his fingers on the man's neck to check for a pulse. He tried a couple different places as Lizzie inflated the blood pressure cuff, then shook his head grimly.

"Nothing," he said, taking hold of the man's wrist to check for a pulse there.

When Lizzie looked over at him for an answer, he shook his head again.

"I can't get a blood pressure on him, either." She looked up at the young man's buddy. "What happened?"

"We were surfing. Real good tides at night around

here. And he fell off his board. Don't know what happened after that. Maybe it hit him…"

"Is he drunk?" Mateo asked.

"We've had a few beers. Nothing serious."

"That's what they all say," Lizzie said to Mateo. "A few beers and a surfboard can get you dead." She said that for the benefit of the young man's buddy. "What's his name?"

"Teddy. Teddy Chandler."

"Teddy, can you hear me?" Mateo yelled, giving the young man a hard thumb in the middle of his chest.

A sternum-rub, as it was called, was a technique used for assessing the consciousness level of a person who wasn't responding to normal interactions such as voice commands. In Teddy's case there was no reaction.

"Call for an ambulance," Mateo shouted, while Lizzie put her ear almost all the way down on Teddy's mouth to see if there was any discernible breathing.

When she could find nothing, she checked for a pulse again. Like before, it wasn't there. So she commenced CPR, placing the heel of one hand on the center of Teddy's chest at the nipple line.

As she positioned herself to start the compressions, Mateo took an IV set-up from her medical bag and inserted it into Teddy's vein—right arm, just below the bend. He attached a saline bag to it, but nothing else.

"Epinephrine could cause severe brain damage," he said, more to himself than Lizzie.

"You remembered that?"

"I remember some of the newer studies stating epi is contraindicated in cardiac arrest."

Lizzie stopped her chest compressions long enough to assess Teddy for breath sounds, but still he wasn't breathing.

Mateo opened Teddy's airway by tilting his head back and lifting his chin. Then he pinched the man's nose closed, took a normal breath, and covered his victim's mouth with his own, giving him two one-second breaths, hoping to see the natural rise and fall of his chest.

Still nothing was happening.

He gave two more breaths, followed by Lizzie, who administered thirty chest compressions. Then they repeated it all.

The second set of compressions caused Teddy to vomit and spit out seawater, and then he sputtered to life, blinking hard, and reeking of far more than a few beers.

"Can I go home now?" the young man muttered, trying to sit up even as Mateo forced him back onto the sand.

"The only place you're going is to the hospital," Lizzie told him. "In a saltwater near-drowning water is pulled out of the bloodstream, and then it pools in the lungs, where it's thicker than normal blood, and can cause heart damage since your heart isn't used to pumping hard enough to circulate the thickened blood."

"In other words," Mateo chimed in, "you may have messed up your heart, so you need to have it checked out."

"Will it hurt?" Teddy asked.

Mateo looked across at Lizzie and smiled. "Probably. But that's what happens when you drink too much and then think you can conquer the surf. It doesn't happen that way, Teddy. Worldwide, one person drowns every two minutes, and while half of those are children, the half that *aren't* children are largely made up of men who take risks. Drinking and surfing is a risk—you got lucky that your buddy knew where to go to fetch a doctor. Normally it doesn't turn out that well."

Lizzie stood and brushed sand from her knees. Mateo

was impressive. Besides that, he was a very good doctor, and for the first time she wondered if there might still be a place in medicine for him. What he'd done and what he'd remembered... Heroic didn't even begin to describe it.

Surely there was a place for him?

Someplace better than where he was now?

Someplace where she wouldn't be so tempted by him?

And, make no mistake. Mateo tempted her in ways no man ever had before.

"It's you they need out there, Doc. Not some other medic. This is Freddy. You've got to go. Got to go... Got to go..."

The soldier faded from view then reappeared in an ambulance, motioning for Mateo.

"Hurry up. Hurry up."

"But I need to be here," Mateo protested. "Incoming."

"Go," his nurse was telling him.

She was pointing at the door where, just outside, the ambulance awaited.

"Go, Doctor. It's your duty. This is Freddy."

But the faces in the hall were blurring together. And the soldiers with those blurred faces were all pointing at the door.

"Go!" they were screaming as he dropped to his knees, shut his eyes, and held his hands over his ears. "Go, Mateo!"

He opened his eyes and he was alone. Just him in the makeshift hospital. And the ambulance. No one to drive him. But the voices—they were still in his head.

"Go!" Mateo screamed, then bolted up in bed, sweaty and shaken.

He knew he had to go, but he didn't know where.

Dear God, he didn't know where.

* * *

Lizzie could hear him scream through her open window. This was his battle to win, not hers. But she desperately wanted to help him through it. Except she couldn't. These nightmares he was having were taking him on a journey he had to walk alone. The answers he needed were there. But they were his to find, not hers to reveal.

She believed that now, as much as she ever had. Still, as she went to her own bed she was shaken. And silent tears slid down her cheeks. She wanted to fight his battles, do away with his demons. But in the end that would only make her feel useful—it would do nothing to help Mateo.

As she laid her head on her pillow and shut her eyes all she could see was an image of someone drowning. Mateo. He was walking into the water and she was the only one there to pull him out. But she couldn't.

That was her nightmare for the rest of the night. He was drowning and she couldn't get to him, the same way she hadn't been able to get to her dad when he was dying. She was letting them down, letting them both down. And she didn't know how to fix it.

CHAPTER SIX

"YOU OK?" MATEO ASKED.

He was concerned about Lizzie. She hadn't said a word in over an hour. Sitting there in the sand, staring at the water, she seemed almost like a statue. A beautiful statue, maybe of a goddess watching over the sea.

"I cleaned up the mess from last night's burnt mahi-mahi and salvaged the salsa to put over something else. But I'm not sure what, since you don't keep a lot of groceries in your pantry."

"Because I rarely eat at home. When Dad was in better shape he loved to cook, but then when I took over we ate very simply. If I couldn't fix it in under thirty minutes, we went out. At least until he couldn't do that anymore. Then, with everything he needed from me in the evenings, I usually just brought something home."

"Did you have someone helping you?"

"I had a couple different people who were available when I wasn't here. One was a student nurse, the other a retired physical therapist. They were good with Dad, but he always wanted me, and sometimes he'd get so belligerent I'd have to leave work to come take care of him." She shook her head. "My father was a lieutenant colonel in the Army, and toward the end he didn't even know his own name."

"I didn't either," he said. "Not for several days. I can't imagine how it would be to lose yourself entirely. Even with just pieces of me gone, I get frustrated. And that's nothing compared to what your dad went through. I'm sorry for that, Lizzie. I suppose we tend to think we're invincible, but the scariest thing that happened to me was waking up in Germany when the last thing I remembered was performing a surgery in a desert outpost hospital. Nobody would tell me what was going on, and I certainly didn't have the capacity at that point to figure it out."

He sat down in the sand next to her, handed her a glass of fresh fruit juice, and took her hand.

"I felt so…alone. I imagine that's how your dad felt when he knew he was losing his memory. It's not an easy thing to face."

She scooted closer and grasped his hand a little tighter. "He wasn't cooperative, either."

Mateo laughed. "Either? Which implies what?"

"You haven't been cooperative. So much so, you got kicked out. And now you're homeless. And, while I'm beginning to see what I believe is the real you, you're still not trying to get better. There's outpatient therapy and private counseling available. It's just a few steps from your door. And yet you've never ventured down there to see if there's anything for you. It's disappointing, Mateo. It's like you enjoy being a step out of time."

"Lucky you took me in, then, isn't it?"

"Is it? I mean, sometimes you act like this is a real relationship. That kiss, for instance. Was it the start of something? Was it meant to be manipulative? What *was* it, Mateo? I spilled my guts to you about how unsure I am and got nothing back. Why is that?"

"Did you ever consider that it might have simply been a kiss? That I'm attracted to you and it just happened?"

"See—that's the problem. You're happy taking the easy way out in the things you do, the things you say. When you walked away from your treatment program did you even stop to think what you were doing? I mean, no one wants to stay in hospital, but if you've got no place else to go—"

"When I was in Afghanistan a lot of widowed women with children came to the hospital," he said, remembering how they would show up out of desperation and hope someone there had a solution for them. "The best we could do was a meal, sometimes a blanket, and the few provisions we could scrounge. It was heartbreaking, seeing all those people with no place to go."

"But that's you," Lizzie said.

"That was me before that particular memory returned. If all these images had been coming back, I might have made a different choice. But I didn't, so here I am. What can I say? I made a mistake. Made several of them. And, at the risk of repeating them, it's easier just to keep myself...isolated."

"Because that's what you think you deserve?"

"I can't answer that because I don't *know* what I deserve or don't deserve."

"That's something best left up to you to figure out. It's a fine line, Mateo. You're doing so much better than anyone might have expected, but you've still got a long way to go. And I'm not going to be the one to tip you in any direction."

"I know. The rest of it's up to me. But I haven't quit, Lizzie. I just don't respond well to pushing."

"Because you've always been in charge and suddenly you're not?"

"That probably explains part of it. But the rest... I know it's not me. At least, I hope it's not." He shrugged.

"I'm not very happy with myself, but I need to know why I do and say what I do before I can fix it."

"If you're not sure of the problem, how can you fix it?"

"Maybe I can't. I don't know. But the one thing I do know is that kiss…it was real. As real as any kiss I've ever had. And I meant to do it, Lizzie. You know, to seize the moment?"

"Am I just a moment?" she asked.

He shook his head. "You've never been just a moment since the first time I set eyes on you. Want to know what I thought at the time?"

"I'm not sure."

Mateo chuckled. "I'll tell you anyway. You'd hurried up and down the hall several times that morning, always in a such a rush. But then one time you poked your head in my door and said, 'Hello.' Then you were gone. I thought you had the most kissable lips I'd ever seen. You were there maybe two seconds, but in those two seconds I knew you were somebody I wanted to know better. And kiss."

"Seriously? You wanted to kiss me?"

"I'll swear on a stack of hibiscus seeds that's what I wanted to do."

Lizzie reached up and brushed her fingers lightly over her lips. "I suppose I should be flattered."

"Not flattered. But hopefully in the mood for another one someday."

"Time will tell," she said, when she'd really intended to say no. But why limit her options? Especially since she *was* attracted to him? So, time *would* tell, wouldn't it?

Mateo put his arm around Lizzie's shoulder and the two of them stood at the water's edge, looking out on the ocean. It was nearly a perfect night. The skies were clear, the waters calm.

"When I was a kid, sometimes we'd go to Lake Chapala or even the Manzanillo coastline to swim. I was too young to realize we were too poor to stay in any of the nice hotels or eat in the nice restaurants the way most of the people were. To me, it was a treat just getting to go. So we'd pile in the car—my mother, my aunt, my grandmother, and her sister—take along packed food, and have the best day playing in the water. Then one time one of the kids from a hotel called me a *pobre niño*. Loosely translated that means poor kid. I didn't understand what he meant, or what he was implying, but I knew it wasn't good. After that we quit going and my mother never explained why. But I don't think she wanted me touched by that kind of ugliness. Then we moved to California and it was all forgotten. But the look of horror on her face that day... It broke my heart and I didn't even know why."

"Kids can be cruel," she said.

"Not just kids. It's in all of us, I think. But most people are aware of how their words can hurt and don't use them maliciously. On nights like this...perfect nights... I think back to how my little piece of perfection was ruined by a couple of words, and I wonder if the kid who used them against me even remembers."

"But they made you stronger, didn't they?"

"Only because I allowed them to. When you're five, though, all you see is something that's been taken away from you when it wasn't your fault."

"Which is why you became a doctor?"

"Actually, we lived in a small flat behind a doctor's office. He let me go in and read some of his books. Most of them I didn't understand, but by the time I was nine I knew that being a doctor was my calling. When he retired he gave me all those medical references, which were horribly outdated, but I loved reading them. I almost got myself kicked out of school for taking one or two of them to class rather than my textbooks. And you?"

"It was all I knew. I was talking serious medicine with my dad when I wasn't much more than a toddler, and by the time I was old enough to choose a career path medicine seemed like the logical choice. I knew it, I loved it, and most of all I knew what was involved. So there was never any doubt."

"Well, I went through the fireman, cowboy, and astronaut phases, but somehow I always tied them into medicine." He chuckled. "For a while I pictured myself making house calls on horseback."

"I have a friend—a nurse practitioner—who makes calls in the mountains in the east, where it's totally underdeveloped. She goes by horse because the roads are impassable."

"Well, then, bring on the cowboy hat and turn me loose."

Mateo looked out on the ocean again and watched a small child who was trying to swim toward the shore. She seemed to be alone, fighting the water, and his instinct kicked in.

Without a word, he suddenly dashed out, dived beneath the waves, and got to the child just as she was about to go under. Pulling her close to his chest, he held her for a moment until her cries quieted and the realization that she was safe set in, then he brought her back to shore, where several people had gathered, watching the rescue.

Lizzie spread out a blanket for the little girl, but stepped back when Mateo laid her there and did a quick check to make sure she wasn't injured. By the time he was finished the beach patrol had pulled up with the girl's mother, who was crying as she dropped to her knees next to her daughter.

"She's fine," Mateo assured the woman, who'd bundled her daughter into her arms. "I'm a doctor and I did a quick check. She's more shaken than anything. But you're free to take her to the hospital..."

The woman wiped away her tears and looked at Mateo. "No, I believe you."

"What happened?" he asked gently.

"She wandered off. I think she loses track of where she is and just..." The woman batted back tears. "Susie is autistic. She's smart. But sometimes she doesn't pay attention. And if I turn my back..."

"I understand," he said, laying a reassuring hand on the woman's arm.

"Sometimes she just gets away from me. She's full of life and thinks she can do anything, but..." The woman scooped up her daughter and followed the beach patrol officer back to his car. Before she left, she turned back to Mateo. "So many people are critical when something like this happens. I appreciate your kindness, Doctor. More than you know."

Mateo stood there for a moment after they drove off, then turned to face Lizzie, who'd come up behind him and now stood there quietly, holding on to his arm.

"Just when you think your problem is the worst in the world, you run into someone who has something going on that's far worse. I used to see that in surgery. Back when I was a resident, sometimes I'd get a little depressed that I wasn't assigned to one of the bright, shiny new medical hospitals—and then I'd get this patient whose life was hanging by a thread. It always made me realize how lucky my lot in life really was."

"I didn't even see her, Mateo. We were looking at the very same thing and I didn't see her."

"I wasn't sure I did, either. It was a gut reaction."

Lizzie blew out a long sigh. "Well, whatever it was, I think I just saw a miracle happen."

He chuckled. "Not a miracle, Lizzie. That was me in my element. Me the way I was and the way I want to be again."

"Do you ever wonder what your life might have been like if you'd chosen to do something different?" she asked. "Like me. I had a music scholarship—I could be playing in some world-class symphony orchestra now. But here I am, and I'm not always happy about it."

"Because…?"

Lizzie shook her head. "I don't know. That's the thing. I always wanted to be like my dad, but in the end he wasn't the man I knew. Of course I wasn't the woman *I* knew by then, either."

"As far as I know I always wanted to do what I do… did. My mother worked hard to get me through school. She even gave up living near her family to relocate to another country, so I'd have a better chance at achieving my dream. But there was that summer I worked on a ranch in Arizona. I was twelve, maybe thirteen. My mother took a job feeding the ranch hands while the real cook was off on maternity leave. By the end of the summer I was convinced my destiny was to be a cowboy, not a doctor. But then, on my very last day, I fell off a horse, broke my arm, and went back to my original plan. I think my mother was glad of that, because she hadn't worked so hard only to see her son herding cattle and mending fences. Not that there's anything wrong with that. But it's not me. Of course, being a surgeon isn't me anymore, either."

"But there's a place for you, Mateo. I'm not sure where it is, or what it is, but skills like yours would be wasted mending fences. Maybe I can help? As a friend?"

"Well, if you find that place, let me know. I'm getting tired trying to figure it out. And so far the road just keeps getting longer and longer, with no guarantees at the end of it. I mean, what's the point of involving you, or anybody else, when nothing about my outcome can be predicted? What could you do to help me, Lizzie? Be specific. What can really be done to help me? Especially when I'm still in a place where when I wake up half the time I have to re-orient myself? What day is it? What time? Where am I?"

"What I can do is make sure you're not going wherever it is you're going alone. The choices must be yours, Mateo. But I can be the support you need."

"Why would you want to tie your life to mine that way? You've already been through something similar once. Why go back for more?"

To give herself another chance?

To go back and find an outcome that wasn't like her dad's?

She hadn't told him the full story yet, but he'd gathered enough to know that she blamed herself for his death. So was this Lizzie's need to find another path the way he was trying to do?

"Because I can," she said simply.

He tilted her chin up and stared into her eyes. So much beauty there, yet so much sadness. Would it even be fair of him, pulling her into his problems when what he could see told him she had enough of her own?

"My previous doctors didn't get me. They were excited when they discovered I still knew how to peel a banana, when what I really wanted to know was how to perform a carotid endarterectomy. You know, the big things—like how to clear the carotid artery of a blockage, how large an incision I should make in the sternocleidomastoid muscle. I know the result could be a stroke, depending on the percentage of blockage, but I can't run through the procedure in my mind without stumbling. What kind of scalpel did I prefer? Or clamp? What kind of impact would the procedure have on my patient's quality of life? It's all there…" He tapped his head. "But not in the way it's supposed to be—which makes me doubt so many other things in my life, including my decision to leave the veterans' facility and come here, only to be so uncooperative that I get kicked out. That's not me. I know that. And yet when I see what I do…"

He shook his head.

"And then to draw you into the middle of it just because you're willing to be there with me… So much of me wants that, Lizzie. But I don't have the right to take over your life that way. I know I'm a problem. I know I do exactly the opposite of what I need to be doing. And to put all that stress on your shoulders, just because I want you at my side…"

"We all hobble through life with one problem or another, Mateo. I think there's something here for you. Not me, per se. But something else. I'd like to be like you are—the one who spots the little girl in the water and saves her before anybody else even knows she's there. And I can help you because what you're going through is impossible to face alone. I'm sure of that. And I do like you, in spite of yourself."

She expected a kiss, and maybe he did too, but instead he reached up, ran his thumb down the side of her cheek to her neck, and then placed the first of his kisses. Butterfly kisses that made her toes curl.

Everything inside her told her to back away, but she was fighting all that was feminine inside her that compelled her harder into his arms, revealing more of her neck to him. And as he took what she was offering her lips parted with a sharp intake of breath.

The sound of her shallow, rapid breathing as he kissed her caused her to desire more. And as if he'd read her mind, he cupped the back of her neck and kissed her deeply, gently, and so quietly she had to open her eyes to make sure he was still there.

He was, and the look in his eyes told Lizzie that he was desperate to explore. As desperate as she was. Which for the first time didn't scare her. Nothing about Mateo did. And that was the problem. The barriers keeping her away from this man had failed, and she wasn't sure she wanted to put them back in place.

No, that was wrong. She was sure she *didn't* want to put them back in place. And again, in another first, she didn't really care.

"You won't get anyplace close to where you want to be if you're alone."

"I've always been alone."

"Not really. You have a mother. I do understand why you don't want to burden her with this. But she knows things you want to know, and maybe reaching out would be good for both of you."

It was breakfast time again, and she was sitting on the beach, eating a bowl of fruit. She'd spent the night in her room; he'd stayed in the *ohana*. But whose choice had it been to remain circumspect? She wasn't sure, to be honest. Maybe it had been mutual. A natural pulling back of feelings for fear they were getting in too deep too quickly.

Well, it sounded good, anyway. But waking up alone hadn't felt so good. So maybe they were just about the moment and nothing else. All she knew was that she'd felt a cold, hard lump in her stomach when he'd walked her to her door and then, without so much as a kiss to the cheek, gone around to the *ohana*.

He shook his head. "I don't want people that close to me."

"Even me?" she asked.

"I don't know. When I'm with you, that's all I want. When I'm not, I'm cursing myself for being so stupid letting you in."

"You sure do know how to flatter a girl," she said, trying not to sound as grumpy as she felt.

"No offense intended."

"As I'm beginning to learn. But here's the thing, Mateo. There's an offer on the table from last night and the answer is simple. Yes or no? Do you want me standing with you? And this time, please don't dodge the question."

He searched her face for his answer, and all he saw was genuine honesty. This was a big step, though. He'd been wandering alone for a long time, and to invite somebody in scared and excited him at the same time. Because he didn't want to walk away from Lizzie. She made him feel...hopeful.

Swallowing hard, Mateo said, "Yes," in a voice that was barely more than a whisper.

"Then that's where I'll stand."

"Until you get too involved for your own good."

Lizzie bent over and brushed the sand off her legs. "That's for you to figure out, Mateo, if and when it happens. Anyway, I'm going down to The Shack to have some juice and forget everything else for a while. You're invited to join me, or you can stay here and eat whatever you care to fix. Your choice."

"Well, with such a gracious invitation on the table how could I refuse?"

* * *

He wasn't in the mood for crowds this early in the day. In fact, he'd hoped to spend some quiet time on the beach with Lizzie, listening to the far-off strains of the waves lapping the shore and watching a ship make its lazy way through one of the channels.

There was so much clutter in his head. So many things darting in and out. And he didn't know which were real and which were not.

Lizzie was real, though. As real as any woman he'd ever met. And their kiss the night before had been about the *realest* kiss he'd ever had. It could have led to more. Maybe it should have done.

But Lizzie was surrounded by barriers that were surrounded by their own barriers and more barriers after that. He couldn't see her letting them down—not for him, not for anyone. Couldn't see her ever giving in to the moment, even though she almost had during their kiss.

"The beach is no place to be alone on a beautiful morning like this, so maybe I'll tag along. Unless you choose to be alone," he said, hoping that wouldn't be the case.

"Does anyone ever really choose to be alone?" Lizzie asked. "Or is that a decision forced on them by circumstances?"

"Guess it depends on the person and what he or she really wants from life. Sometimes I'm in the mood to be solitary, sometimes I'm not."

"But given the choice between the two?"

"Can I choose to be flexible?"

Lizzie laughed. "You can choose anything you like, Mateo. It's your life."

"Not lately it hasn't been."

"Well, it's up to you to fix that, isn't it?"

"You really put a lot of faith in me to do the right thing, don't you?"

When they arrived at The Shack the place was busy, as always, so she chose to sit on a log under a banyan tree.

"You were a surgeon. I'm guessing a whole lot of people put their faith in you to do the right thing. You, too. You *did* put faith in yourself, didn't you?"

"I did. But it went with the job. I owed the people in my care the best I could give them."

"Plus all the military pressures on top of that. Sometimes I think that's what made my dad too old too soon. He never knew how to relax, even when he had time off."

"Do you relax very often?" Mateo asked. "Apart from your vacations, do you ever make time to do something for yourself? Something you enjoy?"

"I surf. Not as much as I'd like, like I said before, but I do get out there on my board once a week, or more, if I can fit it in. So, what do *you* do?"

"Long in the past I played guitar in a little band. I also painted... Nothing fine. Don't have that kind of skill. But I did murals on the sides of buildings. Urban art is what they call it now, and I really enjoyed it. I've always wondered if any of my work is still out there or if some other urban artist has come along and painted over it."

"You should go see," Lizzie said. "Maybe even create something new."

She flagged down the server, who was hustling his way through the growing crowd.

"I'll keep it simple," she told him. "Portuguese sausages and white rice, *lilikoi* juice and *malasadas*. They're like a fried doughnut," she explained to Mateo.

The server looked to Mateo for his order. "I'll have

the same," he said, and then to Lizzie, "I'm trusting your judgment on this."

"Hope that extends to things other than breakfast," she said.

"Well, you didn't go wrong on breakfast," Mateo said, positioning himself under the banyan tree so that, like Lizzie, he could sit and watch the ocean as morning turned into noon.

"You have to watch the portions, though. The food is good and the portions are huge. I usually take enough back with me for another meal or two."

She settled in next to Mateo, too full to move, too early in the day to feel so relaxed. But she was, and it felt good.

"So, tell me about moving to the States," she asked. "Was it traumatic? Because even as many times as I moved with my dad, it just seemed routine."

"After we moved to the States, when I didn't speak a word of English, I would hang around this little grocery store for hours—listening to conversations, trying to pick up the language. And I'd ask questions of anybody who paid the least little bit of attention to me. My school classes were taught in English, so I was getting the education I really needed at the store. In fact, I was there so much the owner gave me a job, sweeping the floors and stocking the shelves. He paid me very little, but he taught me to speak English and speak it properly. It's not easy when the first words you can understand and can speak are the names of various vegetables, but to this day I can pronounce rutabaga better than anyone."

"Have you ever eaten one?" she asked lightly.

"Hell, no. Those things are nasty." He faked a huge cringe.

"Well, finally we agree on something."

"We could agree on something else if you like," he said.

"And what would that be?" she asked.

"That today's a perfect day to walk along the shore, maybe even go wading, but not alone."

"You're a man of vast differences, Mateo. So, tell me... How is taking a walk with you going to make a difference for me?"

"You're tough, Lizzie," he said, taking hold of her hand and helping her off the ground, so she could take her glass back to the bar for a refill of the *lilikoi* juice. "But so am I—and that's what I want to talk about."

And talk quickly, before he backed out. Because his plan was a hard-set plan that she might like or might hate. He wanted to do this immediately, before negative energy zapped him of this little burst of courage. Now or never.

And that worried him, because his life nowadays was closer to the never...

She loved to walk along the shoreline at any time of the day or night. It was a quiet place, a peaceful place. Sometimes, after her dad was asleep, she'd used to slip away for a few minutes and go stand on the shore, or maybe walk into the water until it was up to her knees and simply take in the beauty of the night.

It had been the only time she'd felt in control. During the day, as often as not, her job had kept her off-balance, due to so many different and difficult demands. And as evenings went, the routine had never changed. She'd sit with her dad in the garden for a while as he fussed with the flowers—something he did even when his memory was practically gone. Then she'd fix his dinner, get him ready for bed, and finally tuck him in.

Most nights she'd sit in the hall on the floor outside his door for an hour, hoping he was sleeping. Sometimes he was, sometimes he wasn't. Those were the nights he'd get up and wander, and she'd go after him, and then they'd start the whole evening routine over, because he wouldn't remember he'd already done it once and demand to do it again. Including eating dinner.

Some people had told her locking him in his room would be for his own good. But he was her dad and he hadn't deserved that. She could have hired someone to sit with him at night, but so much of her life had already been disrupted, and she hadn't wanted more of it going by the wayside. So she'd done whatever the circumstances had called for. She'd sat outside his door...sometimes slept outside his door.

Slipping out and going to the water's edge had been a rare and guilty pleasure, because even though she'd gone there to relax one eye had always been on the house.

"So why the walk?" she asked Mateo, as they came to a stop and he bent to slip off her sandals.

"Want to go wading with me?"

The truth was, she did. But after kissing him she was afraid that anything even remotely resembling something romantic would bring about consequences far greater than she knew.

She was attracted to him. But she was also afraid of involvement. There'd never been a relationship in her life that had gone the way she'd thought it would, and while she was well able to wade in shallow water, nothing about Mateo signaled shallow water at all.

"What if I don't want to?" she asked, half hoping he would drag her into the water.

Something like that would be new to her, and being captured by Mateo... Yes, she liked the idea of that. Captured, carried, conquered... All pure fantasy, of course. But nice when it involved Mateo.

"I'm strong enough to carry you."

"You have a twenty-five-pound lifting restriction for a while yet," she answered, wondering why she was protesting so adamantly when part of her really wanted it.

"You're not my doctor, remember? You're just the person I'm living with presently. And telling the person I'm living with that they have a lifting restriction—well… it's something I'd never do. So, in theory, that's information you don't have."

Despite her attempt to stay serious, Lizzie laughed. "I wish I knew what kind of personality you used to have, because I like this one."

"And if it turns out to be the other one? Or one we haven't met at all? Then what?" He kicked off his shoes and headed toward her. "Tell me, Lizzie. Then what?"

"Then we deal with what we're given."

"But what if all my personalities are just part of me, and when you piece them together it turns me into who I really am?"

"Maybe I already like who I'm seeing."

"Seriously?"

"I don't judge people, Mateo. I accept them as they are. Or in some cases don't accept them."

"And you accept me as I am? Even though I'm not sure that person can really be defined yet?"

"Oh, I think there's a lot of definition stacking up. You're just not ready to deal with it yet."

"You know what they say: to everything there is a season…"

"The fine art of procrastination. It can become habitual, Mateo. Just saying…'"

She smiled, then headed toward the water, but Mateo beat her to it, grabbing hold of her hand and pulling her all the way in.

"No procrastination in this," he said, as her head bobbed above the water. "I wanted to do it and I did it."

She splashed water in his face, then started to pull away from him, but he caught her by the hand and held her there, the water just barely touching her shoulders.

"I want to find myself, Lizzie, and I can't do it alone. But it scares me to think how deep I could drag you in."

"Only as deep as I want to go, Mateo. You can't pull me any harder than I let you."

"I was just looking for a place to stay for a few nights, and now this is beginning to sound like a commitment."

"Nothing wrong with commitments. We make them and live with them every day. Should I get out of bed this morning? Coffee or tea with my breakfast? The blue shirt or the white one? Should I let a virtual stranger stay in my *ohana* or let him wander around lost and hope he makes it? We make our choices and those turn into commitments. No, I'm not getting out of bed this morning. I'm committed to staying in bed. And I want to wear the blue shirt while I'm drinking my coffee. Commitment, commitment."

"What about the man sleeping in your *ohana*? Commitment there, as well?"

"Yes, but I haven't figured out what kind."

She wasn't sure she wanted to figure it out. Her dad had always accused her of being too tenderhearted, like that was a bad thing. But it was part of her…the part that opened her up to getting hurt. Like marrying the wrong man because he told her the right story. So her commitment to Mateo—it had to be what worked for him, but also what worked for her. Problem was, she didn't know what worked for her anymore.

"So, let's start this commitment with you doing the

cooking while I clean up after you. And you can tend the flowers since I don't have a green thumb."

"And this is part of your treatment plan?"

"It's called retraining yourself to be disciplined. It's where you start, and I'll add things as I see fit."

"It's also called being your slave."

"That, too," she said, smiling. "Also, what about cars? Are you a good mechanic?"

That one stumped him for a moment, and he frowned. Then he shut his eyes. It was interesting watching him search for a memory, and in her experience, when something triggered someone as her simple question had triggered Mateo, there was usually a morsel there. So she stood thigh-high in the surf and watched the outward signs of his inward battle for a couple of minutes before he finally sighed, then smiled.

"I had a…a… Damn, it was a 1957 Bel-Air. Convertible. Red."

He shut his eyes again and didn't open them as he struggled to find more of the memory. She could see there was more coming back to him, and he was smiling as it returned, which excited her.

"A classic?" she asked, to prompt him back into the moment.

"It was. I found it in an old storage warehouse in pieces. The owner said I could have it."

Suddenly, he opened his eyes and looked at her.

"I remember this, Lizzie. Remember it like it just happened. The deal was I locked up for him… Old Man McMichaels—we called him Mick. I made a deal with Mick to lock up for him every night so he could get home early to his wife and kids. If I wanted to lock myself in and work on the car that was OK with him. And if I sold the car he got half. Except I didn't sell the car. It's… I think it's still in his warehouse. Or could be. He said he'd keep it for me until I came back for it. It runs perfectly. At least it did. And it's the only car I've ever had."

He looked at her and a puzzled expression came over him.

"I didn't remember that before, Lizzie. Why is that something I would have forgotten?

"Even the experts can't explain the workings of the brain. And keep in mind that the farther away you get from your accident and surgery, the better you'll do."

"It does work in mysterious ways," he said. "Sometimes when I was a field surgeon I'd see a brain injury so bad I didn't think there was any hope for recovery, and then recovery was almost instantaneous. Then other times…"

He shut his eyes again. Then shook his head.

"He wanted an aspirin. That's why he'd come in that day. Had a headache. Asked for an aspirin. Died before I could give it to him." He opened his eyes and stared at her for a moment. "I hated brain trauma. Hated what I could see, hated what I couldn't."

"Did you have many patients with brain injuries?"

"Too many," he said. "I'm a… I *was* a general surgeon. I had no business doing neurosurgery. But sometimes it couldn't be helped, if we couldn't get a neurosurgeon in for whatever reason." He sighed heavily. "And look where I ended up. Life can sure play some messed-up tricks, can't it?"

Turning slowly, he looked directly into her eyes.

"But you already know that, don't you?"

"Meaning?"

"Your father. Brilliant surgeon, the way you tell it. Then…" He shrugged. "Did he know, Lizzie? Did he know what was happening to him?"

"At first. And he fought back—a lot like the way you do. With stubbornness and resistance. But as his illness progressed, and more of him got lost, the knowledge of what was happening to him went away as well, taking all those years of bravery and the good things he'd done. That was the worst part, I think. Watching this giant of a man lose the things that had made him a giant. He earned those memories and he deserved to have them. But there was nothing I could do except tell him about the things he'd done. And to him they were just stories. Something that kept him entertained for a little while. But even that stage didn't last long, so after that went away I showed him pictures. They meant nothing to him, though. He didn't even recognize himself."

She swatted back a tear sliding down her face.

"It isn't fair, Mateo. Not to him, not to you, not to anybody. Losing yourself like that…" She shook her head. "But you've got hope. My dad had none and there was nothing I could do about that, even though I tried."

"Did you ever resent him for what you had to do?"

"Sometimes…a little. I think it's natural when the demands become more and more. But in a real sense…no. It wasn't his fault."

"And you: the healer who couldn't fix the person you loved the most." He pulled her into his arms and held her there as the water lapped around them. "I'm sorry you had to go through that, Lizzie. It can't have been easy, and there's nothing else to say except I wish it could have been different for you."

"Like you said, life can sure play some messed-up tricks."

"Why here? Why did you bring him here? Was it just because of the flowers?"

"It was so that a practitioner by the name of Malana

Palakiko could treat him. She's a holistic practitioner who uses light therapy, acupuncture, and natural herbs. Traditional medicine had run its course and I'm...open-minded. She has a little clinic a few miles from here, and since nothing else was working... She's one of the best when it comes to treating various forms of dementia. And, while she can't cure Alzheimer's, she does make her patients feel better, and she's had some good results in prolonging the inevitable. Dad loved seeing her. The thing was, even while I knew there wasn't any good outcome, I wanted to make his life as good as it could be as he was fading away, and I think Malana did that. She was so...kind. Patient. Understanding."

"And his doctors at the hospital?"

"When a case is hopeless, sometimes their efforts are as much for the loved one as for the patient."

"Was it that way for you?"

"Maybe. I just wanted to do everything I could. He would have expected that from me. But so much of his treatment... I think it was designed to make *me* feel better, like I was really doing something good for him. What *was* good for him, though, was sitting in the garden and tending his flowers. I didn't see that at first. I was so busy pushing him into treatments that weren't working." She laid her head against his chest. "I could have done better for him."

"Something tells me you're being too hard on yourself."

"Or not hard enough. I knew he was going to be a huge responsibility and I was willing to make sacrifices. What I wasn't willing to do was find support for myself—and it's out there. I'm not the only one to have done what I did, and if I'd just listened—" Her voice broke and she quit talking.

"Is that why you want to help me, Lizzie? To make up for what you feel you didn't do for your dad?"

That thought had never occurred to her, and she was so startled by it she stepped away from Mateo. "Is that what you think?"

"I'm not sure what I think, to be honest. I know your intention isn't malicious, but…"

"But it might be self-serving?"

"People aren't often as generous and kind as you are. In my experience, there's always a motive. People helped me along because I was a boy with brown skin who had an unlimited future ahead of me. Give me an extra shove and you can claim some of that feel-good motive for yourself."

"That's not me, Mateo. People in my life didn't have motives. In fact, I was hardly ever noticed. As for trying to have a feel-good moment at your expense…" She shook her head vehemently. "I don't know what it takes to gain your trust, but I don't come bundled in motives. My life is a lot simpler than that."

"There's nothing simple about you, Lizzie. Nothing at all. Maybe that's why I'm falling…why I like you so much. You're complicated, yet guileless, and the two put together are an interesting mix."

"How interesting?" she asked.

"Very interesting," he replied as he pulled her back to him and lowered his head to kiss her. "Maybe the most interesting person I've ever met—even if I'm not sure how many people I've met and which ones I considered interesting."

"If you intend on kissing me now's the time, Mateo. Unless you'd rather keep on talking and talking and talking…"

* * *

Even in the near darkness of the evening he could see her sadness. Or maybe it was more that he could feel it. He understood the melancholia that came with the darkening of the day. Remembered it from Afghanistan, listening to the moans and cries in the night coming from his ward. People in so much pain and fear and he couldn't fix them. Some who would never go home. Some who would.

And now there was his own irrational fear of the dark. During the day he could be as belligerent as hell, and blowing off his anger that way worked. But when it turned dark his belligerence disappeared, to be replaced by melancholia and fear. And some of those moans and some of those cries in the night had been his.

And probably Lizzie's as well. Strangely, that hurt him maybe even more than his own pain did—knowing that something far deeper than she would let him know about was pulling her in.

"Care for a swim?" he asked, for the lack of anything better to say.

"I'm always in the mood for a swim," she said.

After the kiss they'd returned to the house and changed into beach clothes, and taken a towel along with them. Now he grabbed her up off the towel and carried her to the water—where he dropped her.

He didn't set her down gently. Didn't even give her the option to go wading. Against her lame protests he carried her out until he was waist-deep, then dropped her. She went under for a second, and when she popped back up she grabbed his hand and pulled him down with her.

"You could be risking my life," he said, laughing.

Her response was to splash him, then dive back under before he could retaliate. But he was strong in the water. As he dived down he grabbed her by the arm and pulled her back up to the surface, then splashed her the way she'd done him.

"Apparently I have some skill at this," he said, then dove back under.

This time when he surfaced he was about twenty yards away from where they'd been before, and he didn't see her.

"Lizzie?" he called, turning around in circles and looking for signs of her. "This isn't funny, Lizzie. Where are you?"

Her answer was to grab him by the ankle and pull him under, then get away before he had time to resurface. Except he'd already anticipated she'd do something like that, so he got himself all the way down to the sandy ocean floor, then grabbed her ankle and pulled her down on top of him. *Fully* on top of him.

He held her there for a moment, before he realized he was enjoying not only the playtime but the feel of his body against hers entirely too much. So he pointed up, then released her, and followed her to the surface. Both came up spitting out water and laughing.

"Just wait until I get you on a bodyboard," she warned him, and she shoved back the hair from her face enough to see that he was staring at her. Up close and personal. Staring with such an intent look that it gave her shivers that were visible to him.

He hadn't meant to. But she was so beautiful he couldn't help himself. Whether or not she was a woman he would have chosen before, he had no clue. But if he were able to choose now, the only woman in his mind was Lizzie.

That was the problem. There might be other things in his mind that would dictate different choices. And even if there weren't she didn't deserve his problems.

As a friend, he appreciated her willingness to help. But as anything else...

"Don't know if I've ever been surfing, or bodyboarding, but the sooner the better," he growled, trying to take those other things off his mind.

And then he dove down and headed underwater for the beach, carrying with him feelings for Lizzie that were far deeper than anything he'd intended.

Was he falling in love? Despite his attempts to talk himself out of it, and all the rationalizations that he didn't want or need that in his life—especially now—was that what was happening to him?

Lizzie headed to the shore as well, wondering when fifteen feet had turned into such a long journey. But it was, and by the time she'd managed to make it to shore Mateo was already standing there in ankle-deep water, dripping wet and looking sexier than any man had a right to—in the dark, in the light, or any other shading of the day.

What am I doing? she asked herself as she stood and walked back to the sand, taking care to keep her eyes averted. *And why am I doing it?*

Because she was attracted to him, pure and simple. She was an adult. There was nothing stopping her. Except common sense. And right now, try as she might, she couldn't dredge it up.

So as she walked past him she turned her head to avoid temptation, and words she hadn't intended to say slipped out. "You look good in the water."

"I wasn't sure you'd noticed."

"Oh, I notice. But I don't always react."

"Sounds very military to me."

"It probably is. My dad always told me to keep my emotions inside, said that people didn't want to see them.

When I did, he called me his brave little soldier, and that was high praise coming from a man who didn't believe in coddling anyone."

"So when you said you'd noticed me…"

"The way any woman would notice a good-looking man. I'm only human, Mateo. Maybe a bit more reserved than you're used to, but I'm normal in all the ways that count." She reached over and brushed his cheek with her hand. "This living arrangement could get difficult because of that. But there are worse things in life than being attracted to a good-looking man."

"Or woman," he replied.

"So if we know it's there between us it becomes easier. At least, it should."

After only a few days, Lizzie was already starting to like having someone there with her. Or was it Mateo she liked having there? Either way, this past year had been so lonely, and having a little noise around the house other than her own was nice. Especially after that kiss…

"Are you sure that's true?" he asked, walking alongside her, but at a safe distance. "Admit an attraction and then hope it can be held at an arm's length?"

"I'm not sure how we're supposed to work. More than that, I'm not sure I know how I *want* us to work. Friends, partners, lov—"

She didn't finish the sentence because this was becoming too deep, and she didn't want a volley of emotions going back and forth between them. Especially when there was every possibility that her feelings were turning into more than she'd expected. He was easy to like, she was discovering. More than that, if she allowed herself to admit it, he would also be easy to love—even with parts of him missing.

But could she go through that again? That was the

question she needed to figure out before she took the wrong step. Because she did know what it was like living with someone who was fragmented. It was difficult, sad, tedious, and moments of joy were so few and far between.

But that had been her dad. Not Mateo. Which led her to an even bigger question. Could she separate the two? There were similarities in their problems, although not that many. And Mateo was caring and warm while her dad had not been. Still, she'd loved her dad because he'd tried to do better. Yet in her mind the similarities were still large. And that was what scared her.

Would there ever be a time when Mateo occupied all her thoughts, as well as her whole heart, and didn't get squeezed out?

"Like I said before, Lizzie, you can tell me to leave anytime. No explanation necessary."

"I know I can." But she wanted him there. Liked having him there. He balanced her out while she went through her own ups and downs and never judged or asked questions. "That's not what I want."

"Meaning you like having me here?"

"I do, Mateo. It's sort of out of character for me, but yes, I like having you here."

He smiled as he watched her make her way to the front door. She wasn't easy. In fact in a lot of ways, she was difficult. But he liked being here with her, too. In fact, he could see that feeling growing the longer he stayed. She wasn't orthodox, she wasn't predictable, but Lizzie was the real deal, and he was attracted to that asset almost as much as he was to her *other* assets.

"Time will tell," he said aloud, as he walked around to the *ohana*. Time and, he hoped, a few more pieces of his memory.

* * *

"You need to go up there, Doc. He's bad and he'll stand a better chance with you."

"I'm not supposed to do this."

Sweat was dripping off his brow, yet he was chilled to the bone. Looking up, he saw the two medics up there working frantically. And they were looking down at him, expecting him to trade places.

"You got an IV in?" he yelled up to them, but his voice didn't carry over the sound of the gunfire that was much closer than he cared to admit. "IV!" he shouted. "Get an IV in him."

They had the equipment with them, and it would be easier for them to use it than for him to carry up more than he had to.

"Get the IV in him, then I'll come up."

Which meant one of them would come down, since the watchtower platform was too small to hold three people, let alone four.

"IV!" he shouted again, indicating the vein in his left forearm.

Finally one of them leaned over and shouted. "Don't come up, Doc. Too risky. We'll get him down to you, then you can—"

As he was shouting a shot rang out, hitting the soldier in what appeared to be his chest.

"What do we do, Doc?" one of the men on the ground asked. "Tell me what to do!"

Then suddenly they were dying.

They were all dying.

"I don't know!" Mateo screamed. "I don't know."

When he looked up again it was Freddy hanging over the edge. Freddy with his chest ripped open. His friend. His only friend out here.

* * *

As he screamed, he woke up in a puddle of sweat. The bedsheets were drenched and his hands were shaking. His memory was returning, and he wasn't sure he wanted it to. What had happened that night…none of it was good. None of it.

Sighing, Mateo left the bed and walked to the window, opened it, and looked out at the stars for a little while.

It wasn't going to leave him. Other things had. Too many things. But this? This was hanging on in huge chunks, tormenting him.

Some memories weren't meant to be remembered and this was one of them. But it was coming back. Damn it. It was coming back.

His screams carried through the night and she couldn't run fast enough to get to him.

"Mateo," she choked, barely slowing as she ran through the front door and up the stairs to his room.

He was standing at the window. Staring out. Not moving. Barely breathing.

"Tell me what to do."

He turned slowly to face her. "They all died, Lizzie. Every one of them, including Freddy. And I was the only one who—" His voice broke, and he sank to the floor. "There was nothing I could do to help any of them."

Lizzie sat on the floor next to him, putting her arm around his shoulder even though he was stiff and resistant. "I'm ready to listen if you're ready to talk."

"But there's nothing to say. I took a risk. Went up the tower when I should have waited. Drew enemy fire and got every one of my ground support killed."

There were so many things she wanted to say—most of them trite. But he didn't need that. So instead she pulled him a little closer and sat quietly, waiting for him to speak again.

It was nearly five minutes before he did.

"Nobody came for a couple of days. The whole area was under heavy fire and they had no idea that one of the casualties was alive. So I lay there, going in and out of consciousness, and I have no idea when I was rescued or what happened after that. The next thing I remember is waking up in Germany. I'd had surgery—I remember that. But I didn't remember my name. Not for days. Or maybe weeks. Then I was sent Stateside, and you know the rest. Belligerent patient. Refuses to help himself."

"Survivor's remorse?" she asked.

"Probably."

Now it was beginning to make sense to her. Mateo was beginning to make sense to her. He didn't want to get better because somewhere, buried deep, he believed he should have died with his men. This wasn't about his memory loss, or his hatred of being a patient. It was about the very essence of a man who carried a burden he didn't deserve.

"Why now?" she asked. "What's bringing all this back now?"

She feared it was something she was doing, or not doing, and she wanted to know.

"Maybe because I feel safe here. The truth is, it's never clear why something surfaces when it does. That's something they've been telling me since Germany. No one really knows why something happens when it does."

"I like the explanation that you feel safe."

"So do I," he said.

CHAPTER SEVEN

BEFORE MATEO, BREAKFAST had always been quick. If she ate it, she never lingered. Most often she grabbed a coffee on the way to work and didn't think about food until her belly told her she was hungry. If it didn't, as often as not she didn't eat.

But this morning she felt like making breakfast for Mateo the way he'd done for her these past mornings. It was simple. Nothing like his elaborate spread. Fresh fruit, toast. And in the casualness of the moment she felt relaxed. Relaxed enough to ask his opinion.

So, over her second cup of coffee, she told him about her opportunity to move from the hospital to a private practice as a primary care provider. She knew it was something her dad would have dismissed as stupid before she'd have been able to get all the words out. He'd actually told her so before his Alzheimer's got so bad.

"Kahawai is really pressuring me. He wants me to buy out his uncle's small practice, possibly expand it, and treat the people who live in the area. He's put me on a deadline now. Says he's going after you if I don't accept."

"Are you happy at the hospital?"

"I'm not *un*happy. It's just that there are so many memories here I'm not sure I want to stay. Not sure I want to go, either."

"Do you have other options?" he asked.

"A few. None that excite me, though. Maybe I'm too picky—or maybe I'm in a place where I shouldn't be making major life decisions yet. Whatever the case, I won't be doing anything without good reason. So, are you up for a bodyboarding lesson today?"

"The best possible scenario is that once I paddle out into the water it all comes back to me and I remember all the medals I won as a world-class surfer."

Lizzie laughed. "I don't recall your name being on any medal list. Which championship was it?"

"See, that's where amnesia comes in handy. All I have to do is say I don't remember, and people won't press for more information. They'll just assume I'm what I claim to be."

"Have you ever surfed, Mateo?"

"Not to my knowledge," he said seriously.

"Well, it's too soon after your head surgery to do anything more than paddle on your stomach. And, while I already know the reaction I'm going to get, I think you should wear a helmet."

"A stylish one, I hope?" he said, taking both their coffee cups to the sink, then rinsing them out before they went into the dishwasher. "If all I'm allowed is bodyboarding, I'll accept that. But the helmet's got to be pretty damned cool."

"Because…?" she asked, biting back her smile.

"Because I'm pretty damned cool, and I don't want my reputation ruined by a helmet."

She liked that little bit of stubbornness in him. It was sexy. But was it really him? And was she always bound to wonder if things were really him?

"Then we'll get you a cool helmet. Pink, purple, neon-green?"

"Black—with stripes. Maybe red stripes. And all the gear to match."

He was really quite funny when he wanted to be, and she enjoyed that, because she needed some lightness in her life. "Whatever you say."

"What if I say that you make me nervous?"

"I'll ask you why, and you'll probably come up with some good lie I'll believe."

"Except I'd never lie to you. Not intentionally."

And just like that the light moment had turned serious.

"I may not be the me who existed before, but no matter who I am I'd never lie to you." He reached out and held her face between his hands. "Your face and especially your eyes are very expressive, Lizzie Peterson. Your eyes would show if you ever lied to me. But you wouldn't do that."

"Are you that sure of me?" she asked, backing away from him. His touch was too real, and it was a reality she didn't want to face.

"What if I said yes? That I trust you more than anyone else I've ever trusted except for my mother?"

"I'm not sure what I've done to earn that, but I'd be flattered."

"Then be prepared to be flattered, because I do." He bent to her ear and whispered, "And I think I always will."

She wanted desperately to ask him what he meant by that, but she was afraid of the answer. She'd said yes to a man once before, then proceeded directly into hell. And, while Mateo was nothing at all like Brad, she wondered about her judgment. Maybe didn't trust it so much. Or perhaps everything stemmed from her need not to be alone.

Whatever the case, she wasn't prepared to give Mateo

an answer to the question she was pretty sure was coming. So she backed away from him.

"Give me half an hour, then we'll meet in the garden and go rent a couple of bodyboards. We have one quick stop to make first. I promised Kahawai I'd look at the clinic."

"So you *are* giving it some thought?"

"Maybe a little. I'm not one to shut down my options the way—"

She stopped. Mateo was his own man and he was going to do what he wanted to do. At least until he believed that asking for real help was a good option. If that ever happened.

"The way I am?" he asked. "That's what you were going to say, isn't it?"

"Let's just say we're not alike."

"But opposites attract, don't they?"

And they *were* opposites in so many ways. Yet they were also so much alike.

"Who said anything about attracting? All I did was mention I wanted to go look at the clinic. You're welcome to come, or you can do whatever you want. It's your choice," she said.

In so many ways, everything was his choice. But she wasn't sure he was ready for all the choices that would come his way.

Time would tell, she supposed.

The clinic was bustling when Lizzie and Mateo entered. The line was long, but nobody seemed put out by the wait. It was staffed by one elderly doctor, who didn't move fast, one medical assistant, and one receptionist. People had brought their lunches and were spread out in the garden outside, eating.

It seemed more like a social gathering place than a medical office, and Mateo liked the feel of that. It wasn't the way he practiced, but he could see Lizzie here, working at a different pace than she normally did, and being happy doing it.

"It's not what I expected," he said, as they made their way through the waiting room to the back, where Doc Akoni looked exhausted as he went from one exam room to the another.

"Two doctors here would be great," he said, assuming Mateo was here to enquire along with Lizzie. "The practice is booming, but I'm too old to keep up with it. My goal is to spend the rest of my years with my wife and do the things we never had time to do before. You know...visit kids and grandkids. Travel... Live out my life in leisure."

"Where do your emergency patients go?" Mateo asked, looking over some of the outdated equipment that was still in use: a breathing machine, an X-ray rig, something that chugged along doing rudimentary blood tests, and a few other gadgets that looked as old as he was.

"There are a couple of hospitals with good emergency care down the coast, if the situation isn't too urgent. And, of course, we can air transport them down to Honolulu when it's necessary."

"How often is that?" Lizzie asked.

"More often than I care for. There are some good clinics in the area, but as far as hospital beds go nothing much around here."

"What about Malakapua Pointe?" asked Mateo.

Lizzie shook her head. "No emergency department. That was never part of the plan."

Doc Akoni escorted his next patient into one of the three exam rooms. "Janis Lawton had her vision for Malakapua when it was being built here," he explained. "And, while we were hoping for some kind of emergency department, she was very specific as to the kind of patient she wanted. Her general care wards and surgeries don't really lend themselves to a broader base of patients with the kinds of injuries and illnesses you see here in this clinic. We're minor. We treat the little things and make referrals for patients who need more than we offer. Nobody comes here expecting open heart surgery, or even an appendectomy."

"Which makes you a country doctor," Mateo said.

He was looking at the little girl who was the next patient in the queue. Her skin was red and blistering. She looked listless and dizzy. And it was clear she was suffering with nausea. Definite signs of sun poisoning.

"Can I help you out with your next patient?"

"You can see all the patients you want. I'm assuming you're the doc everybody's talking about…the one with amnesia?"

"Amnesia in some areas. But many parts of my life are intact—like the part that sees a clear case of sun poisoning."

"You know enough to ask for help if you need it, don't you?" Akoni asked.

Mateo nodded.

"And you can read an X-ray? Because we have a rather outdated machine."

Mateo nodded again.

"Sutures?"

"Yes. I can put in sutures."

"Then it sounds to me like you're good to go. Lab coats are in the back, along with an extra stethoscope. There's one central area for supplies, which I keep locked. We don't dispense medicine because the salesmen prefer to avoid us, meaning no free samples. Also, because we're not a pharmacy, we're not licensed to prescribe. Oh, and don't try to refer patients to…" he nodded sideways at Lizzie "…to *her* hospital. Like I said, they don't do trauma, or any sort of emergency, and there's hell to pay if one of our patients accidentally ends up there. The other places we use are much nicer."

Lizzie raised her eyebrows at his pronouncement. She'd heard him say as much before, but didn't really believe it was that bad. But maybe it was. Maybe it was something she should check into if she went back.

"So, how will you treat her?" she asked Mateo, referring to the child.

"Cool compresses. A lot of fluids. And if that doesn't bring up her hydration level fast enough, an IV. Treat her nausea. Take care of her skin with some kind of medicated moisturizer. And keep her out of the sun for a while. Bed rest for a couple of days if she comes down with a fever or chills, which is likely. Then ibuprofen for that. It's all pretty basic. Nothing to worry about that general care won't take care of."

"You're good," Lizzie commented, genuinely impressed.

"So, for now," said Doc Akoni, "if you need to prescribe any real treatment, and not simply apply a bandage, why don't you run it by me first? Or Lizzie, if she cares to stay. All things considered, I don't think you need close supervision at this level of care, but just to be safe…"

"Not a problem," Mateo said. "It's just like going through my residency again."

"Well, be patient. Things will change," said Doc Akoni.

Mateo nodded, then took the child by her hand and led her toward the exam room, motioning for her mother to follow.

"I could use someone like you around here," said Doc Akoni, on his way into exam room one.

"Even with my condition?" Mateo asked, looking at the old-fashioned whiteboard hanging on the reception area wall, where patients signed their names as they came through the door.

"Even with your condition. If you didn't lose your general skills, this could all be yours."

"Not sure I'm ready to run a clinic on my own. Even one as basic as this."

"Things change, son. You never know who might be standing right behind you, eager to help. All I'm saying is, don't discount yourself. You've got everything you need to do this job, if you set yourself free to do it."

Mateo glanced at Lizzie, who was busy talking to a woman who was obviously well along in her pregnancy. "Mind if I hang around here for a little while and help?" he asked her. "Maybe put the bodyboarding off until later this afternoon?"

He nodded down toward the woman's swollen ankles, and Lizzie acknowledged his discovery with a wink.

"I think helping out would be a good way to spend the morning. Maybe I'll stay and put in a few hours as well. And the first thing... Would you mind consulting with me, Dr. Sanchez? My patient is nearing her thirtieth week, and the edema in her feet and ankles is indeed what's bothering her. Since I haven't worked a maternity case in years..."

Mateo looked at the woman's name on the whiteboard, then found a paper file in a rickety old filing cabinet. He studied it for a moment, then nodded. "Why don't you make Leilani comfortable in exam room two, since it's open? I'll be in shortly."

"You OK?" Lizzie whispered as she passed by him

on her way into exam two. "Can you handle maternity? I know it's a little more than first aid, but…"

"I did it when I was overseas. A lot of the women who lived there depended on us."

"Then you're the man for the job."

"Only if you oversee what I'm doing. I'm not ready to fly solo with anything more than a cut or a bruise."

"Or CPR," she reminded him as she entered the exam room.

That was true. And so many things had come back to him—like why Leilani had swollen ankles. It wasn't part of the scope of a surgeon's responsibility, but he knew. It was coming back to him. All the pregnant women he'd treated in Afghanistan. The complications…the normal but uncomfortable things. It made him nervous and excited at the same time.

Lizzie wasn't sure what Mateo was thinking, and she hadn't intended working here for any part of the day, but Mateo's eyes sparkled with happiness and excitement.

That didn't mean he was finding himself, but it could mean he was finding a new place. But here? In this clinic? Or maybe just in the general practice of medicine?

He certainly was good. Quick. Alert. In tune with the details of his patient. It was the first time he'd showed any kind of hope, and she was glad for that. Glad for him. Actually, she felt so excited that if she were twenty years younger, she might be jumping up and down like an eager child.

Twenty minutes after his examination of Leilani, Mateo said, "Everything looks good. Your blood pressure is normal, baby is the right size, and you look like a first-time mom with a glow."

"What about my swollen feet?" she asked.

"Right…" he said, nodding. "It's called edema, and it's normal—especially in the evening and during warmer weather. It happens in about seventy-five percent of all pregnancies, and once it starts you're stuck with it until you deliver."

"Why?" she asked, and her attention was focused solely on Mateo, not Lizzie, who stood off in the corner, observing.

"Well, it happens when your body fluids increase to nurture both you and your baby. That results in increased blood flow and pressure on your expanding uterus, which is what causes the swelling. Look for it to happen in your hands, as well.

"Then it's really normal?" the young woman asked.

"Perfectly—as long as it's kept under control. However, if it becomes excessive, and comes along with a couple of other things, like increased blood pressure or rapid weight gain, that could indicate a problem, and you'll have to let your doctor know about it."

"Is there anything I can do about it? Maybe take a pill, or something?"

"I think the natural things you can do are better. Such as trying not to stay in one position for a long period of time. Also, elevate your legs when you're sitting. And I always recommend sleeping on your side—your left side—because it helps your kidneys eliminate waste, which reduces swelling. Then, there are other things that might help. Pregnancy-appropriate exercising. Avoiding tight socks or stockings. Drinking lots of water—around ten glasses a day. That helps eliminate the waste in your system that causes the swelling. And comfy shoes. If they feel good, wear them—and skip the vanity shoes.

And, last but not least, cut out excess salt. It causes you to retain water, which is exactly what you don't want."

"It sounds so simple," Leilani said, heading toward the exam room door.

"It is—and it will only last a few more months." Mateo smiled as he escorted Leilani through to the waiting room. "Just use common sense and you'll be fine. But if you think something's not right call a doctor—or a nurse practitioner, if that's who you're using."

"I'm not using anybody," she said. "Doc Akoni confirmed my pregnancy at the beginning, but now when I come here and see so many people waiting I don't stay, because I have to get back to my job. Today I got lucky. You're here and the line is going faster."

"You need regular care," Mateo told her. "For your own health as well as your baby's."

"I'll get it closer to the time."

With that, Leilani disappeared through the door and hurried on her way.

"She doesn't get any regular care," he said to Lizzie, who was standing in the hallway, still watching him.

"A lot of people don't. I saw it when I traveled with my dad. See it here, too. Too many complaints…not enough doctors to go around."

She was proud of the way he had handled himself, and he couldn't have been more spot-on in his examination and in answering Leilani's questions if he'd been an obstetrician.

What Mateo had was a real gift. He remembered things she'd forgotten. Sleeping on your left side—she wasn't sure that was something she'd ever known about pregnancy. She admired what he was doing, looking at something that was new to him, and safe.

Admiring him personally was not so safe. But one

was spilling over into the other and she wasn't sure she knew how to stop it.

Or if she even wanted to.

When the morning was over, and the queue was cut down by more than half, thanks to Lizzie and Mateo pitching in, they decided to postpone their bodyboarding and spend the rest of the afternoon relaxing.

Mateo was glad of that. His headache was back—probably from overexertion. It had been a good long time since he'd worked, and he'd discovered he wasn't in the same good shape he'd used to be when…

Mateo shut his eyes for a moment and fractured pieces of his makeshift military surgery came back to him. Nothing was concrete. Nothing really rang a bell. Except an older nurse sitting at the triage desk… Was she knitting?

"Something wrong?" Lizzie asked as his eyes shot back open.

"Her name was Mary. She knitted…for a grandchild, I think. She was my surgical nurse. Damned good nurse. Knew more than pretty much all the rest of us put together."

"That's just coming back to you?"

He nodded as they took a seat at The Shack, on a lava rock wall surrounding an almond tree. "She was this amazing bundle of energy we all respected. Short, a little round, gray hair, and she could out-move any one of us."

"That's a good sign, Mateo."

"But triggered by what?"

"Something familiar—like working in a congested medical environment this morning. Or something someone said or did. Or maybe one of the patients you treated reminded you of another patient somewhere else? I mean,

I don't know enough about triggers to talk about them, but maybe it's just time. Remember: to everything there is a season…?"

They stopped talking as the server brought drinks—lemonade for Lizzie and something Mateo had called "the usual."

"They know you well enough here to bring you a drink without you telling them what you want? I'm impressed."

"It's a mix of fruit juices—whatever's on hand except banana. It overwhelms everything else, so they don't include it."

"And the bartender just happens to remember that?" she asked.

"He was in the clinic earlier. Suffered a pulled muscle in his neck in a minor injury on the beach breakwaters. I just happened to mention what I liked, and I guess he remembered. Care for a sip?" he asked, holding out his tall hurricane glass to her.

"Should I be jealous that you've made friends here already and the only people I know work at the hospital?"

She took the glass and he felt the soft skin of her hand caress his, maybe linger a second or two longer than it should. Their eyes met, again lingering a bit longer than he'd expected. But he wasn't complaining. Being here with Lizzie like this made him realize there was no place else he wanted to be.

Would she ever consider him something more than a friend? Or just a reminder of what had happened to her father? Those were the questions on his mind right now, and he wanted to ask her, but he wouldn't for fear of her answer.

If she said no, that he could never fit into her life in a different way than he already did, that would devastate him. And if she could never look at him without being reminded of her dad's illness… Well, that would be the last piece of sharp-edged glass dropping to the floor…

"Nothing to be jealous of. I've always made friends easily. When I was a kid I could charm just about anybody to get anything I wanted."

"I never really had time to make friends. Just when we were finally settled in one place, it was time to move on. And now… I haven't changed much, to be honest. It's easier being alone. I can make my life exactly what I want it to be without interference."

"I've never really been alone. Growing up, I was social. Then in college and medical school…let's just say I liked to party. After that, the Army wasn't exactly a place where anyone got to be alone."

"My dad was very 'social,' as you call it. But that never happened to me. He always said I wasn't outgoing enough, and as it turns out he was right. I have my work, though."

"And that's enough?"

Lizzie sighed, then took a sip of her lemonade. "Was today enough for *you*, Mateo?"

"It was different—but I can't really judge it in terms of being enough or not enough. I enjoyed the work, enjoyed getting back to medicine for a little while, even if it wasn't in a surgical capacity."

Lizzie was mellow this evening. No particular reason why, but the feeling had been dragging at her most of the day and now she was ready to give in to it. Let it take her wherever it wanted to.

Mateo had gone with a couple of people he'd met at The Shack to a private yacht party, and even though he'd asked her to come along she hadn't been in the mood.

Instead she'd stopped by the hospital, to have a chat with Janis, but had decided not to go in once she'd got there.

She and Janis lived the same life. They worked. In twenty years, when she reached the age Janis was now, she could see herself being the one with the tiki cup collection, serving tropical drinks to colleagues who dropped by her office. Tonight, that had just hit too close to home, and she'd decided she didn't want to see it, so instead she'd gone home, turned on some soft music and was now reading the latest volume of *Topics in Primary Care*.

The first article that caught her attention was about newly approved disease-modifying therapies for multiple sclerosis. It was an expanding field that was resulting in some exciting outcomes. Next she read about Trigeminal Nerve Stimulation for ADHD in children, but wasn't sure that kind of electrical stimulation was anything she wanted to try. Finally, when she got to an article about initiatives in the management of non-motor symptoms in Parkinson disease, her eyes practically crossed.

But she was too tired to go upstairs to bed. So she shut her eyes and allowed herself five minutes to rest there before undertaking the stairs.

It was warm indoors. The fan overhead was spinning, but still moisture dampened the front of Lizzie's floral green Hawaiian wrap-dress—her favorite for lounging. She stretched out on the chaise, revealing long, tanned legs underneath the dress, then arched back, hoping to catch a little more of the breeze from the fan.

Five minutes led to ten, which led to twenty, which led to an hour—and all she got for spending the extra time lounging was such a vivid image of Mateo she didn't want to interrupt it.

Perspiration was beading between her breasts now, and it wasn't all about the heat.

"Looks like you're having a restless night," he said, from outside the open lanai door.

"Medical journals make me restless," she said, tugging her dress back into place and assuming a more conversational position. "I didn't think you'd be back this early."

"Parties are boring when you don't know anybody there." He stepped inside but kept his distance, going no farther than just barely in the door. "The people seemed nice enough, but I decided I'd rather come back here and spend the rest of the evening with you."

He gave her legs an obvious stare, then moved a few more steps into the room.

"I thought maybe we could go swimming. No one's down on the beach and it's a lot cooler outside than it is in here. Care to go?" He walked over to her and held out his hand.

She was sure he was staring at her breasts. Her dress did nothing but make them more prominent than they already were. He'd caught her looking a way no one was meant to see, and there was nothing to do about it but ignore the fact that she was barely dressed and either go with him or go to bed.

And while going to bed had seemed appealing an hour ago, she was over that now, and her mind was forming a vision of her and Mateo on the beach.

Bold move…but Mateo made her feel bold. And needy. And ready to try something that would make sure she didn't end up serving drinks in pink ceramic pineapples to anybody who happened to be passing by.

So she took his hand, stood, and followed as he led her out the lanai door, not missing the fact that he was dressed in long cargos and a white dress shirt, and hadn't changed into swimwear.

"We didn't turn on the floodlights," she said, as they headed toward the beach.

"Do we need the light?" he asked, stopping and turning to face her. "There's a big moon out tonight, and that should be enough."

The world seemed dreamlike as she stood there, anticipating something…anything. But it was clear from his lack of movement that the next move was up to her to make—if there were to be a move. So, without speaking, she started to undo the buttons on his shirt. One at a time, as her fingers trembled.

This was uncharted territory for her…seduction. The slow headiness of it. Before, with Brad, it had been an act of urgency on his part and she'd been merely a participant. But this was her seduction, and Mateo made it obvious that to keep going or to stop was for her to decide.

He was watching as she continued to unbutton his shirt, making her way down his chest, taking care to brush her fingers over his skin on her journey. Lizzie liked it that he watched her. It made her feel wanted in a way no man had ever wanted her. So with each button, and each deliberate brush of her fingers to his skin, she went one step more, leaning in to kiss what her fingers had just caressed, and listening to him moan as she did so.

"You know you're killing me," he whispered, as she tugged his shirt off his broad shoulders and dropped it on the ground.

"You know that's what I intend to do," she said, smiling softly at him as his hands reached down and gently caressed her back, her arms, her shoulders.

Then he pulled her up and hard to his chest, letting their heated bodies press together.

"My turn," he said, reciprocating button for button, caress for caress, kiss for kiss, and then likewise pulling her shirt off her shoulders and dropping it on top of his, leaving them pressed together skin to skin.

He was looking into her face. "Did you know this was the first thing I thought about when I met you? You were standing there, arms folded across your chest like you always do, assessing me. And my assessment of you, before I even thought about you as a doctor, was that you completed paradise. I'd taken the standard tour and none of it had made a difference, but then there was you..."

"And *my* first thought was that you were going to be trouble."

"Were you right?"

"In more ways than I counted on."

She let him lead her farther down the path to the beach, and to the edge of the water. That was where they stopped, and she removed his cargos and let him stand there in his boxers.

Would this be the thing that ended them? One more step into the water with Mateo and there would be no turning back. Perhaps somewhere in the deepest part of her she'd known this was inevitable. But what she didn't know was what would come next.

This was where the everyday Lizzie would have stopped. Yet this was where the Lizzie who wanted to come out of her shell would begin. Which was she?

As it turned out, Mateo answered that question with his first kiss. It was soft and delicate, just barely there. Lizzie responded with a second kiss—it was more demanding than she'd expected. Harder than she'd known she *could* kiss.

And that was her answer as she took that next step into the water. Then the next and the next. Even though she couldn't have Mateo in the truest sense, she wanted him *now*, and for the first time in her life Lizzie gave in to what she wanted.

In the ocean.

In the moonlight.

In Mateo's embrace.

CHAPTER EIGHT

As the morning light peeked in through the blinds Lizzie opened her eyes and stretched, then turned on her side, expecting to see Mateo there. But he was gone.

After their lovemaking in the ocean they'd returned to the house, running bold and naked, not much caring if they were caught, then showered off the sand and spent the rest of the night exploring, then cuddling, and doing all those things that had finally caused her to sleep in his arms, more peaceful and contented than she'd felt in a long, long time.

No promises had been made. In fact, few words had been spoken. There had been no need. Between them, the emotion had been so raw that words hadn't had any place. They'd both known what this was about: a growing need. Still, waking up with him still there would have been nice, and she was disappointed that last night hadn't extended into the morning.

Dressing, then heading downstairs, Lizzie half expected to see Mateo in the kitchen, or maybe on the lanai, but he was in neither place. He'd been there, though. Coffee was made, and there were fresh muffins sitting out, waiting for her.

So she indulged, and by the time she'd finished Mateo

was there, standing by the sliding door to the lanai, smiling. He was holding a couple of bodyboards under his arm.

"Are you sure you got the right size?" she asked.

"The girl in the surf shop measured me—twice."

"I'll bet she did," Lizzie said, as she did a mental check to make sure.

The board had to come to about mid-chest, and that was where her eyes fixed for much longer than they should have. But what a chest to fix on…

Having Lizzie stare at him like that was nice, especially after last night. But in the full light of day it made him nervous. It also made him keenly aware that he couldn't have what was within his reach. No delusions, no forgetting anything. She deserved what he couldn't give her—a fully functioning man, not just the shell of someone who didn't know who he was, let alone how he was going to work out the rest of his life.

"You do realize that 'bodyboard' has another meaning, don't you?" he said. "It's used in radiation therapy and it allows the intestinal tract to drop out of the treatment field?"

"You really are full of yourself, aren't you?" she asked, laughing.

"It was just something I remembered when I was buying these. Too bad what came back to me wasn't more useful."

"Well, if that's what you want to use your bodyboard for it's up to you. I prefer to use mine in the water, paddling over the waves…"

"Capsizing?" he asked.

"You always turn toward the negative, don't you?"

He shrugged. "Maybe capsizing is a memory."

"Or maybe it's your way of trying to convince me to let you start with a kneeling board, or even a full surfboard. Which I won't do because you've had brain surgery. In case *that* has slipped your mind."

"Wish it would," he said, resisting the urge to reach up and feel the tiny area where the doctor had drilled. "And it wasn't exactly brain surgery. It's classified as a minimally invasive procedure."

"Like I don't know that?"

"Like there's a huge difference between having part of your skull removed and having a tiny hole drilled."

He knew the procedure like he knew the back of his hand—not because he'd had to remove that many subdural hematomas, but because he'd read up on the procedure dozens of times after it was over. It was so simple—drilling a burr hole the size of a dime, inserting a catheter and letting a clot-buster drug drip in. Over several days the clot disappeared, and there was no need for a more substantial procedure, like a craniotomy, where the skull was cut open and the clot was manually removed.

That was the procedure he'd done too many times, and how he wished he'd known more about the other procedure when he was in the field. But it was still new, and in field surgery the tried and true was always the go-to. He'd been in the hospital in Germany when the procedure had been used on him.

Mateo blinked hard to rid himself of the image of what they'd done to him. It was a reminder of too many things he'd known and done as a battlefield surgeon. Things he'd never be able to do again.

"Nope. Can't forget that. It's caused me to part my hair differently."

"Well, if it's of any consequence, the post-surgical notes I read said your procedure was textbook-perfect."

"Not a comforting thought, Lizzie," he said. "Someone tapping into your brain."

"Because you don't like thinking of yourself as a patient? Or because brain surgery, no matter how minimal, scares the bejeebies out of you, like it does most people?"

"One from Column A and one from Column B, please. Being that close to what could easily have been deadly isn't what I care to have come into my mind. It always does, though. And I know I shouldn't complain, since I was one of the lucky ones, but that doesn't make it any easier."

"Did it ever occur to you that if you start your real recovery by accepting the fact that you were a patient, which makes you the vulnerable one, it might take you to the next step, where you'll start dealing with the emotional aspects of vulnerability? And after that...who knows? But your recovery, Mateo, could take a long time."

"Well, it seems I've got plenty of that," he quipped.

"And in the meantime?"

He shrugged. "Take it a day at a time, I suppose. I mean, what else can I do? And don't suggest anything to do with the hospital, because you know how I feel about that."

"I'm not sure you're aware, but I do listen to the things you say and watch the things you do, and you're not helpless. In fact, you function very well. Like yesterday at the clinic. No mistakes—not even any hesitation. Take note of yourself, Mateo. The answers are there. And if they don't come, then start with something that will make new memories. People do it every day."

"But I'm not 'people,' Lizzie. I'm me, and I'm impatient to get on with my life."

"Then *do* it, Mateo. Starting today—right now—look at everything as new. You've got a clean slate. That's a beginning."

"You know, there are times when I really hate your optimism."

She laughed. "Me, too. But I'm stuck with it. And as long as you're stuck with me..."

His lips curved into a suggestive smile. "And how long would that be?" he asked.

"Let's start with a month and see how that works."

"A month? With benefits?"

"Everything's negotiable."

Finally, his full-out smile returned. "Is it? Then tell me what you want to take to the bargaining table to open negotiations, and I'll make sure I'm there with whatever you want."

"I'll just bet you will be," she said, swooshing past him and heading toward the beach. Smiling a smile Mateo couldn't see.

She was magnificent, riding the waves. So much beauty and poise skimming over the surface of the water. And in the instant when she disappeared into the wave on her belly, and then emerged standing, balancing herself, she looked like Aphrodite, the goddess of love, or one of the Greek goddesses of the sea.

This was the most uninhibited he'd seen her. It was as though when she became one with the wave she ascended to another place—somewhere ethereal, somewhere that freed her from whatever it was that kept her bound otherwise.

"You ready for your big adventure?" she called as

she came walking toward him, her tight black swimsuit emphasizing curves he knew he shouldn't be observing and her wild red hair slicked back, exposing the entirety of her perfect face.

Lizzie dropped her surfboard next to where Mateo was sitting and watching, and picked up one of the body-boards.

"It's fun in its own right," she said, holding out her empty hand to pull him up.

But he didn't want to move. He'd spent the last hour watching perfection, and that seemed infinitely more interesting than him being out there, flopping around on a bodyboard.

"Truthfully? I'm good, sitting here watching you."

Lizzie dropped down on the huge, multi-colored beach towel with him, grabbed a bottle of water from the small cooler they'd brought, then smiled.

"Because you're a coward?" she taunted.

And her smile was so infectious he caught it in an instant and smiled back.

"Because you're having a good time, and I don't want to interrupt that for what may be some pretty pathetic attempts to keep my belly flat on a board."

Her eyes roamed down to his belly, then back to his face. "Your belly will be fine," she said.

But it wasn't his belly he was concerned about. Other parts were reacting. All the man parts, as he would expect. And most especially his heart.

Was it beating too quickly? Was his breathing coming a little too shallow and fast? It felt that way, and he wasn't even thinking of her in terms of anything that could cause that. It was simply a natural reaction. A primal urge, he wanted to tell himself. Even though he knew it was more than that.

"What about the rest of me?" he asked.

"Do as I say and you won't have any problems. First, for a beginner, it's best to choose a calm spot, where the waves aren't so high. Maybe a couple of feet, but no more than that."

Mateo scooted a little closer to Lizzie, not so much that she would notice, but *he* certainly did.

"Then wax the board. It should already be waxed, but I prefer waxing myself since it's essential to getting a good grip."

"The whole board?" he asked, even though his mind was more on applying sunscreen to her entire body.

"No. Just the top and bottom third, and the edges."

"For a good grip?" he asked.

He was wishing this was more than a simple body-boarding lesson. Not that he would or could take it anywhere. But something about Lizzie caused him to realize how much he'd missed these past years, and how much he'd forgotten. Smooth skin against his. The touch of delicate fingers. Soft kisses turning wild.

He was putting last night on mental replay and wondering how he was going to manage for the next month. Thinking like this wasn't doing him any good, but he was sure enjoying it. Especially since the object of his attraction—and maybe more—was Lizzie.

He'd never cared much for red hair before; he did remember that. But *her* red hair ignited him. And getting involved with another doctor... That had definitely been off his list, since he knew the ins and outs of that intimately. But he was no longer a doctor, and even if he were it wouldn't matter. Not with Lizzie sitting beside him and their thighs brushing together.

"For staying afloat. Oh, you didn't get yourself a rash guard. Some people like them, because they reduce chafing from the board itself, but maybe that won't bother you."

It wouldn't. Especially if she treated any rash he might get.

"Personally, I like the contact with the board. It gives me a better feel for what I'm doing."

"And the swim fins? The girl at the beach shop said I had to have them."

"Definitely, yes. They'll help you paddle out farther, so you can catch better waves. Oh, and the leash…it attaches to your wrist."

"Seems like an awful lot of trouble just to catch a wave."

"It is—but there's no sensation like it in the world, no matter if you're vertical or horizontal. So, did she sell you a helmet? Black with red stripes?"

"She did."

"And…?"

"And I'll wear it, Lizzie. OK? I'll wear the damned helmet."

He might have argued more with her, but she was so into the moment and he didn't want to break that. She looked beautiful—her eyes sparkling, a slight blush to her cheeks. This was Lizzie in her element, and he was enjoying being there with her even if he didn't so much as get the bottoms of his feet wet.

"Excellent. So, gear up and let's do it. Wade out until you're knee-deep, then put your belly to the board and keep your hips in contact with the tail of the board."

"And my hands?"

He knew where he wanted to put them, but what *he* wanted and what *she* wanted were two different things. Still, he could almost feel her hands skimming down the side of his body, like they had done the night before…

"Top corners of the board. Make sure you keep your fins under water, then paddle out—one-handed or two, doesn't make a difference—until you see the wave you want to catch. For starters, we're going to catch some smaller ones."

This was getting serious. He needed to get his mind back on what he was about to do, otherwise his amateur performance would turn into a clown show because he'd missed one or two vital steps. Of course, mouth-to-mouth from Lizzie sounded pretty good, if that was what it came down to. Especially now that he knew the secrets of her mouth...

"When you do see a wave, point your board toward the beach and start to kick and paddle. The wave will do the rest."

"Sounds simple enough," he said, looking down the beach at all kinds of people surfing and bodyboarding.

He'd been an adventurer. He remembered that. Remembered scaling rock walls, paragliding, even some dangerous sledding in there. Straight downhill, hoping to avoid the trees and the other sledders. But this? It scared him. Not because of the risk, but because he was, like she'd told him, vulnerable. He didn't know if his adventurous side would come back or if he'd turn into one of those people he could see from where he was, who paddled out and simply sat there on the board, too afraid to move.

"You don't have to do this," Lizzie said.

"I do," he replied, taking off his blue floral print shirt. "In more ways than you know."

To prove it to himself and—more—to prove it to her. That was important...showing Lizzie that side of him— the side that wasn't a patient, that wasn't vulnerable, that wasn't so damned disagreeable. It mattered more than he'd thought it could.

Finally, after another mental bout with himself, he slipped the fins on his feet, grabbed his board, and walked to the water's edge. Lizzie was right there next to him, and he found some strength in having her there. But he hadn't always been this way. That much he remembered.

"It's a simple thing," he said. "I've done much more dangerous things than this. Yet I'm not sure I'm ready to take the next step."

"It's not easy, facing your fears," she said, giving his arm a reassuring squeeze, followed by a tender kiss to his cheek. "Especially when you might not even know what they are until they pop up out of nowhere."

"What scares you?" he asked, looking out over the wide expanse of water.

"Lots of things. Making a medical mistake with one of my patients. That may be my biggest fear, because people rely on me, and if I do something to let them down, or even worse…" She shut her eyes briefly, then shook her head. "Horseback riding. Got thrown when I was a little girl and broke some bones in my back. It wasn't a huge trauma, but to this day I've never been back on a horse. Oh, and spiders. You haven't heard a good scream until you've heard me scream when I find a spider on me—or even near me. And some of the spiders here on Oahu are enormous. Like the cane spider."

She gestured, indicating something larger than a dinner plate, which was an obvious exaggeration, and just saying the word caused her to shiver.

It was a cute display, and something he hadn't expected from her. His version of Lizzie taking on the world had just knocked itself down a peg and he liked seeing that side of her. It made him realize that she had her own vulnerabilities, and that he wouldn't be standing out there alone on that sandbar he could see in the distance, holding on to his own bag of insecurities.

Mateo chuckled. "Well, I'll protect you from spiders if you protect me from myself."

"Do you *need* to be protected from yourself?" she asked.

He took a step into the water, then paused. "If I knew the answer to that I'd tell you."

Then he gathered up every bit of courage inside him and marched out until he was submerged to mid-chest. Lizzie followed him and immediately mounted her board, then waited for Mateo to do the same.

"This isn't too bad," he said, once he was belly-down on the board.

"Paddle around for a few minutes. Get used to the feel of it. Sometimes it's nice to just float for a while and let your mind wander."

"Do you do that?"

"Not so much now," she said, paddling over until her board was next to his. "I did when my dad was alive. He was…difficult. Sometimes it felt like I was failing him even though the doctor in me knew what was happening to him."

She paused for a moment, then continued.

"For me, the ocean has curative powers. When I was a little girl, traveling around with my dad, there were several times we lived near a beach. I think that's where I found my balance."

"So Hawaii was a logical place to come?"

"Actually, I lived here before, when I was a teenager. Dad was getting older, and thinking about retirement in a few years, so he transferred to one of the military hospitals here. It was the first time I ever had much of him in my life—which is one of the reasons I came back when he was diagnosed. Some of my best memories were here, and I remembered how much he'd loved it here as well."

"I'm from a little village in Mexico. The people there were poor. My mother was poor, too, and there wasn't enough work for her. Yet she got a sponsor in California, from one of the humanitarian groups, so we came to the States legally and she achieved her dream—which was to see me succeed."

"And now?" Lizzie asked.

"When I'm ready to travel I'm going back. My mother has the right to know what's happened, since she was a large part of my motivation. It's not going to be easy to tell her, though.

Lizzie laid her hand on his arm and squeezed. "So often the right things aren't. But she'll be glad to know that you're safe, and basically in good shape."

"Maybe you'd like to come with me?"

"I might... Mexico is one place I've never been."

The almost-promise made his heart skip a beat. But taking Lizzie home to meet his mother would be no small deal. The people in the village would throw parties, and sing and dance halfway through the night. There would be piles of food, amazing drinks—and all because Margarita's boy was bringing a woman home. Lizzie would love it, he thought.

"If you go with me, prepare yourself for the biggest party you've ever been to—all in your honor."

"*My* honor?"

"They're a friendly bunch of people. What can I say?"

He wasn't about to tell her that taking her to meet his mother would be as good as a wedding announcement.

They weren't ready for that yet. There were still issues to be resolved.

"So, you want to go catch a wave with me now?"

He took in a deep breath. "The waves really are calming, aren't they?"

"And they're calling my name. Mind if I...?"

"Do your thing, Lizzie. I'll be right behind you." Enjoying a view he was pretty sure he wanted to enjoy for the rest of his life.

In preparation to catch a good wave she paddled out a little farther, and found the perfect one that carried her almost all the way back to the shore. It seemed so natural for her. And for him? Well...he paddled out, like she did, found his wave, aimed his board, and rode the wave as best he could, weaving and bobbing in and out of the water until he almost hit shore.

"Wasn't as graceful as you," he said, spitting out a mouthful of saltwater as he stood and grabbed his board. "But that was fun. Thank you."

Lizzie smiled at him. "All part of the service offered to my houseguests. Want to go again?"

"How about I sit here and watch *you* go again?"

"Whatever you want," she said, turning and walking back into the water.

Mateo shut his eyes as the headache overtook him again. It had come and gone for days now, but this one was excruciating, pounding harder and harder, until suddenly everything around him was spinning. The sky, the sand, the water. Himself.

He turned to look for Lizzie, who was just emerging from the water, and waved her over.

"Migraine," he said as she approached.

The brightness of the sun was bothering him. And a

wave of nausea pounded him so hard he fell backwards into the sand.

"Not good, Lizzie," he managed to gasp as she dropped to her knees next to him. "Not good at all."

"Has this happened before?" she asked as she felt for his pulse.

"Yes, but not as bad."

"And you didn't bother mentioning it?"

"It's a headache. Everybody gets them."

She pulled back his eyelids and studied his eyes for a moment, wishing she had her medical bag. His pupillary response was sluggish, and the size from right to left varied, but not by much. It was clear something was wrong, but she couldn't risk leaving him here like this to go get her medical bag.

He grasped her hand. "I think I might be in trouble here," he said, holding on tight.

"I need to get you to the hospital so we can get a scan to see what's going on."

"For a freaking migraine?" he snapped, then clearly instantly regretted his tone of voice. "Just let me stay here and I'll be better in a few minutes."

"Unless it's not a simple migraine. I mean, I don't think it's a stroke, nor is some kind of neuro inflammation at the top of my list, but it could be another clot. Most definitely you've got some changes in brain activity that underlie the chronic pain you've been having, and my best guess—which is all I have at the moment—is that it's connected to your earlier brain trauma. So I can leave you here in the sand and hope it doesn't advance to another level, like a stroke, or I can get you to the hospital to see what's really going on. Your choice, Mateo."

"You know…that's the thing I most dislike about doctors. They take it to the limit."

"How do you mean?"

"It's a migraine. I've diagnosed them and treated them. But you're thinking way beyond that, aren't you?"

"That's why they pay me the big bucks. I'm very good at thinking way beyond what's normal or necessary."

He laughed, then moaned and grabbed his head. "Look, Lizzie. I appreciate the concern, but it's a stinking headache. That's all."

"I hope you're right about that, but in case you're not are you sure you want me to walk away and leave you with an unconfirmed diagnosis?"

She moved closer to him, took his hand, and bent down to kiss him on the lips.

Just before the kiss, she whispered, "I really don't want to lose you, Mateo, and it's not because I'm a doctor who hates losing patients. It's because I'm a woman who doesn't want to lose the man she's falling in love with."

She still needed to figure out how that would play out, as none of her feelings of trepidation had changed. But that was a discussion for another day. Right now, all she wanted was to get Mateo better.

"And if you make the wrong decision and I walk away…it would break my heart. I don't want that happening and I don't deserve it."

That much was true.

That she loved him was also true.

"Get me to the hospital and give me the scan," he said, trying to open his eyes, but failing, as if the sun nauseated him. "Do whatever you think needs to be done."

Blowing out a sigh of relief, Lizzie made the call, then sat there holding his hand while they waited.

One thing was sure. A life with Mateo wouldn't always be smooth. But it would always be good. And she hoped they could get to that point. Because after Mateo there wouldn't be anybody else. For all his stubborn ways, he was the only one she wanted.

When the time was right, she'd tell him. But there were issues to work out before any kind of commitment could be made, and those issues scared her. Neither of them came to this relationship unscathed. Two wounded people... Could that work?

"Are you going to hold my hand when they send me through that long tube of extreme claustrophobia?" he asked.

They were in the changing room and he was expected to put on one of those hideous gowns.

"Seriously? You're claustrophobic?"

"Maybe a little."

She tied him modestly into the green and blue gown he hated so much, then gave him a blanket to spread over his lap as they wheeled him down the hall—*in a wheel-chair*—for his tests.

"I always tell my patients the best thing for that is a shot of vodka—*after* the procedure."

"Hate the stuff," he said, reaching out to take Lizzie's hand once they were in the waiting room.

"Sex works, too," she whispered. "Depending on the diagnosis."

"*Now* we're getting somewhere."

Lizzie was worried and trying to hide it. He could see her struggle. She wasn't very good at hiding her expressions from him.

"It's going to be a migraine, pure and simple. You do know that, don't you?"

"No, I don't." Lizzie sat next to Mateo, holding his

hand as the technicians prepared him for a CT scan. "Look, this isn't going to take long, then if nothing shows we can go home and you can spend the rest of the day sleeping. Now, I'm going to run down to Janis's office for a minute and have a quick chat with her, if you don't mind?"

"Go," he whispered, as if the sound of his own voice hurt him.

"Two minutes—tops," she said, bending over the hard, flat CT table to give him a kiss. "I'll be right back."

She hated leaving him there, but there was nothing else she could do. She needed distance, and a couple of minutes to sort out her feelings. And some reassurance.

"You've got it bad, don't you?" said Janis, joining Lizzie, who was leaning on the wall outside the CT room.

"Depends on your definition of 'bad,'" Lizzie said. "Do I have feelings for him? Yes. What kind of feelings? Not the kind I should be having. Oh, and he didn't want to have this CT," she said.

"Did it occur to you that the man is so scared he doesn't know what he's doing? I mean, to look at him you'd never guess that, but Mateo is...*different*. He's a healer who can no longer heal. He has no home, no place to go, no plans for his future. If I were in his shoes, I'd be scared, too."

"I think he wanted to die."

"He wants to live, Lizzie. He just doesn't know how. If he had a death wish he wouldn't have showed up on your doorstep. To Mateo, you offer hope. And loving him the way I'm pretty sure you do is an added bonus he didn't count on. So give the guy some slack. Back off when he needs it, and stay close when that's what he wants."

Janis's words rang in her head as she made her way

back to Mateo. It wasn't just Mateo who was resistant, though. Or scared.

"So, you ready to get this done?" she asked, as the tech wheeled him into the room and helped him take his position on the CT bed. "Ten minutes and it'll all be over."

"Or starting again," he said.

Lizzie swallowed hard. "If that's how it turns out we'll work through it. I'm not going anywhere, Mateo. So if you start over this time you start with someone in your corner."

She bent down to kiss him, but he caught her off-guard and pulled her almost on top of him, gave her the kiss of a lifetime.

"That was...nice," she said, pulling back from him. "But maybe not appropriate here."

He grinned up at her. "That's just me being true to character."

"Has anyone ever told you you're incorrigible?"

"Has anyone ever *not* told me I'm incorrigible?"

"Dr. Peterson?" blared a voice from the microphone in the next room. "We need to get on with this test. Dr. Sanchez isn't our only patient."

"But way to go," Janis added through the same microphone.

"Now look what you've done," Lizzie said to Mateo as she left the room, fanning herself.

Rather than join her colleagues in the control room, she went to her office to wait, dropped down on the sofa, and shut her eyes until Janis came to talk to her.

"It's a small hemorrhage. Same place as before."

"Because we went bodyboarding?" Lizzie asked, as tears tickled the backs of her eyes.

"I'd say the first injury simply caused a weak spot. I

think this would have happened no matter what he was doing."

"I wasn't cautious enough—just like I wasn't cautious enough with my dad." Finally the tears overflowed, and she batted at them with the back of her hand. "Have you admitted him?"

"We're in the process. Then we're going to fix him—hopefully for good this time."

"With a drip?"

"Clot-busters save lives. And I think there's a lot of life in Mateo that needs saving. And guiding."

"Not my responsibility," Lizzie said.

"When you love somebody the way you do Mateo, *everything* about him is your responsibility. It changes your world, Lizzie. Nothing's the same anymore. But because Mateo is a sick man, you're the one who must step up and assume more than responsibility. You need to step up and accept his love—because he does love you."

"We have a long way to go before either of us can do anything. But I suppose now's as good a time as any to get started."

"*After* the procedure, please. This is Mateo I've got to deal with, and you know how he can be."

She did—and that was a large part of why she loved him. To her, Mateo was nearly perfect. Sure, there were some flaws. But they were such a small part of him, while his kindness and compassion embraced most of him.

Maybe Janis didn't see that, but *she* did, and that was all that really mattered.

Janis took off her surgical mask and threw it in the trash on her way out to see Lizzie. "It's done. He's sleeping peacefully. I need a tropical drink. Care to join me on my lanai?"

"Could I have a raincheck?" Lizzie asked. "I think I'd like to go sit in his room for a while."

"He's mumbling nonsense," Janis warned her. "Something about letting it happen. I'm assuming that means you?"

"I hope it does," she said, then headed off to Mateo.

"Janis says everything went well," she said, sitting down next to his bed. "You've got a catheter in your head, which will stay there several days, but the clot was small and likely just a residual from your initial injury."

He opened his eyes to look at her, managed a lazy smile, then went back to sleep. But he held on to her hand for dear life, and she vowed to stay right there with him until the anesthesia wore off and they were bringing him that green slime they commonly referred to as gelatin.

She recalled his first day there, when he'd asked her to please put on the first page of his chart that he loathed and detested green gelatin—or any gelatin, for that matter. And cottage cheese.

She'd never quite gotten around to doing that.

Lizzie laughed, even though nothing in her felt like laughing.

"Toward the end, Mateo," she said, even though he wasn't awake, "my dad only ate things with bright colors. I suppose he thought the color had something to do with the taste. But when they brought him his tray, if it didn't have something red or yellow or purple on it he wouldn't eat it."

She looked up, watched his heart monitor for a minute, and noticed how perfect his rhythm was. He was a strong man. This would only be a minor setback for him.

"Oh, you're back in your old room. Thought you'd appreciate being here…for old times' sake." She gave his hand a squeeze. "And your old hospital gowns are ready for you, too."

"Do you ever stop talking?" he asked, even though he didn't open his eyes.

"Does it bother you?" she asked, glad to hear his voice sounding so clear.

"No. It lets me know I'm alive and have something to look forward to."

"What?" she asked breathlessly, thinking of all the things he might say. Hoping *she* topped his list.

"Green gelatin."

"Funny thing is, I didn't even know it was happening. It kind of crept up on me, a little at a time."

She was sitting on the lanai with Janis, sipping something fruity from an original brown tiki cup. Janis was sipping something fruity from her favorite pink pineapple. It was late into evening now, and Mateo was still sleeping like a baby while she was trying to figure out the next step.

"I gave his case back to Randy," Janis informed her. "He's not as tolerant as you, so if you know what's good for your boyfriend you'll warn him to shape up or he'll be kicked out of here one more time."

Her boyfriend. Lizzie liked the sound of that.

What would come of it? She didn't know.

But right now that didn't matter.

She had a brick wall to scale before she could do anything.

His head hurt like a son of a gun, and to make matters worse there were five containers of green slime on his bedside table. Just looking at them jiggling at him made him feel nauseated. So did the hospital gown and the no-slide booties someone had slipped on his feet.

"This isn't the way life is meant to be lived," he said to Lizzie as she entered his room.

"They told me you were awake and in your usual good humor." She gave him a quick kiss, then sat down on the edge of the bed. "Has Janis been in to see you yet?"

"Nobody's been in to see me except the green gelatin fairy and you."

"Well, the news is good. The clot was small. It probably resulted from a weak suture put in on the first surgery. And your recovery can be done at my house, if that's what you want."

"What I want is for you to listen to me, and then tell me if I'm right or wrong."

"About what?"

"Your feelings for me. You're in love with me—or I hope you're in love with me—but it scares you because of what happened to your father. You're not sure you can get involved with someone with memory loss again."

"That's very perceptive," she said.

"But is it true, Lizzie?"

"Some of it is. You aren't the same as he was, but sometimes when I see that lost look in your eyes…"

"Have you seen it lately?"

She paused for a minute to think about it. "Not really."

"Your dad's illness wasn't your fault, Lizzie."

He reached for her hand, then pulled her closer to him until they were almost lying side by side.

"I know that. But…"

She bit down on her lip, willing herself not to cry.

"It was a really hectic day. He wanted to go for a walk and I didn't have time. I didn't let his caregivers do it because it was about the only way Dad and I were connecting, and I didn't want to be cheated of that. I promised him we'd go later…like he understood what I was saying. About an hour later I got the call to say that Dad had wandered off. It wasn't the first time, but he always headed toward the ocean, and I was so afraid… Well, we searched the shore for hours and there was no sign of him. The search continued for five days. *Five days*, Mateo. He was out there lost and alone for five days. And then the rescuers found him. He'd gone to Kapu Falls, which was one of his favorite places. He'd actually planted a flower garden there."

"Nobody went there to look?"

"Actually, they did. But Dad had crawled into some underbrush and apparently gone to sleep. At least that was what the coroner said. And he stayed in that same spot for five days. Maybe because that's where he wanted to die, or maybe he was simply waiting for me to come take him home. We'll never know."

She clenched her fists and shut her eyes.

"That's the nightmare I live with every day. And there are so many what-ifs. What if I hadn't gone to work? What if we'd taken the walk he wanted to take? What if the caregiver hadn't turned her back? What if I had one more lock put on all the doors?"

"It's impossible to predict outcomes all the time, Lizzie. Sometimes you're right, but as often as not you're wrong."

"Exactly, Mateo. You can't always predict outcomes."

"Meaning?"

"Meaning that at some point you've got to get on with your life or it will bury you. I was being buried. Not sure what I wanted to do. Yet the answer was always there. I was the one who had to open my eyes and see it, though."

"And the answer?"

"You, me…a beachside clinic. You can't operate anymore, and that may be a reality for the rest of your life. I think you've probably figured out that I've lost the heart for working in a hospital. I want a simpler life, and life's too short not to go after what you want."

"You said you and me in that clinic?"

"The reality is, for now, you'll have to be supervised. I can't predict the future, and I'm not even sure I would if I could. But you're a good doctor and you deserve to be back in medicine. Maybe it's not the way you want, but it's what you can have. And perhaps that's all we really need…what we can have. I think we could build a life around that, if you want to."

"Me as patient, you as caregiver?"

"No. That's not at all what I want."

"Then, as your equal. Someone you don't have to watch day and night. Or at work."

"Why are you twisting this, Mateo? I thought…" She shook her head. "Have I been wrong about this all long?"

"You took in a homeless guy, Lizzie. What's there to twist in that?"

"I thought I took in someone who wanted more from life. Was I wrong?"

She was battling gallantly against the tears that wanted to fall. To finally admit her feelings, then have them slapped back in her face…she couldn't even begin to describe the pain.

"No, you weren't wrong. But I've given it a lot of thought, and…" He paused, drew in a deep breath, then let it out again, agonizingly slow. "And I don't see how it could work with us. I don't want to be taken care of, like you took care of your dad, and I'm sure that's not what you want either. But I'm afraid it's inevitable. Also, I don't want to be watched for the rest of my life, with you wondering if it's the real me when I make a little slip-up. It's got nothing to do with the way I feel for you and everything to do with breathing room."

"I haven't been giving you *breathing room*?"

"You have. As much as I can handle right now. But in the future…"

"You don't have to say it, Mateo. What I saw as the beginning of something that might last was merely a port in the storm for you. But I'm glad I put myself out there for you—because it proved to me that I can do it. It was my choice, and it had nothing to do with my dad." She got up from the bed. "I'll have your things brought to the hospital, Mateo."

"This isn't what I want, Lizzie. I want to figure out how we can be together—not apart."

"What you want, Mateo, is a life that doesn't come with the complications we both have. That's what I wanted at first as well. But we don't always get what we want, do we? Oh, and as for falling in love—it shouldn't be about figuring out how to do it. It should be about how you can't live without the other person. How loving the other person makes you a better person. I'm sorry it didn't work that way for you, because it did for me."

He started to get out of bed, but he was connected to too many wires and tubes, and the instant he tried to stand every single one of the alarms went off.

"I do love you," he said as she headed for the door. "It's just that—"

"And that's where it ends, Mateo. After you tell someone you love them there should be no more words. No qualifiers. But you have a qualifier, and that says it all. I'm sorry this didn't work, because I love you, too."

With that, she was gone.

And he was stuck in a lousy hospital bed, with a tray full of green gelatin which he wanted to throw at the wall.

But he didn't. That was the Mateo who had existed *before* Lizzie. The one who existed after her merely shoved the bedside tray away, slunk down in bed, and pulled the sheets up to his neck.

CHAPTER NINE

Eight weeks later

MORNINGS WERE NOT her friend. Especially now, when she spent every one of them being sick and looking puffy. It was part of the process, her doctor had told her, but that meant nothing when she was sprawled on the bathroom floor, glad for the cool feel of the tile underneath her.

"Come on, Lizzie!" Janis yelled through the door. "It's perfectly natural. If you spend your entire pregnancy this way, by the time the baby gets here you're going to be a basket case."

"Babies!" she yelled back. "Not baby. When he got me, he got me good."

Janis opened the door a crack and peeked in. "You're not even dressed."

"Not getting dressed today."

"So what do I tell your patients?"

"That pregnancy and doctoring don't mix."

Janis pushed the door the rest of the way open and went in. She sat down next to Lizzie, who still wasn't budging.

"Someone should have told me," she moaned.

"Ever hear about using protection?"

"We did. It didn't work—*obviously*." Lizzie rolled over

on her back but still didn't get up. "See how big I am and I'm only two months in. Do you really think I'm in any shape to see patients? I mean, I'm wearing a *muumuu*, Janis. A freaking muumuu."

"Get used to it. The bigger you get, the more you'll come to appreciate your muumuu. Oh, and if you want another, I hear there's a mighty handsome man working in a surf shop a couple blocks over from the hospital. In case you didn't know, he stayed here, Lizzie. He's working hard with a PTSD counselor, as well as sticking to Randy's cognitive behavior program. I'll bet he'd like to see you."

"He knows where I live." Lizzie wrestled herself to a sitting position and leaned against the wall.

"Doesn't he have a right to know about the babies?" Janis asked.

"He does—and he will. But he's so deep into his treatment programs now I wonder if I should wait, rather than throw him another curve ball he has to deal with."

"Have your feelings for him changed?" Janis asked her.

Lizzie patted her belly. "No. In fact, they're growing deeper every day."

"And you expect to work things out sprawled here on the floor in a muumuu?"

"There's a lot to work out," Lizzie said, finally ready to get up.

"Do you know who you sound like?" Janis asked, pushing herself up and heading toward the door.

"No. Who?"

"Mateo. Do you remember when he was full of excuses, not doing anything to help himself, and everybody was getting frustrated with him?"

Lizzie thought about it as she pushed herself off the floor. "I didn't accept his excuses, did I?"

Janis gave her a knowing wink, then left.

And Lizzie put on some regular clothes and decided a walk was in order.

Funny how that walk took her right by a surf shop, where the clerk inside was keeping a whole line of people entertained with stories of his days as a surfer. Like he'd ever even *been* on a real surfboard.

It was such a funny sight, Lizzie laughed...probably for the first time in weeks. This was the father of her babies—the man she loved despite his faulty memories.

Lizzie waved at Mateo when he finally spotted her in the crowd, then waited until he made his way through the crowd to smile at him.

"Looks like you've found your calling," she said, fighting back a laugh. "Talking about your exploits from your days as a surfer?"

"Give the people what they want," he said, taking her by the arm and leading her out of the crowd. "I've wanted to see you. To talk to you about that day. I was overwhelmed, Lizzie. I hope you realize that?"

"You could have come around to apologize," she said, as they sat down on a bench under a banyan tree.

"I did. Every day. Who do you think has been tending your dad's flower garden?"

"I never saw you. And as for the garden... I just..." She shrugged. "I didn't give it any thought."

"Which is why it was getting weedy, and droopy from a lack of watering. I know I hurt you, Lizzie. And I'm sorry for that. But for a while I couldn't live with myself, let alone draw somebody else into my mess. I needed time...and space."

"And?"

"And I've been doing everything I can so that when I finally came back to you, hat in hand if that's how I had to do it, you'd see the differences in me. I wasn't good enough for you then. Maybe not even now. But I'm working on it. Trying new things where old things I've forgotten used to be."

"Like working in a surf shop?"

"If that's what it takes. I know there's a lot I won't get back, and I'm trying hard to come to terms with that. Some days are better than others. Occasionally I get so damned frustrated that all I want to do is go someplace and turn myself into somebody else. Like my surfer persona."

"But you stayed?"

"Because I have to. Because I fell in love with the most wonderful, stubborn, and opinionated woman I've ever known, and to walk away from that would be the worst thing I could ever do in my life. I'm trying hard to fix myself for *me*, Lizzie. But it's also for you. For a future where you won't have to worry about me every minute of every day. For the time when I leave the house and you won't have to pace the lanai and wonder what's happening to me. You deserve that, Lizzie. We both do. But I'm the one who has to fix that. And I'm trying." He brushed her cheek with the back of his hand. "I stayed because I want to prove myself to you. Prove that I'm everything you need and want."

"You have been, Mateo. Every day since I met you. I mean, it hasn't been easy, and I've some adjusting to do myself, but living all these weeks without you…it's been miserable. I've been miserable. And that's not how I want to be. Especially now, because I need an *equal*, Mateo. I mean, we can't predict the future, but we can live for what we have today, and that's what I need. I thought so at first, anyway. But then my need changed into something I wanted more than anything I'd ever wanted in my life, and I didn't see you getting involved in that. In fact, you pushed me away."

"Because I'm not sure yet who I am, and I still get frustrated when I can't pull up a memory. I'm working hard at dealing with myself, but that still adds up to a lifetime of misery for you, and I don't want that."

"Not misery, Mateo. Not if you love someone enough. The way I love you. What I finally realized was that your belligerence is only your way of trying to hang on to the pieces of you that you remember. You're fighting back."

"And I'm scared, Lizzie. Scared to death. But having you there made things better. And my memory of that night in Afghanistan..." He pointed to his head, "I do remember it now. Every bloody detail. How my friends tried to rescue me and died. How I lost my best friend. How I laid there for two days before anybody found me. It's not a pretty thing to recall, but it's my memory, which means it's part of me. And I've found other parts as well. Some good, some not so good. For better or worse, all of it me, though. And as these bits and pieces are returning, they give me something to hold on to. You give me more, though, and I want to earn my way back into your life. Unless I blew it too badly to fix."

"You didn't blow anything, Mateo. I think we were always just two people fighting to get through to each other. Sometimes succeeding, sometimes not." She took hold of his hand and laid it on her belly. "And sometimes going farther than any expectation either of us had."

"Seriously?" he asked. "You're...?"

"Eight weeks along. Healthy and grumpy. Having some battles with my hormones."

"Do you know if it's a boy or a girl?"

"Could be one of each…"

"I did all that?" he said, his pride obvious.

"It took two of us, Mateo. I did have a part in this."

He laughed out loud. "And here I was thinking that being alone, while it isn't good, isn't as bad as I thought it was. I'm assuming you want me involved?"

"I'm wearing muumuus, Mateo. And eating everything in the house. Does that sound like a person who doesn't want her baby daddy involved? Someone has to save me from myself—especially since for breakfast this morning I ate a whole mango pie."

"The whole thing?"

She nodded. "Would have eaten another one if I'd had it."

"Sounds to me like you're going to need that muumuu."

"Not as much as I need you. Will you come home, Mateo? The babies and I need you there. And, more than that, I want you there."

In answer, he pulled her into his arms and kissed her, while across the street Janis sat at an outside café with Randy, watching the whole thing.

"Looks to me like we're about to lose one of our doctors," she said. "I think our Lizzie is about to become otherwise occupied."

EPILOGUE

As WEDDINGS WENT, Lizzie and Mateo's was a small, private affair. Janis stood up for Lizzie and Randy stood for Mateo. They were in the flower garden, surrounded by all the beautiful flowers her dad had planted. Definitely paradise in so many ways.

For the ceremony Lizzie held Robert, named for her dad, while Mateo held Margarita, named for his mother. The twins were six months old now, just getting to the age where they had their own opinions—which were sometimes a bit vocal.

"I think Robert needs changing," Lizzie said.

"And Margarita seems like she's hungry," her soon-to-be husband responded. "Maybe we should take care of that before the ceremony begins, so we're not interrupted part-way through."

"Especially since we've waited so long for this."

She looked back at the small crowd gathering, and at Janis passing out tiki cups full of whatever her concoction of the day was. No one was left without a tiki.

"I think Janis has everything under control for a few minutes."

Lizzie and Mateo dashed into the house to take care of the twins, who'd become the center of so many lives since, for now, they went to work every day with Mateo.

Not to the surf shop, but to the clinic they'd bought. He and Lizzie worked there full-time, loving the life, loving the work.

The clinic was busier than ever, with more and more patients coming through the door every day. The addition of a nursery was a blessing, as Mateo refused to be separated from his family, and now Dr. Lizzie Peterson-soon-to-be-Sanchez was a part of that.

Lizzie still had a way to go in not taking on the blame for her dad's death, but Mateo was always there to help her through the rough spots. And she was always there when his memory lapses gave way to frustration.

"He's going to be here today, you know," Mateo said. "Since we're marrying in his garden."

"Sometimes it's like I feel him here, looking after his flowers. He would be happy knowing you're the one doing that now."

She brushed a tear from her eyes and looked over at Mateo, who had a spit-up towel slung over his shoulder and was holding a baby who was happily indulging in a bottle.

"Guess I should feed Robert, too," she said, tossing another spit-up towel over her own shoulder and giving him his own bottle.

And that was how they walked down the path to the trellis where they would take their wedding vows. A family of four. Everything Lizzie had never known she wanted. Everything she would ever need.

One husband, two children, and paradise.

The perfect life.

* * * * *

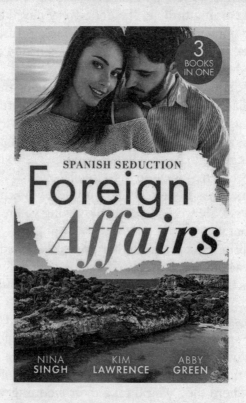

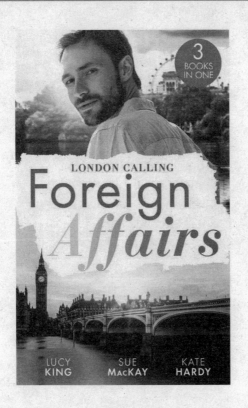

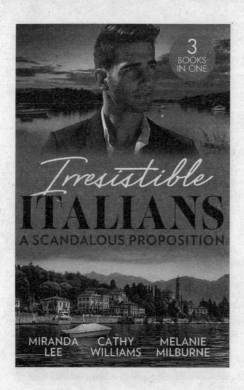

LET'S TALK

Romance

For exclusive extracts, competitions
and special offers, find us online:

f   facebook.com/millsandboon

𝕏   @MillsandBoon

◎   @MillsandBoonUK

♪   @MillsandBoonUK

Get in touch on 01413 063 232

For all the latest titles coming soon, visit
millsandboon.co.uk/nextmonth